THE BURNT HOUSE

Adam Lively was born in Swansea in 1961 and studied history and philosophy in England and America. He has published two novels, *Blue Fruit* (1988) and *The Burnt House* (1989), and a pamphlet in the Chatto Counterblasts series, *Parliament: The Great British Democracy Swindle* (1990). He has also published a novella, *The Snail* (1991). His work has appeared in the anthologies *20 Under 35*, *PEN New Poetry II* and *The Dylan Companion.*

His new novel, *Sing The Body Electric* will be published in June 1993 the year in which he was selected as one of The Best of Young British Novelists.

He lives in London with his wife Diana, and their son Jacob.

D1234428

Adam Lively

THE BURNT HOUSE

VINTAGE

VINTAGE
20 Vauxhall Bridge Road, London SW1V 2SA

London Melbourne Sydney Auckland Johannesburg
and agencies throughout the world

First published in Great Britain by
Simon & Schuster Ltd, 1989

Vintage edition 1993

2 4 6 8 10 9 7 5 3 1

The quotations on pages 261 ad 262 are from Friedrich
Nietzsche, *Thus Spake Zarathustra* (trans. by Walter
Kaufmann, The Viking Press, 1954)

Printed and bound in Great Britain by
Cox & Wyman, Reading, Berkshire

ISBN 0 09 930382 5

TO DIANA

PART ONE

The Journey Out

CHAPTER ONE

One of the first things Bob Morton did when he arrived in England was buy a fire-damaged house in North London. It was a strange move, because New World Broadcasting Corporation had already fixed him up with a luxurious flat in Maida Vale for the year he was to be stationed at their London bureau. Morton had come across the house by chance, on a hot June day. He had been driving aimlessly around the city, getting acclimatised, and had stopped the car to stretch his legs. He had walked on up a hill, noticed a 'For Sale' hoarding, and found himself squinting up at the burnt house, fascinated.

It was in the middle of a tall Victorian terrace, marked out from the others by a grey stain up its facade left by the smoke. It looked as though a giant had reached down and smudged it with a grimy thumb. The boarded-up windows looked like broken teeth. Morton stood on the sticky pavement for a while, in a kind of daydream, just gazing up at it. He returned to the car, then wandered back up the hill again to take another look. It was a quiet street, with magnificent views south across the city. To his own surprise, he had made a sudden decision that he wanted to live there. Next day, he made some enquiries at the estate agent and phoned his bank in New York. He had a survey done, discovered that the damage was not as bad as appeared at first, and inside a fortnight he had bought the place and moved in builders to start the repairs.

Morton, who was anchorman on NWBC's evening news, had come to London to make a series about various aspects of British life. Which aspects, like much else about 'Morton on Britain', was as yet undecided. It had all been arranged hastily following Morton's sudden announcement, a couple of months back, that he wanted to take a break from the news and do some foreign reporting and documentaries. Such is the power of the anchorman that he could have chosen anywhere in the world to muse on – Moscow, Peking or maybe Tokyo would have been the obvious choices. Instead, to everyone's surprise, including his own (he hated preppy Anglophiles), he chose London. It was in keeping somehow with his perverse mood at that time that he should do what was least expected of him. He had been overcome by a creeping restlessness, an unnamable dissatisfaction with the career he had pursued with such success for the past twenty years. He explained this to himself as a consequence of his age. He was approaching sixty and, as retirement loomed on the horizon, it was inevitable that a man who had dedicated his whole life to work should question what it had all amounted to. That was how he rationalised it, but it didn't stop him suspecting that there was more to it than that.

He was utterly without English class awkwardness or snobbery, so was able to strike up an easy friendship with the three men who arrived to work on the house he had bought. There were two young lads, one noisy and one quiet, and a rather dour older man, Trevor, who was a carpenter and plasterer, and who was nominally in charge. Nick, the noisier of the two younger ones, wore a baseball cap and went around bare-chested. He liked to call out and show his muscles to the girls passing on the street. Then there was Aidan, who was the nephew of the owner of the building firm, Terence Healy.

Morton first met Aidan a couple of days after they had started work, when he had to show him some floorboards that needed nailing down in one of the attic rooms. The seat of the fire had been in the basement, which was gutted. As you went up through the house, the damage lessened. The ground floor – a hallway, toilet and one large room – had been badly affected by the smoke and intense heat. The bannisters were charred. The paint and wallpaper were blistered away and the plaster beneath cracked. On the first floor – where there was a large bedroom at the front, a smaller room that Morton was going to use as a kitchen, and a bathroom – the damage was limited to a film of mottled grey soot over the walls and ceilings. By the time you got up to the two attic rooms, there was no evidence of the fire at all. In one of these rooms, there was a casement window that jutted out from the slope of the roof. After Morton had shown Aidan which floorboards needed attending to, they found themselves standing at this window, gazing out at the view. The office blocks of the City poked up through the haze of heat that hung over London. Off to the right, but closer, you could see the Post Office Tower. To the left, the railway lines to Euston and Kings Cross cut a dark swathe through the jumble of buildings.

'When I was a kid growing up in Chicago,' said Morton suddenly, 'I had this picture of London in my mind. See, I used to read a lot of Dickens and Sherlock Holmes. There was always fog, and mysterious figures creeping along the sidewalks. I guess it's not really like that. Do you get fog here in the fall?'

'I dunno.'

'Not a Londoner?'

Aidan shook his head. He had thin lips and a delicate chin. All his features were thin, and he had hippyish, shoulder-length brown hair.

'Like it here?'

''Salright. Haven't been here long. I'm staying with my uncle.'

Morton nodded. He lit his pipe and opened the window to throw the match out. A breeze blew in, and with it the low, constant roar of London. They stood together in silence in the afternoon heat, looking at the view.

'Know what I wanted to be when I was a kid?' Morton continued abruptly.

A fly flew in the window and began patrolling the ceiling in large, aimless rectangles. Aidan shrugged his shoulders. His hair had fallen forward over his eyes, and with a characteristic gesture, he slowly brought his hand up and flicked the hair back behind his ear.

'Al Capone. I wanted to be Al Capone. When I was growing up in the thirties, Capone was still a big deal in Chicago. My father claimed he'd met people who'd known him. I don't know whether that was true, but I sure as hell wanted to believe him. Capone had everything as far as I was concerned. He was a rebel, he had money, the ladies loved him. I wanted to be just like him. I guess at that age you don't think about all the people he killed, all those lives he ruined. How about kids over here? Who do they wanna be? Robin Hood?'

'I dunno.'

'Who did you wanna be?'

Aidan thought. 'Bob Dylan.'

'Bob Dylan's old enough to be your father.'

Aidan shrugged his thin shoulders.

Morton laughed. 'You should have been around in the sixties. You'd have loved it.'

That was how it started. An unlikely friendship grew up between Morton and Aidan Fowler, and whenever Morton came over to the burnt house to check how the work was progressing – he was still staying in the Maida Vale flat until it was habitable – he would find himself passing time with him. They enjoyed each other's company. Morton would do all the talking, and quite often there would be long silences between them. He would reminisce, he would tell Aidan about America, and Aidan would listen and watch him closely with his small, inscrutable eyes. America was the source of everything for Aidan – the films he watched, the music he listened to, the books and comics he read. Listening to Morton was like having that big, dangerous continent step off the screen, up from the record, and appear as flesh and blood before him.

Morton, for his part, was initially drawn to Aidan because he was interested in someone who seemed so much of a throwback. There was a dreamy, far-away, stoned quality to him – though Morton was pretty sure he wasn't on drugs – that spoke to Morton of the time twenty years before when he had first started in television. The connection with that time was made all the stronger in Morton's mind by the coincidence that physically, with his drooping hair and slow delicacy, Aidan bore some resemblance to Morton's younger brother Sammy. Sammy had died in 1968.

Whatever the chemistry, this peculiar friendship was another link in the chain of perversity that had dragged Morton away from his safe position in New York to London, and then to the burnt house. If his colleagues, never mind the millions of TV viewers across America, could have seen how he (the Bob Morton, friend of Presidents and the owners of major league baseball teams) was idling away his afternoons, they would have been amazed. His visits to check on progress were becoming more frequent. As summer deepened, that progress seemed to be slowing to a halt. Various jobs had been started, then abandoned when the materials needed to complete them failed to appear. The three men working on the house, demoralised by the sense that they had been forgotten, took to sitting for long periods in the basement, sipping tea, or eking out what work they could to to fill the long summer days.

The fault for all this, as Morton quickly realised, lay with the owner of the building firm, Terence Healy, and his failure to provide his men with proper back-up. Healy had overstretched himself, taken on too many jobs and hired too many men. Unwilling to delegate responsibility for anything, because he trusted no one and feared that to do so might involve paying them more money, he tried to supervise all the sites himself. He was like the man in the circus who runs around the ring keeping the plates spinning on sticks. Round and round Healy dashed, faster and faster in an ever-widening circle. But the plates were turning more and more slowly, threatening constantly to topple and crash to the ground. And still he added more. Even as the men at the burnt house were slipping into a trough of inactivity, Healy was in a smoke-filled room at the council chambers, negotiating a lucrative contract. Morton was aware of all this, but had been lulled by the summer heat into a mood almost as lackadaisical as that of the men in the house. It was only on a day in August that Morton was galvanised into action, and the thing that did it was the arrival at his office of a letter from his daughter in America.

Dear Bob,

I saw a familiar face on the TV the other day. It was standing in front of the Houses of Parliament in London, and it was you. How are you doing? I was relieved to note that you don't yet talk like you've got your mouth full of cotton wool. Please don't turn into a Brit, Daddy.

Do you know we haven't been in touch since my graduation back in May? It was so great you turned up. I thought you wouldn't. Incidentally, I hope you realise what it was *like* for me, organising things so you and Mother wouldn't accidentally run into each other and start an International Incident? My God!

You probably want to hear what I've been doing since then. (You *do*, don't you?) Well, I went home with Mother and four years' accumulated college junk, and at Mother's insistence got myself a job in the Burger King on Route 20. (Mother believes in vacation jobs like other people believe in the Bible.) Anyway, after a couple of weeks shuffling the styrofoam, it dawned on me that this wasn't a vacation, and I wouldn't be going back to college in the fall. I certainly did not see myself working at the Burger King on Route 20 for the rest of my life, so I cajoled Mother into releasing me, and came to stay with a friend of mine, Susan, who graduated last year, moved to New York, and has (O miracle of miracles!) a sub-let on an apartment in the East Village. So here I am, and does it feel good! (I *hate* suburbia.)

I've been here two months now, getting as close to surviving a New York summer as is humanly possible. The only cloud on my horizon takes the form of strong signals Susan's been sending out recently that at some point she'll want to liberate her fold-down bed. But where to go?

Susan and I have been checking out a season of European films at the art movie-house on our block. We saw one last week that was set in London (it looked cute – all grainy and rainy and black-and-white), and when we were coming out Susan said, 'Why don't you go stay with your father in London? My God, what an opportunity! You must be crazy just sitting in New York.' (See what I mean about strong signals?) Well you can guess where these innocent ramblings are leading . . .

How about it? For a year, until you come back too? I wouldn't be any trouble. You've probably got the idea from what I've said that I've just been bumming around since I got out of college. I haven't. I've been working really hard at my saxophone and getting some dates. I really think I could make it as a musician. I really do. There must be a jazz scene in London. I really wouldn't be any trouble – I'd look after myself and keep out of your way and go to auditions and get work playing and stuff. All I'd need is somewhere to rest my weary head, and some paternal support every now and then. I think I would be really neat for us to be together in London. I've asked Mother, and she said go-for-God's-sake-go-if-that's-what-you-want-to-do-I'm-washing-my-hands-of-you-sorry-I-didn't-mean-that. So now I'm free to go, if you'll just give the word. Of course, I don't want to put any emotional pressure on you, but PLEASE . . .

love,

Laura

Morton had never been close to his daughter. He had married her mother in 1966, when he was thirty-eight and she was ten years younger, and Laura had been born the following year. By the time Laura was two, her parents were divorced. Looking back, Morton couldn't figure out how or why he had got himself into it. There had been a lot of pressure from his parents. He had never had much success in his occasional romantic involvements with women and, especially after his younger brother Sammy went out to Vietnam, his mother was desperate to see her oldest son settled down and raising a family. The thing with Laura's mother had been a 'whirlwind romance'. They met when he was researching a feature called 'Spring in Boston', and by Thanksgiving they were married. Certain scenes from that period came back to Morton even after twenty years with painful force. Their sexual relations had never really worked (except at least once, apparently) and they were both secretly relieved when the pregnancy provided an excuse for them to stop trying. He had felt during those months like he was being rushed towards this goal of marriage and children by forces beyond his control. And the strange thing was that he had the impression she felt the same. During tearful scenes they would sometimes cling to each other like two children being swept down a river. Remembering it now, Morton's main feeling was embarrassment.

Then, when Laura was born, everything changed. They were a married-couple-with-kid. Even their unhappiness was forced underground, replaced by lies and guilt. In 1968, soon after Sammy died, Morton was offered a job at NWBC. It was his first big career break after twenty years in newspapers. Laura's mother refused to move to New York. There was a crisis, and they decided on divorce. Morton's mother had died in the meantime, anyway. She had lived just long enough to hear about the death of her youngest son.

With all that, it shouldn't have been the happiest period of Morton's life. But it was. They were exciting times for a TV reporter. The anti-Vietnam protests were reaching their height. There were student revolts, black revolts, counter-cultures. Morton hustled backwards and forwards across the continent reporting them, burying himself in work to blot out the things that hurt him most – the marriage fiasco, Sammy's death. Morton's reports from that time became classics. In future, retrospectives on the sixties invariably included footage that he had helped shoot. His name was made as a TV newsman, and he had never looked back.

He saw more of his own glittering future in TV news than he did of his daughter. Every two or three months as she was growing up he would dutifully pick her up and take her out for the day. There would always be some third party – never his former wife – there to supervise the handover. He would take Laura out for a walk, to the zoo, later to the movies. When she was a baby she would cry the whole time, then when she was a little older she would just be very quiet, watching him respectfully. When she reached her mid-teens, her attitude towards him changed. She began treating him like a jolly uncle, an elderly buddy whom she could show off to, maybe even flirt with a little. Addressing him by his first name was part of it. Morton couldn't say he felt really comfortable being cast in that role by his daughter, but he couldn't see how to change the nature of their relationship. It seemed easier just to let things take their course. If that was what Laura wanted, then that was how it should be.

Morton had stored up a lot of guilt about Laura. Her mother had been content to make him feel like the faithless husband deserting his family – which was not quite how it was, because it had been, on both sides, a mistake, not a marriage. So he always felt that he had a lot to make up to Laura, that he had to placate her all the time. So as soon as he got the letter he started making plans. Top of the list was the burnt house. He would go down there that afternoon and get things moving. First, though, he called up Terence Healy. Even as he was punching in the numbers, a strategy was forming in his mind. He spoke briefly to Healy, demanding a conference at the house the next morning. Yes, he was going to cook that gentleman's goose. He was going to stuff it, baste it, and roast it.

Carl Davenport, chief research scientist on the Xykon 23/M, was checking a computer printout. He had already checked it a dozen times, and been through a complete instrument check twice. Now there could be no doubt. Suddenly feeling exhausted, he wrote a quick report, filed it, and left the laboratory. Before stepping into the airlock, he fastened his helmet and switched his life-support on.

The doors slid silently open to reveal the surface of the moon. The first thing that one noticed was not the moon itself but the vast planet it orbited, Hubrilius, which filled a third of the sky, even though only a tiny fraction of its vast bulk was visible. The rest was below the horizon, hidden by the surface of the moon. Carl Davenport had seen many strange sights in his twenty years of space travel, but if he spent the rest of his life on this godforsaken spot he would never get used to the sight of the enormous orange planet filling the sky. There was something about being on this moon, orbiting its planet as slowly as an ant crawls over a mountain, that made him feel very small and vulnerable.

Davenport looked away from the planet, with its atmosphere of swirling orange gases, and out into the black infinite. Hubrilius' sun, hidden now in the long night, was an ancient star in the galaxy GX 2391/4, some 40,000 million light years from Earth and counting. Davenport let his gaze wander among the stars that filled the blackness – some nearer, some further away. They gave him a dizzying sense of perspective. There was no hurry. They wouldn't be expecting him back in the Xykon for a while. Davenport let his body relax inside his suit. The Xykon would be returning to Earth in the near future, and as always at such times, Davenport found himself thinking about the long, wonderful human journey that had brought him to this spot.

The first human beings had landed on Mars in 2015, but it was not until the end of that century that a permanent station had been set up there. By that time, too, the moon's advantages over Earth as a base for space exploration were being exploited. By the end of the third millennium, manned spacecraft had penetrated to every corner of the solar system. Permanent stations were in orbit around Jupiter and Saturn. In 2896, the first permanent base was established on the rocky, inhospitable surface of Pluto.

At that point, manned space flight had run up against the great yawning distances of interstellar space. During the fifth millennium, a few expeditions were mounted to Alpha Centauri, the sun's nearest neighbour star. Alpha Centauri is 25 million million miles (4¼ light years) distant, and in order to make the journey the astronauts were put in a state of suspended animation. The expeditions, for a variety of reasons, were not deemed successful. For five millennia the gulf of interstellar space seemed unbridgeable for manned expeditions. Unmanned probes, however, continued to explore the galaxy, and to add to scientific insight. These probes had been developed with ever more powerful propulsion systems, and the 'ballistics revolution' initiated by Carole Szrch (b.8463) produced probes that could travel at 95% speed of light. However, the great advances in interstellar space flight did not come until after the last bastions of traditional Einsteinian physics had fallen. In 10704, Mary Mensah published her New Theory of Space-Time, which among other things laid the theoretical groundwork for faster-than-light travel. The first faster-than-light spaceshift was achieved in 13146, when two craft set out to explore the Pleiades star cluster, some 400 light years from Earth. The expedition was a success, and the last great barrier to the exploration of the universe had fallen.

The next ten millennia saw a massive explosion in space travel, as the Milky Way was explored. Manned expeditions were carried to distances of 200,000 light years. In 15343, the first extraterrestrial life-forms, primitive lichens, were discovered in the globular cluster M22 (constellation Sagittarius). In 18149, a seminal date in human history, the first contact was made with intelligent extraterrestrial life-forms in globular cluster NGC 6205, a dense collection of old stars that orbit the centre of the galaxy. Only a hundred years later, the first intergalactic travel was achieved, when a survey ship reached the Larger Magellanic Cloud, some 155,000 light years distant. Many more expeditions followed to the Magellanic Clouds. In 26250, the first spaceship reached Andromeda galaxy (M31), 2 million light years away. Exploration of Andromeda, M33, Ursa Minor, Draco, and the dozen other galaxies composing the Local Group dominated the period up to 50000, by which time the first expeditions beyond the Local Group were being ventured.

The period up to about 150000 was characterised by the closer contacts between human colonists from the Local Group and the enormous galaxy cluster Coma Berenices, made up of about 10,000 individual galaxies, and 120 million light years distant. In addition, manned probes were exploring galaxies to distances of 500 million light years.

While all this was happening, scientific knowledge was expanding proportionately. Just as man's horizons had expanded from flat earth to solar system to galaxy to clusters of galaxies, so theoretical insights into dimensionality were now enabling this universe to be put properly in context. Although exploration was beyond existing capabilities, it had become firmly established that the universe as it had been known is just one universe of many; that just as there are clusters of galaxies there are clusters of universes; that universes can exercise an influence on one another in exactly the same way as there is gravitational pull, and sometimes collision, between galaxies.

Exploration of the 'the edge of the universe' became more technologically feasible from 215000 with the development of a new breed of research ship, the Xykon and Starkon series. These ships, designed for extended space-time warp, were part of a massive research project aimed at clarifying the rate and nature of our universe's expansion.

Now, in 231418, the Xykon 23/M was the most distant from Earth of all those research ships. Was this, the desolate moon of Hubrilius, where the human journey would end?

The question was a thread drawing all Davenport's thoughts together. What was happening out there? He mentally checked yet again the data he'd been processing in the laboratory. It showed that a gentle shower of sub-atomic particles was falling towards the planet. The shower had started over the last few nights, and was growing more intense. He was at a loss to explain it.

He stayed standing still, gazing up into the starlit intensity, as if by staring long and hard enough he could see the source of those mysterious particles. He sighed, and the sigh sounded close and loud in his helmet. Sometimes he thought he would never figure out the mysteries of that vastness.

Davenport started back across the plain that separated the laboratory from the Xykon. His feet fell without sound on the soft surface-dust. It would be daybreak soon, and he had to get back to the safety of the ship to avoid the harmful radiation of the sun. The enormous bulk of the Xykon loomed ahead of him out of the half-light. It was known affectionately as 'the tortoise', because of its dumpy landing legs, its dome-shaped main body, which housed the crew, and the weird construction sticking up at one end like a head, containing the instrumentation that sliced through the *fabric of space-time like scissors through paper. As Davenport walked the last few hundred yards to the airlock and lift, with the great belly of the ship hanging over him, he was still thinking about those particles. He didn't like mysteries. As he stepped into the lift, he was frowning inside his helmet. The doors slid silently to.*

There was a click. Aidan looked up from the book, blinking in the sunshine, to see Morton holding a camera.

'Hi. Hope you don't mind. I've been taking some pictures of the house. I wanted to do a before-and-after sequence.'

Aidan shrugged his shoulders. He was sitting at the back of the burnt house, on the low garden wall. A fly crawled across the hot concrete beside him.

'What are you reading?'

He handed Morton the book. It was a fat paperback with an illustration on the cover in lurid, over-blown detail, of a spaceship. Beyond it a planet, some stars. The title, *The Voyage Beyond Infinity*, was presented in bold, embossed letters at the top.

Morton took the book and studied it with interest. 'Never heard of this,' he said, 'Any good?'

''Salright. I've only just started it.'

'What's it about.'

'Space and that.'

Morton smiled. 'You don't say.'

Beyond the garden there were more back gardens, and the backs of houses. Beyond the houses, in the next street, some children were playing somewhere. Their shrieks filled the empty blue sky, dying down then bursting out again in the distance to their own rhythm.

'You remember when Apollo Fifteen landed?' said Morton. 'When Armstrong walked on the moon?'

'No.'

'Christ, I was forgetting you'd be too young. You must have seen the TV pictures though?'

'Yeah, of course. I saw a documentary.'

'What did you think?'

Aidan shrugged his shoulders. 'Amazing.'

'It seems like another age. I guess it's the times we live in now. You get nostalgic for the future.'

Silence between them. The sunlight was warm, they could feel it on their faces, but the air had the beginnings of autumn in it, a slight bite that Aidan could feel through his thin T-shirt. A breeze ruffled the downy hair on his bare arms.

'Did you find it hard to believe,' said Morton, 'that they were actually on the surface of the moon, when you saw that film?'

'No.'

'A lot of folks just wouldn't believe it. They thought it was all rigged up in a studio.'

Aidan was looking up into the clear blue sky. A jet, a tiny speck trailing a white plume, was making its way slowly from horizon to horizon.

'We got a lot of letters about it.'

Aidan looked at him. 'How d'yer mean?'

'I work for a TV company, New World Broadcasting Corporation. I guess you might not have heard of it over here.'

'No.' Aidan flicked his long hair from his eyes and squinted up at the sun again.

'For me,' Morton was saying, 'it was just another story back then. Went down to NASA in Houston, interviewed all the big guys in the corporation. Background stuff on the astronauts' families. Maybe I didn't really believe in it myself. It was just another set of pictures. Good ones, of course, but only pictures. When I think about it now . . . You know those pictures they took of Earth?'

'Yeah.'

'Just a blue ball, with cloud swirling round it, rolling through that great emptiness. Boy, what a shot. When I saw that, it hit me what those guys had done. I mean, what an image! That blue planet in all that blackness. When I saw that, I almost believed that stuff you used to hear back then about the new age, the Age of Aquarius.'

'Yeah,' said Aidan, and grinned at Morton.

The older man smiled back, and shook his head. 'Well,' he said, 'a bunch of crap that proved to be.' He pulled a fat wallet out of his jacket pocket, then from the wallet produced a photograph. 'That's my daughter, Laura. I got a letter from her this morning. She's coming over here to visit.'

Aidan glanced at the photograph and handed it back.

'So I've gotta get things moving here. Where are the other guys?'

'In the basement.'

They went down into the basement, and Morton put to the three men his proposition. If they worked directly for him, cutting Healy out, then he would pay them fifty per cent more than they were getting now. He would supply them with all the materials and pay them by the hour for their labour. Aidan agreed immediately, but the other two said they would have to think about it and ring him that evening. In the event, only Trevor, the dour, middle-aged plasterer agreed to Morton's proposition.

The next morning, predictably, Terence Healy was furious. The first thing he did was turn on Aidan, jabbing a finger out and glaring at him down the length of it as though taking aim with a gun.

'I'll tell you this, young Aidan Fowler. If you go through with this, you can fucking well clear out of my house. How does that grab you? Know what it's like finding somewhere cheap to live in this city?'

Aidan frowned and looked at the floor. He hadn't thought of that.

'That's OK,' Morton interrupted casually, 'Aidan's going to stay here.'

'Here?' said Healy incredulously.

'Sure. I need someone to look after the place, stop squatters getting in. Aidan and I worked the whole thing out yesterday. We can make one of the attic rooms habitable easy enough. Be cosy up there, won't it, Aidan?'

'Yeah,' said Aidan without hesitation. He flicked his hair from in front of his eyes and stared at his uncle defiantly.

Later that morning, Morton drove Aidan to his uncle's house to collect his things – his rucksack of clothes and his two precious records, Bob Dylan's 'Blonde on Blonde' and Mahler's Fifth Symphony, which he had first heard in a school music lesson. In the evening, after an afternoon spent collecting materials at builder's merchants, Morton took Trevor and Aidan out for a drink.

As they walked away from the burnt house, Aidan stared around him and felt as if he had been reborn. It was the rush hour, and the streets were filling up with people coming back from work. They spilled off the buses and out of the tube station, streaming past the newspaper sellers who shouted 'Standard' at the tops of their voices, flicking the papers from the pile and taking the money in one deft gesture. People darted in and out of the jammed-up traffic, watched by the bored or angry drivers. If one of the cars was slow in moving on, then the one behind it would give a honk, which set the others off like a gaggle of geese, until the whole street was honking and tooting. These outbursts, and the bright headlights that swept the shifting parade of pedestrians, made the scene festive. Everywhere there was movement and flashing lights and shouting.

They went to a pub on the main street called The Mulberry Tree. It was one of those pub-theatres that had sprung up all over London in the past twenty years. It had been an ordinary working-class pub until ten years ago, when the brewery, who were making a loss on it,

sold it to an American entrepreneur. He had the carpets and formica
tables taken out and the function room upstairs converted into a
tiny theatre. There, night after night, impoverished young actors
struggled through Brecht and Shakespeare, like trying to stage a
wrestling match in a broom cupboard. The pub itself, with its
bright lights, wooden floor, and long bar with brass fittings, made
you feel, as soon as you walked into it, that you were stepping on
to a film set of a Western saloon. The atmosphere of the place was
heightened by the odd mixture of people who gathered there. At the
bar, pin-striped suits jostled with workmen's overalls. It was true
that many of these overalls were suspiciously clean, and surmounted
by confident, button-bright, middle-class faces, but sprinkled around
the tables there were genuine remnants of the pub's plebeian past, old
men who had been there for most of their lives and saw no reason to
change their habits simply because the carpet had been taken away.

When Morton, Trevor and Aidan entered the pub it was just
beginning to fill up. As the three of them came in through the heavy
swing doors, they were submerged in the gentle roar of voices.
They found a table in the corner, by the window, and Morton went
to buy the drinks.

'Cheers,' he said when he got back. 'Here's to the burnt house.'

Trevor sipped his grapefruit juice. He never drank. He had
only come out of politeness. He wanted to get home to see his
wife, who had had an interview that day for a part-time job in
an old people's home. He glanced through the dazzle of light on
the window beside him at the passing crowds. He wanted to get
out there. The noise in the pub, the braying laughter and abrasive
chatter, was beginning to irritate him. He could probably slip off
soon – Aidan and the American were chatting together quite cosily.
It was strange, watching them. They could almost have been father
and son. Morton, talking nineteen to the dozen, was lighting his pipe
and releasing billowing clouds of smoke. Aidan, hunched over his
beer, with his long, straggly hair trailing over his shoulders on the
table, was listening with a frown of concentration. Not that I'd fancy
having Aidan for a son, thought Trevor. Bit of a handful, probably. A
pleasant enough lad, but you could never tell what was going on inside
his head. Trevor stood up.

'I'd best be going,' he said. 'Thanks for the drink, Mr Morton.'

Morton and Aidan watched him thread his way through the
crowd and out the door.

'Every time I look at that guy,' said Morton, jabbing the air with
the stem of his pipe, 'I think of Johnson.'

'Who?'

'Lyndon Johnson. I swear he's a dead ringer, only Johnson used to wear those little glasses. I remember the first time I met him. It was in 1964. That was the first presidential election I covered. It was about this time of year, bit earlier maybe; Johnson was doing this swing through the South. We'd just flown into Austin, and there was this reception laid on – in the airport of all places. There was no air-conditioning, and it was *hot*. I went to the men's room at one stage, and I was just washing my hands when Johnson walks in with a secret service man. He didn't see me at first. He always used to wear a stetson when he went to Texas, to remind everyone he was a local boy. Anyway, I remember he walked into the washroom and the first thing he did was take off that stetson off and kind of fling it down in disgust. It made me think of an actor coming off stage.'

Morton laughed. 'He *hated* that stetson. Anyway, he saw me then, and started chatting to me about how great it was for him to be back in Texas – the kind of garbage he fed to every journalist. He was a real pro. That was the campaign he said, "We are not about to send American boys nine or ten thousand miles away from home to do what Asian boys ought to be doing for themselves." I remember when he said that, and those Texas folk all stood up and cheered him and waved their flags. But he still did it. My younger brother, Sammy, he went out to Vietnam. He was only thirty. A great kid.'

'Vietnam,' said Aidan. 'That's where they had that war, isn't it?'

Morton nodded. 'Say, why don't you go up and get us a couple more drinks?' He gave Aidan the money.

The men and women in suits stood in a circle by the bar, talking loudly at the same time, hurling their confident comments into the centre as though the conversation was a hungry animal that needed feeding. As he made his way through them, mumbling apologies for getting in their way, Aidan flicked his hair nervously away from his face. When he'd got the drinks, he stood at the bar for a moment and sipped his beer. He felt like getting drunk tonight. He felt like listening to Morton talk all evening, and then going up to his room in the empty house and looking out across London and drinking way into the night.

'Look here,' said Morton when Aidan returned to the table, 'are you sure you'll be all right in that house? I'm just worried I've landed you in something you'll regret. You could still patch things up with your uncle and go back there.'

'I'll be all right.'

'Well I guess you're old enough to decide for yourself.' Morton was silent for a moment, gazing thoughtfully at the people in the pub. 'Say Aidan, what do you think about being English?'

'Not much.'

'You mean you're not proud of your country?'

'I don't think about it. I don't think about being English. I'm just a person. Everybody's just people. All that other stuff is crap.'

'That's a nice point of view,' said Morton, chuckling. 'You know what your problem is Aidan? You were born at the wrong time. You belong in the sixties.'

'Mr Morton, can I ask you something?' said Aidan, who was beginning to feel tipsy.

'Sure.'

'What I wanted to know was, why did you tell my uncle we'd already fixed up about me living in the house?'

'Because I didn't like to see him laughing at you. That's an elementary rule of survival, Aidan. Never let people get away with laughing at you.'

'I don't care what he thinks about me.'

'You might not now, but some day you will. I knew a guy, way back, who was a reporter on the *New York Post*. He was just like you. The other guys used to rib him about things – you know, small things. He was the kind who'd turn up at the wrong place for press conferences, or get on the wrong train. This went on for years, because he just shrugged it off. "I don't care what you guys think about me," he'd say. You see, the more he said that, the more they did it – not really maliciously, it was just that he seemed to ask for it. Anyway, one day they found him in a Washington hotel room with a gun in his hand and his brains blasted out. Nobody could figure out why he'd done it – he was happily married, had a couple of beautiful kids. Well. I figured he'd just had enough of it. Deep down he did care, and all those years of it had gotten on top of him. Believe me, Aidan, it's best to nip these things in the bud.'

Morton talked on, about journalists he'd known, and politicians and criminals. Every story he told conjured up an image in Aidan's mind – a lonely hotel room, a confrontation in a stuffy office, a speech to a cheering crowd. He gazed at the grain of the table in front of him, but what he saw unfolding before him was history itself – a vast, shifting panorama. The images that passed through his mind had the quality of old newsreels, that repeat at infinite removes what is accomplished and dead. Yet the images lived. They were a kind of life in death.

Morton said they should be going. He left Aidan at the house and drove back to the Maida Vale flat. Aidan staggered up the stairs of the empty house, watching the images play against the solid darkness. In bright sunlight, a man pulls up at a gas station and gets out to stretch his legs while a Negro works the pump. He screws up his eyes against the light to look across the flat landscape, then glances at his wristwatch before getting back into the car. A cavernous hall with tall, thin windows. Rain beating on the roof. A voice comes from the loudspeakers, 'The President of the United States', and the groups of men in suits and hats turn eagerly towards the stage. Somehow, Aidan made it up the stairs in the darkness. He forgot to look out of the window at London as he had meant to. He got straight into his sleeping bag, curling himself up against the cold and damp, and concentrated on the endless film of America playing in his head.

CHAPTER TWO

On the day that Morton's daughter was arriving in England, Aidan took the coach to the Midlands to visit his family. It was a cold, wet Saturday morning, and the coach sped up the motorway in a cloud of spray. The passengers sank back into their seats and watched the grey veil of rain beyond the windows. Someone in the back row had a radio on, and the jingle of the music was lulling them deeper and deeper into stupor. Aidan grinned to himself. With all that water outside, the coach was like an inside-out fishbowl.

From Birmingham he got a bus, and by the time he reached his home town it was noon. He walked the mile and a half from the bus station, thinking about how much he was looking forward to seeing his older brother, Doug, who still lived at home. Doug had been out of a job since leaving school, and in the last couple of years it had become accepted that he would live with his parents for the foreseeable future.

Home was on an estate off the main road. As Aidan approached the house, a group of kids standing round a motorbike watched him steadily. Aidan didn't know them. A lot of new people had moved on to the estate.

His mother answered the door. She stood looking at him, a slow smile suffusing her face, then took his hand and drew him in without saying a word. That was the kind of thing she did. It had occurred to Aidan sometimes that his mother was not like other mothers, who were always fussing over their children and ruffling their hair, treating them like cuddly toys. On the odd occasions when he thought about it, Aidan found his mother a bit of a mystery. He would catch her gazing out of the window, or humming along to the radio – she loved music, and had a beautiful voice – and it would cross his mind that he had no idea what was going on inside her head. She often had that warm, dreamy expression on her face.

'Hello, Aid, how's things?' Doug had loped down the stairs to greet him.

'Not so bad.'

'Glad to hear *that*.' Doug had a knack of emphasising his words in an unexpected way. Everything he said seemed to carry a double meaning.

Aidan's mother drew him on. 'Say hello to your father.'

His father was watching the football. He stubbed his cigarette out, got up rather stiffly from his armchair, and shook Aidan's hand. Aidan's father never said much. He was a small, wiry man, with a diffident manner and a worried, almost haunted look to his eyes. The only person he ever really talked to was his wife.

They had lunch, as always, in the kitchen. And as always on a Saturday, they had shepherd's pie. Through in the living-room, the television talked to itself. The cooking had steamed up the windows. They sat around the small table in a pleasant, cosy warmth.

'How are Uncle Terry and Auntie Eileen?' asked Aidan's mother. 'I hope you've not been a trouble to them.'

'I've moved out of their house,' said Aidan. 'Gone somewhere else.'

'Where have you moved? Where are you living?' His mother put her knife and fork down.

'With this American bloke, Mr Morton.'

'An American?'

'Yeah.'

'But why, Aidan?'

'Well,' he offered, ''cos we're working on his house.'

'But what about Uncle Terry? What does he say about all of this?'

'Oh he doesn't mind.'

'Martin?'

Aidan's father waved his knife dismissively. 'I can't tell him what to do.'

Mrs Fowler looked back at her son. 'Who is this Mr Morton? What does he do?'

'He's on the television.'

'Well I've never heard of him.'

'He's only on American TV.'

Aidan's mother sighed, shook her head, and began to eat again. There the matter rested. After lunch, Aidan helped with the washing up, then went up to his brother's room.

'Got out of that one all right, didn't you?' said Doug, glancing up from his magazine with a sarcastic smile.

'What do you mean?'

'All that stuff about Uncle Terry. He kicked you out, didn't he?'

'No . . . how do you know?'

''Cos I'm *not* stupid.' Doug leapt up from the bed and cuffed Aidan over the head with the magazine. 'Come on, let's go down the pub. *You* can tell me all about it.'

Outside, the clouds had broken up. The trees along the main road glistened with moisture in the sunshine. Doug was talking eagerly about a band he'd seen recently in Birmingham. Aidan was enjoying the sound of his brother's voice, which he had known so long it seemed like a part of him. They were heading for The Horse and Jockey, where Doug had been taking Aidan for years. Built in mock Tudor style, it was separated from the main road by a large car park. It was the kind of place that catered for the passing trade. A board by the side of the road advertised hot and cold food at the bar, and apart from a few local residents the most regular customers were travelling salesmen. Inside, it was spacious and sumptuously fitted with imitation red velvet. The eyes of the drinkers blinked at the light that was diffused through the pub by the large, frosted windows.

Doug marched over to the bar, his brother trailing behind him, and planted himself down on a stool.

'Oy, George,' he shouted to the barman, '*stop* rifling the till and come and get us some drinks.'

The barman turned round. His white shirt billowed out before his beer belly like a spinnaker before a hefty breeze. He sidled along the bar slowly, grinning.

'Well, if it isn't the great unwashed.'

'Yeah, yeah,' said Doug, rather irritably. 'Just get us a couple of pints, will yer?'

George promptly reached up for two glasses and began filling them. The ritual greeting was over. 'Expected you in earlier. Done the crossword already,' he said as he pushed them, foaming, across the counter.

'Yeah, well it was a big family occasion today. We were killing the fatted calf for the prodigal son here.' Doug jerked a thumb at Aidan, who grinned. George turned away.

'Cheers, Aid.'

'Cheers.'

There was a pause, and Aidan looked at his brother. Doug had never been a tear-away at school – in fact he'd looked scholarly, with his glasses and his solitary habits. But exams hadn't been his strong point. Once he'd started failing, and known he was failing, he'd attached himself to the group of more daring boys who drank in the pubs and rampaged through the town at night. Once school was over, the group split up. Its members got cars, or jobs, or girlfriends. Only Doug remained, touring the old pubs and waiting for an old mate to turn up. He drank a lot. His face, which used to be thin and taut like Aidan's, had puffed and sagged. There were dark rings beneath his eyes. But Aidan could see himself in Doug, especially in his thin lips. And, of course, their hair was the same, straggling down to their bony shoulders.

'This American bloke's great,' said Aidan.

''As he *got* a gun?'

'Course not.'

'Just jossing yer.' Doug grinned and, with one nervous movement, flicked his glasses up his nose and sipped his pint. Aidan smiled back and drank his.

'You know anything about Vietnam, Doug?' said Aidan after a pause. 'What was that all about?'

Doug whipped off his glasses and said in a deep imitation-American voice, '*Shit. Sighgone. Onler Sighgone. Everer tarm ar wake urp ar think arm back in the jungle.*'

Aidan laughed. Doug could always make him laugh. 'What was that?' he said.

'God, you are pig-ignorant.'

'Well, what's Vietnam then?'

'I'll tell you what Vietnam is. Vietnam's why I asked if your American mate's got a gun. That's right, isn't it, George – these Americans are crazy.'

George, who had wandered along the bar to catch the end of this conversation, smiled indulgently.

'They come in here when they've lost their way to Stratford,' Doug continued. 'That was a laugh with those two last week. They come in here and ask George, "Is this a genu*ine* tavern from Shakespearian tarms?" And you know what this old crook says? "Of course, Madam. This has been the drinking place of kings."'

'Well they might have bought a drink,' protested George.

'If I hadn't put them right.'

'Bastard.'

'I was just *being* an honest citizen. I said to her, "In actual fact, I doubt if this pub's as old as you are." They didn't like

that *at* all. They looked a *bit* confused. The old man gave me a
nasty look, and she kind of pursed her lips up like a . . . *sphinc-
ter.*'

'Losing me all that trade,' said George to Aidan. 'If he didn't drink
so much himself I wouldn't let him back in.'

'Well we've got to have a bit of excitement around here sometimes,' said Doug. 'Bloody backwater. My brother's living in London. He's moved in with a Yank.'

'That right?' George looked at Aidan with his bleary eyes.

'Come on then, Aid,' said Doug. 'Get us another drink.'

Forty minutes later, with two more pints inside them, Aidan and
his brother left the pub and started walking home. The air, after the
stuffiness of the pub, tasted cool and fresh.

'What you doing tonight?' said Doug.

'Dunno.'

'Wanna go to a party?'

'Yeah.'

'Remember Gary Wilson? He's getting engaged to some bird.
Should be a laugh. Unless you want to watch TV with the dinosaurs.'

'No. I said, I wanna go.'

'You'd be *into* that would you?'

'Stop fucking me about. Yeah.'

Doug laughed.

When the two brothers got back to the house, they found their
mother and father watching the horse-racing. The electric fire and
cigarette smoke made a warm fug.

'What are you boys going to do this afternoon?' asked Aidan's
mother.

'We're gonna burn the town hall down,' said Doug.

His father smiled faintly. As Aidan followed his brother out of
the living-room, he looked back and noticed that his parents were
holding hands.

Upstairs, Doug flicked the switch of the electric fire and put
a record on. It was Pink Floyd's 'Dark Side of the Moon'. A
doleful guitar began pounding from the speakers. Doug, sitting
cross-legged on the bed, laid the record sleeve across his knees,
pulled a pack of Rizlas from his pocket, and began taking a cigarette
to pieces.

'What'ye doing?' said Aidan.

'What d'yer think? I'm rolling up.'

'What about them?'

'No problem. They never come in here. 'Sides, they wouldn't know what it was.'

Doug softened the lump of cannabis resin with the flame of his cigarette lighter and crumbled some of it into the tobacco.

'Here, wanna light that candle?' He passed Aidan the cigarette lighter.

Aidan took the candle down from the bookcase, set it on the floor, and lit it. A sweet smell touched his nostrils. The candle, fixed in the centre of an old plate, was burnt half-way down. At its base was a mess of wax, ash, and matchsticks.

'What yer playing at? Turn out the light then.' Aidan leapt up, and the room, plunged for a moment into gloom, focused around the flame of the candle.

'Put that one on.'

Aidan got up again and switched on a small bedside lamp. It illuminated a pile of dirty clothes on the floor.

Doug finished rolling the joint, by stuffing a small piece of cardboard from the cigarette box into the end, and lit it. A cloud of strong-smelling smoke billowed out across the bedroom, and Doug took a deep drag.

'Yeah,' he said in a deep, slow voice. 'Burn it down.' After a couple more puffs he passed the joint to his brother.

Aidan, holding it between his thumb and index as his brother had done, took a drag, and was seized by a pleasant sense of relaxation. Hundreds of vivid thoughts surfaced in his mind.

'Hey Doug,' he said. 'You should come down and visit me in London. You could stay with me in this old house. You could meet Mr Morton – Bob.' Once the idea occurred to him, he had a mad enthusiasm for it. His tongue started running away from him. 'You'd really like him. He'd like you. He's done all this stuff, like going to all these places in America and meeting these people and being on the TV. He's really interesting, he's got all these stories—'

'Hey, don't bogart the joint.' Doug leant across and took it from between Aidan's fingers.

Aidan shut up. He felt stupid for having talked so much. He looked up at his brother, who was reading the record sleeve. Above him hung a psychedelic poster, black with swirls of fluorescent colour. To his right, at the foot of the bed, was the window. The curtains had only been half opened; they had obviously been like that since Doug had got up that morning. For some reason, this detail set Aidan thinking. It made him feel intimate with his brother. He thought of him waking that morning and reaching down the bed to pull the curtains apart just far enough for him to see down into the back garden. It was late afternoon now, and the column of sky between the curtains was perceptibly darkening. The year was slipping slowly further into Autumn. A strange sequence of thoughts passed through Aidan's mind. The bedroom was cosy and warm. The music surrounded them. The day had hardly entered the room, just seeping in through that crack in the curtains. Night had joined hands with night, sleep with sleep.

Doug was grunting. Aidan reached out and took the joint from his outstretched hand. It was almost finished. He shivered when he pulled on it. His head began to buzz again.

'Doug, what do you think about being English?'

'What?'

'What do you think about England?'

'You're daft. What kind of question's that?'

'Bob asked it me.'

'Who's Bob?'

'The American bloke.'

'So he *has* got a gun.'

'Shut up. He asked it me.'

'And what did you say?'

'Not much.'

'What?'

'That's what I said.'

'And what did he say and what did you say and what did he say . . .' They both laughed.

'What do you think of England, Doug?' They were both still giggling.

'What did he say?'

'Not much.' They roared with laughter. 'Well?'

'It's the pink bits.'

'What bits?'

'The pink ones. I told you.'

'What are they?'

'On the old map at school. *You* remember. You've got Pinky and Perky. Pinky – that's us. Then you've got Perky. That's the Germans. And the Russians.'

'I never heard that.'

'That's 'cos you *never* listen. Bloody hell, they'll never learn you. Is your Yank a Perky?'

'No, he's—'

'He's a Porky! Could be a Perky, you know.'

'Shut up. He's all right.'

'OK, OK. Cool it. He's a Pinky really.'

For a moment Aidan felt foolish, then he smiled. He liked his brother. 'What about another joint?' he said.

'There speaks a true Pinky,' said Doug, reaching for the record sleeve.

'Let's shut up about that now.'

They smoked another joint. But the mood between them had soured, and now they went into their own worlds. The room felt stuffy to Aidan. He heard the stupid music for the first time. *Hanging on in quiet desperation is the English way.* Everything seemed cloying. He was sick of it all.

'Oy, Doug. I'm going out for a bit.'

Doug grunted. He'd gone back to reading the record sleeve.

Aidan went downstairs. As he tiptoed through the hall, he heard his mother shout from the kitchen, 'Douglas?' He ignored her, and closed the front door quietly behind him.

It was cold outside. Aidan zipped up his denim jacket and set off towards the end of the estate. There was more light than he'd thought there'd be. When he looked at his watch, he was surprised at how little time had passed in Doug's bedroom. He'd walked down this way many times before. You used to go over some allotments to get to the canal, but now there were new houses and behind them a muddy track that led to a rubbish tip. The path was still there, but now it wound between garden walls. Aidan picked his way through the puddles by the orange light that flooded across from the street lamps on the estate. His sensations, coming from the stuffiness of his brother's bedroom, felt acute. Once on the towpath of the canal, he turned right towards Baileys, where he had worked until the beginning of the year. Baileys was an iron foundry and manufacturer of industrial transformers and generators, the largest employer in the town. Aidan's dad had worked there himself for fifteen years until, two years ago, he had been made redundant. Baileys had been bought by a bigger company, and although they kept people like Aidan, they were laying off a lot of the skilled workers. Aidan's dad hadn't had a job since. When Aidan got shown the door too, it didn't look like he would be able to get work, not even in a shop or a MacDonalds. Then his mother got in touch with Uncle Terry, her brother, whose building business in London was doing well. Within a couple of months, Aidan found himself living in his uncle's house in London, labouring for him.

Now, looking up at Baileys in the chill evening air, Aidan felt an exhilarating mixture of strangeness and familiarity. The part of the factory that backed on to the canal dated from the time when the canal was still used for transporting the iron. Imposing brick walls rose sheer out of the water, slightly sinister in the half-light. A couple of lights had been left on inside, throwing into silhouette the enormous dark shapes of the machines. A constant drip fell from some broken guttering into the canal far below. Aidan could picture vividly in his mind what it had been like in there during the day. The work had been boring, but he had liked looking around at everything while he worked, exploring the shapes and spaces made by the metal and concrete, watching the strange juxtaposition of the rows of unfinished machines and the men and women who serviced them along the production line, who bent sometimes right inside them to tighten bolts and put on washers. The memory fascinated him. His ability to recall it so vividly fascinated him. Here he was, standing by the canal in the twilight, but inside his head something completely different was going on. It was past, yet here it was, repeated in his head in a different, transparent form. Who could say that it was finished? The past, the present and the future came together in Aidan's head as things not different, but of the same substance.

He walked on. He felt as if he had discovered something important. He wanted to tell someone about it. Doug might understand, but he wouldn't want to talk about it. His mum and dad – they would listen, but they wouldn't understand. They would just think Aidan was ill or depressed about something. The only person who he could think to talk to about it was Bob Morton. And didn't he have something to do with it? That first night in the house, after he had talked to him about America – it had been the same then. Aidan had seen things in his head then, things that he had never experienced. He pictured Bob Morton now – his wide, expressive mouth and large eyes. But above all, there was his voice. All Aidan's sense of possibilities centred around him.

'Doug, hang on a moment,' said Aidan as they left the room to join the rest of the party downstairs.

Doug halted on the landing and turned slowly round. 'Whassit?' he said.

'I wanna talk to you about something.'

'Christ. You're like a fucking old woman.'

Music pounded from the bedroom and from downstairs, crashing together around them. Aidan nervously lit a cigarette.

'I dunno why you let those people say that stuff,' he said, blowing the smoke towards Doug.

'You *are* full of crap.' Doug turned away, stumbling slightly on the stairs.

'Well I wouldn't . . .'

'You're fucking drunk,' snapped Doug. He continued down the stairs, then at the bottom, with a drunken change of mind, turned to confront Aidan. 'What'ye fucking talking about, anyway?' he demanded.

Aidan slumped down on the stairs. He was feeling drunk. 'Those people up there were laughing at you.'

'Balls.'

'She called you an old hippy. She was laughing.'

Doug leant forward and, gripping Aidan's hair, shook his head. 'We was *having* a *joke*.'

'Get off me,' said Aidan, pulling his brother's hands away. '*They* were having the joke. They were laughing at you.'

There was a long silence between the two of them. Some people pushed past them to get up the stairs. Aidan puffed on his cigarette and stared at the carpet. His brother was staring intently at him, and it was making him nervous.

'So what?' said Doug eventually.

'They were *laughing* . . .'

'Yeah, I know that. But so what?'

Aidan began to say something, but Doug interrupted him, 'You think I care what they think of me? Stupid cunts.'

'You might not care now, but some day you will.'

Doug laughed mockingly. 'What the fuck are you rabbiting on about?'

'Don't let people get away with laughing at you, Doug. It's a rule of survival.'

Doug looked at his brother for a few moments, then slowly began to smile. 'I know what all this is about,' he said. 'It's something to do with that American bloke. It's something Ronald Reagan said to you, isn't it?'

'That's got nothing to do with it . . .'

'What's going on between you and him? Why're you always going on about him?'

'I'm not . . .'

'Yes you are. What is it, he fancy you? Not a couple of queers, are you?'

'Fuck off, Doug.' Aidan pushed past him to the door.

Outside, he stamped along furiously. Christ, he thought, Doug's just as bloody stupid and set in his ways as Mum and Dad. Just as stupid and blind to what's really there. Anything new, anything different, and they'll shut their eyes to it or just laugh at it. Perhaps I did go on about Morton, but at least he's something *different*. That's what they can't stand.

When he got back to his room, Aidan read.

Davenport had been thinking about Earth when he first got back to his room in the Xykon. He always felt nostalgic for Earth when he took his books down, as he did then. He'd bought these theoretical texts when he was a student, and taken them with him everywhere since then, treasuring them. They were his bibles. Usually he took them down just to leaf through them, like chatting with old friends. But this time it was different. There was a sense of urgency. Every now and then he looked up from the books to make some notes, or to study the display screen where he'd called up the report he'd just written in the laboratory.

He knew his way around the books intimately, but he'd never looked in them for what he was trying to find now. As his desk lamp shone on hour after hour, cutting a funnel of light through the darkness of his tiny room, Davenport studied with unflinching concentration. The vast bulk of the ship around him gave its usual low hum. He worked his way through Urq-Bernhardt's Beyond Cosmology, *Qu's speculative and flamboyant* In a Grain of Sand, *and many others. He even went back to Mensah's* New Theory of Space-Time.

After many hours, he switched off the display screen and slumped back in his chair, exhausted. He couldn't be sure, of course – there was no evidence – but he had a horrible feeling he'd glimpsed the cause of those strange particles falling towards the planet. He listened to the quiet hum of the ship. Whom could he tell? Whom should he talk to? He'd never felt more alone, more isolated from his colleagues. He was still thinking with the back of his mind about Earth.

Two days later, Davenport was tannoyed to the communications room. He had sent a message to Starkon 243/P. This Starkon research ship, stationed 4,000 light years away, was Xykon's link with the rest of the universe, and with Earth. Paradoxically, it proved harder in some respects to put radio signals through extended space-time warp than it did a massive spaceship. Communication breakdowns were not uncommon. All Xykon's links with Earth, with the Milky Way, and with the Local Group came via the Starkon 243/P.

When Davenport arrived in the communications room, he found the technicians standing in a group around the printout console. The message was in:

Starkon 243/P. 19. 5/37. Received Dr Davenport's inquiries concerning sub-atomic particle shower. We have been reviewing situation in conjunction with Starkon 174/X. Report as follows: We have had no communication with any Milky Way or Andromeda station for 25 Standard Velocity Time Periods. We have had nothing from Starkon 169/T or 131/S for 22 and 20 SVTP respectively. All these stations, in the last bulletins we received from them, gave data on mystery sub-atomic particle shower. Our readings on this are higher than Xykon's (see data appendix). The particles appear to be the product of a hitherto unknown form of high energy nuclear fission. We are still investigating. We have been directing our NER (Neutron Emission Radar) at the area of Local Group, and have come up with following results: We are getting no readings of matter forms in this area. This area, and all Universe Sectors 2.46 and 2.93, appear to have been crossed by an expanding cloud of high energy and low density at sub-atomic level. The NER further indicates the expansion of this cloud through areas formerly occupied by Starkons 169/T and 131/S. We are checking for any malfunction in the NER.

Although it contained no more than the confirmation of his worst fears, Davenport stared at the communication in disbelief. He rubbed his eyes, which felt tired, and read it again. It was true. Earth, the Milky Way, the Local Group, and a sizeable chunk of the universe, had quite simply disappeared.

CHAPTER THREE

It was neat. One moment the plane was surrounded by cloud, the next it had dipped down, and underneath her there was England – England just like she had imagined it, with green fields and cute little villages. That moment, she knew she had made the right decision coming here. Some of her friends back home had thought she was crazy to go to Europe with no plans and no job. If they could just see how wrong they were, Laura thought, as the plane banked, lurching another chunk of suburbia into view. If they could just see, they would know she had done the right thing. She turned excitedly to say something to the old man next to her, but he had his eyes closed. He was gripping the armrest fiercely. Laura sighed, and took her father's letter out of her pocket to read again during the last few moments as the plane came into Heathrow.

Dear Laura,

Got your letter yesterday, and have I been busy since then! Enclosed is a ticket for a flight on September 16th. I'll meet it. I've been pretty tied up with the house. I'm already talking about it as though you're familiar with it. It's where we'll live. I call it the 'burnt house' because, well, because it's burnt. But it was a small fire, and the damage isn't as bad as it looks at first. I think I kind of took pity on it. If you want something 'grainy and rainy and black-and-white', like you said in your letter, then the burnt house is it – the authentic London experience.

I've been having it repaired, only the contractor's been way too slow, and now that you're coming

I have to get things moving. So I've sacked the contractor and started doing things myself. I don't think I trusted him right from the start – he's one of those Irishmen who pretends to be English. Anyway, we went round some builder's merchants yesterday afternoon, and I did some math and I reckon it's going to come out a *lot* cheaper. Your old Pa was not, as you know, born yesterday. It'll mean more time, of course, getting the materials, but hell, there's more to life than making TV programmes.

You want to play music when you come here, then that's what you should do. I just want to say, honey, that I think anything you decide to do with your life is great and fine by me. I mean that.

On second thoughts, I want to put in an exception to that. *Do not,* on any account, have anything to do with the slimy, rotten business that I've ended up in. Last week, they finally got around to throwing a welcoming party for me at the bureau, and never have I witnessed such an obscene orgy of back-stabbing and brown-nosing. During the first half hour, just about everybody sidled up to me to ingratiate themselves and say the vilest imaginable things about their colleagues. Well, I'd had just about enough of that, so I grabbed my old buddy Don Hexter (remember him from NY?) and we snuck off and got fried at the local pub. Maybe your old Pa isn't so old after all!

It'll be great to see you again, honey. Like you say, it'll be neat, us being together in London.

love,

Bob

He met her at the airport and drove her into London. A light rain was falling. Through the spray sent up by the cars, Laura took her first look at England. She loved this time of year. For her, the fall meant a new start, a new college year, a new set of objectives. Now there was no college, of course, but instead there was this. She didn't mind the rain. She didn't mind the drab parade of London's suburbia. It was new, it was different, and that was what counted.

He took her to look at the burnt house. She got out of the car and gazed up at the fire-blackened facade. It was still raining – a light, persistent rain that was like thick, clammy mist. She stood beside her father on the pavement and looked up at the house, at the boarded-up windows and peeling paintwork, and all of a sudden she felt very tired. The initial excitement of her arrival had evaporated, and now she was just conscious of having travelled thousands of miles and missed a night's sleep. She was not in the mood to be dumped in front of a derelict building and told that this was to be her home for the next few months.

'We cannot live here,' she said flatly.

But Morton hadn't heard her. He was marching up the crumbling stone steps and unlocking the blackened front door. Laura heard it open with a whine of complaint from the hinges. She followed him along the hallway, which was lined with building junk. Morton's voice echoed as though in a cave. They went down some rickety stairs into a dim basement.

'This is the part I'm really excited about at the moment,' he was saying. 'Trevor and Aidan are building an interior wall there' – he pointed at a pile of grey blocks – 'so it'll be two rooms. I think I might even have it as a self-contained apartment. Come and see the rest.'

Back up the stairs she followed him, feeling tired and mentally battered by the strangeness of everything around her. Morton didn't notice. He was too busy giving her the guided tour. They slowly made their way up through the house, until at last they reached the attic rooms at the top.

'My God, Bob. You haven't been sleeping here have you?'

They were in the front attic room. In the corner furthest from the door, on an old mattress, was a sleeping bag. It lay like the discarded outer skin of a snake, the way a sleeping bag looks when someone has left it in a hurry. Beside the bed was an empty milk bottle. The foil top was piled high with small cigarette butts. Rolled across the bare floorboards were a couple of empty tins. One had held tuna fish, the other peas.

'No, we'll stay in the Maida Vale apartment for the moment. Aidan's living here.'

'Who's Aidan and why's he living here?'

'Sorry, honey, didn't I tell you? Aidan's one of the guys who's working on the house. Well, he's just a kid really. It's a long story, but he's got nowhere to stay right now. So I said he could sleep here.'

'He's not some kind of weirdo, is he?' She had picked up a couple of Aidan's old science fiction books and was looking at their lurid covers.

'Of course not. He's a good kid. You'll like him.'

'So where is he now?'

'He's gone to see his folks out of town. He'll be back tomorrow.'

Laura put the books down and picked up Aidan's records, the Bob Dylan and the Mahler. She turned them over in her hands and said, 'Look, Bob, this is all very interesting, but is there somewhere clean and warm where I can just lie down and get some sleep. I'm really beat.'

'Sure. We'll go back to the apartment.'

On the way to Maida Vale, Laura lost it. She didn't know why, or how it happened. She made some comment about her father's driving, and when he asked her what the matter was it just came out.

'Nothing's the matter,' she said irritably. 'Nothing at all. It's just that everything's so weird here. What's going on? I come all this way to be with you and I find everything's just weird. I'm sorry, I can't deal with it. I mean, what are you doing with that house? What possessed you to buy it? And that boy – what's he doing there? Why do you suddenly take this kid in and have him staying in your house?'

'I like him,' said Morton. 'He's different.'

'He sounds weird to me. How long is he going to *be* there, for chrissakes?'

'Laura, this isn't like you. You're usually more tolerant than this.'

'And this isn't like you. What's happened to you since you came to this stupid country?'

Morton dropped her at the apartment and went on to the NWBC studios. Laura crept miserably into the spare bed and slept. She slept deeply, without dreams. When she woke, a couple of hours later, he wasn't back. She opened the curtain and looked out the window. The rain had stopped, the sky had cleared, and the light was fading fast. She felt better for having slept, but bad now for having said such dumb things to Bob. She would cook dinner for him to make amends. She picked up the money and keys he'd left on the table and went out to find some shops. As she clattered down the stairs of the apartment building, she started scat singing the tune to 'Softly as in a Morning Sunrise'.

By her first impressions of Maida Vale, she could have been in practically any city in the world. She stood for a moment on the wide street, the traffic sweeping by her, and tried to decide which way there might be shops. It looked the same in every

direction: rows of smart, five-storey apartment blocks, each with
sun-terraces and a little stretch of grass and a large car park. There
were no people anywhere, just the cars swishing past on the wetness
of the road. She set off to the right, which she reckoned, more by
instinct than calculation, was the direction of central London. The
anonymous apartment blocks continued. Once, she saw a man in a
fur coat hurry out of one of them, get into a black limousine, and
drive away. After a quarter of an hour, when she was on the verge of
giving up and returning to the apartment, she saw off the main road
a street of small, terraced houses. That looked more hopeful. She
turned into the street, and halfway along it she found a tiny grocery
store, its windows hidden behind a metal grille.

Inside the store it was warm, and smelled of spices. There were
just two narrow aisles, and the shelves were packed with a confusing
jumble of food, detergent, toilet paper, frying pans, packets of clothes
pegs. Behind the checkout counter, a plump-faced Indian man was
watching a tiny black-and-white TV. He glanced up when Laura
came in, registered her presence, then turned back to the screen.
There was no one else in the store.

Laura picked out some groceries and took them to the checkout.
The Indian man tore his gaze from the TV and tried to arrange his face
to look alert and eager to serve. It was a game show he was watching.

'Boy, am I glad I found you guys,' said Laura, dumping her wire
basket on the counter. 'I thought I wasn't going to find anywhere
around here.'

'Yes,' the man said, smiling at her nervously.

'This neighbourhood's a real wasteland, isn't it?' continued Laura.
She felt like some conversation. 'See I don't really know my way
around. My father's staying in an apartment just round the corner,
and I've just arrived this morning from the States. Seems like this is
the only shop in the area. You must get real crowded, if the whole
neighbourhood comes here.'

The man was silent for a moment, as though he expected Laura to
continue. Then he shook his head. 'No,' he said apologetically, 'not
many people. Not very much business.'

'Too bad,' said Laura. 'I guess they all go down to the mall. Do
you have mall near here?'

There was a pause. 'I do not think so,' said the man, in a
tone that made it clear he wasn't at all sure. He began ringing
up the items and putting them in small white plastic bags. Laura
paid.

'Thanks very much,' she said. 'I guess I'll see you around.'

'Thank you,' said the Indian man. As she turned to the door, he added, tentatively, 'Have a nice day.'

Laura encountered Aidan for the first time two days later. She had arranged to meet Morton at the burnt house after he had finished work at the studio. She spent the day going round the tourist spots – St Paul's Cathedral, Trafalgar Square, the Tower of London – and by late afternoon she was bored and tired. She had seen these places so often on film, all she felt was mild surprise when they were there before her in stone and mortar. It was almost dark by the time she had made her way by tube out of central London and up to the burnt house.

It looked grimmer then ever in the fading light, completely dark but for a glimmer from the first floor. The door was unlocked. She called out in the hallway, but there was no reply, only a dull echo. She could hear faintly some music coming from somewhere upstairs. As she stumbled in the darkness, her hand reached out and met the stairs. The bare wood was covered with dust and grit. She coughed into the musky, dark air. This house was too much. As she made her way up the stairs, she was careful not to touch the walls.

The music was a kind of quiet nasal moaning, backed by jangling guitar. Laura stood listening to it for a moment on the landing. Bob Dylan. She thought about knocking on the kitchen door, then just opened it and went in.

Aidan was sitting by the window. The music was coming from an old mono record player that sat on the table. The window was open, and the boy's feet were resting on the sill. A cold draught blew through the room.

'Hi. You must be Aidan?'

He looked round. 'Yeah, I suppose I must.'

'Yeah, well I'm Laura. Bob's my father.'

Aidan nodded.

'Did he . . . tell you I was coming?'

'Yeah.'

'I'm really beat. I went round all the tourist traps today. Thank God I've got that done. Now I can forget about them and concentrate on being a real Londoner.'

There was a pause. Laura sat down at the table and looked at him. He was wearing jeans and a denim jacket, and had that pinched look of someone who isn't dressed warmly enough.

'Aren't you cold with that window open?' she asked.

''Salright.'

'Suit yourself.' She picked up a book that lay in front of her on the table and laboriously read its title out loud. '*The Voyage Beyond Infinity*. Are you reading this?'

He nodded. He was rolling a cigarette now. She watched him. He was nodding in time to the music.

'Any good?'

''Salright. I only just started it.'

'I read *The Longest Journey* at college. I guess this must be a sequel?'

'I dunno.'

'I was kidding.' Pause. 'Are you a trekky?'

'A what?'

'Back home we have people called trekkies. They're crazy about "Star Trek", you know, they dress up as the characters and stuff. I guess you don't have that here?'

He didn't reply.

'Sorry, I didn't mean to be rude or anything. I . . . was just kidding.' She fell silent, and they both listened to doleful Dylan. Then she started again, brightly. 'I was only asking because I saw you had more of this kind of stuff upstairs. I guess you must be really into it?'

He shrugged his shoulders.

'I was just interested because I've never tried it myself. Somehow all that stuff about weird planets and space rockets just turns me off. Do you know what I mean?'

He lit his hand-rolled cigarette, picking off a piece of tobacco that had stuck to his lip.

'Do you ever read, like, ordinary books?'

'How d'yer mean?'

'You know, with characters and stuff, talking to each other.'

'You get that anyway. You read a book for something different.'

Laura pondered this for a moment, then looked at her watch. 'He's late. He's always late. Say, Aidan, would you like to come out to a pub? Is there one near here? I haven't been to a pub yet.'

Reluctantly, Aidan agreed to go with her. The only pub he knew was the one where he'd gone with Morton that first night. Laura left a note for her father telling him where they would be.

The Mulberry Tree was quiet. The barman was leaning up against the sink, reading a novel by Gide. Around the bar there were just a few regulars, men in their thirties who looked older – an accountant, a lawyer, an antique dealer, the man who owned the secondhand bookshop a few doors down. They watched with aloof interest as Aidan and Laura came in and sat alongside them at the bar.

Laura looked around for a few moments, then exclaimed, 'This is great! How did you find this place? This is the *real* London. A real London pub. It's just like I imagined it.'

'What do you wanna drink?'

'No, let me. What do you drink?'

'Pint of bitter, please.'

'A pint of bitter,' she repeated to the barman, who had stored his Gide carefully among the gin bottles, 'and I'll have . . . the same. 'When in Rome,' she added gaily. 'Now, Aidan, you've got to tell me all about yourself. Or do you want me to go first?'

Aidan shrugged his shoulders.

'OK, my name's Laura and I'm twenty-two and I graduated from college in the summer and I don't quite know what to do with my life although I think I want to be a musician. Familiar story, eh? Oh yeah, and I'm really excited about being in London because I've never been to Europe before. I guess that covers all the main points. How about you?' She grasped her beer glass with both hands and took a swig.

'Cheers,' said Aidan.

'Well?'

'Nothing really.'

'How do you mean, nothing? Oh no. Don't tell me. You're reserved, right? I knew it. My mother warned me. All Englishmen are reserved.'

'I just work for your dad.'

'But the *real* Aidan? That's what I'm after.'

'I dunno what you mean.'

'Sorry, I was just kidding again.' He looked annoyed. She thought she'd better change the subject. 'Hey,' she cried, 'they have music here.' She pointed to a tiny stage in the corner. There were a couple of stools on it and a microphone. 'Excuse me, barman! Barman! Can you tell me what music you have here?'

The bloke with the ear-ring leant across the bar and started talking with her. Aidan turned away, relieved not to have to answer her questions any more. She talked to you like you needed to be jollied along, chattering as if all hell might get out if there was a break in the conversation. Aidan had known a couple of teachers like that at school, the posh ones. They tried to smother you by talking very fast and very friendly. Still, she was all right apart from that. She was quite funny. She didn't look much like Morton. Her face was a different shape, and her hair was a different colour, and long and frizzy. She had a long, bony nose.

'Say, Aidan, it looks like I might have my first gig. I just have to find someone to play with, do an audition, and I'm in. You don't play the guitar or anything, do you?'

The barman had gone to serve another customer. Aidan shook his head.

'Pity. Oh well, I'm sure I'll find someone. I'll just have to keep coming back here. Anyway, this is such a great place. And the guy says they do plays upstairs. Can you believe it? And it's so close to the house.' She stopped. 'Oh yeah. The house. Aidan, is Bob serious about moving into that house?'

Aidan shrugged his shoulders.

'I mean, how do you deal with actually living in that place? It's so icky, with all that grunge on the walls, and dust everywhere. It gives me the creeps. How long do reckon it'll be till you guys have got it sorted out, you know, like a proper house?'

'I dunno.'

'Well I've just got to tell Bob there's no way I can move in there the state it's in at the moment. No way. He's crazy. I mean, what was he doing buying it in the first place? He must be out of his mind. He's got a perfectly good apartment in Maida Vale laid on by the corporation. Why he has to go and buy that dump . . . it beats me.' She took another deep gulp of her beer. 'Boy, this stuff's quite something. It's stronger than the beer back home, isn't it? Sorry, I guess you wouldn't know. I'm so beat. I went round all the tourist places today. Oh yeah, I told you that already. What else? I unpacked my saxophone yesterday. Even that sounds different here. *Everything*'s different here.' She laughed and drank some more beer. 'How do you get on with Bob? He's a pretty crazy guy, isn't he, my father? He's taken a real liking to you, you know that? I mean, it's not like him to invite people in off the street and have them live in his house. He can be quite tight-fisted underneath that Joe Sixpack-everybody's-my-buddy routine. Hey, there he is now.'

Morton had come in and was standing near the door, peering round the pub.

'Bob! Over here!'

Morton came over. 'So you guys are getting to know each other? That's great.'

Aidan wanted to get away, but Morton insisted he stay for a while. He had another half, then left Morton and his daughter to themselves. He took a circuitous route back to the burnt house.

He liked walking along the streets, looking into the lit rooms. As he passed, domestic scenes flashed before his eyes of couples, families, lovers, friends, in argument, joking, in intimate exchange. I'm different from them, he thought. The thought pleased him. I have no one else. I live at the top of the burnt house, and above me there is just the roof and then the sky and then space. He stopped, and looked across the street at an upper window where a girl was standing before a mirror putting a jacket on. She was getting ready to go out. She gave the jacket a gentle tug where it had got crumpled at her shoulder, then quickly picked up something and went to the door. The light went out. For some reason, it made Aidan inexpressibly happy to think that he would never see the girl again.

Davenport sat at a table on the stage, watching the crowd come into the massive central hall at the heart of the Xykon. It took quite a while for the fifteen hundred men and women to file in and settle down. There was an excited buzz of conversation. This was the first mass meeting there had been for some time.

'OK, guys,' Davenport said into the microphone when they were seated. His voice boomed around the hall. 'If you could just quieten down, we'll begin.' The voices in the crowd died to a murmur and disappeared. There was a silence. Davenport began to speak.

'I know that rumours have been going around about our losing communications with Earth, and I expect you've guessed that that's got something to do with why I've asked you all to come along here this evening. Now what we're going to discuss here is probably the most important thing we'll ever have to talk about, so this is what I propose. I'll give my summary of the situation, and my proposal, then we'll have questions and comment from the floor.'

You're stalling, he thought. Quit stalling. For chrissakes get on with it and get it over. He looked down at the expectant faces. He could feel a lump in his throat.

'We've been in touch with Starkon 243/P,' he continued, 'and according to their scanners, the whole of the Local Group has ceased to exist.'

Davenport hadn't meant to pause at that point, but he found himself needing to swallow. For a moment the audience was silent, then a noise like the wind blew across it as shocked faces turned to each other and started talking.

'What the hell do you mean, Davenport?' a man shouted angrily from the back.

'Listen. Calm down,' said Davenport. The audience were immediately

silent and attentive. 'It appears that the Local Group has been replaced by an expanding field of high energy and low density.'

'You mean an explosion?' asked a voice from the crowd.

'Yes,' said Davenport. It was time to be frank, 'The Local Group does appear to have been blown away.' He paused for a moment for this to sink in. This time there was no noise. Not a sound. 'Furthermore, this annihilation is sweeping through our universe – like an explosion. Some of you will be familiar with a theory put forward by Urq-Bernhardt many millennia ago. He proposed that just as galaxies can collide, with catastrophic consequences, so too can universes. The crudeness of our knowledge of dimensionality has precluded extra-universal exploration, and hence made it impossible to prove or disprove Urq-Bernhardt's theories. Until now, that is. I believe that this annihilation, this explosion that is sweeping across our universe, that has already engulfed Earth and the Local Group, is the result of exactly the type of universal collision postulated by Urq-Bernhardt all those years ago.'

'What about us?' came a voice from the audience.

'Us? We must survive, I suppose. We must set the Xykon on the strongest possible space-time warp away from the explosion. It is advancing towards us at enormous speed, but we can keep ahead of it.'

'When do we stop?' shouted someone else.

'Stop? We don't. We can't. We keep going. I've made some preliminary calculations, and at most the Xykon would be able to come out of warp for a generation. Then it would have to go back into warp and continue.'

'How do you mean, a generation?' Several people were shouting different things at once.

'I mean that this journey, this flight from the explosion, is endless. It's our bequest to our children, and our children's children, and their children, and so on into infinity. For ever.' He paused, and almost magically the hubbub in the hall died down. 'Some of you may have heard about the sub-atomic particle shower.' His voice was softer now, more relaxed and conversational. 'It was that that first gave me a clue as to what was going on here. I remember when I was a kid in Kansas, if there was a big storm coming you'd get these puffs of wind that'd throw dust up in the air. You always got a lot of dust in the air before a big storm.' His voice had died away almost to nothing, and the hall was perfectly silent and still. Fifteen hundred people were absorbed in vivid memories of the Earth they would never see again, 'I know it might sound like a desolate prospect, this never-ending flight from the explosion.' Davenport's voice was soothing now, then rising in a passionate crescendo. 'I can only ask you to think of our forebears, all those millennia ago, who with their reckless spirit crossed the great plains of America in horse-drawn wagons. Now it is our turn. The torch is passed to us. Before us lie the infinite plains of the *unexplored universe. We must cross them. The journey will never be over, but we must make it, or else the human spirit will surely be extinguished.'*

Davenport hung his head, surprised at his own eloquence. He closed his eyes. The hall was very still. Then someone started clapping. Someone else joined in, then a third, and the applause grew until the whole audience was clapping and stamping their feet. The noise was like a collective howl of sorrow, fear, and something almost like hope.

CHAPTER FOUR

London was coming to life around her. The more Laura looked around, the stranger and more wonderful everything became. The people were secret and enclosed. She couldn't figure out their sudden moods, the melancholy silences that would grip them, then be swept aside by bursts of absurd conviviality. They were as changeable as the weather they talked about all the time. In October, the city was buffeted by storms that swept in from the Atlantic. Wind and rain lashed down the streets and against the windows. In the street markets, great pools of water would collect on the plastic sheeting that covered the stalls, and when the rain was through and the sun had come out again, the stall-tenders would prod the plastic from below with broom handles so that the water cascaded down on to the tarmac. The winds would sweep the showers across quickly, then tear the clouds to shreds that skidded madly across the sky. Everything was driven by an exhilarating cycle of transformation. After the unnatural torpor of summer, it was as though this northern city were coming to life, were breathing more freely at the prospect of winter.

At her father's insistence, they had moved into the burnt house. Laura tolerated that better than she thought she would. There was electricity in the house now, and hot water. She still had occasional arguments with her father about what a crazy thing he had done buying it, but they did little to spoil the overwhelming thrill she felt at being in this foreign city. Early one morning, before her father was awake, she got up and went out of the house. The streets were quiet. Above her was clear, bright blue, while off to one side an enormous swathe of cloud, tinged with pink, arched from one end of the sky to the other. She felt the cold air tingle the insides of her nostrils. She walked on, until she came to a small park on a hill.

The park climbed up over the hill, an expanse of grass lined with trees. She started walking across the springy ground. She was feeling an amazed happiness. The world suddenly seemed like a miracle, a ball rolling through the empty infinity of space. It carried around it this swathe of atmosphere, with its gift of life. Life. She could almost taste it. The light was weak and pale, a northern light. It stretched up way past the houses, way beyond the city, across lochs and fjords, up into mountains. It was from mountains that it came – a thin, airless light. First light. Her blood was tingling with excitement. She felt like she could carry on walking up this park for ever, to Scotland, further north to where this light that stretched above her was from. She strode on, breathing deeply, almost running.

But the park didn't go on for ever. There was a road at the end of it. Laura was so wired up, so drunk on the fresh, early-morning air, that she didn't hear the taxi approaching. She just stepped gaily out on to the glistening wet tarmac. The first she knew was that something huge and black had shot into the corner of her vision. Then it was up against her, swerving and squealing. The driver slowed to a stop, jerked down his window, and shouted angrily at her, 'You tired of living?' Laura, who'd hardly registered it had happened, laughed and shouted back, 'You must be kidding. I love life. I love it!' The driver slammed his window up again and drove off, shaking his head.

It sometimes seemed to Laura that Aidan Fowler was tired of living. Maybe he was tired after working all day on the house, but anyway he never showed any enthusiasm for anything. It seemed that he was content just to drift along. She had tried asking him about what his goals were, what he wanted to achieve in life, but all he would do was shrug his shoulders in that infuriating way of his. But she liked him anyway. He was different. She had never met anyone like that before. Occasionally, she got him to have a drink with her at The Mulberry Tree, but usually he said he couldn't go out because he didn't have any money.

There were Americans, of course. Laura had plenty of acquaintances from college, friends of friends, who were studying or working in London. During her first month in the city, she called some of them up. They would meet. Once or twice she brought them back to the burnt house – Americans were always curious to meet her father. But she quickly got bored of them. She hadn't come all the way to London to hear the same voices as back home.

There were different voices in The Mulberry Tree. She had got to like the pub. It seemed to contain all the quirkiness she found attractive in the English. When Aidan wouldn't go with her, she

would go in there by herself in the early evening, when she had
finished practising her saxophone. The first couple of times she did
that, it was to find out if she could play there. But as she got interested
in the people, that fell into second place. There were a group of
regulars, barflies, who would be there everytime you went in. Their
membership would change a bit now and then, but fundamentally it
remained the same group that had been there the first time she had
gone to the pub with Aidan.

The early evening was the regulars' prime time, when the pub
was practically empty and they could quietly read their newspapers
or books, or banter with the barman or, more rarely, with each other.
Later on, when the pub filled up, they would seem diminished,
swamped. Some of them would stagger home, while those that
stayed looked a little pathetic, clinging to the bar while the crowd
washed around them. In the early evening, though, they looked
almost dignified, perched on their stools. There was rarely any
sustained conversation, because each respected the others' privacy.
After going to the pub for so long, they had come to an unspoken
understanding. Conversation, usually caustic and ironic in tone,
would start up suddenly between them, then just as quickly stop
and be forgotten. They would all return to their drinks and their
private preoccupations.

When Laura first began to sit with them, perched alongside them
at the bar, sipping a half pint of the English beer she had come to like,
they hardly deigned to notice her. Then after the first three or four
times, they began to give her a nod of greeting when she came in,
as though she had become so familiar, such an accepted part of their
world, that they didn't even need to exchange words. Laura found
it all very mysterious, but quaint and refreshing after her American
friends, who talked incessantly.

The first of the regulars to speak directly to her was Philip. He
was in his thirties, though he looked older, with a haggard, slightly
drooping face. He drank heavily, and as he drank the life would drain
out of him and he would grow more and more silent. At the start
of the evening, Laura had noticed, he would be quite sparky. That
was when the people connected with the theatre upstairs would be
coming in, the actors and their friends and hangers-on. They would
gather at the end of the bar and behave theatrically, throwing their
arms about and laughing loudly. They were hip, and Laura was
interested in them, would have liked to talk to them. But she also
liked listening in to Philip's dry comments. 'Oh darlings,' he would
say wearily as they began to trickle in the door. 'You know, there's

more acting goes on down here than up there in the theatre. It's more convincing, too.' Then the theatre people would move on, and as the evening progressed, and Philip got drunker, he would say less and less. He would just give a lopsided, knowing smile when somebody else said something. Then even that would go, and he would end up just staring straight ahead – in the middle of all the noise of the pub, his jowls drooping about his fleshy lips – as though he had come up against a wall.

So it was early in the evening that he spoke to Laura that first time. It must have been about her fifth visit to The Mulberry Tree. He turned to her and said, 'I suppose you're American?'

'Yeah,' she said, smiling. 'I am.'

He tutted and nodded his head, then said, 'What's the secret? Why are Americans so bloody happy all the time?'

'Who says we are?'

'All right. Correction. Why do you pretend you're so happy?'

They had got talking after that, and Philip told her all about himself. He had been a schoolteacher, and now he ran the secondhand bookshop a few doors down the street. He loved books. He was always reading something in the pub – Trollope or Ford Madox Ford, something slightly old-fashioned like that. He went on about how the shop was going bankrupt because so few people these days could read, never mind be interested in buying books. But he would never go back to teaching, he said, because he hated kids. He liked talking about children, about how evil they were and how you could see in them, in a kind of pristine form, all the loathsome things about people generally. At least, he said, as people grew up they learnt to cover up the worst things about themselves. Laura listened with interest. She had never thought about kids that way before.

The other thing he liked talking about was his student days. He had gone to Cambridge, and although he only ever made sarcastic comments about it, the way he kept coming back to the subject gave Laura the impression that that had been the most vivid period of his life. Nothing since then had lived up to it. He was a sad character, but intelligent and also quite gentle, and Laura liked talking with him while she watched the pub fill up with the London crowd.

But then a couple of weeks later, after they had talked maybe half a dozen times, something happened that meant they didn't see each other any more. Laura, for the first time, had gone into The Mulberry Tree at lunchtime. She had been practising her saxophone, but the noise of hammering and drilling made by Aidan and Trevor had eventually driven her out of the burnt house. There was a thick mist outside, making everything still and silent. It smothered the sound of the traffic and gave everything a moist, clammy feel. Laura went into The Mulberry Tree to warm up. Sheets of grey pressed up against the windows. There were only a few people in the pub, and Laura saw Philip sitting at his usual place at the bar. He was reading a book.

'Hi, Phil.' She went over to him. 'I didn't know you hung out here at lunchtime.'

'Well, now you know what a dynamic young entrepreneur I am, don't you?' He said it in his usual dry tone.

'How's the shop?'

'No sodding idea.'

'Business not good?'

'Two schoolboys looking for smut. They didn't find any. I keep that stuff back for myself. Hardly what you'd call a profitable morning.'

'I guess not.'

'So I've come in search of solace.'

He bought her a beer, and another for himself. The traffic outside sounded more distant than usual, as though the cosy interior of the pub had drifted somewhere far away. For some reason, they were both in high spirits. The freakish weather seemed to give everything a surreal, irresponsible edge. They quickly finished their beers, and Laura bought some more. Philip was telling her stories about the strange types who came into his shop.

'Christ, Phil,' she exclaimed. The beer was going to her head. 'You think you've got problems! Imagine what it's like living in a ruin. I'm not kidding – a ruin. The place is so goddamn primitive. And the noise and the dust – it's incredible. Add to that the two lunatics I'm living with. First there's my father, who's turned distinctly weird since he came to this country. He used to be, you know, the standard middle-class executive type, maybe a bit more intelligent than most, but now he's decidedly weird. I mean *strange*. For a start, he's bought this goddamn house. That's the thing I can't figure out. Oh well, anyway he spends all his spare time pottering around it planning all the things he's gonna do to it.

'So there's one lunatic, right, my father. The other is this kid called Aidan. Did you see him – he came in here with me a couple of times? He's kind of skinny with long hair and button eyes? Oh well, I guess he's pretty inconspicuous. Anyway, Aidan is so spaced out he's hardly even on the same plane of reality as everybody else. I mean, have you ever tried sustained communication with someone who exists in an alternative universe?' She laughed. 'You have to be very, very patient.'

Philip laughed too. He didn't laugh often, but when he did it sounded boyish and pleasant. He insisted on buying some more drinks. The pub was more crowded now, and everybody seemed to have had life injected into them by the close, cold mist that lingered on outside.

Laura was smoking cigarettes, which she didn't normally do, and listening to Philip talk about the eccentric characters he'd known at college. Philip seemed to have known lots of strange, larger-than-life people, almost like mythic figures. Laura liked hearing about them.

She looked at her watch. 'My God. Look at the time. Shouldn't you be getting back to your shop?'

'No. What for? What's the point? The bloody shop can wait. Let's have another drink.'

'I don't think I should. I'm feeling pretty drunk already.'

'That's the idea. Come on. I'm having one.'

'OK. It's kind of fun, isn't it, getting drunk in the middle of the day?'

'It's one of the great discoveries of our age.'

She laughed uproariously at that, though she didn't quite know why. It wasn't that funny. 'Cheers,' she said. 'Here's to secondhand literature.'

'May it rot.'

Later, they got on to music. The pub was emptying again, and one of the barmen was wiping down the tables. They were conspicuous, sitting at the bar, puffing manically at cigarettes and talking loudly. It was obvious that they were quite drunk. Laura was talking about her ambitions to be a jazz musician. 'You'll probably think this is really pretentious of me Phil, but I just know I could be a musician. I get such a buzz out of playing.'

'I've got a couple of jazz records. What are they? Ben Webster, that's it. Big fat black guy. Have you heard him?'

'I know the name. Come to think of it, I've never actually heard him.'

'Why don't we carry on the party? I've got a bottle of wine at home. I could play you some Ben Webster.'

Laura puffed on her cigarette, squinting at him through the smoke. 'Yeah,' she said, 'that'd be great.'

They stood for a moment out on the pavement, in the mist. Laura looked up, and through the grey haze, the curtain of moisture that drifted around and over them, she could see blue sky.

'Hey Phil,' she said, loudly, so passers-by glanced at her, 'Look there. Look up there. You can see blue sky.'

He mumbled something she couldn't make out and wandered off down the street. She followed him. He lived in a small flat above his shop. It was cold and sparsely furnished, and smelt of damp paper. He turned on the gas fire and they sat in front of it and drank old, bitter red wine.

It was warm in front of the fire. Through the grimy window, Laura could see the mist-shrouded blue sky again. Ben Webster's tenor saxophone was thick and sweet and old-fashioned. If she'd been sober, Laura wouldn't have liked it, would have got restless for something cleaner, with a sharper edge. But she was drunk, and somehow the combination of the soupy music, the wisps of mist floating by the window, the heat of the gas fire, was covering her in a fuggy, not unpleasant gloom. She tried to shake it off, lighting a cigarette and turning brightly to Philip. He had reached his silent stage, staring intently at the worn carpet.

'Say, Phil,' she said. 'What was I saying back there about my father?' He looked up at her, then back at the carpet. 'You know, I was saying he was kind of crazy? Well I don't want to give you the wrong impression.'

She could hear herself talking, watch Philip as he listened gloomily to her. It was so dumb, why couldn't she stop? She didn't even know this guy. What did he care what her father was like?

'I mean, he's a really nice guy in fact. You should meet him. All I meant was, the only thing that really bugs me about him sometimes is the way he talks to you sometimes like he's on TV. Do you know what I mean? But you probably haven't seen him on TV, have you? No, I guess he's pretty much an American phenomenon. All the time when I was growing up, even at college, it was always "Are you *really* Bob Morton's daughter?" It was like, I'd come home from high school and sit down with the rest of America to watch my father reading the news, or interviewing someone really famous. And he's good at it. Everybody loves him. They can't resist him when he turns on that smile and lets his eyes twinkle. What I hate is when you realise he's doing it to you, like you were the other side of a TV screen, or a camera. We had a joke about it when I was a kid, the two of us. He'd say something special, just for me, and then he'd say it like he would for the 'gap' – that was our word for the 'Great American Public'. He could really make me laugh. And he could say it special, for me. I hate that feeling that he's talking to you like he talks to millions of other people. I hate him then. It's like he's all surface. Do you know what I mean? Like a TV screen.' She paused. 'Fuck it, I don't know why I'm telling you this. We Mortons talk too much.' She suddenly felt very ashamed. She closed her eyes and hid her face in her hands. The room started spinning backwards violently in her head. She felt as though she was crying, but there weren't any tears. She was just screwing her face up out of confusion and momentary unhappiness. She sniffed anyway, and glanced at Philip. He was looking at her.

'Look,' he said, embarrassed, 'Are you all right? Why don't you come over here and sit next to me?' He stretched out an arm. It was a clumsy, drunken gesture, mixing lust and pity.

'Really, no thanks,' said Laura, and put her hand down on to an ashtray, 'I've got to go.'

'Don't go. You don't understand.'

Laura saw his pleading expression, his thick, fleshy lips, as she heaved herself to her feet. He reached towards her again, and as she stumbled for the door, the last thing she saw was the wine bottle tip over.

The rest of that day was awful. Laura felt hungover and irritable, confused and a bit guilty about what had happened, or almost happened, or not happened, with her and Philip. She had an argument with her father, and snapped at Aidan for stinking the kitchen out with his hand-rolled cigarettes.

But the next day, after she'd had a good long sleep to get the beer and wine out of her system, she felt much better. She dropped into The Mulberry Tree, but Philip wasn't there. Nor was he there on the next day, nor the one after that. He had stopped going there entirely. Laura thought about going into his shop to talk to him, but then she passed him on the street and he pretended not to see her and crossed to the other side. Whatever it was had happened – and nothing had, after all – he didn't want to be reminded of it.

It became one of those mildly unpleasant incidents you forget about. It quickly faded, and Laura started taking her music more seriously, practising her saxophone regularly and hustling to get a chance to play at The Mulberry Tree. She was a good sax player. She had had excellent teachers, and had a natural feel for melody and rhythm. If she had a weakness, it was in her harmonic range. She had never really bothered to sit down and learn all those complicated substitution chords that a post-Coltrane player is meant to know. To a certain extent, she could get over that just by flair, but only to an extent. It was symptomatic of something more general in her playing, which was that although it was great as far as it went, it only went so far and then just seemed to give up because it couldn't be bothered to go any further. The real problem was that she had never had to stretch it. Her parents looked after her financially, and at the back of her mind, unspoken but underlying her whole attitude to music-making, was the thought that it was really just a hobby.

Eventually, she got her chance to play at The Mulberry Tree. A pianist was looking for someone to share a spot with him, and she got it. He was a competent but unexciting player, and together they could run smoothly through a set of a dozen standards. The best thing they did was an outrageously bluesy version of 'Tea for Two', with a heavy walking bass.

Laura was getting a buzz from playing in public again, but she was also frustrated at playing background music. It was a noisy, drinking crowd. Then one night, she got a break. After they had finished the set, a small, fat man came up to her and congratulated her on her playing.

'Very witty playing,' he said. 'Very *witty*.' He said 'witty' quickly, spitting it out with evident relish. He had an extraordinarily round head and a red face, crisscrossed with broken veins.

'Stanley Morgan's the name,' he said, and shook her hand.

'Laura Morton.'

'And a very honourable name that is for a jazz musician to have.' He beamed at her. 'Now Miss Morton, I'm in the same line of business as yourself, and the band I play with has recently been bereft of its saxophonist. I think you would be just the performer to fill that sad void. Would you be at all interested?'

'You're asking me to play in a band? Are you *kidding*?'

Laura leapt up the octave, then down again. She strided up and down, all the time edging her way along the chromatic scale. She felt very happy, and full of music. On Saturday, in a couple of days, she was playing her first gig with Stan Morgan's band, at a pub in Bloomsbury. And over the last couple of weeks, she had been going out to hear jazz all over London. She had heard everything from old men puffing away at 'St Louis Blues' and the 'Saints', to young men scrabbling feverishly at 'Chasin' the Trane' or wallowing in moody things of their own. Some of it she liked, some of it made her laugh. She felt like she was bursting with music. And tonight, in addition, she was going to have dinner with her father. She felt like she had hardly really talked to him since she had come to London.

As she played, Laura gazed at her father's things stacked up on the bare wooden floor. She had taken to practising in her father's room, the big bedroom at the front of the first floor, during the day. She did this mainly because the acoustics were good, but also for another reason. She didn't know what it was. Perhaps it just felt comfortable, made her feel nearer him.

She put her sax down and went next door to make some tea. She had got to like the thick, strong tea that the English drank. You could get quite high on it. Downstairs, the men were working. She didn't know what they were doing, but every now and then there was a thump, or the scrape of something being dragged across the gritty floorboards. Occasionally, there was a burst of whistling, or the low drone of Trevor saying something to Aidan. They would be stopping soon. It was already dark outside.

Laura sat down at the table and sipped her tea. In front of her on the table was Aidan's book. Its cover stared vacantly up into the room. She picked it up and read:

After the meeting, Davenport was sitting in his tiny cabin with his assistant, Steve Schroeder.

'I still can't believe it,' said Schroeder.

'You'd better.' Davenport leaned back against the wall and rubbed his face, feeling exhausted. They were sitting next to each other on the narrow bed.

'But . . .' Schroeder began.

'Don't. It's true. We've run all the tests we can, and then some.'

'No, I was just wondering about this flight, about keeping the Xykon going away from the Explosion. I mean, how do you motivate people to keep going when there's no end to it, when there'll never be any end to it, for anyone? Isn't there any hope at all . . . of escaping?'

'None. Hell, what did you expect me to suggest? That we stick around here until we get blasted to nothing? No, there's no hope.' There was a long silence. 'Except maybe – no, forget it.'

'You've got to tell me now.' Schroeder grinned at him.

'It's nothing really. Just my own theoretical speculations. You must promise not breathe a word of this to anyone, ever. You know how ancient mariners, when they still thought the Earth was flat, used to fear falling off the edge of the world? Well, we still don't know what happens at the edge of the universe.'

'But that's ridiculous. The universe is infinite in this mode of space-time. Everybody knows that.'

'Yeah, but what is infinity? We know nothing about it. By its nature, it's beyond human comprehension.'

'Do you mean that . . . something happens?'

Laura looked up. Aidan had come into the room.

'Hi, Aid. Say, this book of yours is kind of goofy, isn't it? "The universe is infinite in this mode of space-time." I mean, come on, he cannot be serious. Do you reckon the guy who wrote it ever gets embarrassed writing prose like that?'

Aidan shrugged his shoulders. He sat down at the table and rolled himself a cigarette.

'Do you want a cup of tea? I just made some.'

'Yeah, thanks.'

She poured him some tea. 'Are you doing anything Saturday night.'

'No.'

'Well, how would you like to come hear me play? I've got my first gig with this band.'

'Yeah, OK.'

'That's great. Do you like jazz?'

'No.'

'Oh well. Listen, I've gotta go now. I'll see you later.'

Three quarters of an hour later, Laura was at the plush London headquarters of the New World Broadcasting Corporation. The receptionist told her to go straight up, as her father was expecting her.

The two people in the lift, a man and a woman, held the doors for her, and she got in with them. They were in the middle of a conversation, and when she joined them they stopped. But after they had surreptitiously checked her out, and not recognised her, they carried on where they had left off, only in subdued voices. They were both American.

'Where did you hear all this?'

'You know – a bit here, a bit there. Put it all together.'

'It wasn't Frankson gave it to you? You know what he's like.'

'I'm not that dumb.'

'So where does that leave us? If they're pensioning him off by sending him here, it doesn't say a lot for the status of this operation, does it? I mean, what does it say about *our* prospects? I always knew Tokyo was the hot posting.'

'Don't get so paranoid. It's completely different. He's on the way down, and we're on the way up. We've just kind of met in the middle.'

They both laughed.

'But how come he's on the way out? He used to be their blue-eyed boy.'

'He's gone crazy. Celia in Planning was telling about some of the projects he wants to follow up for this series.' She raised her eyebrows

and shook her head. 'And then there's that house he's bought . . .'
The doors opened at their floor and they got out, still talking.

Laura stared in disbelief as the doors slid silently shut. They were talking about her father.

Chapter Five

The view from the veranda, through the thick but beautifully clear perspex walls, was magnificent. It was almost sunset, and some workers were making their way back along the trail that led from the station into the jungle. They looked anonymous and somehow comical in their heavy radiation suits and breathing apparatus, Marquaiana watched as the last of the group lumbered into view out of the gleaming white foliage. She was trying to tell which one was her fiancé, Rachon. She couldn't. Her gaze left the men and wandered across the gothic landscape.

The steep hills, densely vegetated and dripping with moist heat, piled up towards the horizon. From the veranda one could only see the ground right below, where it had been cleared around the entrance to the station. Beyond that there was just the unbroken upper canopy of the forest. Not that the canopy was uniform, for here and there the superior fronds of styrex plants shot up into the sky, their enormous diamond-shaped leaves of the palest yellow, drooping and threatening to buckle under their own weight. The top of the white forest was tinged now with the greenish-blue glow of sunset. Marquaiana never tired of this moment. The glow seemed to start at the heart of the sun, a bright blue ball on the horizon, and spread out across the white carpet of leaves like liquid.

Her reverie was interrupted by a soft groan. She turned round and looked tenderly at her grandfather.

Carl Davenport was lying on a simple bed of neutralised styrex wood. His soft brown eyes started up into the sky, which was now suffused with green. For a moment he opened his mouth, then closed it again. His ninety-year-old faced had shrunk around its bones. Every now and then, the breeze from the fan ruffled his delicate white hair.

'Are you all right, grandfather?' said Marquaiana. She crouched down at his side.

Davenport slowly turned his head. Then, when his faraway brain had registered his granddaughter, he smiled.

'Dying,' he said quietly. 'Apart from that I feel just fine.'

Through the perspex could just be heard the low, intermittent hum of the drachmas. From time to time their translucent forms flitted close to be veranda.

'What are you thinking about?' Marquaiana asked after a pause.

'Earth,' said Davenport. 'There aren't many of us left who . . . who were there.' He smiled to himself. 'All gone now.' He turned his head again to look at her. 'It does me good to . . . to see you, Marquaiana. There were times in the old days, just after we found out about the Explosion, when we wondered whether it was worth carrying on. What did we have to look forward to? A lifetime of running away. Of course, there was some idealism. We never heard from Starkon, so almost certainly we were the only humans left in the universe. It was as though we had been chosen. The Elect.' The old man spoke softly, his voice dropped to a whisper. 'And yet, why struggle for survival with no end in sight? It wasn't the struggling – the years of flight, the calculations and arguments about how long we could stay on a planet. It wasn't that in itself that was so awful. It was the idea of its endlessness. The idea that neither we nor our descendants would ever find a home. Some did . . . give up. But the rest of us realised that it wasn't just for us to decide. Looking at you now, I know we were right.'

Marquaiana reached out and held his hand. Davenport smiled again.

'But what a life you've been born into,' he continued. 'You'll never know what it was like in the old days. Before long you'll leave this planet, and it'll be left behind you and completely forgotten. What would be the point of remembering it? It will go. And you'll fly on, and stop, and fly again. Always behind you will be the great wave of annihilation, and in front of you only restlessness and forgetting.'

Davenport fell silent and closed his eyes. Marquaiana looked at him fondly. He was a sweet old man, but he did talk such a lot of funny nonsense. She gave his hand a little squeeze. It was stiff between her fingers. She started in alarm, and leant over him. He had stopped breathing. He was dead. She flung his hand down and turned away in fear and disgust.

Aidan, sitting at a table in the corner of the pub, put down the book and squeezed some water from his hair, watching the brown liquid trickle down onto his denim jacket. He had been working late with Trevor, repainting the back wall of the burnt house. His hair and hands and clothes were covered with brick dust and old mortar.

He went to the loo for a wash, and when he got back Laura had arrived, her saxophone case banging and clattering through the swing door. Behind her came a gust of damp air.

'Oy, shut the door, will you?' shouted the man behind the bar. 'It's perishin' in 'ere.'

'OK, OK,' snapped Laura as she struggled to unjam herself from the door. She got herself a drink and sat down with Aidan, pulling an *A to Z* out of her bag.

'I'm not sure how to get to this place,' she said, frowning at the map. They'd arranged to meet in this pub near Euston Station and walk together to where she was playing.

Aidan watched her as she pored over the book, flicking impatiently from the maps to the index and back again. She was still in a bad mood. He had noticed her bad mood over the last couple of days.

'All right?' he said.

'What?' she looked up crossly.

'You all right?'

She smiled. 'Yeah. I'm sorry.' She put the book down. 'We'll find it. I just feel kind of edgy tonight. I guess I'm a bit nervous.' There was a long pause, and they sipped their beer. 'Actually, you've probably noticed I haven't been myself recently.' She sighed. 'I had a bad time with Bob the other night – you remember we were having dinner.' She stopped. 'Aidan, do you mind me talking about this with you? I just have to talk with someone about it.'

He shrugged his shoulders. 'I don't mind.'

'What happened was, when I got to the studios, I got into the lift with these two people, and they were talking about Bob. At first I didn't realise who it was they were talking about, they were just talking about this guy who was, like, losing his position in the corporation – you know, they figured he was on the way out. They were being really nasty, laughing at him and stuff. Then just as they got to their floor they mentioned the house – they were saying he was crazy to have bought it.' She smiled. 'Well maybe they did have a point there. Anyway, that's when I realised who they were talking about. It was so weird, overhearing it like that. I told Bob about it and would you believe it he just wasn't interested. He didn't want to know. He said he didn't care what people thought or said about him. That's not the Bob I know. I kept trying to tell him what those people had been saying, but he just would not listen. We had a kind of argument about it. I just got so mad at him. Then we made it up. But I still feel strange about it. For chrissake, that was his job they were talking about. I just don't understand his attitude since he came here.'

They sat in silence for a while, then Laura said, 'I feel better now. Thanks. I guess things aren't so bad. He said he might come along to the gig tonight. And we're going out together again next week. We're going to a concert with a Member of Parliament called Charles Tetchley and his family. Pretty exciting, huh?' She looked at her watch. 'My God we're going to be late.' She threw back her drink, collected up her stuff, and they made for the door.

A warm, damp wind blew. Laura's coat flapped against her legs, and a black rubbish bag billowed along the road in front of them. The clouds that speeded overhead were luminous white against the dark blue sky.

'So you don't like jazz, Aidan?' she said, raising her voice against the wind.

'Not really.'

'Have you ever heard any?'

'My dad's got a couple of Acker Bilk records.'

Laura laughed and gave his arm a squeeze. 'Oh boy,' she said, 'are you in for a treat.'

They crossed the Euston Road, where the cars hissed on the wet tarmac and the neon lights were smeared into the puddles, and entered the no-man's land between it and Bloomsbury. Laura dug the *A to Z* out of her bag again, and after a couple of false turns they found The Man in the Moon. A notice in the window read 'Jazz Tonight. Stan Morgan Quartet.' The word 'Quartet' had been crossed out, and 'Quintet' written above it.

It was a large pub, divided into a bar and a music room at the back. Between them was a wide doorway. The music room had a small raised platform in one corner, and on the platform were an old upright piano, a double bass and some chairs. Two spotlights, suspended from the ceiling, were trained on it, and round the walls, which were painted red, were black-and-white photographs of people playing jazz.

'Christ,' said Aidan, looking round at the tables packed with people, 'aren't you nervous?'

But Laura hadn't heard him. She was waving to someone at the bar. 'I've got to go,' she said. 'You find somewhere to sit down.'

Aidan bought a pint and went through to the music room. He sat down near the back and looked around. The platform, the spotlights and the photographs around the wall gave the room a theatrical atmosphere. The members of the audience glanced every now and then at the empty and brightly lit stage. A man staggered up to it with a drum kit under his arms, and there was some clapping and an explosion of laughter from one of the tables.

Through the wide doorway, Aidan could see Laura standing at the bar with a group of men. The group started making its way into the

music room and through the tables towards the stage. There was more
ironic applause, but the musicians, still chatting amongst themselves,
ignored the audience. They clambered on to the platform, shading
their eyes and staring crossly at the spotlights. A short, fat man with
a red face, clearly the boss, climbed painfully down again and went
back to the bar to get them turned down. When he returned, he got
stuck with one leg up on the platform, and Laura had to help him
up. They looked comical standing next to each other – Laura tall,
with her saxophone dangling from her neck, and him short and
self-important, with a trombone between his pudgy fingers. The
pianist reminded Aidan of an actor who was always in old comedies
playing a schoolmaster, with a big moustache on a hang-dog face.
None of them looked how Aidan expected jazz musicians to look.
They thumped, rattled and honked for a couple of minutes, then the
trombone player called them to order and, without waiting for the
audience to quieten down, nodded to Laura to begin.

Aidan recognised the tune. It was 'Night and Day'. Laura played
it slowly first, in a free tempo. The pianist blocked in the chords,
while the drummer produced a shimmering effect with his sticks
on the cymbals. If it had been any other jazz tune Aidan wouldn't
have recognised it, but 'Night and Day' had been on his mother's
treasured record of 'Great American Showtunes'. Aidan could see
the cover now, with its top-hatted figure – teeth gleaming and arms
outstretched – against a background of the Manhattan skyline. He
could remember his mum singing it. And when he was about six she
had starred in *Salad Days* at the amateur dramatics. Dad had helped
with the lighting. He hadn't ever thought about that. And now, just
because of this tune that Laura was playing, that his mother used to
sing, the memory came to him clear as anything. There he is in shorts,
sitting next to Doug on the wooden chairs of the church hall. His
mum's up on the stage beside the piano. There's a bloke playing the
piano, and another telling her how to sing her song. And after all the
rehearsals, the evenings of being told to sit quietly at the back of the
hall, or of kicking a football around at the back where the dustbins
were kept, there is the performance, and the strange sight of mum in
beads and funny clothes, with lots of lipstick on.

The music was going faster now. Laura flew up and down her
instrument, spraying notes at the audience. Many of the notes were
strange and dissonant. Behind her, the drums chugged on, and the
trombonist, who hadn't played yet, slapped his thigh in time. She
grew more frenetic, bouncing at the knees and almost getting her
hair tangled in the keys of her saxophone. Aidan didn't really like

her music. You couldn't call it beautiful. It seemed she was fighting the other musicians all the time instead of playing with them.

But the audience loved it. When she stopped, and the trombonist took over, they clapped and cheered widly. It jolted Aidan out of the dreamlike state into which he'd fallen. He looked round the room. Straight away he spotted Morton standing just inside the doorway. Morton happened to glance back at that moment. He came over.

'Hi, Aidan. Say, Laura's doing a pretty good job out there, isn't she?'

Aidan nodded and moved over to make space for him at the table.

'I had to hang about at the house waiting for the telephone engineers. We've got ourselves a telephone now. Pretty good news, huh?'

Aidan couldn't think of anyone who'd want to ring him. Also, he preferred the burnt house when it was cut off, when it was different. He didn't want it being like everywhere else. He didn't want it part of the system.

Morton was sitting down now, tapping his fingers on the table. It was the trombonist's turn. The slide of the trombone shot in and out as he glided and snarled his way through the melody. When he had finished, the drummer banged and crashed by himself. Just when Aidan thought it was never going to end, the drummer gave a kind of drunken yell, and all the others joined in to play the tune again. Then they stopped. Before the applause had died, they had started on another number.

'It's strange to hear Laura play these old tunes,' said Morton, leaning closer to Aidan to make himself heard. 'I mean, like this tune.' He paused for a moment and listened. '"Take the A Train". Godammit, this is the music of my youth. I was dancing to this tune way before I even met Laura's mother. And now here's Laura playing it. That's passing time for you. You like dancing, Aidan?'

'No.'

'Too bad. Still, I guess things are different these days. I don't reckon I'd be a dancer myself if I was young now. Ever since the sixties it's been do-your-own-thing. Where's the fun in that? In the old days you asked a girl to dance, and you danced with her, alone. You didn't all dance together in a group. Maybe I'm being sexist or old-fashioned, but I like the man to lead and the girl to be in his arms. It was the sixties did it. That's when the whole thing changed.'

Aidan rolled himself a cigarette. Usually he liked listening to Morton, but sometimes, like now, he didn't. Sometimes he was boring.

Morton seemed to sense that Aidan was losing interest. He picked *The Voyage Beyond Infinity* up off the table and said, 'I met Arthur C. Clarke one time. Sixty-one it must have been, at a conference I was covering. Nice guy.' He paused. Aidan lit the cigarette, said nothing. 'I'll tell you who was a big science fiction fan, and that was Bobby Kennedy. I remember when I got back to D.C. after that conference, he wanted to know everything about it. Crazy about the stuff, he was. He'd read it all. Not that he'd let it go public, mind you.' Morton chuckled. 'He absolutely forbad me tell anyone about it. "Bob," he used to say, "if it got out that I read science fiction it would be the end of my political career. People would think I believed in UFOs. They'd think I was a nut. I'm keeping a lid on this one." I hope you're not thinking of running for parliament, Aidan?'

Aidan shook his head. 'They're a bunch of bastards. They're just interested in power.'

Morton laughed. 'I guess you can't argue with that. You could have a point, though. I've known dozens of politicians in my time – some of them quite well – and in not a single case have I felt any lasting attachment. It always seemed like they were on guard, watching what they said. Watching you watching them. And it wasn't just that I was a reporter – it seemed as if they were like that with everyone. They had to be. Except that in some cases, the really successful ones, there didn't seem to be anything behind that mask. They were all surface. Like Johnson – he was the consummate politician. I only saw his mask slip once. That was one time when I saw him throw his stetson down in the washroom. He was in Texas . . .'

'Shall I get another round?' Aidan interrupted. He suddenly wanted to get away from Morton.

'Sure, let's have another beer.'

It was difficult to get to the bar. The people who stood in the way were so fixed on the music they didn't notice Aidan when he asked them to move. He had to push through them. Suddenly, everything – the crush of people, the noise, Morton's endless talk – felt to Aidan like one big weight. It was crushing him. He struggled on, treading on people's toes and jogging their arms so that they split their beer.

He made it to the bar. He was just on the point of ordering the drinks when everybody around him started clapping. The band had stopped. Aidan looked round at the stage. Laura was giving a bow, and the trombonist was shaking spit out of his instrument. When the spit was out he went up to his microphone, and his deep voice boomed out around the pub, 'Thank you very much, ladies and gentlemen. We're going to take a break now for a cup of tea.' The people around Aidan at the bar laughed and clapped again. The musicians clambered down from the stage and, led by Laura and the schoolmaster pianist, started threading their way through the audience towards the bar. Morton was coming out of the music room too, to meet them. Aidan, watching them approach, had suddenly had enough. He slipped through the crowd and out of the door of the pub.

'Congratulations, Mr Morton,' said Stan Morgan, when Laura had introduced them. 'Your daughter's going to make a lovely little musician.' The two men, pumping hands, beamed at each other. 'Her taste is perhaps a bit advanced for old has-beens like us – '

'Hasn't-beens, more like,' added the pianist lugubriously.

–'but she has been restraining herself admirably and keeping a tight rein on those fantastic flights of the musical imagination that might confuse us humble souls brought up on Miff Mole rather than Manfred Mann.'

'Manfred Mann?' said Laura incredulously.

'Forgive me,' said Stan, hand on chest, 'I speak from ignorance.'

'Here's to you, Stan Morgan,' said Morton. 'I haven't heard trombone playing like that since Jack Teagarden in '63 – one of the very last concerts he gave, I believe.'

Stan, by way of expressing his pleasure, raised his short but substantial bulk up on to his toes, then gently lowered it again. 'No, Mr Morton,' he said, looking at the ground and shaking his head, 'you place me in illustrious company indeed, and I only wish I was worthy of your praise.'

'You guys,' said Laura with a grin, looking first at Stan and then at her father.

'You may laugh, Laura – ' said Morton

'Gee, thanks.'

'–but one thing your generation has lost is a sense for the niceties of social interaction. I was just touching on this point with Aidan – he was here a moment ago – '

'I shouldn't think he was too impressed with that,' said Laura.

'Aidan is better at listening than you are.'

'You should respect your elders and betters,' announced the pianist.

'Politeness,' continued Morton, 'is the lubricant of social discourse.'

'Like Castrol GTX,' suggested the pianist.

'A good point, Mr Morton,' said Stan, 'and soundly put. I hope you're paying attention, young Laura?' He grinned at her across his beer.

'Why don't you save your wind for the trombone, Stan?' she said, and patted his stomach.

A few minutes later, Stan looked at his watch and said with a sigh, 'Well, lady and gentlemen, I'm sorry to have to tell you that we must return to our musical duties. To your instruments! Mr Morton, it's been an honour and a pleasure to share your company, and I hope to repeat the experience before too long.'

Farewells over, the musicians trailed back onto the stand, arranged their instruments, and launched into 'I Want To Be Happy'.

The tune didn't reach Aidan, who was several streets away by now. He had stopped on a corner, partly to catch his breath and partly because he was wondering if he shouldn't go back. He stood for a minute, panting and undecided. Then, with an unconscious gesture of dismissal, he walked on.

He was lost. He had deliberately lost himself when he ran away from the pub. It exhilarated him not to know where he was, among the official-looking, forbidding buildings. He ran his hand along a black iron railing and looked up at the dull brick facade. He didn't know what it was – perhaps a Ministry or a part of the University. It didn't matter. The street was deserted, and only in the distance could he hear the hiss of traffic on wet tarmac. He looked up past the facade into the night sky. He had left the pub, and all Morton's talk, far behind him.

After a few minutes he came to Kings Cross. When he got to the front of the queue at the ticket office he found he hadn't got enough money. Also, he had left his tobacco in the pub. He climbed back up to the street and started walking north. He didn't mind having to walk. He didn't mind anything. As he climbed the hills into North London he felt something slip off him. His steps were lighter, but he walked more slowly. It was a long way to the house, and he got lost again. When he finally made it back he found the house quiet and in darkness. He didn't know what time it was. He didn't know if Morton and Laura had already come back and were asleep, or if they were still at the pub, or somewhere else. He didn't mind. As he groped his way up through the house, he didn't even pay attention to whether it felt like a house that is empty.

CHAPTER SIX

Jeremy Tetchley stepped out of the cinema, past the lurid posters, on to Brewer Street. He walked away quickly. 'Peep Show', 'Live Peep Show', 'Private Booths', 'Erotic Bed Show', 'Massage Parlour'. His eyes flitted about. He went into a peep show, came out, and walked on quickly. His heart was beating fast. He stopped. What to do? He felt excited and sick. He lit a cigarette and looked at his watch. It was opening time.

He worked his way through the crowd in the pub and bought a drink. He half expected people to turn and stare at him. It was as though he were marked. The thought excited him. His guilt and self-disgust excited him. This is like a deep hole I'm falling down, he thought. Only there's no bottom to it. I'll just keep falling. He found a seat and stared into his beer. I'm drowning, he thought. No, it's more like one of those wheels with a mouse running round and round inside it. And I'm the mouse. He took a swig of beer and smiled wryly. What the fuck did it matter, anyway? That's what the people who'd sneer at him didn't realise. What the fuck did it matter? He looked around the pub. Most of these blokes did the same thing. He grinned to himself. They didn't feel like he did about it. They could just come in here afterwards and have a chat or joke with the barmaid. Peasants. He felt nothing but contempt for them.

He got up and had another drink, then another. He glanced at his watch. Shit. He was late. The pavements were crowded, and he had to dodge out into the traffic. He ran down Charing Cross Road, along the side of Trafalgar Square, and only slowed down to a walk once he was on Hungerford Bridge. A train thundered by beside him. Up ahead, the Royal Festival Hall, its lights blazing, rode like a battleship into the Thames. Jeremy looked down the gap between the footbridge and the railway lines, into the dark, fast-moving river. You'd be

65

sucked under in a few seconds if you jumped. You'd never know a thing. But they would. They'd be sorry.

'I can't think where he can be,' muttered Margaret Tetchley. She flashed a smile at Laura.

'Jeremy's just finished university,' said her husband lazily. 'He hasn't really decided what he's going to do next. I'd like him to go into politics, of course. Mind you, in a way I'm quite relieved he's shown no ambitions for that – the way he talks sometimes, you wonder if he wouldn't end up on the other side.' He laughed.

'I was just telling Laura about Jeremy,' put in Margaret Tetchley sharply.

'Anyway, there are plenty of alternatives. He's very bright, you know. There's law school, or the city . . . I've always thought advertising would be an interesting area for him. He's good with words. I don't have to tell you that the media's where the future lies, do I, Bob?' Charles Tetchley Conservative Member of Parliament for S—, gazed serenely across the foyer of the Festival Hall. Nothing pleased him more than to mix business and pleasure. It was pleasant to sit in this comfortable chair, nursing a gin and tonic and looking out at the lights along the river, and it was important to be pleasant to this American television journalist.

'Looks like you've got things pretty much mapped out,' said Morton.

'Sorry?'

'For your son.'

'Oh, I wouldn't say that,' said Tetchley modestly.

'It's so nice to sit down and relax before a concert, isn't it?' said Margaret Tetchley to Laura. She was trying to draw her back into a separate conversation.

'Yeah, sure,' said Laura, concentrating on what her father and Tetchley were saying.

'I dunno, Charlie,' said Morton thoughtfully. 'Have you got to the stage in life when you wonder what it was all for? I have. I look back on all that drive and ambition and wanting to get places, and I ask myself, "Well, so what? Where's the beef?" Do you know what I mean?'

'I really can't see anything wrong with wanting to better oneself. 'That's what keeps civilization going. If people didn't have enterprise . . .'

'Sure,' said Morton, waving Tetchley aside just as he was about to launch on one of his favourite speeches. 'You can want to build a bridge, or write poetry, or fly to Mars. But a *career*? That's the idea I've come to dislike, that slow, blinkered crawl to the top.'

Laura was listening to this conversation with increasing unhappiness. She couldn't understand her father these days. His reaction to what the people in the lift had said was only part of it. He never talked excitedly about his work like he used to. Now he just talked about that damned house. And he had taken to coming back from work early sometimes to work on it, which was totally unlike him. Then there was the stuff he was saying now. It upset Laura. It was as though her whole conception of him were being destroyed.

'But, Bob, that's so hypocritical,' she blurted out. 'What have you done but "crawl to the top", as you put it?'

'Your daughter's quite right, you know, Bob,' said Tetchley. 'I mean it's all very well for you to sit in your ivory tower and make pronouncements, but out there in the real world—'

'That's not what I meant at all,' snapped Laura.

'Sorry if I misunderstood,' said Tetchley, and pursed his lips.

'What I was getting at was the complete opposite. What I meant, Bob, was that it's you that's lived in that "real world" and played by its rules. You've never really turned round and done something different. So you can't suddenly say now, "It's all crap".'

'Why not?'

'Well . . . you just can't.'

'Just because I'm getting old doesn't mean I can't change. Why *can't* I turn around now and say "It was all a mistake"?' He opened his hands and smiled at her.

'Why can't you? Because . . . because where does that leave me? Was I a mistake? If you've got a past, you've got a responsibility to it. You *can't* just turn your back on it.'

'Well perhaps we should start making our way to the box,' said Margaret Tetchley brightly. She picked up her handbag. 'If Jeremy's coming he can find us there.'

'But, honey,' said Morton, 'I was only talking about careers and stuff. I wasn't talking about you.'

'I never know what you're talking about these days.'

'Well,' said Margaret Tetchley, 'I really do think we should make a move.' She led Laura away, and glared back at her husband.

Charles Tetchley roused himself as if out of a kind of stupor. 'Yes,' he said jovially, 'off we go. Children, Bob. They're a terrible problem. I gave up trying to control mine years ago.'

'My problem's with the kid trying to control me,' said Morton.

'Oh quite,' said Tetchley. 'Absolutely.'

When Jeremy arrived, the last concert-goers were hurrying across the foyers, urged on by electronic bleepers, to the doors of the auditorium. The sound of clapping could be heard. Jeremy knew where his parents' box was. They used it for entertaining most Sundays, though sometimes they just left it empty or lent it to friends. He scampered up some stairs and along a corridor. The clapping, which was for the leader of the orchestra, had stopped, and there was silence. The orchestra sat still on the platform. Then there was a larger burst of applause and the house lights were dimmed, as the conductor, preceeded by the soloist, a leading black American soprano, walked out between the violins. At that same moment, Jeremy slipped into his parents' box. His mother, who was sitting by the door, was the only one to see him. She motioned him to sit down, and shoved a programme into his hands. Throughout the music she glanced at him fussily.

At the front of the box were Jeremy's father, a girl with long frizzy dark hair whose face he couldn't see, and a short oldish man wearing a bowtie. They were looking down at the orchestra expectantly. Jeremy wiped his face. He was trembling and out of breath. He could smell the smoke and beer on himself. Then the music started. It came from very far away, from nowhere. Once it had started, it seemed to Jeremy that it had always been there and that there hadn't been a moment when it wasn't in existence. It was like a vast, timeless ocean made suddenly and vividly present. The violins rocked like waves, and then almost immediately a woman started singing in German.

The music enveloped him, and he relaxed into it. (Or almost – he wished his mother would leave him alone and stop staring.) It was sad, wistful music. As soon as he started listening to it, the hard, cynical person he had been in the pub cracked, and he almost felt like crying. He was like a little boy again. The woman's voice, soaring above the orchestra, than falling back into the rocking arms of the violins, seemed all-forgiving. He was overcome with relief and exhaustion. As the music went on, he began thinking about the journey he used to make home from boarding school for the holidays. There had been a certain kind of yearning he had felt during those journeys – after the cruel pressures of school – for unconditional acceptance, for a complete embrace. And when he was at school, he used to send himself to sleep by pretending he was a fallen hero, and that he was being nursed by a beautiful woman. He would curl himself into a foetal ball, close his eyes, and imagine a scenario. They were always different, and he was good at inventing new ones, but it might be something like chasing a bank robber in the street. The robber would turn and shoot him in the leg or stomach. He would be lying on the hard pavement, and the woman would rush to him and kneel at his side to comfort him. Later she would visit him in hospial and stroke his head and ask him how he felt. Silently, for fear that one of the other boys in the dormitory would hear him, Jeremy would mouth the words that would have passed between them.

Morton heard the first song with only half an ear. Music, especially classical music, was not his strong point. When he found himself at concerts he would spend his time reading the programme. On this occasion, Morton first noted with satisfaction that the singer was from Chicago. He regarded Chicago as the most American of American cities, and was proud of having been born there. His Chicago origins played a large part in his public image, and did much for his popularity. The American public liked a man to have roots, but a connection with New York, say, or Boston or Los Angeles, might have run into regional antagonisms. Chicago was just the town where they played hard ball.

Morton read the programme. 'Richard Strauss completed his 'Four Last Songs' in Montreux in September 1948.' Morton knew enough about music to be surprised at the date. This sounded like it had been composed in the nineteenth century. Morton had been in Germany, near Wiesbaden, in September 1948. He had just finished his training as a radio operator, and been flown out there. He was twenty, he had never been out of America before (he had only been to New York twice). He had hated it. Mostly what he remembered was the cold, the mist on the flat German countryside, and the depressing barracks where they lived. That was the time of the Berlin Air Lift. You could hear the big-bellied transport planes thundering overhead at night. They were sending them in sometimes one every three minutes. The Germans seemed frightened and distant. They didn't know what was going to happen to their country. It was strange to think that while all that was going on, old Richard Strauss was down there in Montreux writing his songs, utterly oblivious. Listening to it, you'd never think the two world wars had happened. There was a *fin-de-siècle* feel about it, a whiff of Old World corruption.

Morton read on, but the programme booklet was disappointingly slim, and he had finished it by the end of the first song. So he put it down and listened to the music. The second song had an Alpine feel. The violins were high up, like thin cloud, and beneath them the orchestra was cavernous and vast. The woman from Chicago started singing. Her second phrase, two descending triads, was like the theme tune of 'Jesus Christ Superstar'. Through a peculiar association of ideas (musicals and mountains), Morton found himself thinking of 'The Sound of Music'. Julie Andrews running timelessly across a sunlit meadow. Yeah, the music fitted it pretty well. It was like film music. Only better, probably. They had had music like this in the forties when Hollywood got a craze on historical romances, usually with a European setting. The English aristocrat would be languishing away thinking about his girl, the Marchioness of this or that, who was awaiting the tumbrils in Paris. That's when they'd have this music. Then the young man would rouse himself, leap up from his chaise-longue, and vow to cross the channel to save her. At that very moment there was a surge of activity in the cellos. Morton chuckled out loud.

Charles Tetchley heard him and glanced sharply across the box. Like all Americans, Morton was too loud. Still, he had to be tolerated. He was the kind of man one had to make oneself available to. That was why Tetchley had originally suggested they meet, and subsequently issued this further invitation including their respective families. Still, he could have done with someone less fond of the sound of his own voice. Like interfering in decisions about Jeremy's future – that was an insolent piece of nonsense. And his daughter was not much better, far too full of herself. Quite a looker, though. He stared down at the orchestra again, pushing the Mortons to the back of his mind. The orchestra's uniform pleased him, as did the regimental up-and-down sweep of the violinists' arms. Most of all, though, he liked to watch the conductor. He liked the conductor to be a heroic figure, like a great general above the battlefield. He liked him to look the part. The week before, there'd been this little Jewish chappy conducting, and he'd been quite awful – all hunched up and jumping around. This one was much more like it, with his head upright, his silver-grey hair brushed back and his chest thrust out. Charles Tetchley would have loved to have been a conductor. A conductor was a kind of hero. The musicians beneath him worked away at their own little parts, but it was the conductor who had the vision to see the whole thing and the leadership to guide those placed in his charge. He stood at the front of the orchestra like a figure-head, or like a warrior in battle who bares his chest to the sword. Of course, the picture was spoiled rather by the singer. Tetchley couldn't resist giving himself a little smile. She did look pretty ridiculous – apart from anything else, she was so bloody *fat*!

Laura, sitting between the two men, noticed both her father's chuckle and Tetchley's reaction to it. She smiled to herself. Her attack of unhappiness about her father had blown over, and now she was thinking, as she liked to, about music. As a child, she had played the clarinet in youth orchestras, but she had always preferred playing jazz. In classical music, it seemed, the emphasis was on the vertical placing of the notes; everything had to be strictly *together*, as coordinated by the conductor. Jazz musicians tended to come at things from a different way round, thinking first about the rhythmic drive that propelled the band through the harmonies. She liked it that way. Every now and then you'd hear a concert hall piece played like that – spontaneously, the way Toscanini used to conduct. But not often. Yet, thought Laura, that must have been the way Bach or Beethoven sounded when they improvised. By its nature, that couldn't be reproduced.

The last song opened like a quick-blossoming flower. The horns boomed across the hall, and the violins began their slow, aching ascent. Against the woodwind's sustained, sombre chords, the two violin parts were held almost in suspension. They climbed, then as they fell they twirled around each other like falling leaves. The horns sounded again. The violins gave way, and the song began. Laura was thinking about Aidan. He was elusive. She usually had no time for people who seemed ungenerous with themselves, but Aidan was different somehow. There was something strange there. She was beginning to get an idea why Bob liked him. Yet it was out of character for him too, for he, notoriously, liked people to be 'up front'. But then you couldn't say of Aidan that he wasn't 'up front'. That was just it. You couldn't tell if he was keeping something back or if that was all there was. With him, it all seemed more fluid than just those two alternatives could allow for. But fluids run away. That was the problem with Aidan, thought Laura. He ran away.

The woman had stopped singing. The dark chords had returned, without the violins this time. It seemed that they would go on for ever, getting darker and colder. Then above them, on two flutes, there was bird-song. It was repeated, and again, then the piece was over. It was as though at the end of a long, wearying journey one had glimpsed paradise.

The second half of the concert, a Beethoven symphony, didn't move Jeremy like the first had done. There was a rectitude and integrity about the music that made him feel uncomfortable. He sat with his elbows on his knees, and rubbed his nose in shame. His life was poisoned. He hadn't even been able to look at the American girl, Laura Morton, without stripping her in his mind. She had talked to him so trustingly in the interval, and he had smiled and said clever things back, when all the time for him, in his mind, she had been no different from the pictures on the screens in Soho. And she had had no idea how he was looking at her. For a moment the thought of that innocence excited him, then he was revolted at his excitement. So Jeremy's misery went on. Each thought, mixing attraction and repulsion, turned back on itself in a pointless, endless involution.

But things were never actually as bad as they seemed for Jeremy. After the concert, as the party of Tetchleys and Mortons walked to a nearby bistro, he was able to talk easily with Laura.

'I've heard of your father, you know,' he said smoothly.

'You have?'

'Of course. He's the Walter Cronkite of the 1980s, isn't he?'

Laura laughed so loud that her father and the older Tetchleys, who were walking some twenty yards ahead, looked round to see what the matter was. There were moments, such as this, when Laura was aware with a sense of exhilaration of being in a foreign country. The mist wrapped itself around the lampposts. She laughed into the cold, damp air.

'Hey, Bob,' she shouted, 'this guy reckons you're like Walter Cronkite.'

Charles Tetchley, looking back, frowned. Bloody loud-mouthed girl, he thought. Don't they teach them any manners over there? His wife, walking at his side, thought much the same – only she also thought it was a shame, because Laura was pretty, and would be nice for Jeremy.

'Well ask the young man if he'd care to step inside with me and we'll sort that out,' Morton shouted back. But the joke was weak. He seemed dispirited.

The three older people turned and walked on, ignoring each other. To Laura they were funny, like an absurd caricature of three people not getting along. Charles Tetchley had his head turned huffily away from the others, pretending to survey the architecture of the South Bank. His wife watched him anxiously, then glanced at Morton, who was studying his shoes as they scuffed the pavement. Every now and then she coughed or shivered her shoulders, as though that might make up for the lack of conversation.

When they got to the bistro, Tetchley took charge and ushered them all to a table he had chosen. It was dark, with a candle on each table. Somewhere in another part of the restaurant a saxophone and guitar were being played. Laura, with Beethoven's rhythms still charging through her head, asked if they couldn't move nearer the musicians. They did, much to Tetchley's annoyance. He had taken a strong dislike to the American girl.

The table at which they settled was in an alcove. Jeremy found himself sitting on a bench at the back of it beside Morton. For a while, after the wine had been ordered, they sat together in silence. Laura, sitting at the mouth of the alcove with her back to them, listened intently to the music. Beside her, the older Tetchleys were having some kind of argument through clenched teeth.

'Laura plays the saxophone herself,' said Morton eventually. 'She's damn good, too. I heard her play just last week.'

'Really?' said Jeremy. 'That's great. The sax is *the* really hip instrument at the moment. I mean jazz is almost boringly trendy right now.'

'That right?' He looked at Jeremy with interest. He was dressed entirely in black. His wavy brown hair had been cut into a geometric shape, shorn hard at the sides. 'You seem to know a lot about what the fashions are.'

'Christ,' said Jeremy, 'you can't avoid it. I mean you're just bombarded with images and prescriptions about how to behave all the time. It's all really predictable – what the music is, what the clothes are, what the politics are. I mean it changes all the time, but only like a mouse on a tread-wheel. It just goes on and on. Everybody reads the same magazines and hangs out at the same places to watch each other. It's really claustrophobic.'

Morton screwed his eyes up to peer through his pipe smoke. 'I can't tell whether or not you like it. Do you want out?'

Jeremy laughed. 'God, I wish that was an option. Like I said, you can't avoid it. I mean I suppose you could kind of drop out and join a commune in Wales, but that's so disgustingly hippyish.'

'You've got yourself a real dilemma there,' said Morton. 'I'm glad I never had to face that.'

For an unpleasant moment, Jeremy wasn't sure how seriously he was being taken. 'Yeah, well America's different,' he said. 'I went to school there for a year. To be perfectly honest with you, I couldn't stand it – it was so boring. I mean, things drive you a bit mad here, but at least there's something going on. In America everybody dressed the same, talked the same.'

'That's because it's a democracy,' said Morton.

'I don't see how you make that out. I mean, Britain's a democracy.'

'So they say.'

They were silent for a while. Jeremy felt all right when he was talking, but as soon as he stopped there was a bout of guilt and self-pity. His parents had finished their argument, and his mother was smiling at him stupidly. He lit a cigarette.

'Actually,' he announced, 'neither of them's really a democracy.'

'Yeah?' said Morton. 'How do you figure that?'

'I mean people just get their opinions straight from the TV or the papers. It's the media that really controls things.'

'That right? But you're an intelligent young man – I'm sure you don't believe everything you read in the papers.'

'Of course I don't, but . . . well, I've been lucky to have had a good education.'

'Yeah,' said Morton, 'but there's the problem. You reckon that people who haven't had an education like yours are gullible and believe anything that's told them. How do you know that you don't just believe that because your teachers told you it? It could be a product of *your* upbringing.'

Jeremy nodded, puffing on his cigarette. It was the kind of tortuous train of thought that appealed to him. 'You could have something there,' he told him.

'Damn right I could,' said Morton.

After the meal, the Tetchleys and the Mortons went their separate ways. Morton drove Laura to the burnt house, while the Tetchleys got a cab back to Dulwich.

'Thank God that's over,' said Charles Tetchley as they sped down the Old Kent Road. 'I'm afraid they were rather unbearable, but it was important for me to put on a show for that Morton fellow.' He smiled at his family. 'Thanks for your support.'

'That's all right, darling,' said Margaret Tetchley. Then she added, 'It must have been very dull for you, I'm afraid, Jeremy.'

'Not really,' he said. 'I thought they were cool.'

Charles Tetchley snorted. 'Each to his own taste.'

'Yeah,' said his son acidly, 'That's right.'

CHAPTER SEVEN

The tower on Paan was a mile high. It had taken five years to build, and was designed to last at least fifty. It housed all the Xykon crew.

The Council had decided that according to the OSV (Overall Survival Velocity), the colony could remain here fifty years. Then they should leave, pressing on away from the Explosion. Hostilities had broken out with the natives of Paan as soon as the Xykon had landed. The Paanites had a backward civilization. Their machines for sub-orbital flight were quite sophisticated, but space flight had hardly been attempted. Yet they fought fiercely and rejected all offers of negotiation. The humans of the Xykon warned them about the Explosion. Over the generations (the Paans existed on a short life-cycle) the imminent apocalypse entered Paanite religion. But it did not, as had been hoped, weaken their resistance. They fought on. To annihilate the whole Paanite population would have wasted precious energy resources, so the humans decided to build the tower, and retreat to its safety.

The tower's foundations reached a mile underground. Like the Paanites themselves, the tower was streamlined in the shape of a wing against the wind that hurtled constantly around the planet. Otherwise the vibrations would have been unbearable. The top quarter of the tower, high above the surface of the planet, was for the defences. An integrated system of radar and lasers, of which the scientists were very proud, provided total protection both for the tower itself and for the bunker next to it that housed the precious Xykon space-time ship. This barrage of technology faced a series of ever more sophisticated Paanite aeroplanes, but they never got through. Thus it was that the Paanites spent their last precious generations before the Explosion battering uselessly at the armoured tower.

Aidan put the book down and breathed deeply, feeling his chest expand. The air was cold. He stretched his arms behind his head, feeling the muscles tighten. Working on the house had toughened him. He got out of his sleeping bag, put on his shirt and jeans, and went downstairs. The wooden floorboards were rough beneath his bare feet.

He went down to the first floor kitchen and put a pan of water on the camping stove. He pulled up the sash window, leaned out to look across the back gardens, then sat down and rolled a cigarette while the water boiled. It was a beautiful day. The sky was cloudless. You would have thought it was summer, if it hadn't been for the cold draught coming in by the open window. Aidan opened the old mono record player and put on the scherzo of Mahler's Fifth Symphony.

It was his favourite movement, a rustic, outdoor waltz that somehow seemed to be heard from a great height. Listening, he looked sleepily out of the window. The steam from his tea rose before his eyes. On the other side of the back gardens was the rear of another terrace of houses. All the curtains were drawn. Everybody was still asleep. The french horn was playing the kind of tune you would whistle out walking. It was odd to think of the rows of people lying in their beds with their eyes closed. What were they dreaming about? They were in their own vast, private worlds. They were untouchable. The horn, cocksure and comical, sauntered across a universe of sound. Beyond the sleeping people was the cold blue sky. Aidan thought about the difference between the sky and the limitless spaces inside the people's heads.

'Whence do we come? Whither does our road take us? Why am I made to feel that I am free while yet I am constrained within my personality as in a prison? What is the object of toil and sorrow? Will the meaning of life be revealed in death?' That was what Mahler said once. Aidan had learnt it by heart off the record sleeve. He was still thinking about this when there was a noise at the door. Laura came in. She was still in her nightdress.

'Aidan,' she said, 'you are the only fruitcake I know who listens to Mahler at half-past seven in the godamn morning.'

He looked up. 'I'll turn it off if you like.'

'That's OK,' she said, stretching her arms above her head. 'I was awake anyway. Kind of glad to have someone to talk to. I feel so wired up. I couldn't sleep.' She slumped down in a chair. 'Do you have a spare cigarette?' Aidan passed her the one he'd rolled. She lit it. The violins slid into a suave melody. Laura, her bare feet on the kitchen table, tugged on the hand-rolled cigarette. The smoke from it drifted up to the newly painted ceiling.

'I met such a dishy guy last night,' she began. 'His name's Jeremy. Jeremy.' She tried it out in a different tone. 'Jeremy. God, it's such an

English name. His father's a Member of Parliament for the Conservative Party. Can you believe it? But Jeremy's not at all stuffy. He's kind of radical, in fact. He's got one of those haircuts that are shaved at the sides. And he's got a cute snub nose and completely gorgeous almond eyes.'

Aidan patiently rolled himself a cigarette.

'Still, I guess you don't want to hear about my crazy crushes. Do you think I could call him up? Would that be "terribly forward"?' She laughed, and took a jabbing puff at her cigarette.

'I dunno.'

'My God, perhaps I'm in love.'

Her words were almost lost in the apotheosis of the scherzo. The bass drum had begun to beat a tattoo, the violins had entered with a whirling dance, and the rest of the orchestra had flung themselves against each other. Now the horns charged back across the universe, the violins flying off them like water from the backs of galloping horses. The trumpets tightened the tension, the horns brayed to the heavens, one last time, and the movement ended with a loud thump.

'Christ,' said Laura. 'I'm exhausted. Normal people put on something like Pachelbels Canon first thing in the morning.'

'You didn't have to listen to it.'

'I didn't have a lot of choice.'

'Sorry.'

Laura laughed. 'That's OK,' she said, 'I never did like Pachelbel.' She stubbed out her cigarette. 'Know something? I think I will call Jeremy. I'll do it tonight. Why the hell not? We live in a liberated age, don't we, Aidan?'

'Dunno.'

'But you know what it's like to feel liberated, don't you, Aidan?' She leant across the table towards him. She seemed strangely excited this morning. 'You're a free spirit. Those crazy books you read, and you've always got your head in the clouds. You know how to cut loose.'

Aidan just shrugged his shoulders.

Laura laughed again. 'You're also one of the most infuriating people I've ever met. Say,' she continued, changing the subject without thought, 'when do you guys plan to be finished on this place?'

'I dunno.'

'You must have some idea. I tell you, I'm getting so sick of living in this squalor. Doesn't it bug you? It's really getting to bug me.'

There was a pause. She found herself joining Aidan in gazing out of the open window. The sun was above the houses now, flooding the back gardens with thin autumn light. Somewhere in the street behind them there was the bang of a car door, then the cough and roar of the engine starting up.

'Say, I never asked you. What happened to you last week at The Man in the Moon? You just disappeared.'

'I came back here.'

'But why didn't you tell anyone you were going? I don't understand.'

'I just wasn't into it.'

'It was kind of rude. I think Bob might have felt hurt. You two were talking together, and then you just left without saying a word.'

Aidan didn't answer. Laura's thoughts had already moved on. 'Jeremy's father was really icky. He wants Jeremy to be an advertising executive or something big in business. I just can't see it. Don't you think it's really awful when parents bully their children into doing particular things? Bob's always been really good about that. He's always encouraged me to do my own thing.' She paused, then chuckled to herself. 'God, you should have heard Jeremy talk about some of his father's friends, these Conservative types. He was so funny. That's what I really like about England. You can be completely outrageous about things and it's just accepted. In the States, people are so sincere and reverent about everything. They take themselves way too seriously.'

There was a pause. Laura waited for Aidan to reply, but he didn't. She stretched back in her chair. She was feeling comfortable.

'You know, Aidan,' she said, 'this place feels great after America. America's like a desert. Everything's the same. All the people are the same. Shopping malls, TV, guys with baseball hats and guys with little alligators on their sweaters. Everywhere it's the goddamn same. Everywhere you go, people say the same goddamn things. It's like they're all on the same narrow track called "success" or "personal development". You know the kind of thing I mean. But here I feel like everything's opened out. It's weird, because it's the States that's meant to be the big country, the land of opportunity and all that. But I feel like everything's wide open *here*.'

As she spoke, Laura was gazing out of the window, over the rooftops, into the clear blue sky. The sky was the same everywhere. This sky reminded her of the summer camp in Vermont she had been sent to when she was in fourth grade. The kids would sit outside the wooden cabins sunning themselves in the afternoon heat. Suddenly, Laura felt nostalgic for American voices. Perhaps she was enthusing about London just because it was new to her? Perhaps what she was feeling didn't have anything to do with London at all? She looked at Aidan, as though in him there could be some answers. For a moment, all her thoughts focused on him and his strangeness. He seemed very far away.

'What are you thinking, Aidan?' she said.

'I was thinking about what you was saying just then. It's funny, 'cos it was the same for me, only the other way round. 'Course I've never been to America, but when I met your dad what he talked about was like a new world to me. You know, the way he talks about stuff that's happened to him. It sounded fantastic. Better than this dump. I'd like to go there sometime.'

When Aidan finished speaking he frowned, as though he was annoyed at himself for saying it. Laura was amazed. She had never heard him say so much all at once.

'I guess it's just a question of what you're used to,' was all she could think to say in reply.

Aidan didn't answer. He seemed to have slipped back into his own world. His outburst and then his silence seemed so strange to Laura. But after a while she got bored of waiting for him to say something else, and went upstairs to practise her saxophone. Then Trevor arrived, and Aidan had to go downstairs to begin the day's work.

It was half-past three the same day. The afternoon had sunk to its lowest point, and it seemed like it would never haul itself up out of this trough to evening. Aidan had had a pint in the pub at lunchtime while he read his book, and now the beer had spread through his blood, dulling his senses and making him tired. He and Trevor were plastering the basement rooms. Mingled with the sound of the radio was the scraping of their trowels on the boards on which they carried the plaster, then a kind of squelch and a patting as they spread the plaster and firmed it onto the wall. Aidan moved lethargically backwards and forwards between the wall and the bucket of plaster, which he stirred slowly with a stick. Every now and then, when he recognised the tune they were playing on Radio Two, Trevor would burst into energetic whistling. He glanced over his shoulder to see how Aidan was getting on.

'Don't let it dry,' said Trevor.

Aidan started out of his daydream. He wet his trowel and dampened down a patch that was dry and flaking off the wall. His mind wasn't on the job. It kept drifting off to think about anything but what he was meant to be doing. He couldn't even concentrate on what the DJ was saying with such false gusto. For a long time he had a picture in his head of the classroom at his primary school, with its miniature wooden tables and chairs and the walls plastered with paintings. The sun was always streaming in through the windows, and it was always the middle of an afternoon's monstrous expanse. It seemed like they were all his childhood was – sunshine and aching boredom. Not too different from now, he thought, as he plastered the wall and listened to the stupid radio.

'Watch what you're doing,' said Trevor. He grabbed Aidan's trowel from him. A lump of wet plaster had fallen from the wall into the brick dust that coated the floor. Trevor deftly scraped the plaster up, wet it, and smeared it back on to the wall, firming and smoothing it.

'Half asleep, you are,' he said, annoyed. He chucked Aidan's trowel into the bucket of water. 'Go and make us some tea. Might wake you up a bit.'

Aidan wiped his hands on his jeans and started up the stairs.

'And don't go boozing at lunchtimes if you can't handle it,' Trevor added after him.

But he wasn't angry. When Aidan returned with two mugs of tea, he gave him a couple of his biscuits. They sat together on the stone steps that led up from the basement to the pavement. It had clouded over since the morning, but the cloud was high, and there was still some hazy sunshine. The burnt house loomed over them.

'Tell you,' said Trevor after a while, 'I wouldn't fancy living in this place.' He gazed thoughtfully up at the facade of the house. 'Not the state it's in.'

Aidan was expecting this. Trevor was always bringing the subject up. He didn't say anything in reply, and they sipped their tea in silence.

'How are you getting on in there then, Aidan?' Trevor began again.

'All right.'

'Mr Morton treat you all right, does he?'

'Yeah.'

'What about his daughter, that Laura? She seems like a nice girl.' Trevor winked.

'We get on all right. There's nothing like that.'

'I was talking to her just the other day. Friendly girl. Then they're all friendly, these Americans, aren't they? And Mr Morton, he's a good sort. Young Laura was telling me all about him, about his work and everything. Dotes on her father, that girl does. I suppose Mr Morton's famous in America?'

'Suppose so.'

Trevor squinted up into the hazy sunshine, looking up at the facade of the house again. 'I wouldn't fancy that, would you? People recognising you on the street and stuff? You wouldn't feel your life was your own. And what about the family? Doesn't seem fair on them. I expect Mr Morton was glad to get away from it for a while, coming over here where he isn't so well known.'

Aidan didn't know what Trevor's problem was. He was usually a miserable old sod, but as soon as he got on to this tack he really got going.

'Me, I believe in keeping yourself to yourself,' he was saying now. 'I mean, I like Mr Morton all right. He's a good man to work for. But I can't understand why he does that job. Do you reckon he really enjoys it?'

'Don't ask me.'

'Still, he seems to like you well enough. Perhaps you'll get famous too.' He gave Aidan a friendly nudge.

They both stared down at the steps beneath them.

'Tell you,' Trevor continued after a pause, 'you could've knocked me down with a feather when Mr Morton says "Aidan's gonna live here." Knocked the stuffing out of your uncle, too, I can tell you. I mean it's hardly usual, is it? Having one of the gang living in the house you're doing up? Living with the boss? Still, I expect they do things different in America.'

He was always saying stuff like that. But if he didn't like Aidan living in the burnt house, for whatever reason, then that was his problem. Aidan didn't see why he should get into an argument about it. There was nothing to argue about.

Trevor was silent, stirring the brick dust at his feet with a stick as if trying to work out another line of attack. Then he frowned, threw the stick down, and swigged off the last of his tea.

'Back to work.'

By the time they knocked off that afternoon it was raining hard. Great swathes of dark, low cloud had met. The light was dimmer.

'Fuckin' cats and dogs,' Trevor muttered as he hunched himself up and dashed out along the spray-filled street. He never had owned an umbrella.

Aidan went upstairs. Laura was at the kitchen table, doing something to her saxophone with a small screwdriver.

'You'll never guess what I've just done,' she said.

'No.'

'I phoned that guy Jeremy. The one I was telling you about this morning. Don't you think that was pretty brave and courageous of

me? And you know what? He's coming over here later. I couldn't
believe it. He just said, "That would be really nice. Shall I come over
this evening?" He's got such a cute accent.' She laughed.

Aidan made himself a cup of tea and took it upstairs. The rain was
drumming on the roof. He picked up the book.

*Chuck Davenport spent his days, and many of his nights, near the top of the
tower in the OCC (Operations Cordination Centre). This was the
nerve-centre of the tower's defence system. From there, all the incoming
Paanite missiles and aircraft were monitored, and defensive lasers deployed
against them. The OCC also had one of the very few windows in the tower,
enabling one to see the Paanite world outside. It was made of massively
reinforced perspex, to protect it against the debris of exploded Paanite aircraft
that the howling winds hurled against the tower. An automatic cleaning
mechanism had been fitted to the outside to clear it of dust and organic debris.
The view from the window was bleak but magnificent: hundreds of miles of
rocky plateau. In the far, far distance, with a telescope, could be made out the
Paanite base from which the air strikes were launched.*

*Chuck Davenport had fought his way up through the Administration to
become Chief Executive Officer for Defence Operations. He was the youngest
ever to hold that post. But then he came from a good background. The best
background. His great-great grandfather had been Carl Davenport, first leader
of Xykon. Not that Chuck ever thought about his ancestor, except in so far as
the fact could be used as a minor but potentially useful assertiveness weapon.
This fifth generation of Xykon crew were hard people. The whole meaning of
the journey was base survival. They had lost all connection with a time when
life could mean more. So the dead, the ancestors, were simply those who had
not survived. Death was something to be ashamed of. It was a sign of failure.*

*In this colony of hard people, Chuck Davenport was one of the hardest.
He, after all, had fought his way to the top of the tower. Now it gave him a
nervous satisfaction – nervous because failure was so horribly possible and in
the end so inevitable. He sat in front of the computer screens and coordinated the
tower's rock-solid defences. He didn't like to be disturbed. That was why he
was so annoyed when the intercom opened up and he was told that his
grandmother, Marquaiana, had come to see him.*

CHAPTER EIGHT

It was still raining. In the West End the streets were crowded. After a beautiful morning, the weather had turned. The traffic moved slowly, the headlights lighting up the falling rain. Morton was making his way from the NWBC studios on the Tottenham Court Road to Piccadilly, where he would get the underground north to the burnt house. The rain wasn't falling straight, but slanting across, swept by a wind from the south west. Morton, holding his umbrella out in front of him to protect himself, was finding it difficult to manoeuvre through the crowded streets. Everybody was impatient, hurrying as quickly as possible to get out of the rain. It was at times like this that Morton wished he had glasses, or, better still, that his eyesight hadn't gotten as bad as it had.

He crossed Oxford Street and started making his way down through Soho. Big black taxis roared in the narrow streets. There were blasts of music from the shop doorways. A hundred fruit machines jangled out into the night from the open front of a leisure arcade. Everywhere neon signs blazed at each other across the narrow chasm of the street. 'Girls Girls Girls' shouted one. 'Live Nude Revue' another. 'Male/Female Double Act'. Morton hurried on, and as he crossed the street, dashing on to the pavement to avoid a taxi that was bearing down on him, he collided with someone who was emerging just as quickly from one of those neon-lit doorways. Morton, being the smaller of the two, half fell to the ground, grunting as he stumbled on to the upturned ribs of his umbrella. The rain ran down his neck. The man who had bumped into him helped him to his feet, and for a moment they stood face to face, bathed in the orange light from the sign above the doorway. 'Porno Cinema/Bed Show'. It all seemed to happen incredibly quickly to Morton. Before he had had time to apologise, or thank him for helping him up, the man, who had never been more than a blur to him, had suddenly dropped his arm, mumbled something, and disappeared down the road.

Morton's thoughts returned to the interview he had done that day. It had been a session with an 'eminent' English novelist for the *Morton on Britain* series, asking him to expound on the state of the nation. The idea had been foisted on him by Don, his producer, who knew everything there was to know about television but whose grasp of reality was impaired by seeing everything through the lens of the media. Even what he knew about books came from reviews of books, programmes about books, reviews of programmes about books. Morton by contrast prided himself on being a reporter.

Morton had dutifully read the man's latest novel, and hated it. The guy wrote like P.G. Wodehouse, only he took himself seriously. Once he was in the studio, it turned out that he knew nothing about anything and everything about nothing. He spoke in contrived, self-deprecating aphorisms. England, he thought, was probably becoming a nastier place, and the fact that the masses wouldn't buy his books was corroboration of this. But anyway, he wrote for himself. Morton had wanted to drop the whole thing, but Don thought it was great and really English. Morton's questions to the novelist had had an undercurrent of mockery.

Sitting in the underground train, joggled to and fro, he was suddenly overcome by a wave of exhaustion. He always found appearances in front of the camera draining, and particularly on a day like today when he'd had to work so hard to get decent product. When he had first started out in television, nearly twenty years ago, he'd felt split. It was him, Bob Morton, sitting in front of the camera asking the questions, but it had also felt like he was *playing* Bob Morton. That had panicked him. He had felt as though he was losing his identity. But then Sammy had died, and as Morton threw himself more and more into work, he had found that split disappeared. Like a good 'method' actor he was able to project and identify himself totally with how he was moving and speaking in performance. It never stopped being hard work, but it had got so he could switch it on and off without worrying about it. Only since coming to London those doubts, that feeling of strangeness about what he was doing in front of the camera, had come back. And in idle moments he found himself thinking back a lot to '68, that exhilarating, terrible year when he had started working on network TV and Sammy had died.

The train pulled into the station. Watching the playback of the interview that afternoon, Morton had felt sick of seeing himself on that screen. it had brought back his first reactions to observing himself, all those years ago. Initially he had been excited. He had made it. He was on network TV. Then it had felt weird, even scary, like the camera was stealing his soul.

The lift, as usual, was out of order, so Morton had to walk up the grimy spiral staircase that led from the underground tunnels to the surface. He stopped halfway up, still thinking about what it had been like watching the playback, to get his breath back. The other commuters streamed up past him. It had been so strange. It was hard to describe. It had been as though he were dead. There he had been, preserved up there on the screen, moving and talking. But he wasn't really there at all. Morton started up the stairs again. That was what it was like when people died. Other people carried pictures of them in their heads. There would be snapshots, maybe home movies, too. He had a snapshot of Sammy in his wallet. Christ, thought Morton, when I die there'll be so many damn pictures of me left over, they'll hardly know I've gone. He was chuckling to himself as he came out of the station into the wet again.

The rain was harder. It slid in rivers down the slate roof of the burnt house. It gathered in the blocked-up guttering. It seeped through into the house where the slates were cracked and where the concrete filleting had crumbled away. Aidan had put down his book. He was watching a yellowish damp patch in the corner of the ceiling. He could almost see it grow. And he could sense the dampness on the wall behind his head. He breathed the taste of wet plaster. Him and Trevor would never be able to put this house to rights, Aidan thought. It was hopeless.

The rain drummed on. Aidan found it oppressive. He got out of the sleeping bag, flexing his muscles, and went downstairs. Laura had just gone out with that Jeremy bloke of hers. Aidan had heard him arrive, then both of them laughing and talking in stupid loud voices as they clattered out of the door.

Aidan got some food out of the fridge and ate. The processed cheese was like plastic. He sat at the open window and watched the rain drip on to the sill. Outside it was black and wet. Damn, he thought. He was feeling restless, trapped. It wasn't that he wanted to go out to the pub or meet people or anything. It was *everything* that made him feel trapped. This house was trapping him. He put his Dylan record on and rolled a cigarette. The record crackled and hissed. He had had it a long time.

Dylan's voice sounded lonely against the surface noise and the patter of the rain on the window sill. Aidan was just beginning to feel better, when the door downstairs slammed. He recognised the tread on the bare floorboards. It was Morton. He listened to the footsteps come up the stairs, then pause on the landing outside. Then the door opened.

Morton hesitated in the doorway, blinking in the light of the naked bulb, listening to the plaintive voice from the old gramophone.

'Hi Aidan,' he said. 'I thought maybe there wasn't anybody here.'

'Laura's gone out,' said Aidan. 'She went out with some bloke called Jeremy.'

'Really?' He didn't sound interested. As he sat down heavily at the kitchen table, he seemed unusually subdued, even sad. 'How're you and Trevor getting on with the plastering?' he asked.

'All right,' said Aidan. 'I think there's water coming in the roof.'

'Know something, Aidan? From time to time I ask myself whether I did the right thing, taking on this place.'

Aidan didn't reply. There was just the sound of Bob Dylan's voice, and behind that the guitars, and behind that the sound of relentlessly falling water.

'I heard this song before,' said Morton. 'What is it?'

' "Desolation Row." '

'Who's the singer?'

'Bob Dylan.'

Morton smiled. 'Oh yeah. Bob Dylan. He's the guy you wanted to be when you grew up. Remember you telling me that, upstairs, back in the summer before you moved in?'

Aidan nodded.

'Well, do you still want to be Bob Dylan?'

'How could I?' said Aidan.

Morton didn't reply for a while, and they listened to the guitars and to the song continuing to spin itself out. Then he said, 'I remember when you used to hear this guy's songs all the time – back in the sixties. When I first started out in television, one of my first assignments was to do a feature on what was called the "counter-culture". So off I went with a camera crew to Haight Ashberry and Berkeley, then back to some of the places on the Lower East Side. My brief was to explain it all to the folks in Dakron, Ohio, or wherever. Not that there was much to explain, in a way. A lot of them were nice suburban kids. You can't cover up good breeding, even with bandannas and beads. Anyway, whenever we went into these little clubs and cafés, there'd always be some guy with a guitar trying to be Bob Dylan, doing his own version of . . . what was that song, something to do with the wind?'

'Did you get into it?' asked Aidan, ignoring Morton's question.

Morton laughed and began filling his pipe. 'Not me. I was too old for that, even back then. I was going on forty. Anybody over thirty was the enemy. I guess from our side of the fence a lot of it looked kind of ridiculous. And it scared people too. The camera crew I worked with on that feature – you should have heard some of the things they said. They hated hippies. But then cameramen are always jumped-up hard hats. For someone like me, I guess there was a kind of vicarious excitement in it. A part of me was resentful that I'd missed out. It seemed like for those kids something was really happening. Everything was being thrown in the pot. Everything was up for grabs. It seemed for a moment like you could put a question mark against anything. You could disapprove of what was happening there, but that didn't seem relevant. They were in touch with something bigger that was happening all around. Equally, it didn't seem to make much sense just to agree with them. There wasn't really anything to agree with. It was chaos. Either you were in touch or you weren't. You were with them or you weren't.' With a great puff of smoke, Morton lit his pipe. 'And I wasn't. Hell, I was a TV anchorman.' He laughed. 'You can't be a TV anchorman *and* be in touch.'

He was quiet, tired of talking. He puffed at his pipe and gazed out of the open window at the darkness and the rain, listening to the endless, hypnotic spinning out of Dylan's song. It was cold with the window open, but it was good to feel the cool, wet air on your face. Morton felt comfortable sitting with Aidan. You didn't feel like you had to make conversation with him.

When the record was finished, Aidan put it on again. It was his favourite song. It was very strange. You couldn't make out what it meant. That was what he liked about it.

So that was how they spent the evening. They listened to 'Desolation Row' over and over again. It was as though normal life had been suspended while the rain continued to pour down outside. Morton hardly spoke a word. He just stared out at the rain and listened to the music. Aidan had never seen him like that before. Usually he talked all the time. Aidan just sat there doing nothing too. He was tired from work. Once when he glanced across at Morton, he saw that he had dozed off. Later on, Aidan cooked some beans on toast. While they ate, Morton asked him a few questions about how the work on the house was going, then lapsed into silence.

After they had eaten, Morton got up and began slowing washing up. He was still at the sink when Laura and Jeremy came back in. They could hear them banging in through the front door, joking and laughing about the rain and how wet they had got, clomping up the stairs. Laura burst into the kitchen first, with Jeremy close behind her. They both laughed and flopped down at the kitchen table.

'Hi, you guys,' said Laura. 'Isn't this weather just awful?' She laughed. 'My God, I'm sounding like a Brit, going on about the weather.' She looked at Jeremy, and they both burst out laughing at some private joke. They brought in with them the warm, beery smell of the pub.

'You two have a good time?' asked Morton from the sink. He hadn't bothered to turn round when they came in.

'Yeah, it was great, wasn't it, Jeremy? We went to The Mulberry Tree. My God, Aidan, you're not listening to this Dylan album again, are you? Don't you *ever* get tired of it?'

Aidan shrugged his shoulders.

'Is that what it is?' groaned Jeremy. 'Heavy man, and all that.' He chuckled, and Laura rapped him playfully on the knee.

'Aidan and I have been having a good time listening to it tonight,' said Morton. 'It brings back a lot of memories for me.'

'Mr Morton, you can't be serious,' protested Jeremy. 'How can you like this stuff? It's so portentous and humourless. As for the sixties and all that hippy stuff, the whole thing makes me want to vomit, quite honestly.'

Morton was silent for a moment. Then he said, 'Well, I guess it was all a long time ago. How's your dad doing? You know I'm interviewing him next week.' He had finished the washing up. Now, wiping his hands dry on a dish cloth, he turned to face the others.

'Oh, he's busy bossing the country around – ' Silence.

Something strange had happened. Jeremy had suddenly gone quiet. Aidan looked up from the cigarette he was rolling to see what the matter was. It looked like Laura's posh friend had forgotten what he was saying. He was just staring at Morton. He had gone all red in the face.

'Well I guess that's what he's there for,' said Morton uncertainly. He too had noticed something strange in Jeremy. He was looking straight back at him.

The silence was broken by the phone ringing out on the landing.

'I'll get that,' said Laura, and she went out.

'Yeah,' said Jeremy in a constrained voice, 'I suppose that's right.' He swallowed.

Laura had come back in. 'Aidan, it's for you.'

Aidan went out on to the landing. He was relieved to get out of the kitchen, out into the dark quietness of the rest of the house. He shut the door behind him. He sat on the stairs and picked the receiver up off the floor.

'Hello.'

'Aidan? Is that you?' It was his mother. Her voice was distant.

'Yeah. Hello, Mum.'

'Thank God I've found you. I had terrible problems getting hold of this number.'

'Sorry. The phone hasn't been in long.'

'Why haven't you been in touch? Why didn't you send us your number? You promised you would. Uncle Terry didn't know it. I rang him up, because we hadn't heard from you for so long. He's very annoyed with you, Aidan.'

'Sorry,' said Aidan.

At the other end of the line, his mother sighed. 'Well at least you're all right,' she said. 'You *are* all right, aren't you?'

'Yeah.'

'I had terrible problems finding this number,' she repeated. 'You see, we hadn't heard from you for so long, so I rang your uncle Terry. He didn't know the number. So I had to find it through the place where the American gentleman works. You've no idea the time I had trying to find this number. I had to ring all these television companies.'

'Sorry, Mum.'

'Why didn't you write to us, or phone us? You will keep in touch in future, won't you?'

'Yeah.'

'Doug's here. He wanted a word with you. Mind you keep in touch. Look after yourself, love. Bye.'

'Hello. Aid?'

'Hello, Doug.'

'Who's been a *bad* boy then? Listen, I'm thinking of hitching down to London soon for a couple of days. This place *is* getting right up my nostrils. Be all right for me to crash at Ronald Reagan's house, won't it?'

'Should think so.'

'Thassa boy. Give us the address.'

Aidan dictated the address of the burnt house to his brother, and they hung up. He stood, and considered for a moment going back into the kitchen. Then he turned away and went up the stairs to his room. There he listened. The rain had stopped. He went over to the casement window, flung it open, and felt a gust of cold wind on his face. The sky had cleared. The weather had run full circle, back to the clear and cold it had been that morning. An eerie white light from the moon was like water on the rooftops. The moon illuminated the remaining clouds, which were high and streaked into tatters by the wind. Aidan forgot where he was for a moment. He felt like he was part of the sky. He looked down at his sleeping bag, where his book lay open.

One day, Chuck Davenport's grandmother Marquaiana came to visit him in his control room high up in the tower. The old woman was tiny and very frail. Something about her appearance annoyed Chuck Davenport. He wanted to reach out and snap her stick-like arms.

'Hello, Marquaiana,' he said in a loud voice. 'Why have you come to see me?' It seemed natural to shout at the old woman.

The old woman didn't reply. She was concentrating on keeping her balance as she shuffled across the floor towards him. Something seemed to prevent her lifting her feet off the ground. Chuck got up to help her. In his impatience, he almost pushed her into the chair opposite him.

They sat facing each other. The old woman still didn't acknowledge his presence. Now she was shifting her bottom around on the seat to get comfortable, tugging at her tunic where it had got rumpled. All her movements were slow and dignified. Finally she looked up at him and fixed him with a gaze of surprising intensity.

'I've come to say goodbye,' she said.

Chuck had never heard anything more extraordinary. 'I'm afraid I don't quite understand,' he said with a nervous and apologetic laugh.

'I'm dying. You're my last direct descendant, and I've come to say goodbye to you before I die.'

Chuck roared with laughter. He chuckled and wiped the tears from his eyes. 'Bye then,' he said in a comical voice, waving across the desk, and roared with laughter again. 'But Marquaiana,' he said, when his amusement had died down to a grin, 'people die all the time. Why are you making such a fuss?' There was even a note of sympathetic interest in his voice.

'I'm dying,' she repeated stubbornly. 'I'm going forever, so I wanted to take a last look at my family. I wanted to say my farewells.'

Chuck Davenport frowned. There was something rather repulsive about her. She'd lost her teeth, which meant her consonants were indistinct. When she parted her wrinkled lips to form words, her mouth described an unpleasant black void.

'Look, I'm afraid I'm a busy man,' he said, and glanced at the computer screen beside him. 'Much as I'd like to pass the day with idle chat . . .'

'You don't feel anything.' The voice that came from the frail old woman's

body was surprisingly, annoyingly, strong.

'What do you mean, "feel"? This is the most preposterous conversation I've ever had. So you're dying. There's nothing I can do about that. Old people like you are enough of a burden on the colony's resources without wasting the time of busy executives.'

'You want to forget me.'

Chuck looked at her with distaste. He wished she'd go, but she was sitting there as immovable as ever.

'I wasn't always like this,' she continued after a pause. 'I want to tell you about your great-great grandfather, my grandfather.'

There was a knock at the door. It opened slowly and Morton entered, looking around him uncertainly.

'Hi, Aidan? You weren't asleep, were you?'

'No.'

'I just wanted to take a look at the damp you said was coming in.'

The patch had grown. At its centre it was pale yellow, while its extremities, where the water had advanced across the ceiling and down the wall, were brown. The wallpaper was beginning to peel.

'Hmm,' said Morton. 'I guess we'll have to see what we can do about the roof.' He stood for a moment in the middle of the room. 'Don't you get cold with the window open?'

'I like the cold,' said Aidan.

Morton stepped over to the window and looked out.

'You sure get a good view from up here. Seems like you can see most of London.' There was a long silence. 'You did well not to go back in there after your phone call. There's something strange about that Jeremy guy. After you'd gone, he started getting quite aggressive with me about hippies and stuff. If it hadn't been for Laura, I think I might have got mad at him. You see, my kid brother was kind of hippyish, at least he was towards the end. He was nearly ten years younger than me, one hell of a bright kid. He was a journalist too, worked on a paper in California. Well in '66 they sent him out to Vietnam to cover the war there, and that completely changed him. He just dropped out. Started running around with a pretty wild crowd. Hung on to his job for a while, then got fired. He died in '68 in a car crash. The post mortem showed he was doped to the eyeballs. He was almost like a son to me, because of the difference in our ages. When somebody as close to you as that dies, it changes the way you look at the world. It's like you're detached from everything. Because you're thinking all the time about what might have been instead of what is. I was like that for about a year, at least. That was about the time I was doing that feature about the hippies I was telling you about. I guess at any other time I'd have dismissed them as spoilt middle-class kids, most of them. I'm a pretty hard-nosed guy, really. But I was thinking all the time: *what might have been, what might have been.* I began to understand something important, which is that you can only understand the world if you can imagine it could be different from what it is. Like Sammy could still be alive. And other "what ifs" started coming to me, like "What if you weren't a TV anchorman? What if you were twenty years younger? What if you were the other side of that fence?" I don't know why I've started thinking about it again these days. Ever since I came to London, it's like I've had a jolt.' Morton, still leaning on the windowsill, looked round at Aidan. 'You're a funny guy,' he said. 'You never say much. It's like you're a bit detached from things yourself.'

'Best way to be,' said Aidan awkwardly.

'Could be,' said Morton. 'I've always wanted to be the centre of the show. Always performing. It's hard to get out of the way of things after a lifetime. People expect you to be first with the joke, first with the story. "What's new, Bob?" they say. "Tell us about it." Of course, you wonder whether they really care. But you still get up and do your act.' And he was doing it even now, mesmerising Aidan with his flow of talk. 'So it goes on. They're so used to you doing it, so used to all the gestures and all the tricks, that you wonder if they might have forgotten you're really there. Well, I won't bore you any more. You get some sleep, young Aidan.'

Aidan watched him go out of the door, then lay down on the sleeping bag with his book.

'I was there when Carl Davenport died,' said Marquaiana, concentrating hard on her words. Her old, frail body leaned forward slightly. 'That was before we came here. I'd never seen someone die before, and it frightened me. No: not just frightened me. I wouldn't be bothered about it if it had just been that. It disgusted me.' The old woman hung her head and fiddled absently with the material of her tunic. 'I've been thinking a lot about it,' she continued. 'I have a lot of time to think. You see, my reaction . . . I think the process started with my generation. Mine was the second generation after the Explosion. Ever since the Explosion, the colony has been on the move. In another generation it will be gone from here.' She waved a hand at the bleak landscape of Paan beyond the window. 'For ever and ever – or at least as long as we can foresee – the colony will be moving on, always moving just ahead of a great wave of annihilation. The whole purpose of the colony, of our existence, is this ceaseless flight from death. She paused, shaking her head. 'No wonder I was so

revolted at the sight of my grandfather lying there dead. No wonder you don't want to have anything to do with me. I'd hoped I might be able to . . . to pass on something, to hand something down from my grandfather to you.' She sighed, exhausted after having said so much.

Chuck had listened to her attentively. He was not, in fact, a stupid man. But he remained genuinely puzzled as to why his grandmother had come to see him.

'I don't understand what the problem is,' he said. 'We live and work for the good of the colony. I defend the tower so that the colony will survive and be able to leave here and move on. I won't be around by the time the colony leaves this godforsaken place, but I'll have played my part. It's just a question of how you look at it. Like the business of your dying. It's an attitude of mind. You think about dying, you think morbid thoughts, so you're dying. It's as simple as that. Death's a state of mind. You bring it on yourself.' He gave her a kindly smile, then glanced at his computer screen. 'You'll have to go now,' he said. 'There's an air strike imminent.'

Aidan got up and closed the window before going to sleep. It was becoming colder.

CHAPTER NINE

When Jeremy bumped into Morton outside the strip club in Soho, it was as though the bottom had fallen out of his world. What he feared most had happened. Someone he knew had seen him coming out of one of those places, and now his shame would become public. His parents would know. In that moment of confusion in the rain, looking at and being looked at by the immediately familiar face, it was as though he were looking into a mirror of respectability, and seeing beamed back his own depravity. It was all over in seconds. Jeremy had felt a shock of recognition, like a sudden sickness racing through his body, but hadn't been able to put a name to the face. He had dropped the man's arm – he had been helping him up from the pavement – and hurried away towards the underground, fumblingly lighting a cigarette. In the tube he had played the scene over and over again in his mind, trying to remember who the man was. The worst of it was that it was someone to do with his father. As the train rattled on, and he still couldn't put a name to the face, he began to think that he might have made a mistake. Perhaps it had just been a moment of paranoia. He had grasped at that. Out of relief, he had drunk a lot with Laura Morton. She was fun, even if ridiculously enthusiastic about everything. Then they had gone back to the house, and her father had been there. Morton had turned round from the sink, and Jeremy had suddenly seen who it was he had run into in Soho. Everything had crashed about him again.

Over the ensuing days and weeks, Jeremy examined these mental snapshots over and over again, till they became as sick and familiar as a recurring nightmare. 'You know I'm seeing you father next week?' Morton had said, and then he had turned around and looked Jeremy straight in the eyes. What had that been? A warning? A taunt? Jeremy had no doubts that Morton had recognised him right from the start.

So why hadn't he just said 'Didn't I see you in Soho earlier this evening?' Because it was too sordid to bring out into the open? Or too trivial to be worth bothering about? Or was he playing a game with Jeremy? Yes, that was it. He was playing him like a fish on a line. Morton mut have seen Jeremy's embarrassment, his discomfort. Jeremy could remember how his cheeks had burned, his throat gone dry. He relived that moment of shame again and again, turning it over and over in his mind.

Occasionally in the past, sitting through some interminable pornographic film in a small, stinking cinema, it had crossed Jeremy's mind in a perverse way that the sole, real reason why he was doing it was so that eventually he should be discovered, and all the shame and derisive laughter in the world be heaped on his head. Now it was actually going to happen, he didn't feel so good. What would Morton say to his father? 'There are some things I think you ought to know about your son'? Or, laughing, 'Say Charlie, you'll never guess where I ran into your son last week'? Or maybe he would say something about Laura: 'Thing is, a father's gotta look after his daughter's welfare, see she doesn't fall into unhealthy company. It's none of my business what your son does with himself, but in so far as it affects my Laura . . .'

Yes of course, it would be Laura that Morton would be most worried about. She was always going on about her father, so they were obviously close. Perhaps he had told her about seeing him in Soho. Or maybe he would just tell Jeremy's father, protecting his daughter from the whole sordid business. Whichever way, he wouldn't want Jeremy seeing Laura again. Strangely, this thought gave Jeremy some heart. It seemed to give him some room for manoeuvre, a chance to defend himself and maybe even get back at Morton.

But these moments of hope were rare. Right from that first moment when Morton had turned round, and that electric shock of recognition had sparked between Jeremy and the American's face, it had just been a treadmill of paranoia, the same questions and fears coming up over and over again in ever more convoluted forms. Sometimes it almost seemed to Jeremy as though the questions were physically wrapping themselves around him, choking him. The precious middle-class home in Dulwich, his parent's stuck-up respectability, oppressed and annoyed him even more than usual. During the days, when his parents thought he was out job-hunting, he drifted around Soho, in and out of the pubs and the porno cinemas, on his usual round. All the time he was distracted, hardly there at all. He was waiting for Morton's meeting with his father, for that catharsis. In the meantime, it was as though he had an itch on the brain that he constantly needed to be scratching, scratching. In the evenings he would return home, tired and ashamed, and despise his parents for not knowing what their own son was really like.

The day came and passed, and nothing happened. His father said nothing, just congratulated himself on getting on TV. He hardly mentioned Morton. But Jeremy didn't feel any relief, it didn't make things better. It made them worse. New questions arose. Why did Morton not tell his father? Or if he had told him, why was his father saying nothing? Was he laughing behind Jeremy's back too? These questions nagged him constantly. There were few things to distract him from them. Although he had graduated in the summer, he had already lost touch with most of his college friends. He didn't see many people. In the evenings, his father lectured him on how he should think about his career. He offered to fix up lunch for him with his old friends in the City, or in chambers, or in publishing. But Jeremy would have nothing to do with it. He knew what his father's friends were like, those pleased men with minds as unbending and blind as steel. For a while, at college, he had thought that the aversion he felt towards them and their world was political. He went to some meetings, but the self-importance and posturing he found there sickened him almost as much. And when he saw Labour politicians on the TV, with their executive suits and their watching, careful eyes, it seemed as though they were exactly the same as his father's friends, but with flatter accents. They all frightened him. Sometimes everything frightened him, and sometimes it filled him with contempt and anger. His anger, intimate and unspoken, began with his parents and radiated outwards. If only he could articulate it, he thought. If only he could define what it was that angered him, then people might take notice. As it was, he flailed around hopelessly, like a skewered insect waving its legs in the air. Everything was shit.

The issue of Jeremy's career made things bad enough between him and his father. But about a week after Morton had done the interview something happened that made them even worse. Over the summer since he had left university, at his father's insistence, Jeremy had learnt to drive. He had disliked and shown no flair for it, but out of boredom he had persevered. In the end, at the second attempt, he had passed his test. Occasionally, Charles Tetchley went to Westminster by taxi, and on those days he encouraged his son to take the BMW out for a spin. It was his way of making overtures of friendship. He wanted his son to be a driver. Charles Tetchley believed in as many cars, and as much driving, as possible. For him, the car was more than just a means of transport. It was an article of faith, a positive force for good. It encapsulated all those things – individual power, technology, sleek body-lines – that he prized most dearly.

Jeremy hated driving the BMW. He was alarmed at the surge of power that a touch on the accelerator produced, and scared of scratching its shiny, silver-grey surface. But reluctantly, under the pressure of his father's amiable bullying, he had agreed to take it out that day.

It was dull and overcast. Spots of rain fell on the windscreen. Jeremy spent five minutes getting the car out of its parking place, manoeuvering very carefully to avoid touching the other cars. When he was out, he turned on to the main road and headed south, towards Crystal Palace. Other people in Jeremy's situation – with a free afternoon and a full tank of petrol – might have behaved differently. They might have been enticed by the signposts inviting them to Kent and the south coast. They might have relaxed, lowered the window, switched on the radio, and put their foot down. But Jeremy was nervous. To begin with, he was anxiously checking the oil and petrol gauges. He drove slowly and hesitantly. Then instead of enjoying the sensation of travelling, he began thinking again about Morton. He always came back to his humiliation. It was almost comforting, the way it was always there. It was something you could depend on, like fiddling with a loose tooth when you were a child and knowing that you could produce a little stab of pain, a spasm of the nerves. He went over it again, over each microsecond of agony and exposure. And then that hippyish boy had gone out to the phone. Jeremy had forgotten his name. He had been witness to Jeremy's humiliation too. And Laura. Did Laura know? He had to see her again, if only to discover that. But even if she didn't know, she had seen him naked, unmasked, in his worst moment. Jeremy opened his jaws wide and gave a kind of groan. His knuckles were white on the steering-wheel. He drove twice around Crystal Palace Park. His mother, he remembered, used to drag him down here to look at the fake dinosaurs. There were a lot of kids about now. The schools had just got out. The traffic crawled.

When he got back to Dulwich, he felt even more hemmed in than when he had gone out. The drive had done nothing for him. He went fast for the first time along the street towards home, but when he got there he found that the parking place outside had been taken. The only other space he could find was further down the street, between a builder's skip and a Range Rover. It was smaller. Jeremy could feel his palms sweating. He wasn't any good at parking. He hated it. He revved the engine to give himself confidence, then began. In his nervousness, he forgot that it's easier to back the car in first. He drove the car forward, turning it into the space and straightening out too soon. That left him parallel to the kerb, half in and half out. He looked over his shoulder to reverse, and in a moment of panic didn't know what to do next. He seemed to be stuck. He didn't know which way to turn the wheel. A car slowed up to pull out and pass him. Its driver looked at him with amusement. Jeremy lifted his foot from the clutch, forgetting that the gear was engaged. The car leapt forward and hit the skip with a bump.

Out of the corner of his eye he saw some net curtains twitch and a pair of hostile, bespectacled eyes look out at him from one of the houses. His mouth was dry now. For God's sake, he thought, calm down. His breathing was coming quickly. As he backed the car away from the skip, there was a scraping noise. He steered the back end of the car in towards the pavement, so that the front was now sticking out into the road. Christ, he was getting nowhere. He tried going back a bit further to correct, misjudged it, and hit the Range Rover with a sickening crunch. A couple of pedestrians on the other side of the road had stopped and were watching him. Jeremy was boiling inside. Tears pricked his eyes. He kept seeing Morton's face. He edged forward again, and from behind he heard the tinkle of broken plastic tumbling to the tarmac. That sound snapped something in him. He swung the steering wheel round. The car surged forward and slammed into the skip. He wrenched the gear in reverse and drove back into the Range Rover. He was laughing now. He slammed his father's car violently backwards and forwards into the skip and the Range Rover until it was good and parked. In the gutter was a fine scattering of broken plastic. Bumpers and radiator were buckled. A group of passers-by had stopped on the pavement, and were now approaching the car to take collective action. Jeremy cut the engine, got out of the car with a slam of the door, stuck two fingers up at the people, and ran off down the road.

He went straight to the off-licence, bought four cans of lager, and sat in West Norwood cemetery. At opening time he went to the pub. He felt better, swamping his anger and frustration. One thought kept coming to the surface: especially now, after this, he had to get away from his parents and live somewhere else. By the time he got home he was drunk. As soon as he closed the front door behind him, his father came charging out of the living-room.

'I could murder you,' he shouted. 'Six hundred bloody quid's worth of damage! The whole lot's coming out of your allowance.

And first thing tomorrow you're going round to the Bantam-Smith's at number 37 to explain yourself. It's their Range Rover you damn near wrecked.'

He had stopped right in front of Jeremy. Jeremy could smell the sweat on him. He had discarded his jacket, and his tie, wrenched loose, was skewed to one side. He wore the blue and white striped shirt that he liked to wear in the Commons.

'You've been bloody drinking, haven't you? I suppose you were spliced when you caused that mayhem out there? Come on, Jeremy, you've got a good deal of explaining to do.'

He took his son by the arm and began leading him across the hall. Jeremy tried to shake himself free, but his father only gripped harder. For a moment, like a terrible chasm opening up beneath them, there seemed to be the possibility of a physical confrontation. But Jeremy submitted, trying by remonstrating to maintain his dignity as his father steered him into the living-room. His mother was there, looking concerned.

Charles Tetchley parked his son before his wife and himself.

'Well?' he said.

'Well what?'

Tetchley, almost uncontrollable with rage, began to take a step forward. 'Don't you get cheeky with me,' he yelled. 'Why did you smash up my car?'

'Look,' said Jeremy, slouching on to one leg in an exaggeratedly relaxed way, 'you don't *really* want to know what happened. This is so stupid.' His voice was comic in its forced reasonableness. The way he waved his hands around as he spoke revealed his over-wrought state. 'All you want to do is humiliate me as a kind of punishment. That's all you want.'

'Jeremy . . .' his mother began in a serious voice.

'My God,' her husband interrupted, 'sometimes I wonder what kind of child we've produced.' He went to the drinks cabinet. Jeremy turned to leave the room.

'Stay right there,' his father snapped. 'We haven't finished with you yet.'

Jeremy, perversely, was almost enjoying all this attention. He gave a deep sigh and, adopting his slouching posture again, waited for his parents to speak.

'G and T, darling?' said Tetchley gruffly.

Jeremy couldn't help smiling at his father's tone.

'Wipe that grin off your face immediately.' Tetchley held up a bottle of tonic and jabbed a finger at his son.

'Jeremy,' said his mother, 'we just want to understand.'

'C'mon, don't patronise me,' said Jeremy, shifting his weight to the other foot.

'Don't speak to your mother like that.'

'She was . . .'

'Jeremy, we just want to get this thing cleared up.'

'And you're damn right we want to punish you. You're like a little bloody hooligan. When I think of all the advantages you've had, all the love and affection your mother and I lavished on you. And all you can do is turn around and throw it in our faces.'

'Charles – '

'No, darling, he's got to be told. There are millions of children in this country who'd give their eye teeth to be in your shoes. And all you can do is mooch around sponging off your parents. Well it's about time you faced up to the responsibilities that go with your position.'

Jeremy laughed. He was in better spirits now. 'What does that mean?' he asked with as much sarcasm as he could muster. 'You mean I should be like you?'

'You could do a lot worse.'

'I'd rather smash up cars,' said Jeremy, with a sudden surge of anger, 'than strut around in a suit preening myself in front of a lot of other flabby, middle-aged toffs.'

'Right, that's enough,' said Margaret Tetchley firmly, stepping between father and son. 'Off you go, Jeremy. You can go up to your room or something. Your father and I want to be on our own.'

As Jeremy slammed the living-room door behind him, he could hear his father's raised voice. He was shaking with nerves.

He spent the next day in Soho. Looking at pornography and becoming excited by it had become for Jeremy a habit, like smoking cigarettes or picking one's nose. He took as little real pleasure in it as one does in those. To say that he looked at pornography because he liked the female form would be like saying a smoker smokes because he likes how tobacco plants look. In fact, women frightened him, and the sex act itself disgusted him slightly. It disgusted him even more when it was called 'making love'. But then disgust was what he was coming to enjoy, disgust with himself and with everything. Disgust seemed like something almost warm and protective. It gave him an identity and a way of looking at the world. It also kept his mind busy. No train of thought is too tortuous for disgust. To humiliate himself more, his disgust coiled itself around and around the fact that Bob Morton had seen him in Soho. Everything reminded him of it. When he heard Americans on the TV or radio, it was as though they were part of a conspiracy with Morton. And then there was the thought that Morton had told Laura. That drove him almost mad. It nagged at him more than anything else.

In a strange way, smashing up his father's car acted as a catharsis. It seemed to make things better. He started getting in touch with some friends, seeing whether anybody knew of somewhere he could live. And at last he rang Laura.

'Jeremy,' she said, 'It's great to hear from you. I thought you'd forgotten all about me.'

She did sound pleased to hear him. Maybe her father hadn't told her. It was hard to tell. He asked if she wanted to meet.

'Yeah of course, that would be great. Say, I've got a really big gig coming up next week. You said you wanted to hear me play. Do you want to come? Yeah? That's great.'

They made the arrangements and hung up. Jeremy sat for several minutes looking at the phone and listening to the stillness of the house. His father was at Westminster, and his mother doing her voluntary work at a local charity. The house was empty. Laura had sounded like she didn't know. But then had she spoken a bit nervously, as though she did know but didn't know how to handle it? Or perhaps Morton hadn't told her, had just assumed that Jeremy wouldn't dare bother his daughter again. He worried on at it.

CHAPTER TEN

Laura blew a long, low note on her saxophone. She felt her diaphragm stretch, so that her belly filled out and touched the boiler suit she liked to wear when playing. If she wore jeans or a skirt, then this movement was constricted at the waist. She extended the note and ran it into the first phrase of 'Round Midnight'. She snatched a breath and dashed down the chromatic scale from top to bottom of the instrument, then played a rippling, turning-in-on-itself figure from bottom to top. She swung the instrument away and massaged her lips with her teeth. Her breath was coming more deeply and steadily after blowing. There was a good tingling sensation on her lips. She rattled the keys with her fingers and felt with elation her sense of command. She could play anything.

She turned towards the window and began a string of fast blues riffs. The sash window was slightly open. From below came the sound of scraping and banging. Aidan and Trevor were working on the ground floor. The crisp, cold air blew in, and Laura looked out as she played. It was almost December now, and only a few yellow leaves clung to the branches of the two beeches across the road. Laura had watched these trees all through the fall. They reminded her of the great transformation of New England, when the whole landscape turned flaming orange and yellow. The two beeches across the road, alone and surrounded by solid English brick houses, their leaves turning and dropping, were so like home in miniature that they brought it back to her how far she had come. They were across the road and thousands of miles across the world. Quite often she had this sad, wildly romantic sense of being a stranger here. It was an odd, thrilling sensation. It made her want to stretch out her hands to feel and understand the hard, jagged foreignness of what was around her. She sensed it walking back from the tube in the evening after a storm, when the clouds had cleared and the clear deep blue was stretched from one end of the sky to the other. Then, the small, boarded-up brick shops and wet pavements would make her laugh and want to cry, as though forgiving them. And she would have this feeling too at gigs when she was being admired and people were joking with her about her accent, or when she was playing and watching at the same time the English faces respond to her playing her foreign music. Everything about her became different to her. The world suddenly shone with its apartness.

As Laura wandered up and down in front of the window, her fingers and lips and lungs spelling out the blues, a whole train of images, from the leaves of New England to the faces in an audience, passed through her head. But she kept coming back to the faces that would be in the audience later that evening. Jeremy would be among them. Imagining the audience made her feel good. It had always been her way of controlling her nerves before playing in public.

From fast blues she switched to long held notes and slow melodies. Time sped without her noticing it. Beyond the houses, the sun kissed the horizon and the sky around it blushed. Then, quickly, darkness seeped in from beyond the sky. Laura was playing a chant at the bottom of her instrument, to practise her control. Down there, her whole throat and chest seemed to vibrate in sympathy. She reached a point of stillness, and then stopped. It was time to go. She packed up her saxophone and left the burnt house, heading for the tube station.

Aidan heard her leave. He was sitting in the kitchen, resting his feet on the windowsill. As soon as he had knocked off work, half an hour earlier, he had come up here to hear her playing in her father's room next door. He liked her saxophone better when it was on its own, without all the drums and other stuff. In fact he liked Laura herself better when she was on her own. When she was with other people she showed off in a loud, nervous kind of way. He hadn't liked her much when she'd first come, and he still didn't understand the way her and Morton were together. It was like she wanted something from him. He listened to her clumping heavily down the uncarpeted stairs, her saxophone case banging the banisters, then returned to his book.

The Xykon colony left Paan a lifeless ruin. The last generations of natives, had pounded furiously at the Tower. To cover their escape during the Great Departure, the human colony had installed a massive nuclear bomb and timing device in the top of the Tower. As the enormous Xykon spaceship surged up through the buffeting winds and out of the atmosphere, the bomb went off. All life of Paan was destroyed for ever. But then the end was coming anyway.

Xykon shot through space and time faster than light, and without sound. The actual movement was inconceivable. No one can imagine how empty space is. Or how cold. Or limitless. It's not like the air we breathe. Compared with space, the air we breathe, piled up in the sky till it becomes blue to the eye, is crowded and dense. Outer space is black and nothing. And no one can imagine how long are the times and distances in space. Think of a journey, a simple travelling from A to B. Now forget it. Space is a void where nothing man or woman can think of could apply.

Generations passed, many thousands of lives played out within the solitary confines of the ship. There were diversions – films, 'culture' and the rest. But gradually, through the years and over the generations, a collective claustrophobia began to take hold of the society. The stillness of the ship as it shot across the universe; the sense of that great emptiness before and behind them; the knowledge that their journey was without end even for the generations to come – all these began to oppress the people, especially the young. The social bonds began to break.

The greatest problem aboard the ship had always been work. There was none. Of course, useless toil could be invented, and people could be encouraged or forced to do that. But only the very unthinking would submit for long. So the diversions and entertainments became more lavish. The spectacles of film and light and sound that were served up in the three great auditoria became more spectacular. But gradually, and especially for the young, that was not enough. They wanted more meaning. A group of them took the dangerous step of seeing their diversions not as diversions at all, but as the aim of life. They became hedonists. The group grew. At first, the Administration had not noticed them. (It was easy to miss things in the great rabbit warren that was the ship.) Then, when they did notice them, they patronised them, seeing in what the young people did another useful diversion. Then they began to get scared.

A heavy trade in drugs developed. This, too, was encouraged at first by the Administration as a harmless form of entertainment. But the drugs got no better. With nowhere to go, no place to walk except the corridors and halls and rooms of the ship, nothing to see except the Administration's bland entertainments – with nothing outside them, in short, the young were beginning to turn inwards and expand their minds with chemicals. They could sit for hours, days at a time, and without seeming to move – much like the ship, in fact – travel millions of miles in the slow blink of a drugged eyelid. The walls of the ship might be closed, but inside their heads there were open, sunlit spaces.

A circle of five young people were on the floor of a small storage room. It was one of those half-forgotten places in the labyrinthine ship where non-vital spares were stored. Around the young people were stacked boxes of electronic circuit boards. One of their number was a junior stores operative, and he had *given the others access to this place. They didn't speak, but every now and then, when one caught another's eye, they would smile softly, or occasionally one of them would emit a low hum, and the others would join in. They were without the usual apparatus of pleasure associated with such gatherings. There was no music in the background, no pungent smoke in the air, no drink and burbling talk. A bulb above them picked out everything with a bright white light. Periodically, the tannoy crackled into life from a loudspeaker in the corner of the ceiling. 'Maintenance crew 12 report to Computer Centre, Forward Deck 15, Level 3' 'Second screening of latest "Star Dynasty" update to commence in Auditorium 2 at 8.00.' Very occasionally, there would be an ironic smile in the group at these abrupt and urgent messages. But on the whole their minds, with such vast distances to cover, moved too slowly for humour.*

All of them except one sat comfortably with their backs leaning against the piled-up boxes. This one was a thin, tense girl with cropped brown hair. She crouched on her haunches, staring down between her knees at the floor. She had been in this position for two hours, since they had taken the drug. Her name was Faina.

In the pitted surface of the plastic floor-covering she thought she could see the reason for everything. Not that she saw it as symbolic in any way, nor was there a logical progression by which she went from the fact of the plastic floor-covering to an articulate conclusion. Just the presence beneath her of that mute, trodden-on object was enough to fill her with an overwhelming sense that she was looking at everything she needed to know. Staring at the floor more intently, it reminded her of the Earth mountains she had seen in the ancient films. Faina enjoyed these films. Most people didn't – they were bored of them, and preferred the computer-generated entertainments. But Faina dreamed of them, the teeming cities and oceans, hills and forests. Again, it wasn't exactly that the plastic floor-covering looked like the mountains to Faina. There was nothing distorted about her vision. The connection between them was at some abstract, indefinable level. Her thoughts travelled quickly, so quickly that they were absorbed pre-articulately, experienced in a rush. She felt weary with wisdom.

'Faina Davenport report to Deputy Deck Officer 421 on Rear Deck 19, Level 7.' The tannoy clicked off again. A slow stirring swept through the group.

'That's your brother wants you, Faina,' said one of them quietly, after a long pause.

'I know,' said Faina. Her voice was so distant that the words sounded more like a general statement than a reply. She was still staring at the floor.

She stood up, 'I'll be back,' she said, and left. The others smiled softly to each other.

Faina made her way across the ship like a sleepwalker. She stood in lifts, walked along corridors, climbed escalators, and was sped along on moving walkways. When she reached her destination, she hesitated outside the door as though surprised to find she had arrived. She could remember nothing of her journey. She watched her finger travel to a button beside the door and press it. Then she waited. The video camera was pointing down at her. Right now her brother would be looking at the screen beside his desk to see who was outside the door. He would let her wait a few seconds. Then the door snapped open, and he got up to greet her.

'Faina,' he said rather formally, 'I'm so glad you could come.'

Faina wandered into the centre of the room. She smiled pleasantly, looking round at the tastefully decorated office, with its plants and sculptures.

'I'm tired,' she said, and sat down on the floor.

Pete Davenport, disconcerted by the look of troubled seriousness that was suddenly on his sister's face, wandered over to the tanks that made up his mini-zoo. Mini-zoos, a delightful domestic feature, were one of the perks of middle-ranking office. From behind the glass, a cloned lizard creature gazed insolently back at him.

'I wish you'd talk, instead of just sitting there with that dumb expression on your face,' he snapped irritably.

'. . . telling me something, telling you something . . .' *Faina chanted quietly.*

'What the hell is that meant to mean?'

'That's right,' *said Faina with a grin, but looking at him steadily,* 'the hell.'

'Let's stop fooling around. I asked you here because pretty soon my name'll be coming up for promotion to the Central Council. I mean to be appointed, but there is no chance of my being so if you continue to behave as you do and associate with the kind of people that you do. Before any appointment is made, the most extensive research is carried out on candidates' family and associates, to look for security flaws. As soon as they discover that I have a sister who . . . behaves as she does, then my career in the Administration will be finished.' *He left a moment for this to sink in.* 'I'm sure you wouldn't want to cause the end of a promising career.'

'I'm not sure,' *said Faina. Again, her voice made it sound more like a general statement than a reply.*

'But I don't understand,' *said Pete in exasperation.* 'Why do you do this? Why are you mixed up with those useless people? You're perfectly intelligent. If you cleaned up your life, and I got on to the Council, I could get you a good job. In the Cultural Section, maybe. Our family has a tradition of loyal service to the Colony stretching back to before the Explosion. Are you going to be a part of that, or are you just going to be a spoiler? Are you going to do what's right, or are you going to say, "No, I'm going to do just what I want and stand* *in the way of everything?" '*

Faina was about to speak, but Pete interrupted her. He was carried away and excited by now. 'You people make me sick,' he spat. 'Of course, you expect everything to be done for you. You expect the ship to run. You expect all the services and amenities that the Administration provides. But are you ever grateful? Like hell. All you think about is yourselves. You never consider your duties and obligations to future generations, or the debt you owe to those who came before and brought us to where we are now. You're so narrow-minded, you can't even understand our historical mission to keep mankind alive, to survive into eternity.' He was red and spluttering with rage now. 'All you're interested in is living for the moment. Living for the fucking moment!' With a manic laugh, he turned away again. The lizard gazed at him uncomprehendingly.

Laura was playing that night in the Queen's Head, in Barnes. It was a large pub by the river, one of the very best jazz venues in London. In a short space of time, Laura had begun to make her way as a musician. While she was playing with Stan Morgan, word had got round and people had come to hear her. She started getting invitations to guest with other bands, or to do feature spots with resident rhythm sections. She found less and less time to play with Stan Morgan. But Stan didn't mind. 'When you're playing the Blue Note in New York, Miss Morton,' he would say jovially, 'don't you forget that it was old Morgan who first gave you a foot up the ladder.' And then he would slap her paternally on the back.

What people liked about Laura's playing was her melodic sense. She could move her fingers fast, but what really pulled her through was her feeling for the melodic arch. Other sax players played in disconnected spurts, or fell back on old formulae, but Laura had a sense of direction. She was a bluesy player, and happiest at medium or slow tempi. But on top of that, when she was inspired, she could play hypnotic, mantra-life riffs and off-key arpeggios, scything up and down the instrument, against the beat.

The music room of the Queen's Head was crowded, the other musicians already warming up on stage, when Laura arrived. She hardly had time to greet Jeremy, who was standing at the bar. Their first number, according to custom, was a medium tempo blues. After the 'Straight No Chaser' head, the leader of the band – an alto player called Dave Prince – took a long solo. Laura was nervous. Although she had rehearsed once with this band – just beginnings and endings – she had never heard them play in public. For a moment, as she listened to Prince take off, she was frightened of being out of her depth. He played rather like Charlie Parker, using a lot of rippling, forward arpeggios. A couple of choruses into his solo, he went into double time and set up a pounding, asymmetric riff with the drummer. It was impressive. Laura tapped her foot and waited her turn. When it came, after tumultuous applause for Dave Prince, she started slow and soulfully, setting herself apart from what had gone before. The drummer switched to brushes. She thought carefully about each phrase, not rushing into things to begin with. The audience all seemed to lean back in their seats. As she played, Laura fixed her eyes over their heads at a point somewhere on the back wall. Only occasionally would she allow her glance to dip down into the field of faces. And even then she took nothing in through her eyes.

Jeremy, watching her through a sea of heads from the bar, was so transported by the music that for a while he forgot everything that had been troubling him. Then it all began to come back. Laura had been perfunctory in greeting him. Had Morton told her? Straight away, Jeremy could picture the scene. Had Laura been shocked? Or had she and Morton (more likely, this) had a good laugh? Jeremy could imagine how Morton might phrase it, the bastard. He might well have told her earlier this evening, when Laura happened to mention to him who she was seeing. In that case, she wouldn't have had a chance to ring Jeremy and cancel their meeting. Or maybe she really wanted to see him in order to confront him and demand that he explain himself? This last thought alarmed Jeremy, but was somehow more palatable than the others. Well if that's what it was, and he was going to have to give an account of himself, then he would need some fortification. He bought another pint and began drinking it greedily. What with the music thundering through the room, he could hardly tell he was getting drunk. In fact, things seemed to be getting clearer. He began spotting things he hadn't noticed at first. There was applause, and the band started another number. He imagined that Laura was catching his eye every now and then – and every time she did so, it seemed that she played one of those ironic, mocking phrases she went in for. Yes, that was definitely what was happening. Christ. He had to get out. He even took a few unsteady steps into the crowd, towards the door, then remembered his cigarettes, returned to his place, and forgot about leaving.

At the end of the first set, Laura came over to Jeremy and kissed him on the cheek. So she didn't know. Jeremy felt first a rush of relief, then a thrill at all this adult kissing-on-cheeks (it was the kind of thing his parents did), then self-loathing such as he had never felt before. He was such a fraud. Which, of course, was just how he liked to be. He was telling her that everyone in the pub fitted the stereotype of the pot-bellied, middle-aged jazz buff. She laughed, looking flushed and excited from playing. Every now and then, she grasped Jeremy's hand or arm, as though she was drunk as well and needed support.

'And look at the blokes in the band,' he continued. 'They're wearing flared grey-flannel trousers. Honestly, I mean the music's good – but that bass player's shirt's too much. I didn't know shirts that ugly were actually legal.' Laura giggled, leaning against Jeremy to control herself. Jeremy wished she wouldn't touch him. It made him feel funny, and every time she touched him his self-hatred boiled up again. 'No, you're not going to get anywhere in this business,' he continued, talking faster and faster, 'unless you're fat, male and forty. Look at these blokes. They look like train-spotters.'

After a few minutes Laura returned to the stand, elated. Dave Prince's band was the best she had ever played with. She had felt at home right from the moment in her first solo when she had ended a phrase on a bluesy growl, and the drummer had replied with a crack on his side-drum rim. By the end of the first set – partly physically, from the hard blowing – she had felt high. Colours were crisper, and objects themselves, not just their light, seemed to impress themselves on her retina. Talking to Jeremy, she had found she couldn't help staring at his hair. It was dragooned into a stylish cut, but within those limits it fell naturally into lovely curls. She wanted to reach out and run her fingers through it, and could barely restrain herself from actually doing so. She felt fidgety. Then there were his eyes, which seemed to brush back towards his temples, and his delicate lips. She wondered what it would be like to run one of her fingers along his lips, then up his cheeks to where the bone was prominent beneath his beautiful eyes.

Laura played her best in the second half. To a certain extent, because she was a new face, she stole the show from Dave Prince. Jeremy, safe in the knowledge that Morton had told his daughter nothing, unwound and began watching her with a relaxed and proprietorial eye. He didn't have much of an ear for music. What interested him more was the look, the style of things. None of these musicians, Laura included, dressed how jazz musicians should dress. They should dress in black, with clean, strong lines. Laura was such a good player, it was a pity she wasted her time playing in this kind of outfit. If she was with a younger band, maybe playing something more modern, with a steadier beat, and if the whole thing was packaged right, then she could go far.

Jeremy stopped with his beer glass at his lips. Fuck it, yes. That was it. He would ring Tony Baldwin. He hadn't seen him for months. Jeremy was suddenly seeing a way out of his hopelessness, his indecision about what to do with himself. He would manage Laura Morton. He would put together a proper pop band featuring her, and promote it. Tony would help. Tony had his own video company, his own recording studio. Everything would be great. Why hadn't he thought of it before? He would go into the music business. His parents could stick their respectable careers and professions. He gulped his beer excitedly, smiling at the thought of how his parents would react when he told them he was going to manage a rock band. That would really boot his father up the backside. Jeremy wasn't even hearing the music now. Tony had a house in Clapham. It was a big house, Jeremy remembered, with lots of rooms. Tony would be bound to let him live there, at least for a while. They had got quite friendly when Jeremy was at college. He had even helped out at a couple of shoots for Tony's videos. And they had gone round the clubs together. He would ring Tony in the morning.

At the end of the final set, Jeremy whistled and clapped louder than anyone. He was on top of the world. The audience began to crowd out of the door, and Laura, after chatting for a few moments with the other musicians, came over to Jeremy. The bar was closed, but the landlord let the musicians stay behind for a few drinks. It had been a good night. Except for Laura, they sat on stools at the bar, while the barman started sweeping up around them. Laura sat apart at a table with Jeremy. Every now and then, the musicians threw teasing comments across the room about Laura and her 'sweetheart'. Laura grinned back at them, or, in mock annoyance, shouted back, 'Will you guys can it?' then laughed as her fellow-musicians took off her accent.

Jeremy ignored them. He had more important things on his mind. Excitedly, but with determination, he was preparing Laura for his plans. He got irritated when she was distracted by the other musicians.

'Listen, this is important, Laura. What we've got to do is break away from these middle-aged, middle-class people telling us what to do. The young should stick together. You could be leading your own band. And you could be in a band that's really in touch with what's happening on the streets. The trouble with these guys,' he waved a hand towards the bar, 'is that they've lost touch. Basically, they're fucking straight.'

Jeremy only really forgot himself and all his problems when he was talking. And when he was into his stride, he could be very persuasive. It helped that Laura was tipsy. She had been thirsty after playing, and had bought a pint. She had drunk that quickly and got another. She slid fast from euphoria into drunkenness.

'God,' she interrupted Jeremy after a while, 'this is weird, because I was saying to Aidan the other week how the thing I really *love* about England is the way you've got some culture, you know like youth culture. I mean in the States there might have been some back in the sixties, but now except for some punk in LA or New York which is just copied from London, all the kids are like miniature adults. All they want to do is go to Law School or Business School, and then they're going to be just like Mom and Pop. It's like, in the States there's only one place to go. And God, I don't want to go there.' She laughed, grabbed Jeremy's arm, and hugged it to her chest. 'Don't let them send me there, Jeremy.' She laughed again.

'No, well that's it,' said Jeremy, withdrawing his arm to light a cigarette. 'You join me in getting this band together, and we can make a completely new start. I mean this stuff's all very well,' he waved towards the other musicians, 'but we could do something that would be a total concept. The whole thing – the music, the style and everything – would be a statement.'

Laura nodded eagerly. She had one elbow on the table, and her chin rested on her hand. As Jeremy talked on, she swayed a little towards him, smiling dreamily. His words were giving her that feeling of foreignness she loved. At one point, she completely forgot herself and, gazing into his face, reached up and stroked his hair. Jeremy started visibly. Laura's hand on his head felt hot and clammy. Her whole body seemed to be giving off a kind of stifling heat, directed at him. She removed her hand and, in her drunkenness, it was as though it had never been there. She continued to lean towards him, so that as he talked her face was only inches from his.

They were the last to leave the pub. Out on the street, by the river, Laura shivered and took Jeremy's arm.

'Why don't you come back on the train to the burnt house? We could have some coffee. You're never going to make it all the way down to your parents' place.'

But Jeremy resisted, and eventually Laura went over the road to the station alone. Jeremy set off to walk along the river to Hammersmith, where he could get a bus.

There were no lights along the footpath, but the sky was quite clear, so that shafts of white moonlight lay across the way ahead. The road veered away to the right, until the sound of traffic was only a distant roar. Down to the left, below the river bank, could be heard rustlings and the occasional quack of a duck. The air was laden with dank river smell. Unnoticed by Jeremy, bats fitted to and fro along the edge of the river.

He was still thinking about his conversation with Laura. His head was spinning with plans and ideas. Then, with a jolt, he became aware of his surroundings. He was scared. It was dark, and the path was lined on either side by trees and dense undergrowth. There would be no chance of spotting someone, a mugger, a madman, hiding next to the path, waiting. He walked on quickly, suddenly feeling more sober, guiding himself by following the gaps in the trees above the path. The trees were silhouetted against the moonlight, so that he was following a strip of silvery dark blue sky that kept receding ahead of him as he stumbled faster and faster along the path. But there was no attack. Gradually, as he got into the rhythm of walking and the city seemed more and more distant, his thoughts and fears slipped away. He was mesmerised by the window of moonlight above him between the two rows of trees. The trees rustled and rattled in the wind, and for a moment, with a sense of revelation, he realised that what he was afraid of was not muggers, but the very darkness and wind and trees. He felt this for just a moment, with something that was like relief but stronger. Then, as he emerged from this patch of wildness up on to Hammersmith Bridge, the feeling deserted him. His brain tightened again, forgetting, and he hurried forward beneath the orange neon lights to insert himself once more into the city.

CHAPTER ELEVEN

When Tom Saab came to Faina's room, on her brother's orders, she was recovering from another trip. For the past six hours she had roamed far and wild, through jungles, across wide praries and sun-drenched deserts. Now she was back on the ship with the knowledge that she had never left it. She stared at the ceiling, her brains fried from the drug. She was numb, frustrated at not even being able to feel depressed. She couldn't feel anything. She answered Tom Saab's greetings and questions monosyllabically, uncurious as to why he had come. She knew him only as an old friend of her brother's, always in his shadow and toadying to him. The conversation ground to a halt, Tom looked uncomfortably at his feet, and Faina leant back on her couch.

'Pete and I had a terrible row the other day,' said Faina.

'Yes, he told – ' began Tom, then stopped and looked down at his feet again in confusion.

'I felt really bummed out about it,' continued Faina, ignoring him. She was glad of someone, a virtual stranger, to talk to. 'He wanted me to straighten out my life-style. I think he was really worried about me. But I just can't. Or I don't see any point. Do you ever look around the ship and ask yourself "What are we doing this for?" Maybe not. I know, I know: "The Xykon's voyage is the fulfilment of humankind's unique mission to survive. Amidst the annihilation of everything, humankind is the shining beacon that will live on into eternity." We all learnt that little ditty as children. But I just can't believe in it any more. It's so abstract. What's it got to do with these rooms and corridors? I want to live, and if I can't do that, I'd rather die than be in this limbo.'

Faina fell silent. She fiddled distractedly with the light-fitting above her head.

'You really are down, aren't you?' said Tom after a pause.

'Yeah,' snapped Faina.

113

'Well I shouldn't worry about what Pete says. He probably doesn't mean it.' There was a long pause. 'If you really are feeling low. I've got something that could give you a lift.'

Faina looked at him. 'You?' she said, disbelievingly.

'Sure, I've got a friend who works in the labs. He's been putting together these new opiates. I tried this one myself. It's something else. You wanna try it?'

'What, now?'

'Sure, why not?'

Faina swung her feet to the floor and sat up on the couch. 'Yeah, why not? Let's do it.' She took the pill that Tom gave her and swallowed it. She laughed. 'You're a real mystery, Tom,' she said. 'You're the last person I'd imagine to be carrying expanders.' She lay back and looked intently at the ceiling.

Tom bit his bottom lip and watched her anxiously.

'That feels pretty good for starters,' she said in a whisper. The ice-cold numbness was already creeping up her legs. Soon it would reach her heart.

Aidan was in the central valley of the burnt house's roof. On either side of him, the roof rose then fell away again towards the street and, at the back, the garden. When he crouched down, these peaks gave him some protection from the cold wind that buffeted the house. London lay grim and vast as far as the eye could see, until it disappeared into the damp winter haze. It looked completely still, the tower blocks in the centre and to the east like monuments, like tombstones amongst the tangled undergrowth of streets and houses. Closer to, the view resolved itself into hundreds of chimneypots spread across the rough terrain of the roofs like tree stumps that had survived from a great forest fire. Some of the buildings in the middle-distance were probably landmarks, but Aidan didn't know them. He didn't really know London.

Over the still city, the sky was violent and active. Air rushed around Aidan's face, biting into his clothes and flapping his hair into his eyes. Smaller clouds skidded overhead, spitting moisture down at him. He watched a great swathe of grey cloud move across from the west. The rain beneath it raked the streets.

For a moment, the sun was revealed, and cast a bitter, warmthless light on the scene. Then a shadow swept the city and everything was grey again.

He watched a plane, a jumbo jet, move slowly up the sky, as though weighing at every moment the distance between itself and the ground below. He had never been in a plane. Three or four years ago, his dad had talked about taking them to Spain, but then he had been made redundant, so they hadn't gone. He watched the plane lumber upwards, disappear into cloud, emerge again, then disappear for ever. Perhaps it was going to America.

'Aidan!'

Morton's voice came from deep in the house. A minute or so later, his bald head appeared through the trap door.

'How're you guys getting on up here?'

'Just been putting some new filleting on this wall. Trevor's gone to buy some tiles.'

Morton glanced at the book in Aidan's hand. 'Left you to mind the fort, huh?'

'Something like that.'

Morton heaved himself up out of the trap door and looked around. 'London. Not a bad little city, I'd say.'

They stood beside each other in silence for a few moments, looking at the view.

'Trevor thinks the roof's all right,' said Aidan. 'Just needs a few new slates.'

'You guys are doing a great job on this house, you know that? I'm getting really attached to this place. I'm thinking of having a party here soon, like a house-warming. I'll ask some people from the office. If you've got anyone you want to ask, feel free. I'm sure Laura'll bring some of her musician friends.'

'Can my brother kip down here for a couple of nights? He rang me up last week and said he wants to come to London.'

'Sure. No problem. Tell him to come for the party. Why don't we make it two weeks on Saturday.' He paused. 'I guess you'll be going back to your family for Christmas?'

'Dunno. I haven't thought about it.'

'Well you're more than welcome to stay here if you want, but Christmas is the big family festival. I'm sure your parents'll want to have you there.'

Aidan didn't reply.

'I hope you won't mind me saying this, Aidan,' Morton continued, 'but it doesn't seem like you're very close to your family.'

'Suppose not.'

'I mean, if you ever want to talk about it . . . I guess your father losing his job must have put a strain on things?'

'Dunno really.'

'Well, like I say, you can stay here if you want.'

'Thanks.'

Aidan gazed out across London again, feeling uncomfortable. He didn't like Morton asking questions like this. The whole point of Morton was that he was different, exotic, nothing to do with the world Aidan had grown up in. And now here he was talking about Aidan's family instead of New York and California and Vietnam.

Two of the cracked tiles that needed replacing were on the side of the roof that sloped towards the street. It wasn't a steep slope, but if you did slip off there would be a three-storey drop on to the iron railings by the front door. When Trevor returned, after Morton had gone back down into the house, he tied one end of a rope round his waist, the other round a parapet.

'Hard to credit,' he said, as he tied the knots, 'but some blokes'll do a job like this without a rope for safety. Silly buggers. You seen that bloke around here in a wheelchair? He used to be a roofer. Broke his back.' He examined the rope, which looked old and frayed. 'Not that this would take my weight for long. Best I could find.' He laughed. 'You make sure you haul me up good and quick if I fall.' Aidan grinned back at him.

He watched Trevor climb down the roof and prise out the first old tile. The sun had come out now, and the wet roof glistened. Trevor's hammer echoed across the rooftops. Another plane was mounting the sky, its windows flashing. The hammering stopped. Aidan glanced down and saw Trevor edge his way along the roof to the next tile. The plane could just be seen among the clouds, sparkling in all that moisture as the sun hit it. Trevor's hammering had started again. As the plane approached overhead, its roar reached the roof. Aidan watched, grinning into the sunlight that splashed the roof, willing it upwards. He was with it. It was escaping the ground, just like Aidan had wanted to escape the drab world in which he had grown up for Morton's world. As Aidan watched the aeroplane, he felt as though if he could only reach out and jump from the roof he could catch it and join it. For a moment he was dizzy. He could actually see the distance between himself and the plane, and between the plane and clouds through which it passed and the ground. He could do more than see the exhilarating, yawning distance. It was as though the distance was entering and becoming part of him.

In a rush, things crowded back in on him. He noticed the rope beside him taut, straining at the parapet. He looked down. Trevor was lying flat on the lip of the roof, his entire body pressed into the tiles, his hands and feet pressed into the wet, sloping surface to gain a grip. He had slipped down almost to the edge. Even his face was pressed down, cheek flattened, into the wetness. His eyes glared up at Aidan. He raised his head and shouted hoarsely, 'Pull me up!'

Aidan grabbed the rope and heaved Trevor up till he was able to crawl to safety on his hands and knees. Once he was safely back beside the parapet, the older man crouched silently for a few moments, his head hanging, running his hands through his hair. His hands were shaking.

'You're a right one,' he said abruptly. 'I thought I told you to watch out, not gape at the bloody sky. Christ.' He dropped his head again and once more began running his hand through his hair.

Aidan stared in horror as it sank in what had almost happened. 'Why didn't you give us a shout?' he asked weakly.

'I did. I couldn't make you hear, could I? In a world of your own, as usual. I'm telling you, this is the last time I work on a roof with you. Sometimes I wonder if you're really all there. I reckon you've got something missing upstairs.'

'Sorry,' said Aidan.

'Sorry? What's the bloody use of sorry? You nearly had me killed there. Come on, let's go and do those floorboards.'

They said nothing more about it. Trevor was too angry, and Aidan was too horrified and guilty. He kept imagining Trevor tumbling over the edge of the roof, spinning, arms and legs flailing, down on to the railings below.

He played the thought over and over again in his mind, until it got mixed up with his feeling of dizziness as he had watched the plane ascend through the clouds. It even became exhilarating in the same way.

When they had done the day's work, Aidan retreated to the top of the house. Up in his room, he kept coming back to that image of Trevor tumbling down from the roof on to the railings, and of the plane arching slowly up through the clouds. He lay on his sleeping bag and looked up at the damp patch on the ceiling. At least that wouldn't be getting bigger now the roof was fixed. Morton would probably want him and Trevor to start decorating the place soon, scrape off all the soot and blackened wallpaper and paint it over with gleaming new paint. Aidan didn't want the place changed. At least, he didn't want to be there when it was changed. He liked it how it was, blackened and bare. The burnt house. Once it was smartened up it would be like any other house. It would be like the house he had grown up in, crammed with useless objects, stale with permanence. He had come here to get away from that, and now it was all going to start again.

All afternoon the noise of Trevor and Aidan hammering downstairs had been driving Laura crazy. She stopped practising her saxophone and sat at the window, watching it get dark. It wasn't just the noise. Everything about this godawful house seemed to get her down. When it rained, as it was now, it smelt damp. It was always gloomy. And everywhere, on all your clothes, in the bath, in your hair, was this yucky film of dust. And it was cold.

She was expecting Jeremy. Since that evening at the Queen's Head, ten days ago, she had seen a lot more of him. He had rung her up the next day and they had gone for a walk. Then they had gone out together a couple of evenings. The second of those times they had kissed on the lips. It was so cute the way he wanted to help her get on in the music business. He had a kind of boyish enthusiasm about it. Occasionally, Laura had reservations about playing pop. But as soon as she heard Jeremy talk about it, she felt herself being nudged along by his keeness. She could never resist enthusiasm.

The happiness Laura suddenly felt as she sat waiting for Jeremy was almost like excitement, but with no goal, no satisfaction, in its sights. It was weightless. It tumbled forward like an object spinning through outer space, propelled perpetually by nothing but its own unimpeded movement. It was like the buoyancy of an improviser, leaning in and out of the harmonies, playing with them. Irony almost like cruelty. She had a tune going in her head as she thought this, riding the rhythm section. That was partly what she liked in Jeremy. She could see in him the same kind of excitement, a kind of fidgetiness. Swing. She couldn't help comparing him in that respect with Aidan, who always seemed so inert. Thinking about their individuality like that made the fact that they were both British seem even more strange. Again she had that almost physical sensation of being a foreigner, of rubbing up against her surroundings in a way she had never done before. In America, it seemed to her now, you could slip through life and never feel anything, never make contact.

The hammering downstairs had stopped. She heard Aidan's footsteps climb slowly up to the top floor. Then there was just the patter of the rain outside. Sometimes the burnt house felt claustrophobic. She was losing patience with her father's obsession with the place. He had announced to her this afternoon, after coming back early from the studio again, that he was going to have a house-warming party. What was there to celebrate about a dump like this, she had wanted to know. But now, thinking about it, a party didn't seem so crazy. She would invite everyone she had met since coming to London. That would make it seem almost like a rite of passage.

A couple of minutes later, when Jeremy banged at the door downstairs, Laura was bubbling with excitement about the party. It was the first thing she told him as she led him up the bare wooden stairs to the kitchen.

'Well, I hope that Aidan kid doesn't invite loads of hippies,' said Jeremy. 'If there's one thing I hate it's hippies.'

Laura laughed. 'Don't worry. I think it'll mainly be colleagues of Bob's. That's bad enough. Have you ever been in a room full of drunk TV executives? It's obscene.'

When they were in the kitchen, Jeremy brought things back to his plans for a band.

'I saw that friend of mine Tony again today. I've definitely got him interested. He's given me somewhere to live as well. He knows a lot of musicians. He's been thinking of launching a new package anyway. I want you to meet him as soon as possible.'

'What's this place you're moving to?'

'He's got a house in Clapham. I'll be able to organise everything from there.'

'God, you're so lucky. I'd love to move out of this place.'

'Yeah. So I'll fix something up with Tony. What about tomorrow?'

'You're really wired up about this, aren't you? I don't know, Jeremy. If I'd wanted to play pop, I'd have learnt the guitar.'

'You'll have the artistic freedom to play just as you want to play,' said Jeremy seriously. 'You'll be able to play just like you do now, only it'll be in a different context. You see, the trouble with the bands you've been playing with now is that they've got no image – you know, like an identity. They've got no profile.'

'OK, OK. I'm convinced. You could ask anything in that cute British accent of yours and I'd agree.' She leant forward and kissed him.

'You'll see Tony tomorrow then?'

'Sure. This house of his – does it have any more spare rooms? I'd do anything to get out of this place. It's really starting to bug me.'

'I don't know. It's quite big. But it's hard to tell, because people tend to drift in and out. And anyway, wouldn't your father be a bit upset if you moved out of here?'

'I hadn't really thought about that. I guess he would be kind of upset. But don't worry. I'll talk to him about it. I'm sure he'll understand. I'll have to be careful how I put it, because he's really proud of this house.'

'Yeah, ask Tony tomorrow, after we've talked about the band.' Jeremy brought things back to that again, telling her more of his plans. Laura, holding his hand in hers, was only half listening. She was thinking about how great it would be to live in a house in – what was the name of the place? It sounded like 'clap 'em' – with Jeremy. So the party would be a kind of goodbye to the burnt house for her. Yeah, and good riddance.

Jeremy stayed for quite a while. They kissed a couple of times. Jeremy sensed her desire, but felt repulsed by the physical sensation of her tongue in his mouth. He knew she wanted him to stay longer, but he managed to get away. As he walked down the wet, wind-blown street to the tube station, he imagined with pleasure what Morton's reaction would be to his adored only daughter moving away from home to be with a degenerate.

Laura was left flushed and excited. She sat for a while at the table, staring at the soot-stained walls, and imagined Jeremy's swept-back eyes and the feel of his slender fingers as they had lain in her hand. She didn't really know what she was frightened of. It was something like looking at a magnificent view and, mixed up with the beauty of the view, being scared of the height. It was fear of an emptiness that might reach far below all this fulfilment.

She turned off the lights in the kitchen and went upstairs to her bed. As she lay there, she was flooded with a warm feeling of lonelinesss. She rolled on to her side and hugged her pillow close, then brought her knees up to her chest and hugged the pillow with them as well.

CHAPTER TWELVE

Generations had accepted the Xykon's mission and the decisions of the Council. But things were beginning to change. First there were a series of scandals involving officials, beginning with the revelation that Peter Davenport, a middle-ranking official, had had his sister poisoned. On the other side, there developed out of the hedonists' sub-culture a political movement that questioned the ship's ultimate purpose. This movement attracted an increasing number of the younger generation. The Council hoped at first to contain it, but in the end, weakened internally by the scandals, they had to recognise the movement. They were split in their attitude. Suddenly, it seemed, there was an almost euphoric atmosphere of questioning and openess. It looked like anything was possible.

Liberal elements in the Administration organised a series of debates on fundamental issues affecting the future of the colony. The last of these dealt with the question of whether the colony should in fact have any future.

'It has been assumed,' a radical spokesman for the youth movement summed up. He was a confident young man with long black hair and a moustache. The packed auditorium listened to him respectfully. 'It has been assumed for generation after generation, ever since the Explosion, that the people of this colony would do as they were told: that they would deny themselves and turn their backs on their own happiness for the sake of future generations. But what were they giving future generations that was so precious? More of the same. Each generation would inflict on itself the misery of this stifled existence – ' he cast his hand around the auditorium – 'so that their children, and their children's children, could experience that misery too. Well that looks like vindictiveness to me, not selflessness.

'I want to make an analogy now, so that you'll know exactly what I'm talking about. You've all read in the history books about money and banks. Back then, the person of virtue was the person who stored up money in the bank for his descendants to enjoy. But then, presumably, if those descendants

were virtuous, then instead of enjoying it themselves they would store it up some more and add to it for their descendants. So nobody would ever enjoy it. The capital would sit there, piling up into eternity while generations scurried around it, feeding it. It's like that with us, I think, only what we're storing up is not money but existence itself. We're piling it up, not so that it can be used or enjoyed, but just for the sake of piling it up. Because what we're always told about the purpose of Xykon is that it's all about survival – the survival of life.

'But is what we're preserving life? As it is, the purpose of our existence is solely to perpetuate itself. I don't call that life. Life should have a purpose beyond itself. What I say is that we should take the existence that has been given us and use it to live. Over the past few generations, I'm told, Xykon has passed many good planets where it could have stopped. I say we should stop at the next good planet we come to and live. Yeah, and let our children live. And maybe our children's children. Then the Explosion can catch up and end it all. But at least someone will have lived. I know you've heard this proposal before and I know you've heard the Council's response. They'll say it's suicide and murder. They'll say that their position is pro-life. But what I say is that there's a difference between life and existence. What I say is that it's us who are pro-life. All we want to do is live – yeah, and then die.'

The spokesman sat down, and about half the hall applauded enthusiastically. The vast auditorium was filled with the hum of conversation. Up on the platform, the spokesman for the Administration rose to make his reply. He was known as a liberal, and had been carefully chosen for his appealing manner.

'I want to thank my colleague,' he said, smiling at the younger man, 'for setting out so clearly the dilemma we all face. I'm sincerely glad that we have the opportunity to debate these matters, for perhaps our greatest hope lies in our ability to continue having discussions like this.

'Straight off, I want to make plain my agreement with my colleague on one fundamental matter. I agree that life on this ship is limiting, frustrating and unsatisfactory. According to the experts, if Xykon is to survive, then we're stuck with it. My colleague here suggests as an alternative that we accept that the colony will end, and hunker down on a congenial planet until the end comes. I can understand the attraction of that, particularly if one compares it with the apparent irrationality and futility of perpetuating our present state of affairs into eternity. A long time ago, people used to believe in an all-creating, omniscient God, and I guess that from the point of view of such a God my colleague's suggestion might be the best thing to do. But there is no such God, and we as individuals have no right to take such decisions. For what of the people who came before us, and who might come after us? The former restrained themselves from taking that

*decision, and if we take it ourselves then we will be denying the latter
the opportunity of doing the same. We would be setting ourselves up as
arbiters of past and future. We will have rubbished the existence of both our
ancestors and our descendants.*

'*My colleague says that life should look beyond mere existence. But
don't we look beyond mere existence when we continue a joyless existence
for the sake of an invisible and unattainable goal? I agree with him: we
should look beyond our own miserable existence on this ship. It's only by
looking beyond it that we can make sense of it. But it's my colleague, I
would argue, who is limiting himself to delving within existence for some
ellusive happiness and fulfilment. Who knows, perhaps it would not be so
idyllic and fulfilling on this utopian planet of his, when we are relieved
of all our responsibilities and are just waiting for the end? Would we be
any better off then? No, you've got to look beyond the actual conditions
of existence to make sense of it. And that's what we do when we consider
Xykon's mission.*'

'Aidan! Say, Aidan, are you up there?'

He put down *The Voyage Beyond Infinity*. 'Yeah,' he shouted back,
'I'm here.'

'Come on down. Your brother's arrived.'

Aidan hurried downstairs. He found Doug and Laura in the front
room on the first floor. All Morton's things had been stacked at one
end. Already there were garish paper chains and ribbons hanging in
loops from the ceiling.

'Hello, Aid,' said Doug. With exaggerated care, he lifted a red
paper ribbon that was dangling in front of his face, and grinned at
his brother.

'You two guys look so alike, it's incredible,' said Laura.

'*You*'d better believe it,' said Doug. 'Has he been behaving
himself?' He jerked a thumb at Aidan.

'Sure, he's been great.'

'He hasn't been *mis*behaving himself?' Doug looked at her intently.

'I couldn't say. Maybe you'd better ask him that.'

'Don't – ' began Aidan.

'No,' interrupted Doug, 'let the girl speak, Aid.' Then he added
confidentially to Laura. 'My brother and I had a bit of an argument
last time we met, 'cause I said he was having homosexual relations
with your father.'

'But that's—' began Laura in an outraged tone, then laughed.
'You're even more weird than Aidan, you know that? Not in the
same way, though, thank God.'

Doug pointed a finger at Laura in a dramatic fashion. 'No one,' he said, slowly and portentously, 'is weird in the same way.'

Laura laughed. 'Two of you,' she said, 'and I'd go crazy myself. Now why don't you put your bag up in Aidan's room? I've got to sweep up in here.'

Doug picked his army camouflage rucksack off the floor. 'Where to?' he asked Aidan.

'Up the stairs and straight ahead.'

'Is he always like that,' whispered Laura when Doug had gone, 'putting on that weird attitude all the time?'

'I dunno,' said Aidan gloomily. 'He's probably nervous. That's why he's trying to shock you. He'll calm down.'

'I sure hope so,' said Laura. She went over to the portable record player, which she had moved from the kitchen, and put on some jazz. Then she resumed sweeping the floorboards.

Doug returned. 'Mind if I roll a joint?' he said, and sat down in the middle of the floor.

'Sure you can,' said Laura, 'so long as you don't set light to all this paper and you save some puff to blow up the balloons.'

Doug took off his denim jacket and laid it across his lap. Beneath the jacket he was wearing a Hawaian shirt. It was sky blue with green parrots and red palm trees.

'Boy,' said Laura, 'that shirt really makes a statement.'

'What,' said Doug in a laboured way, 'it's saying is "Why-don't-you-two-'guys'-sit-down-here-cos-it's-really -hard- to- roll- a-joint-with -people-standing-around-making-you-feel-bad-about-it?"'

'Gee, Doug,' said Laura drily, 'the last thing I'd want is for you to feel bad about anything.'

She and Aidan sat down on the floor with him. Above their heads, the brightly coloured streamers fluttered slowly in the cold draught that came up the stairs. Doug, nodding his head in time to the music, pulled out a packet of cigarettes and some rizlas, and began rolling his joint.

'This you playing, Laura?' he said after a few moments.

'No, it's Cannonball Adderley.'

'But I thought Aidan said you played the saxophone – sorry, the *sax*?'

'Yeah, but that doesn't mean I'm playing on every record you hear, does it?'

Doug continued nodding his head, crumbling the cannabis into the tobacco. 'No,' he said after a long pause, 'I suppose it doesn't.'

When Jeremy arrived a few minutes later, they were stoned. He looked at the bright-coloured ribbons, smelt the sweet tang of the drug-smoke, and felt sick. 'I hope I'm not early,' he blurted out at the up-turned, dreamy faces.

There was a silence. Not any kind of a silence – a tense silence or a mournful silence – but just an absence of movement.

Then Doug said, 'But you haven't come far, have you?'

Laura giggled. She couldn't have said what it was she found funny or what Doug might have meant by the remark.

'Well,' began Jeremy rather irritably. He paused. In his right hand, wrapped in purple tissue paper, was a bottle of wine. He saw himself waving it around foolishly. 'Actually, I've come all the way across London,' he mumbled quickly, and plonked the wine in front of Laura on the floor.

They burst out laughing. Even Aidan grinned.

'What's so funny?' demanded Jeremy. He couldn't help the note of petulance in his voice.

'I'm sorry,' said Laura, trying to straighten her face. 'Doug, you've got the stupidest sense of humour.'

Doug shrugged his shoulders, pulling on the remains of the joint, then blowing a long stream of smelly smoke out into the festival of ribbons above his head.

'Say, Doug,' she added, 'why don't you roll another so Jeremy can get high? He's feeling excluded. Come and sit down, Jeremy.'

'Don't bother,' said Jeremy wearily. 'I'll stick to cigarettes.' He crouched awkwardly next to Laura.

There followed another silence. Nobody had bothered to change the record when it had finished, and now the only sound was the drip of rain from outside. Laura, Doug and Aidan were stunned into inarticulacy – the red, yellow, green, orange, blue streamers and the rough-grained floorboards were so impressed upon them as to push their minds further and further back into tangled roots, or to release their thoughts like a spring, so that they flew off at untraceable tangents. Jeremy watched them carefully, with a mixture of fascination and disgust.

'God, I haven't got high since I left the States,' said Laura, and she lay back on the floorboards and gazed up through the streamers. Suddenly, she sat bolt upright again. 'It's weird how many different accents there are in this country,' she burbled. 'I mean, the way you two talk is completely different from Jeremy. I guess that's because you come from a different area. What do you call it? Yeah, the Midlands. Is it like the Midwest? I mean, the way Jeremy talks is what we'd call in America a "British Accent".

I had no idea British people talked like you two.' She laughed. Doug laughed too.

'*You'd* better believe it,' he said.

'Come on, you guys. Why do you talk so different?' There was a pause. She laughed again. 'Tell me.'

'Actually . . .' Doug began, imitating Jeremy. Everyone except Jeremy laughed.

'You guys,' said Laura, and lay back again on the floorboards. 'You know, everything's so different here. It's got a bite to it. It's like everything in America's . . .' She searched the dangling ribbons for a likeness. 'Smooth surfaces.'

'Smooth,' said Doug, imitating her.

'You all talk in funny voices. It's like you're all actors, playing at being Englishmen. You're all playing character parts. Back home, everyone wants to be the romantic lead. My God, I'm talking rubbish.' She'd lost her brakes now, words tumbling and tripping off her tongue and lips without control. 'I was walking in Clerkenwell the other day, through one of those street markets, and I don't know, everything seemed so *real*. Kinda coarse. I don't mean in a bad way. Everyone was carrying those plastic carrier bags you have here. We don't have those in supermarkets in the States.'

'Only an American could be sentimental about plastic bags,' Jeremy commented, with a wry smile at Doug and Aidan. They ignored him. Laura didn't hear.

'I mean *everybody* carries around plastic bags in this country. It's surreal. Why? What's with plastic bags?'

'For their shopping?' Doug suggested.

'It's crazy. In the States, people just go to the mall on Sunday and fill up the trunk with groceries.' She giggled. 'They don't go footling around the streets all the time with plastic bags gripped in their sweaty palms.'

'The maul?' said Doug. 'Would that be Pall Maul?' He winked at Jeremy.

'I'm going to get some fresh air,' said Jeremy. He had just stood up, when there were footsteps outside the door. Morton came in, tottering under the weight of a large box, his teeth clamped around the stem of his pipe. He put down the box, puffing clouds of smoke, and was introduced to Doug. He told them all a funny story about the guy in the liquor store thinking bourbon was a kind of brandy.

Jeremy helped him to bring in the boxes of drink from the car. Up in the kitchen, they unpacked the bottles and poured peanuts into bowls. From next door came the muffled sound of jazz on the record player. Jeremy was glad to be away from them, sitting there like a bunch of hippies. He had felt soiled, somehow, just looking at them. He was disgusted with Laura getting involved with that.

Not that being with Morton made him feel any more comfortable. But at least between himself and Morton he felt a kind of bond. It was almost as though the American were implicated in Jeremy's guilty secret. Jeremy watched him closely, searching him for signs. But Morton was a sly operator. He was playing Jeremy along, giving nothing away. Jeremy would have loved just to come out with it. 'OK, Morton,' he would say. 'Why don't we stop pissing around? I know you saw me that time in Soho, coming out of the porn place. Well I don't care. You can tell who you like. I'm not ashamed of myself.' But he couldn't. He was afraid of Morton.

'Laura told me about the place in Clapham,' said Morton. 'I guess you'll be looking forward to moving away from home. You'll have more opportunity to do your own thing.'

Jeremy froze. Everything that Morton said, absurdly, seemed spiked with double-meaning and mockery.

He felt a sudden desire to fight back. 'I'm just sick of the way they live,' he said defiantly, 'with their empty middle-class values. My father talks like some kind of Thatcherite text-book. Every other word is "productivity" or "streamed-lined efficiency". He's so smug and narrow. He thinks his whole life is one big profit margin. I'm sick of it.' Jeremy ripped open another packet of peanuts. He wanted deeply to shock Morton and show him that he didn't care what Morton knew or could say about him.

'Well it's kind of healthy that someone your age should be impatient with home life and want to get away,' said Morton implacably. 'I should go for it.'

Jeremy smirked inwardly at the Americanism. 'Will you miss Laura,' he said, 'when she moves to Clapham?' He felt as though he was tiptoing out on to thin ice. Since Laura had first suggested moving with him to Clapham, Jeremy had became obsessed with the idea. He had easily persuaded Tony to give her a room. In Jeremy's mind, getting Laura out of the burnt house was a way of getting back at Morton.

'Wanna drink, Jeremy?' Morton was holding up a bottle and examining its label. 'Thought I might check out whether this Scotch is drinkable.'

'Yeah, thanks.' Jeremy waited tensely while Morton poured out two measures. They raised their glasses.

'Course, I'll miss Laura not being here,' Morton said. 'But then she wants to get out there and experience what London's got to offer, so I'm not going to stand in her way. And Aidan'll be here, so I won't be all on my own. He's a good kid, isn't he?'

'Yeah.'

'Well I hope you two can make a go of it in the music business. I guess that's different from just being a musician, like she is at the moment? I hope she hasn't inherited a kind of showbiz streak from me. I'd hate to have inflicted that on her.' And on and on he talked, cheerfully.

Jeremy sipped his whiskey and felt his spirits sink. He sunk further and further down until, floundering at the bottom, he scraped up some mud and flung it angrily up at Morton. 'Yeah, well,' he interrupted, *à propos* of nothing, 'Laura and I just want to cut through all that business bullshit. We're not interested in business. That's what's so perverse about this society, that everybody's running after money in this endless rat-race. All that running after money – wealth-creation, my dad calls it – it's all meant to be such a great, brave, macho thing to do. But what they're doing really is running *away*. People like my dad, the way he sees things deep down is like there's this big black force closing in on him, and he's got to keep on running and running to stay ahead of it. He thinks perhaps if he runs fast enough, makes a *bit* more money, then he'll be able to forget about that black force that's catching up on him. But deep down, he knows it'll always be there, inside his head.' Jeremy swigged off the rest of his whiskey and glared aggressively at Morton. The liquor scorched his throat.

Morton sipped his Scotch, looking at Jeremy sceptically. 'I've got to tell you, I've been here before, Jeremy,' he said. 'Back in the sixties, America was the richest and seemingly the most successful country in the world. Then, in the middle of all that abundance, a lot of the young people turned round and said, "We don't want to be part of all this materialism and spiritual impoverishment, especially when there's so much injustice in the world. We're going to – what was that phrase? – turn on, tune in, and drop out." And that's what they did for a while. But it didn't last. Trouble was, they thought they'd change the world just by living in a different way themselves. But nobody really gives a damn how people live. They can live how they like. There've always been nutcases, that's what other people'll figure. You don't change anything that way,'

'I didn't mean all that sixties rubbish,' Jeremy interrupted angrily, 'sitting around smoking pot like they are next door. That's just hedonism. It makes me sick. "Live for the moment, man, 'cos we're all gonna die." What I meant was . . . was that that black force doesn't even exist really. If only people would realise it. It's all in their heads – even theirs – he jerked his thumb again at the wall that separated them from the front room.

'I think you're kind of hard on people,' said Morton. 'Why don't you have another slug of this. It's all right, isn't it? I've tasted worse.'

'Yeah, I'll have some,' said Jeremy, and held out his glass. The bastard's laughing at me, he thought.

'Well Jeremy, I still can't figure out what it is you believe in.'

'Me? I . . . I don't really believe in anything. I'm kind of an anarchist.'

Morton did laugh at that.

Power is certainty. When people are unsure of the future, those that can provide certainty will prevail. The period of liberalism didn't last long. The reactionaries in the Administration gained the upper hand again and, in an equal and opposite reaction, the youthful dissidents developed their dissent. The small society of the ship seemed to be splitting apart.

Tom Saab, never discovered for his part in Faina's death, began to rise through the grades. He organised a movement calling for the release of Pete Davenport and other officials convicted of corruption. Meanwhile, the atmosphere on the ship grew bizarre and thrilling. Walking through the long corridors and passage-ways, the wide, low-ceilinged public spaces, you would come upon groups of men and women who glanced at you suspiciously. What were they doing? Talking. Plotting. Sometimes seeming to perform strange rituals. Large crowds would gather, unbidden, for no visible purpose, and mill around the public spaces until Security was sent scurrying down the corridors to clear them away. But then, hours later, another gathering would spring up somewhere else. What were they doing? The event was all – like a long, drunken party, a happening, that leaves nothing, but marks and celebrates the passage of now. Exotic

'Oy, Aid.'
    tales took them
'God, he's deaf. AID!'
    far away
No use. 'What's up?'

Laura was opening the window to let out some of the smoke – Doug had lit another joint – and as she did so, the paper chains and streamers danced in the currents of air. Aidan felt light-headed from the dope and from following the black print as it crawled

across the page. All the colours swam together. 'What's the matter?'
he said.

'Christ, you're dead to the world, you are, when you're reading
that bloody book. Haven't you finished it? You were reading that
when you came home. That was months ago.'

Aidan shrugged his shoulders and began rolling a cigarette.

'What's it about, Aid? What's the *theme*, eh?'

'Dunno.'

'God, they should put you on the telly. You're bloody gold-mine
of information, you are. Anyway, it's *extremely rude* to read in
company.'

Aidan smiled into his roll-up.

'Can *you* imagine, Laura, what it was like with a brother like this?'
He pointed at Aidan. 'It was like living with a terminal idiot. All he
does is grin like a bloody wind-up doll.'

Aidan couldn't help smiling more.

'Well I think he's cute,' said Laura.

'About as cute as a scrag-end of mutton. Besides, I thought you
said we looked the same. That mean you think I'm cute too?' He took
a triumphant puff on the joint.

'I wasn't talking about the way he looked. I meant . . . he was
kinda noble.'

Doug laughed wildly. 'Noble? Are you kidding? He looks *more*
like a bloody dosser. Anyway, aren't I noble?'

Laura looked at Doug, with his thick-rimmed glasses, his straggly
hair dangling over the Hawaian shirt, his impish eyes. She laughed.
'Yeah, sure you are,' she said.

'And here's *your* prize for giving the correct answer.' He handed
her the joint.

There was a silence. The record had finished, and through the wall
they could hear Morton's gently-modulated voice droning on in the
kitchen. Suddenly, Jeremy interrupted, sharp and loud, 'Yeah, well,
Laura and I . . .' and then the words were lost. Doug glanced at his
brother and smirked. Laura noticed this with irritation.

'Jeremy's helping me break into the rock music business,' she said
'He's got a lot of contacts.'

'That right?' said Doug. 'I thought you played the saxophone –
sorry, the *sax*.'

'I do.'

'That right?'

'Christ, I wish you'd stop saying that. You're laughing at Jeremy
for some reason, but actually he's really smart.' She took another

drag of the joint, and felt her head swim, her tongue loosen. 'He's showed me a lot of opportunities I'd have missed if I was on my own. He's taken me to the right pubs and the clubs where all the interesting people go. There's so much going on here, in the arts, in film, music, video, street fashion. There are some really radical things happening that you just don't get in America. There's no culture in America. I don't know why you two guys don't get hip to what's happening here. It's all around you. It's happening. Before I came here, I thought of America the way you're brought up to there – this big, wide-open country, the country of opportunity. And I guess I thought England was this cramped, narrow little place, that had all this history pressing down on it and crushing it. But since I got here, it's all . . . it's all changed around. Now I think of America as the place where people restrict themselves. They're so ambitious, but along such narrow lines. They just think between parallel lines. It's like there are so many more options here. There's a richness. It's in everything, the way people talk, the way they behave. I don't know, it just makes me want to get out there and join in.'

There was a pause. 'Sorry?' said Doug. 'I *didn't* quite catch that?'

'I even love your sarcasm.'

Doug took the joint from her, smoked in silence, then handed it on to Aidan.

'I heard what you said,' he began. 'Thing I couldn't figure out was, it was like you were talking about a different country from the one I live in. All that stuff about richness and opportunity. If you asked me to think about England, I tell you what I'd think. I'd have this picture in my mind of our dad sitting in his armchair. It's three o'clock on a Tuesday afternoon – it's sunny outside, but the curtains are half drawn – and our dad's watching the racing on the telly. He'll sit there for another couple of hours, till our mum comes shuffling in to ask him if he wants a cup of tea. She's been listening to the radio in the kitchen. That's all they do. That's England for you.

'I've got nothing to do either. Know what I do some days? I walk out to the by-pass, stand up there on the fly-over, and watch the traffic go by on the motorway. I mean, it's better than the racing, isn't it? I like those big lorries – think about where they might be going. Hardly a fitting occupation for a healthy, virile young gentleman like me, is it? And look at Aid there. Why do you think he's got a head full of empty space? Why do you think he's always got his nose stuck in one of them stupid space epics? 'Cos he's bored out of his tiny mind, that's why. Always has been. He was raised to it. It's his *inheritance* – his heritage, you might say.'

'I'm not bored. I'm all right,' said Aidan.

'Blimey,' said Doug. 'It talks. I thought you were one of them aliens.' He flicked his glasses up his nose and grinned. Aidan grinned back at him. They had never looked more like brothers.

CHAPTER THIRTEEN

Charles and Margaret Tetchley were the last to arrive at the party that evening. They had had an argument. The garage had lent Charles a Porsche while the BMW was being repaired, and Charles loved to drive it at every opportunity while it was in his possession.

'I don't think it's a good idea tonight,' his wife had said. 'You're bound to drink at the party, and I'm certainly not driving back.' Tetchley had become petulant. They had stood in the hall for twenty minutes arguing about it. In the end, they phoned for a taxi and sat in silence during the long crawl across London.

When they arrived at the burnt house, the door was answered by Doug. Doug had appointed himself doorman.

'Invites,' he snapped, holding the door ajar and peering tipsily out into the rain.

'Is this Bob Morton's house?' Charles asked brusquely.

'Could be,' said Doug. 'Invites.'

'For God's sake, give him our invitation,' said Margaret Tetchley. 'I'm soaking.'

Swearing, Charles Tetchley fumbled in his pockets for his wallet, then shuffled through his plastic till he found the invitation. Doug watched him.

'There. Now let us in. Where's Morton?'

Doug took the invitation and shut the door.

'What are you doing? For God's sake, let us in,' shouted Tetchley, thumping the door.

After a lengthy pause, Doug opened it and looked at the Tetchleys sternly. '*Please,*' he said, 'hands off the woodwork. You can come in. Sorry about the delay – I was checking it isn't forged.' He waved the

133

invitation under Tetchley's nose. 'I'm sure you appreciate the need for security. Sir.'

'Quite,' said Tetchley, and he marched past Doug into the house. Margaret followed her husband, glancing at Doug with distaste. The large room off the corridor was dark. Beneath their feet were bare floorboards that creaked, and scattered around the room, on the mantelpiece and on milk crates, were candles. It looked like a shrine. Beside one of the candles at the far end of the room, a youth sat cross-legged on the floor reading a book. He didn't look up, but even without seeing his face he appeared remarkably similar to the youth who had let them in the door.

'Are you sure we've come to the right house?' Mrs Tetchley whispered to her husband.

'Of course we have,' he said, and marched off into the corridor again. 'Damn Americans.' Margaret Tetchley followed him out of the room, and only then did Aidan look up slowly from his book.

Out in the corridor, the Tetchleys found that the first youth, the one in the vulgar shirt, had disappeared. From upstairs came the sound of laughter and conversation. 'Come on,' Charles snapped at his wife, as though she were the cause of all this nonsense. He began mounting the stairs.

The party was in full swing, The old record player crackled jazz in the corner, but was drowned out by the roar of talking and shouting. About forty people had come, filling the ribbon-festooned front bedroom and kitchen. Some had spilled out on to the landing, and it was past these that the Tetchleys squeezed as they arrived. Most of the people had been invited by Morton from NWBC London or through work, like Tetchley. These wore dark suits or smart dresses and make-up. Most of them were Americans. Then there were about ten who were rather different – shabbier and more diverse – and who'd been invited by Laura. She had asked everyone she knew in London, apart from contacts from college. She'd even put an invitation through the door of Philip's shop, but he hadn't come. Those that were there were musicians. They made occasional forays to mix with the bulk of the party but otherwise stuck together. Stan Morgan was there, his face flushed, wearing a purple corduroy jacket and a bowtie. At his side, as ever, was his imperial-whiskered pianist. They both clutched large tumblers of scotch.

The noise was so deafening that people had to shout at each other from inches apart. Even then, words were missed, misunderstandings made, so you had to repeat everything louder this time, so that the noise went up another notch and everybody had to speak up some more. It seemed like the room might explode.

At the centre of it, moving like a whirlwind through his guests, was Morton. In his arms he carried four bottles – Scotch, gin, red and white wine – with which he plied every glass. Crowded and barged on all sides, he managed at the same time to shake hands, smoke his pipe, light other people's cigarettes, slap backs, describe in the air the latest design of autocue, hug shoulders and keep up a steady stream of gesticulatory conversation.

'Hi, Charlie, Maggie.' He slipped through the crowd to where the Tetchleys stood in the doorway. In one deft movement, he transferred two bottles to the other arm, shook Tetchley's hand, and removed his pipe to kiss Tetchley's wife on the cheek.

'Charlie, how'ye doing? Maggie, good to see you.'

Mrs Tetchley winced. She hated being called Maggie.

'Hello, Bob,' said Tetchley. 'Young Jeremy here, is he?'

'Sure, he's over the other side there.'

Through the forest of heads and glasses they could see Jeremy leaning against the wall next to the record player. In front of him, Laura was dancing to the music. Every now and then, she took Jeremy's hand and tried to drag him away from the wall to dance with her.

For a few seconds, Morton and the Tetchleys watched their children in silence.

'Come into the kitchen,' said Morton, 'I'll find you some glasses.'

On the landing, Doug came up to them. His Hawaian shirt was half hanging out of his jeans.

''Sorright,' he said to Morton, jerking his head at the Tetchleys. 'They're orright. All their papers are in orrer.' He grinned, swaying slightly before them.

'Thanks Doug,' said Morton, 'that's great.'

''Sorright, *Bob*,' said Doug.

There was an embarrassed pause, as Doug just remained standing there, blocking their path. Then Morton noticed Doug's extended glass, and topped him up with red wine. Doug moved on.

'That young man let us in the front door,' said Tetchley. 'Eventually.'

'That right?'

'Is he . . . a friend of Laura's?' asked Margaret Tetchley.

'Well I guess you could say he's a friend of mine. He's the brother of Aidan, who lives here. Aidan's been working on the house. You should meet him – don't know where he's got to right now – he's not the kind of kid you'd touch base with every day, I should think.'

'I think we "touched base" with him downstairs,' said Tetchley in a cool tone. 'He was reading a book.'

'What on earth were all those candles doing down there?' asked Margaret.

The kitchen was quieter and less crowded than the front room. A man sat on his own by the window, and a couple talked quietly in the opposite corner. The table was strewn with bottles and glasses.

'I was talking to Jeremy the other week,' Morton continued. 'It looks like he and Laura are going steady.'

Mrs Tetchley gave a nervous laugh. '"Going steady,"' she said. 'Such a quaint phrase.'

'Quaint notion, I guess,' said Morton. 'Jeremy seems very keen on the music business. Laura and he have got great plans. Will you be disappointed he's not following a professional career, Charlie?'

'Of course not. Glad to see he's showing a bit of get-up-and-go. Just what this country needs. I can't say I like all that thump-thump music myself – pretty damned awful, isn't it? haha – but for goodness sake, there's a market for it, isn't there? I mean, if Jeremy can make a go of it, then why the hell not? I know Jeremy. Beneath all that sullen unpleasantness – which he picked up at university, I may add – there's a good old-fashioned entrepreneur bursting to get out.'

'That right?' Morton contemplated his Scotch for a moment. 'What do you think about them moving into this place in Clapham?'

'About time he got out there into the real world,' said Tetchley.'Can't have him sitting at home becoming a mummy's boy.' He laughed.

'You never told me,' said Margaret Tetchley, turning on her husband. 'When did he say this about moving away from home?'

'Oh, a few days ago. I rather assumed he'd told you himself.'

'Well, he didn't. What's this house he's moving into? Whose house is it?'

'Some chap he knows. I don't know the—'

'Charles, I want to talk to him right away. Excuse us please, Mr Morton.' She took her husband's arm and started for the door.

'Sorry about this, old boy,' said Charles Tetchley to Morton as he was led away. He gave him a look of resignation.

Morton joined the man who sat looking out the window. 'Don,' he said, 'how'ye doing?'

'How am I doing? I'm sick of this goddamn English weather, is how I'm doing. Take a look at that.'

The window was open. The night outside was black as pitch. The rain couldn't be seen, but was heard as a ceaseless pattering, smelt and felt as a dank coolness gusting through the open window.

'I mean, I like rain to be rain, right?' Don continued. His drooping jowls wobbled a little as he gestured vigorously at the offending weather. 'In the States, when it rains it rains. You getta good storm, and the slate's wiped clean. You can start over. Here, it just kinda dribbles on and on.' He glanced round the room and lowered his voice. 'Like the people.' He rested his chin on his hand and scowled out at the steady drip drip of water down from the gutter on to the windowsill. 'You going home this Christmas, Bob?' he continued.

'Back to the States? What for? I've got nothing to go back there for. I've got everything I want here. I've got this house to finish renovating yet.'

Don Hexter glanced around him at the walls and ceiling with little interest, but as though he hadn't noticed the room up to now. 'I still can't understand what you were doing when you bought this place. Why do you want a ruin?'

Morton chuckled. 'I don't know. Perhaps I wanted to build something for once in my life.'

'Bob, give me a break. Don't talk in riddles. Anyway, what's the point if you're only here for a year or so? I don't get it.'

'Who says I'm only going to be here a year?'

Don shrugged his bulky shoulders, as though the matter were not worth pursuing, and looked out at the rain again. 'Wasn't that Charles Tetchley you were talking to back there?' he said.

'Sure.'

'Have you told him the context his interview's gonna be used in? Does he know how the programme's shaping up?' He gave Morton a sly smile.

'He's not here on business,' said Morton briskly. 'Point is, his son's dating Laura.'

'No kidding?'

'They're moving in together.'

'She leaving this place?'

'Yeah.'

'Don't blame her. I'd do the same. I think you're a fruit cake, living here.' He looked gloomily out at the rain. 'Guess you'll be sorry to see her go?'

'Oh, she's gotta do what she wants. She's a grown-up now – she'll be all right. You want to know a secret, Don? And mind you never tell Laura this. It's almost like I've lost interest in her as she's grown up. Not that I don't care what happens to her. I do. Just that when kids grow up, it's like they become different people. You know what I love about kids? You can't predict what they're going to do. They surprise you. Now, nobody ever surprises me. Everyone I talk to, I can predict moment to moment what they're going to do. People move down narrow paths. Adjusted – that's what they call it. When Laura was a kid, she reminded me of a hose when you let go of it and it leaps about across the yard jetting water in every direction. Then she grew up, and it was like it was all smoothed out. I know this sounds bad, but I felt like I was watching her become like everyone else. And at the same time, I figured she could cope. She wasn't grating against the world. She was adjusted. So yeah, I'll miss her, but I figure she'll be all right.'

And then the fighting started. At first it was just pushing and shoving when Security arrived to break up the spontaneous gatherings. Then the resistance became more organised. Pete Davenport – whose release Tom Saab had obtained, and who had become Head of Security – ordered his men to use greater force. He issued them with weapons. Some of the men used the weapons enthusiastically and with relish. Others laid down their weapons and joined the protesters. Or took their weapons with them.

Protest spread to key areas of the ship. Technicians downed tools. Research projects – long-term monitoring of the Explosion, for example – fell by the wayside. As the crisis grew, hardliners in the Council became dissatisfied with how the situation was being handled. There was a desperate power struggle. Tom Saab was removed as Head of the Council and replaced by his old friend Pete Davenport. Davenport was happy to take a harder line.

Repression made things worse. The violence escalated. Running battles broke out along the corridors, and from behind closed doors could be heard screams. Walking down one of the ship's long passageways, one might come across evidence of a recent incident – an acrid smell in the air; a fragment of material from a tunic, or a shoe lying on the floor; a smear of blood down the wall. Often, an eerie silence fell over the whole ship as it continued its lightning journey across the universe. People didn't trust each other. Then the fighting would start again.

Thus the last survivals of humanity, perhaps the last survivals of intelligent life, careered wildly through space without purpose or direction. And tore themselves apart – almost. For glimmerings of reason remained. Up through the chaos seeped the realisation that this could not continue. When people thought about how utterly alone they were in the unimaginable vastness of space, they grew strong in the conviction that they must not fight. It was so strange, so wrong, to think of the cold wastes of emptiness and then of this ship full of life exterminating itself. It had to be stopped. Not just the killing and fighting – the ship itself had to be stopped. For it was the ship, and its endless mission, that was the original source of conflict.

So the terms of debate had changed. It was as though Davenport and others who thought like him had been by-passed, their ways of thinking made redundant. They lost their grip. Some scientists began independent work, scanning space ahead for solar systems, surveying planets and their atmospheres. They no longer looked back. They were looking ahead. It seemed almost that they had forgotten about the Explosion. It was no longer a question of whether the ship should stop, but when, and where. There was excitement in the ship, a feeling that after all something was going to happen.

'Real party-goer, you are.' Doug slumped down next to Aidan, his back against the cold plaster of the wall. ' "Something was going to happen," ' he read over Aidan's shoulder. 'About time too, isn't it? You just finished that chapter, then? Time something happened. Fucking right. That what *you* think then, Aid? You think something's gonna happen? *That* what you think?'

'You're pissed.'

'And you're fucking boring.'

They sat for a while in silence. The candles, spread out across the room, glowed like stars. Through the ceiling they could hear, quite faintly, the jazz on the record player, and an occasional braying laugh.

'Your mate Morton's a *bit* of a laugh,' said Doug eventually. 'Real life and soul.' He turned to Aidan and saw something strange. Aidan was biting his bottom lip, as though in pain. He was still staring straight ahead at the candles, but his face was taut and strained. Doug, through his blur of darkness, thought for a moment that his brother was hurt, or going to be sick. Then he realised he was holding back tears. Doug didn't know what to do. Instinctively, his hand went out to Aidan, but it hesitated and only brushed his denim jacket. 'Whassa matter, Aid? It's not that book, is it?'

Aidan's mouth stetched into a painful grin. 'Course not,' he said.

'What is it then?'

'Nothing.' Aidan flicked the hair from his eyes again, almost defiantly this time. 'By the way,' he continued. 'I'm moving out of this place.'

'Is that *it*?'

'Just thought I'd tell you.'

They were silent again. Doug glanced at his brother with some concern, and saw that his lips were pursed. He was frowning into the candlelight.

'Why do you wanna go, Aid? This place's all right. And like I said, that Morton bloke's a laugh.'

'Yeah, I know. That's what I thought when I first met him. You know, he was *different*. The way he talks, in that cool voice, and he tells you stuff about America and all the places he's been and the people he's met. I got into all that. It was *different*.' He frowned harder into the candlelight. 'It's like what you were saying earlier about how boring it is at home, just sitting around watching the TV. I thought I'd got away from all that. Now, I feel like I'm carrying this prison around inside me all the time. It's getting just like home. Feel it closing in around you all the time.' Aidan's hands went up to his head in a nervous, helpless gesture. He ran his long, bony fingers through his hair, sweeping it back behind his ears. 'That's why I had to get away from home. I just couldn't get into it. It's like that now.' He swallowed. 'Sometimes I feel like I'm a million miles away.'

'Where you gonna go?' Doug asked softly. 'What about this job?'

'I dunno. I've got a couple of ideas.'

'Well you watch out, Aid.'

Aidan nodded.

'C'mon then.' Doug stood and gave Aidan his hand to pull him up from the floor. 'You wanna get pissed.'

On their way upstairs, they came across Stan Morgan and Tony, his moustached pianist. The musicians were draped drunkenly over the bannisters.

'Greetingsh, revellers,' cried Stan down the well of the stairs.

The Fowler brothers trudged up towards him.

'I've seen you before, haven't I?' Stan continued, his face bunched up into a frown. He jabbed a finger at Aidan as he and Doug reached the landing.

'I heard you playing your trumpet,' said Aidan.

'I remember now,' replied Stan with a lot of exaggerated nodding. 'You must be the young man who dashed off so precipitously. Very pleased to make your acquaintance. Any friend of Miss Laura Morton is a friend of mine. A very fine saxophonist.'

'Too fine for us,' added Tony, with a mirthless chuckle.

'It's a trombone, by the way. And you,' Stan continued, turning to Doug, 'you look like you must be this gentleman's brother.'

Doug and Stan shook hands. 'Nice to meet you,' said Doug politely. 'And you look like you must be completely pissed.'

Stan didn't hear him, because at that moment the door of the front bedroom was opened, releasing a roar of party noise. It was Morton coming out of the room. He glanced at the four people standing on the landing and gave them a perfunctory wave before disappearing into the kitchen. Aidan detached himself from the group on the landing and followed him.

The noise of the party was different now. At the beginning, it had been the sound of excited, effervescent chatter. Now it was a machine-like roar, an extended howl of drunkenness that moved, open-jawed, between the propped-up guests. They were propped up against the walls, against each other, clutching their glasses as though they were hanging on to a cliff-face. The guests were slack-jawed and jerky in their limbs – like Jeremy, who was dancing now with Laura. His parents had gone. He flailed his arms out of rhythm, and Laura, watching him, thought he was funny. Or, at least, she followed his every move with a look of bewilderment, and laughed when he glanced at her. There'd been an argument with his parents which she hadn't quite understood. She couldn't tell whether they really wanted him to move out or not. She couldn't understand what the argument was about. And Jeremy's attitude was weird. What was it he wanted from them? It was like he was looking for approval and chastisement at the same time. A part of her wanted to help him, while another was happy just to dance with him, holding his hand sometimes and moving her arm in synch with his.

Some of Morton's colleagues were also dancing now. Two of them danced together, parodying Jeremy's flailings. They all laughed, and shouted, and sang along self-consciously with the record that spun round and round beneath the needle. When they weren't laughing or shouting or singing, their expressions were serious and vacant, as though they were concentrating very hard on something they didn't quite understand. None of them understood; they endured. Between them, the noise of the party they had made ground close and flat. But at the door it cascaded out, free, to the landing, where Doug was introducing bemused Stan Morton to marijuana; and out through the kitchen, where Aidan was telling Morton that he was leaving the burnt house; out of the open window, which threw back cool gusts of air, into the dark, dank back gardens. And other parties all across unimaginably vast London – hundreds, thousands of parties on this December Saturday night – spun their confused, blended cry out to an unhearing night sky. And later – when Laura had sex with Jeremy for the first time among the empty bottles – the sky was growing colder, until it was storing in its heavy clouds not rain but snow and ice.

PART TWO

North

CHAPTER FOURTEEN

In January, the rains that had washed through a mild December became snow. The deep Atlantic depressions continued to move across, a new one off the shores of the British Isles every other day. But now their fetch was shorter, and the west winds they brought were colder and more unstable. In London the snow hardly settled. When it did, it quickly turned to slush on the pavements and under the wheels of the traffic. The skies overhead would clear towards evening, and there would be a pale sunset, broken near the horizon by the jagged tops of distant cumulus. Morton noticed this once or twice when he happened to wander up to the attic room that Aidan had occupied.

So went the pattern for most of January, a regular rhythm of winter storms. Then the seamless web of wind, rain, sleet and snow was broken. Thousands of miles away in Siberia, where the snow fields reflected away the light of the sun without warming the earth, dense masses of freezing air accumulated. With increasing pressure, this intensely cold air spilled over and moved south. It reached Scandinavia, then crossed the North Sea, only warmed a fraction by contact with the water, and settled over the British Isles too. The snow that had been left by the last Atlantic storm froze.

Cigarette smoke, sealed off from the wind outside, drifted through a tangle of people and equipment. Jeremy Tetchley was watching Tony Baldwin anxiously through it, scrutinising him for any reaction to the music that thundered across the still air of the recording studio. The music bounced on. It was almost Victorian in its sentimentality, but driven by motor rhythms and glossed over by a swill of electronic sound. Tony Baldwin seemed to have no reaction at all. He brought out his Filofax and started leafing through it, jotting a couple of things down. Jeremy admired his cool.

Tony was a self-making mogul, an entrepreneur of style and youth fashions. He had started out, in his youth, selling T-shirts and ethnic jewellery across market stalls in Camden and Notting Hill. From there he had moved to flogging records and, eventually, setting up this studio. And from there it had been a short step to making videos too. Jeremy had first met Tony when Tony had shrewdly hired, at no cost, an old school friend of his, now fresh out of film school, to direct a couple of these videos. Jeremy, with time on his hands one college vacation, had hung around at shoots and got to know the Cockney barrow boy who was running the show. Tony, for his part, liked Jeremy's sense of style, and his accent and background appealed to the snob in him. For a couple of months they had gone clubbing together, pissed up against walls all over Soho, and thereby forged a bond, like dogs.

Jeremy liked the way Tony had so many different surfaces. The group Jeremy and he had got together around Laura was just one facet, one tiny element in the kaleidescope of Tony's business dealings. He was a collection of secrets and strategies. Jeremy liked the fact that none of his surfaces connected. None of his sets of contacts had knowledge of each other. That gave him an air of mystery and danger. Jeremy wanted to emulate that, to be a complicated and intricate person. He was collecting his secrets.

At the end of the song, Tony sprang from his chair as though released from chains. He congratulated Laura and the other musicians. Then without delay he made his excuses and slipped out the door, a tall, slim, figure dressed in black, with a pony-tail. Jeremy could imagine him going back to his office in Soho to make some late phone calls, putting his ear to the web of connections he had spun across the city. Jeremy, who along with Laura had moved into his house in Clapham, was happy, for the moment, to be caught in that web.

The musicians packed their instruments and left. Jeremy and Laura went to a nearby pub, where they sat talking excitedly about the future of the band.

'I've got a great name for it.'

'What?' Laura gripped his arm in anticipation.

' "Wow".'

'Just "Wow"?'

'Yeah.'

'That's crazy.'

'I know, it's great. Unpretentious.'

'Like the music.' Laura giggled.

'Direct. Sunny. Young. We want something with a bit of colour.

People are getting bored of all that black-and-white. We want something more baroque, more post-modern. Pastiche.'

'Like "Wow"?'

'Laura, this is serious. If we don't get the image right, we'll get nowhere. We're living in a hall of mirrors.'

But Laura couldn't help laughing. It was as though she had been in a dream for the past few weeks, since moving into the house in Clapham with Jeremy. She could hardly remember it, the whirl of warehouse parties and nightclubs. Sometimes, in the depths of January, they had hardly seen daylight from one week to another. Her world was bathed in a beautiful, bright neon glow. Jeremy's swept-back eyes, his elegant cheekbones, were bathed in it now. Laura reached over to touch, and said, 'I've got a great idea. You should be on stage with us when we do our first gig. You're such a cute dancer.'

'Don't be silly. I'd look stupid.' He flinched involuntarily at her touch, and she withdrew her hand and said dreamily, 'Oh well, it doesn't matter.'

And it didn't. That was the beautiful thing. As they left the pub, the doors belched heat and cigarette smoke into the raw winter darkness. Laura gripped Jeremy's arm tightly as they walked, and for a moment, against the freezing air, he seemed to accept her touch.

Morton put the phone down. It was the third time he had tried to reach Laura that evening. There never seemed to be anyone in at the house in Clapham. A few days ago, he had got that Tony guy, the one who owned the place. He had asked Morton a lot of questions about TV, looking for openings. A pushy guy. Still, it was Laura's business where she lived. Morton just wished he could get hold of her once in a while.

He felt restless. The bare, discoloured plaster of the walls seemed to stare at him, waiting for him to do something. He went out on to the landing, flicked on the electric light, and started up the stairs to the top floor. Halfway up the first flight, he stopped and listened. He must have stood there on the bare wooden stairs for five minutes, listening. He was acutely aware of the big empty house stretching away underneath him, stretching below the ground into the basement. It was an old house, maybe a hundred years old. He thought about the people who had lived in it, who had walked, or run, up these stairs. He stood and thought about them almost as though he were listening for them, trying to catch their footfalls. But there was nothing. He was listening so hard, he could no longer even hear the snow-muffled swish of traffic a street away. He was glad there was no noise. Perhaps

I'm not listening for the creak of a floorboard at all, he thought. Perhaps it was this silence I was listening for. The silence had substance. It seemed to fill the well of the stairs from the bottom. For the first time, Morton thought about the old woman who had lived here, who had died in the fire in the basement. What had she been like?

He turned and carried on up. When he reached the top landing, he stopped again. This would have been the servants' quarters once, he thought. It was dark, but from the front room, the one which Aidan had occupied until a few weeks ago, there came a weird white light. Morton stepped forward and entered the room. Moonlight was on the floorboards. It came through the window not like a liquid suffusing the walls and ceiling, like sunlight, but shafting and clearcut. He walked over to the window and looked out. The cloud cover had been torn apart by northern winds, letting the bright full moon fill everything with its whiteness. It irradiated the whiteness of the snow. The buildings looked like crystalline castles. Morton, his face close up to the window so that he could sense the icy cold of the air near the glass, felt like a child again. For a moment he felt a child's thrill. He smiled to himself and shook his head. What was happening to him this evening? His mind was like this old house, populated by thoughts and memories that moved about inside of their own will. That thought fell away as his gaze focused more closely. On the surface of the glass was a thin skein of ice crystals. As he watched, his warm breath melted it away.

The surface of the planet looked unreal through the woman's thick visor. Seen from within the computer-controlled environment of the suit, it was like watching one of the familiar film shows on the ship. Only the feel of the rocks through the thick soles of her boots brought home to her that she was actually stepping out on to real ground. She was the first.

She walked forward past the massive landing-leg of the ship, picking her way carefully over the rocks. She didn't want to fall and tear her suit. She walked on, and once she was out of the great shadow of the ship, she climbed laboriously to the top of an outcrop and looked around.

The ship had landed in a broad, shallow valley. Perhaps a great river had once flowed down it. Now it was dry, carpeted with massive boulders. But there must have been some moisture under the surface, because here and there were trees, tough-looking things with big, twisted trunks and waxy pale green leaves. In the far distance on either side, rocky hills rose sharply from the flat surface of the valley. Beyond them, obscured by evening mist, there were mountains. It was late in the day. The sun was strong but slanting across the scene, etching the shadows of the boulders into the clear light. Above, the sky was vast and unbelievably blue, darkening towards the horizon furthest from the sun.

The woman drank in the view, then began her work, fumbling with excitement as she swung her instrument bag off her shoulder. Atmospheric conditions had already been analysed from within the ship. She checked these again, and measured the gravitational force. It was the same as Earth's — somewhat more than that artificially maintained on the ship. Very carefully, she climbed down from her perch and set to work on the floor of the valley. She found a spot without too many rocks and sat down on the ground, spreading her instruments in a circle around her. Following a routine she had rehearsed in detail as the ship had approached the planet, she gauged the soil's radioactivity levels, toxicity and moisture content. It took her an hour. Everything was OK. She relayed the results back to the ship, giving detailed figures, then gathered the instruments together and stood up. She felt stiff, so she did some stretching exercises. Her breath sounded loud inside her helmet. The heavier gravitational pull had made her body feel different.

She turned to start walking back to the ship. While she had been working on the thin, wind-blown soil, she had been so absorbed that she had almost forgotten about the ship. Now it looked unbelievably startling and out of place, towering over her in the empty landscape. Of course, she had never before seen the outside of the ship in which she had been born and grown up, had only seen pictures of it. She found it hard to relate its gigantic size to the stones and rocks around her. Standing high on its landing-legs, the enormous ellipsoidal bulk of its body seemed almost to straddle the valley. The whole thing tilted slightly to one side where on touch-down one of the legs had slipped down a canyon.

The woman climbed up on to a boulder to get a better view again. As she hauled herself on to the top, she thought she saw something, a lizard perhaps, flick away out of the corner of her vision. From her new perch, she could see how far she had had to walk to escape the shadow of the ship. She looked at her watch, and saw that she had been out of the ship for nearly three hours. From this distance she could see the upper surface of the ship, whose grey metallic sheen gleamed in the sunlight. The winking lights — red, white and yellow — looked absurd in the brightness. Here and there on the surface of the ship there were tiny dots moving about. They were groups of men, technical crews, inspecting the exterior for atmospheric-entry damage. They seemed to take no interest in the vast landscape that the ship had entered.

As the woman's gaze travelled down over the ship, she noticed the long ladder hanging from the belly of the ship down to the surface of the planet. That was where she had come from. She would have to climb it when she got back. It made her tired, just thinking about it, in her heavy suit, against this gravity.

She had a few minutes before she should start heading back for the ship. She made herself more comfortable on the boulder, propping herself up on one *arm and looking round at the landscape again. It was beautiful. She wanted to make closer contact with it, to take her helmet off. It was strictly against orders, but suddenly, looking at this new world, all the orders seemed silly. She had taken the readings herself, and the atmosphere was safe – like that of Earth, which meant that it was close to that produced artificially on the ship. She sat up. Her hands moved to the catches at her neck, then hesitated. If it was discovered that she had contravened such an important order, there would be a disciplinary hearing. She might lose her rank. But then that kind of thing had been mattering less and less on the ship over the past months. There had been a kind of revolution. And now, on this new planet, it wouldn't matter at all. Quickly, her thick gloves fumbling with the catches, she undid her helmet and took it off.*

The environment – the sensation of the planet in its feel and sounds and smell – flooded and overwhelmed her. She almost fainted. The heat was like that of a blast-furnace, except that it seemed to belong to the planet intrinsically, having the planet's smell and sound wrapped up in it. It was as though the planet were a live thing, smothering her with a blast of its hot, personal breath.

Ke-che-ka Ke-che-ka Ke-che-ka. A train rumbled along the track below, distracting Aidan from the book. He liked it out here. The wind from the north-east, laced with snow, was battering and throwing into confusion the tops of the trees. Some small birds got up from the undergrowth of bushes and scrap metal, and were swept sideways before controlling their hurtling flight, making it to the other side of the steep cutting.

He came here most lunchbreaks, where the streets petered out into a wasteland beside the railway line. There was an electricity sub-station amid a nest of pylons, and the remains of a breaker's yard. Further down the line there was a cement works, but apart from that there were just the railway tracks, and fences, and thick, wild vegetation. From where Aidan sat, on an upturned, rusty water tank, you could see the turrets of St Pancras, barely half a mile away, and beyond them the buildings of the City poking the sky. It was the same view as from the burnt house, but much closer up. From this place, Aidan felt central London tower over him, as though he were a supplicant sitting at the feet of the city walls.

He got up and put *The Voyage Beyond Infinity* into the plastic bag he'd been using to keep his arse dry. Eager for warmth, he started back.

When he got back to the warehouse, he found everything quiet. The other blokes were sitting on cardboard packing cases, sipping from plastic cups.

'Aidy, baby,' cried Phil. A couple of the younger blokes smiled. Phil was a joker.

'Wotcha,' said Aidan. He sat down and began rolling himself a cigarette. An atmosphere of heavy boredom hung in the air. Outside, from time to time, a lorry ground its gears as it made its way up the narrow street to one of the warehouses. Inside, it was warm and cosy, even though the wind occasionally rattled the metal screen at the front. The men were hemmed in on all sides by towering piles of cardboard boxes which had been delivered that morning. Along one side of the warehouse ran a wide workbench, and at this bench stood the warehouse manager, an ex-military man. While the other men sat gazing vacantly at the floor or at the endless brown boxes of electronic equipment, the warehouse manager ostentatiously carried on working, thumbing through a pile of invoices. He wore an official-looking brown coat. Every now and then, he would pause at a particular invoice and examine it, sometimes scribbling mysterious marks with his stubby pencil. Since he was the only thing that moved in the warehouse, attention gradually focused on him.

'What you doing, Captain?' said Phil the joker. 'Writing yer memoirs?' There were sniggers around the warehouse. Nobody knew the warehouse manager's real name, because everybody always called him 'the Captain'. No one knew whether he really had been a Captain.

'Got to get these invoices done this afternoon,' said the Captain firmly, 'or we'll have the office on our backs.'

Phil made a face of mock awe and horror, raising another laugh. 'The Office' was the administrative centre of the electronic firm's distribution network. Although it was situated just a couple of hundred yards down the street, and was supposed to organise the activities of the warehouse, the men in the warehouse knew 'The Office' only as an alien and threatening force invoked by the warehouse manager. The only direct contact with 'The Office' came on the odd occasions when a secretary was sent, stilettos tip-tapping on the concrete, to deliver a message to the Captain.

'I don't reckon it's invoices at all,' said Phil. 'I reckon it's your memoirs. "What I Did In The War", by the Captain. What *did* you do in the war, Captain? You working in a warehouse then?' The others laughed.

'That's enough of that, Tait,' said the Captain, firmly but trying to suggest with his voice an attitude of amused tolerance. Phil and the Captain had a strange relationship. The older man treated the younger like a mischievous but promising private, the kind who stepped out of line but would prove loyal when it came to the crunch. The other men, and the protagonists themselves, knew that this didn't correspond with reality.

Really, the warehouse manager was scared of Phil Tait. That was where the humour of the situation lay. But there was another reason why the other men laughed at Phil's jibes. Deep down, though none of them would have admitted this, they were all scared of Phil. There was something cruel and anarchic in his humour, and no one knew how deep it ran or where it could lead. His face was hard and bony, with a big nose and eyes set far apart into a jutting forehead. He was always grinning derisively, and the way he looked at people suggested to them that he might whip out a punch at them at any moment, or crack their noses with that hard forehead of his.

The only one who didn't laugh at Phil's jokes was Aidan. He seemed to have some kind of dispensation. Phil's attitude towards him was subtly different from that towards the other men. He mocked them, of course, but there was something gentler, almost tentative, in the way he did it, as though there were a special, polar fascination that the ineffectual, long-haired kid had for the physical bully.

'Right then, lads,' said the Captain. 'Back to work.'

'Righty ho, Captain,' Phil shouted back in a burst of animal high spirits. The other men laughed and slipped from their perches on the boxes to begin work again.

The boxes that had been delivered that morning, containing calculators and digital watches, had to be unpacked and the contents transfered to smaller boxes. Then these smaller boxes had to be put in the basement cellar to await . . . something else.

The Captain arranged his men at their various tasks, giving Phil the easiest and best job of throwing the boxes down the stone steps into the cellar. Aidan was sent down into the cellar to receive the boxes and stack them up. Within a couple of minutes they were all into the rhythm of their work. Even the Captain mucked in, sealing up the smaller boxes with grey tape before handing them to Phil, who handed back a cheerful insult.

Down in the cellar, Aidan was soon lulled into a semi-doze. It was warm, and the naked bulb in the middle of the ceiling burned very brightly. Upstairs, the radio had been switched on to sickly-sweet Radio One. He took off his denim jacket. The boxes came tumbling down the steps from Phil's unseen hands. Aidan gathered them from in front of the steps, then scampered quickly out of the way to avoid being hit as another one came hurtling down. He scurried backwards and forwards, mesmerised by heat, light and monotony. His mind wandered. For a while he thought about *The Voyage Beyond Infinity*, pretending to himself that the light bulb was a broiling desert sun.

After a couple of hours there was a tea break, more banter, then everybody started the final stint of the day. At five to five, the Captain went round all the men asking who wanted to do overtime that evening, and at five the day was over. Only Aidan was staying on with the Captain. They sat side by side at the workbench and started packing watches. It was an easy job. The ladies' watches had to be taken out of the boxes in which they had arrived from the factory, then fitted into little plastic display cases ready to be packed up again and sent to the department stores. The Captain had switched off the radio, and for a few minutes the two of them worked in silence, their hands moving over and over the same twenty-second task.

'He's a cheeky monkey, that Philip Tait,' said the Captain eventually. He chuckled and glanced nervously at Aidan to see what his reaction was to this, to see whether Aidan had swallowed the false offhandedness.

'Yeah,' said Aidan, and carried on working.

After a few more moments, the Captain continued, 'Mind you, funnily enough, he was right about what I did in the last war.' He chuckled to himself at this coincidence. ''Course, most of the war I war too young to do anything much – younger than you. Then in '44 I was called up, and I served in the Royal Engineers warehouse at Dover. Shipping stuff out to France, we were. Stayed on after the war, served Queen and country for fifteen years, then after I'd got out I went into the warehouse business, and I've been doing it ever since. Some of these young blokes, like that Philip Tait, they might think I'm just an old fool, but let me tell you, I've got a wealth of experience behind me. There is *nothing* about this business I don't know. Stock control, book-keeping,' he counted them off on his fingers, 'postal, packing, economical use of space – it's all up there.' He tapped the side of his head. 'How old do you reckon I am, Aidan?'

Aidan shrugged his shoulders. 'Dunno.'

'Go on, have a go. How old do you reckon I am?'

'Dunno.'

'I'm sixty. Surprised? Bastards over there in The Office are gonna want me to retire next year. Know what I'm gonna do? I'm going to take their money and go. Yeah, 'cause I'm not finished yet. I'm going to set up on my own. Cousin of mine's got some property in Dagenham. There's a place he got would be perfect for a little packaging business. Just perfect.' The Captain lapsed into silence.

'How old did you say you were, Aidan?' he continued after a while.

'Nineteen.'

'Nineteen, eh?' There was another silent. 'And how long've you been working here?'

'A month.'

'I've been watching you, young Aidan – there's not a lot I don't notice in this warehouse – and I've liked what I've seen. You're a grafter.' He prodded Aidan's arm firmly with his finger. 'And that's a rare thing these days, believe you me. Anyway, I've got a proposition for you, young Aidan. I dunno whether you've got any plans – perhaps you're going to go to college like all the other kids these days, lot of good it does them. What I'm offering you is a partnership. Like I said, there's a good chance I'll get this place in Dagenham, so I'm looking for someone else, a younger man, to come into partnership with me. What do you say? How do you fancy the warehouse business?'

For a moment, Aidan was too surprised to say anything. He stopped working on the watches and turned to look at the Captain, at the older man's rheumy, yellowing eyes.

'I dunno, Captain,' he said. 'I'll have to think about it.' He knew immediately he didn't want to have anything to do with it.

They worked on without speaking again. As the silence closed in around them, Aidan began to wonder whether he hadn't imagined the whole bizarre conversation. But when they'd finished, and the Captain had filled in Aidan's time sheet, giving him an extra hour on the side, he added to him, 'Don't forget what I said, young Aidan. Dagenham.' Aidan turned and escaped as quickly as he could through the hatchway door into the street.

He thought about Dagenham on the way home. He stopped at the local pub and sat at the bar, thinking about the Captain's proposition, about how people were always pestering you with one thing or another. They couldn't just let things be. The harsh wind outside smeared snow across the frosted glass windows. There was a new barmaid just started that night, but Aidan hardly noticed her as she served him his pint. Some Irish country crooned from the juke box. He looked around. On Friday when they had a singer in, and someone playing the electric organ, the pub would be full. But tonight there were only a few customers. They sat staring straight ahead, like people in a train, as though they thought they might get somewhere just by being in the pub, as though the pub was a spaceship shooting through a gale, and they were its passengers.

Aidan's gaze flicked away from them, past the barmaid, to the bar. Above the upside-down spirit bottles, he noticed for the first time two framed photographs. One was of the pope. The other was of a bloke with short hair. Underneath him was printed 'John Fitzgerald Kennedy'. He had heard that name before. He was one of the people Morton had talked about. Whenever Aidan thought about Morton, he felt a twinge of guilt – because of leaving the burnt house suddenly like he had. He pushed Morton from his mind, but then found himself thinking about the Captain again. Why couldn't they leave him alone? Just leave him alone. He hadn't asked for any of this.

He slid off his stool at the bar and left the pub, leaning into the biting wind. His digs were just round the corner. When he first started at the warehouse, he had still been living at Trevor's house, where he had moved from the burnt house just after the New Year. Then one night he had been in The White Horse after work, and an old bloke had come up to him and asked him if he knew anyone looking for a room. He had been glad of the chance to move out of Trevor's place.

The house he lived in now was in a lonely terrace at the end of a street. The wind, tearing down towards the railway line, flapped the low wooden gate. Snow had formed a drift against the rusting motorbike that stood in the front garden. He went upstairs to his room – past the quiet chatter of the TV in the landlord's living-room – and switched on the electric fire to disperse the chill.

Gradually, over the following days, everybody from the Xykon spaceship emerged on to the surface of the planet. At night, hundreds of campfires twinkled across the floor of the valley. The colony had broken up, dissolved into small groups huddling around the fires that kept out the cold desert night. The woman sat before one of these fires, watching the wood burn, listening to it hiss and crackle. The sparks it sent up were smothered quickly by the vast blackness of the night sky. The stars sprinkled overhead seemed to mirror as though in a dark pool the camp fires spread far across the valley. The spaceship was behind them somewhere, forgotten and obliterated by the darkness.

Most of the others in her group had fallen asleep, exhausted. They had felled and chopped up one of the curious, thick-trunked trees to make the fire. Every movement in the heavy gravity was a strain. It would take years to get used to it, thought the woman. Years. She looked away from the fire, up at the stars. But were there years? The Xykon colony had ceased its journey, had stopped and made its stand on this planet. At some point, the Explosion, with its wave of all-evaporating radiation, would hit them and sweep them into oblivion. But when? On board, monitoring and analysis of the Explosion's progress across the universe had dwindled to nothing over the past weeks. And now it hardly seemed to matter. In the old days, on the ship, it had. Escape from the Explosion had been behind everything, had given meaning to their lives played out hurtling through space. Now, in the stillness of the desert night, the Explosion seemed unimaginable. It was already being forgotten. The night brought other things. The woman started thinking about the desert, about other valleys and about ranges of hills stretching far away into the distance.

CHAPTER FIFTEEN

Morton had had a hard day. As he climbed the stairs from the underground, through sodden clumps of discarded newspaper, his breath came short. A draught howled down the stairs from the outside, making his cheeks numb and his lungs feel as though he was swallowing chunks of ice-cream.

Even Morton, who had grown up in the Midwest, was impressed by this winter weather. It was almost as cold as Chicago. As he wandered from the station to the burnt house, he prodded with his feet the piles of snow that lay here and there on the pavement. They were rock hard. When he got back to the house he put the TV on. 'Britain remains in the grip of the worst cold snap for twenty-five years,' said the newscaster. 'Temperatures plunged below −10° centigrade again in many parts of the country, and bitter north-easterly winds added to the misery. For the first of our regional reports, we go to Debbie Cornhill in East Anglia.'

Morton poured himself a Scotch. After the news, a chat show came on. He switched off the TV and rubbed his tired eyes. All day he had been reading autocues, putting the finishing touches to the continuity pieces for his first three shows. His face felt tired from being expressive, his jaws from talking. It was a relief now not to have a camera pointing at him.

The blow heater was making him sleepy, swamping him with waves of warm air. Soon he was asleep and dreaming. He was walking across a vast, flat plain. He was walking towards a group of people that gradually loomed closer and closer out of the bright, sunlit distance. As he approached them, he became aware that his mind's eye was like a camera filming the scene, that he was there but not really a part of what was going on. He was like a cameraman moving through a crowd, filming it. As he came up to the group, they looked up and laughed and said things to him. But he couldn't hear them. It was like watching TV with the sound down. One of the happy, smiling faces looking up at him was that of Sammy, his younger brother. There were other young people with him – a girl with long hair and an open, healthy face, and some others. They were sitting on the grass, talking and laughing together. For Morton it was a scene of unbelievable sadness – not because Sammy was dead (he wasn't, in the dream), but because Morton was distanced from them in just the same way as someone watching TV is distanced from the events actually taking place beyond the screen and cameras. Morton tried to break through to them, circling wildly around them on the grass. He tried to break through whatever it was – not just the glass of a lens – that separated him from them. There were moments of panic, then the whole thing dissolved in darkness.

Morton woke confused and depressed. He looked at his watch. He been asleep for only a few minutes. He stood up impatiently and glanced around, looking for something to do. On the table was a pile of junk – old newspapers and magazines, an instruction manual for the new boiler, circulars that nobody had bothered to throw away. He started sorting through it. At the bottom, beneath a letter from an estate agent asking if he wanted to sell his house, were Aidan's records. Morton picked them up and gazed at the covers, at the imposing, elderly German conductor who was conducting the Mahler, and at Bob Dylan's boyish features. The sight of the records jolted him out of his torpor. For a moment, he could see Aidan as clearly as if he had just walked into the room – his denim jacket hanging loosely on his bony shoulders, his expression defensive, almost hurt. Morton frowned with annoyance. It was typical of the kid to drift off leaving his possessions lying around. What should he do with them? He didn't even know where Aidan was.

He had been hurt by Aidan's sudden decision to leave the burnt house. In retrospect, Morton could see that he had begun to feel protective – almost paternal – towards the boy, and that perhaps that had been in part the cause of Aidan's wanting to move away. Aidan had stayed on over Christmas, keeping himself to himself, then moved out after the New Year, saying he was going to stay with Trevor for a few days. Trevor himself had stopped working at the burnt house soon after that. He had found himself a regular job with a firm.

Laura had also moved out after the New Year. That left Morton alone in the burnt house, and although he was sad at first to see the little household break up, the solitude grew on him. And although at first he also worried about getting some other men in to help with the renovation of the house, the half-finished state of the repairs grew on him too. He had the essentials – light, heat and water. For the rest, the walls remained in their grey, smoke-stained condition, but he had come to appreciate that as a reminder of mutability, of where the house had come from. For the moment, Morton was content to draw out the process of repair, enjoying its openendedness. He was more interested in the journey than in the destination.

He stood there at the table, indecisively, holding the records. To hell with it. He poured himself some more Scotch, sat down, and immediately started thinking about the dream he had been having. Why had the sky loomed so large? The plain had been dead flat, and the sky vast and arching over him – a corny, technicolour sky, with lots of blue and the sun beaming down between puffy white clouds. All that had seemed more important somehow than the stuff about Sammy.

He stood up again, lifted the sash window, and leant out into the cold night air. His breath came in freezing clouds. The houses opposite, across the back gardens, had their curtains drawn. It was a clear night with the stars bright. You hardly ever saw them like that in the city. What am I doing? Morton thought. I must be mad, at my age. I'll catch pneumonia. But the air felt good, swept away the sleepiness that had been overcoming him again. Once again, he found himself thinking about Aidan, without irritation this time. Aidan had liked to look out of this window. Morton used to come into the room sometimes and find the kid just sitting here, gazing out at the sky, his head stuck ridiculously out into the freezing night. Morton smiled to himself. He'd been a good kid. Something about the thought of him made Morton feel better after that day of fast talk and pointing cameras.

He pulled his head in from the window, closed it, and turned away. For the first time in ages he noticed the photograph he had taken of Aidan the summer before. It was propped up against some pans on a shelf above the sink. He took it down and looked at it, remembering the moment. Aidan had been sitting on the wall out the back, in the sun. His head had been bent over his book, his hair falling down over his face. As Morton had taken the picture, Aidan had looked up, squinting slightly into the bright sunlight.

He sat down. The waves of warm air from the blow heater were having a soporiphic effect on him. He switched off the heater and sat in the quickly chilling silence, listening to the burnt house. Like all old houses, it creaked occasionally as its timbers expanded and contracted. They would be contracting now, shrinking themselves up and tightening against the hard, cold air.

Maybe Morton had offended Aidan in some way? He didn't know. It was hard to tell with British people. They weren't upfront. Anyway, Morton was sorry he had gone. He had been a breath of fresh air. It was hard to explain why, because he had rarely said anything. Maybe that was just it. Morton could feel himself getting tired sometimes of good communicators. Everybody he met through work was articulate. In the television world, if you couldn't say quickly, precisely and forcefully what it was you wanted and why you wanted it, then you were sunk. Maybe that was just how life was. If so, then God help the Aidans of this world.

Morton turned the heater back on again and leaned back in his chair, wondering where Aidan was now. A smile spread across his rubbery, expressive face. Of course. Aidan had gone back home to his folks. Why hadn't he thought of that? It was obvious. Why had he assumed that Aidan would run off by himself? Because, thought Morton, he had had a romantic image of Aidan. He had seen the boy as a loner, a drifter who had cut himself off from his family and had to make his own way in the world – not just materially, but emotionally and spiritually too. It was understandable in a way. The kid said so little, you could project just about anything on to him.

Suddenly, Morton felt annoyed with himself. What he had just thought about Aidan was too glib. He wasn't even sure it was true. And he hated the way he could hear himself say it. He could hear his voice slipping into a reasonable, professional mode, as though it had a life of its own. The sentences in his mind followed on from each other smoothly and easily, like they did in front of the camera. He stood up and started walking up and down the small kitchen. He really had been hurt by Aidan's leaving the burnt house. Ever since coming to London, Morton had yearned for a new start, something different. London had seemed to invite change. Yes, and somehow Aidan had invited a kind of change. Morton had never met anyone like him before. He was someone – almost, it seemed, a blank, a *tabula rasa* – on to whom people projected their own feelings and hopes. When they looked at him, they saw not Aidan but a strange mirror, a vision of themselves-as-they-might-have-been. Morton had seen someone disengaged, unworldly, even saint-like. And now here was Morton rattling about in the old, burnt house by himself.

He stood stock still in the middle of the room and considered. He tried seeing things not as others saw them, but as he honestly saw them himself. He couldn't say that he was unhappy. Indeed, he couldn't remember a time in his life when he had thought he was unhappy. The world had always been too full of possibilities for Morton. Even the walls around him, mottled to a strange landscape by the action of the fire, spoke to him of something other, of a new realm of possibilities. In a way, Morton was just fine.

He went over to the phone and punched in the number of the house in Clapham.

'Hello.'

'Hi. Could I speak to Laura Morton, please?'

'Yeah. Is that you, Mr Morton?'

Morton could hear voices and music in the background. 'Yeah,' he said.

'Hello Bob. It's Jeremy here. How are you?'

'OK, yourself?'

'All right. Sorry about all the noise. We're having a party, well just a few friends really. Laura's very well. I'll get her if you like. I'm sure she'd like a word. She's just in the other room.'

Morton listened to the bang and clunk as the receiver was put down. There was thirty seconds of background babble, then another clunk.

'Hi, Bob,' said Laura.

'Hi, honey. I just called to see how you're doing.'

'I'm OK. Sorry about the noise. Can you hear me? There's a party going on here. Yeah, I'm doing fine. We got copies of our single today, and it's going into the shops next week. Can you believe it? That's why we're having a celebration. I'll drop one round to you, and I really hope you like it. It's pretty funky. How's everything your end? Keeping the "Gap" happy?'

Morton laughed. 'The "Gap" doesn't need me to keep happy. Anyway, the first show's going out there in a few weeks.'

'That's great. God, I wish I could see it.'

'Well I guess I could show you a copy in the office. Or there's talk of a British network buying one of the programmes.'

'No kidding? On British TV? That would be great.'

There was an awkward pause, the line silent.

'How's everything at the house?' said Laura. 'You heard anything from Aidan?'

'No. I guess he's just gone his own way, disappeared into the winter mists.'

'Yeah, well I'd better go. Don't want to be a party pooper.'

'OK. Take care, honey.'

Putting the phone down again, Morton wondered why he had called her. He hadn't said what he had wanted to say. But then he hadn't known what that was. He had hoped that the act of talking to her would bring it to him. The mood almost of elation with which he had picked up the phone to make the call had gone. The heater was making him sleepy again. He switched it off, stood feeling the air grow colder and colder, then switched it on again and, with a sigh, sat down again by the closed window.

'That was Laura's father on the phone,' Jeremy announced to everyone when she came back. 'He's a kind of American Richard Baker.'

'God, what an awful thought,' said one of the two women at the far end of the room.

Laura laughed it off. 'Well I don't know who this Richard Baker is,' she said.

'He's an English version of your father,' said Jeremy, and turned to the others with an ugly, triumphant cackle.

Laura looked round for somewhere to sit. She had been sitting on the floor next to Jeremy but he had stretched out while she was gone, taking her place.

'Hey, Laura, come and sit here,' said the other woman at the far end of the room, and patted the sofa she was sitting on. Laura joined her.

She was called Karen. Laura had met her a couple of times before. She seemed to be a friend of Tony's, but was a homely, wholesome kind of person. She wore tight jeans, a colourful blouse and her face had a pink, well-washed look. She didn't seem like the kind of person Tony usually hung out with, the sharp, worldly kind.

'Is your dad really on the telly?' she said, sipping at her wine and giving a kind of squirm to make herself comfortable in the conversation.

'Yeah, he's what we call an anchorman. He does the newscasts and stuff for one of the major networks.'

'I saw a programme about American TV,' said Bev. It was Bev who had responded to Jeremy's quip. 'It was absolute shit. It made me so fucking angry. Just hundreds of adverts and consumerist crap. And the news was so fucking biased and right-wing. I couldn't believe it.' She gave a kind of snort and stuck her nose back into her paper cup, angrily gulping wine.

Laura looked at her sitting on the floor with her knees drawn up, at her close-cropped punk hair and black jeans, and wondered what to say. It wasn't the first time that this had happened, that she had been attacked simply for being American and been expected to defend herself for it. But she still hadn't learnt what to say, how to deal with the situation. It made her angry, though she wasn't sure who or what at.

'Yeah, I think it's a lot of bullshit too,' she said weakly. Bev gave her a sceptical look.

'Well I like the adverts sometimes,' said Karen with an apologetic giggle. 'I think they're really funny sometimes.' As she rocked with her laughter, the sofa heaved a bit, and she leant momentarily against Laura. Laura could feel the heat of her arm through the thin blouse.

Karen shook her head as though trying to shake the funny thought out, then was still. The three of them were silent for a while, listening to the pounding music and the talk coming from the other end of the room.

'C'mon, Dave, of course you're a fucking yuppy. I know.' It was Jeremy, shouting across the room and jabbing his finger at a lanky, blond-haired youth who knelt on the floor and rocked forwards and backwards on his heels, puffing nervously at a cigarette.

'No I'm bloody not. For a start, if you're really a yuppy you have one of those Filofax things, and I'd never get one of those.' Dave's tone was vehement, but he smiled broadly as he said it as though dismissing a gratifying compliment.

'I'll tell you who really is a yuppy,' said a third man sitting at Jeremy's feet. 'Andrew Taylor.'

'Yeah.'

They all talked about the absent Andrew Taylor, each trying to outdo the other in disparaging and sneering comments. They laughed a lot.

'I hate yuppies,' said the man at Jeremy's feet when they had finished.

'Yeah.'

The three women at the other end of the room listened to all this. Laura heard Bev mutter, 'Public school wankers,' to herself.

'How long have you been going out with Jeremy?' asked Karen with a cosy, conspiratorial smile.

Laura hesitated. She hadn't really thought about herself and Jeremy in those terms. 'Going out' basically meant sex – that was easy enough. But there was something else implied in the way that Karen asked it, something significant that didn't seem to apply to her and Jeremy. His braying voice came across the room again, banging on about yuppies. For a moment, as Karen and Bev looked at her, waiting for a reply, she felt a bit ashamed.

'Only a couple of months,' she said.

'Well, I think he's ever so dishy,' said Karen. 'You are lucky.' She laughed, then slapped her knee and added, 'Stop it, Karen.'

Her laughter was infectious. Laura noticed that even Bev was smiling. They watched Tony came back into the room. He'd been going in and out all evening.

'How long have you known Tony?' asked Laura.

'Hey, don't get the wrong idea,' said Karen. 'I'm not going out with him. Oh he's all right, but I wouldn't trust him an inch. I was at school with him, in Newham. He's always kept in touch, mind. Always keeps in touch with everyone, Tony does.'

'How about you, Bev?' said Laura, trying to build bridges. But Bev, staring at her feet, couldn't have heard her above the music.

'Oh Bev knows Tony through Jeremy,' said Karen. 'They were at college together. He's terribly clever as well, isn't he – Jeremy?'

'Yeah,' said Laura vaguely. She wished Karen would stop going on about him. She wasn't jealous – far from it. She was just annoyed that Karen seemed to think she had to be nice about Jeremy in order to be friendly. 'How about you, Karen?' she said. 'What do you do?'

Karen laughed, heaving back on to the sofa. 'Christ, you don't want to know about me. What about you? Playing in a pop group, got a record out. You'll probably be on telly soon, too. And you've got Jeremy.'

'Fuck Jeremy,' Laura snapped without thinking. There was an awkward pause. Laura glanced up and saw that Bev had been listening, smiling to herself.

'Ooo,' said Karen. 'Can I really?'

They all three laughed and got on much better after that. Laura spent the rest of the evening talking with them. Karen, it turned out, was a temp. And Bev, who had finished college the summer before, was unemployed. Laura had assumed they didn't know each other very well, and had just happened to be sitting together at the party. But it turned out they shared a flat. Bev seemed like an unhappy person. Laura guessed she looked to Karen for support, because she seemed generous and trustworthy. When, later, Laura saw them out the door, Karen whispered to her that she thought Bev really liked her. Bev was just shy, she said. Laura watched them disappear into the night together – Bev with loping strides of her monkey boots, Karen shuffling her feet busily along the icy pavement.

'Laura, shut the door, will you, love,' Tony shouted from the sitting-room. 'It's bloody freezing.' Somebody said something else, quieter, and she could hear Jeremy laugh.

Laura went upstairs. Tony, Jeremy and a couple of others were carrying on drinking, but she didn't feel like being with them. It had been so nice chatting to Karen and Bev that she didn't want to risk spoiling it.

She went upstairs and sat on her bed. Her sax sat on its stand in the corner of the room. Looking at it gave her a pang of guilt. She hadn't practised much lately. Playing with the band was easy; the chord changes were simple, and she could coast along without any effort. So she hadn't been working, she had just enjoyed the attention and the rushing around at night and people wanting to talk to her because she played in a real band with a single coming out. Things had rushed past so quickly that nothing individual had seemed to have any significance. It was all a blur, a sometimes beautiful blur, of lights and drinks and cigarettes. And music, measuring out each night at clubs and parties with its pounding beat. It was quiet now, for a moment. From downstairs there was just the faint boom of Jeremy's voice, then another, then laughter and silence. It was as though this evening the whirling cycle of hedonism had come to a stop for Laura, like putting a brake on a spinning wheel. What had previously been a blur could be seen clearly. It made her uneasy. She didn't understand Jeremy. Something seemed to take him over when he was drinking, laughing with that twinkle of mockery in his beautiful eyes. It seemed to Laura sometimes that she might be slipping into chaos. The bonds that kept things together might be breaking. At first, Jeremy and Laura had gone everywhere together on their nightly rounds. But in the last couple of weeks there had been confusions and missed messages. Several times Laura had found herself left behind in Clapham. The thought occurred to her now that Jeremy had always taken her for granted.

Exhausted, she began to slowly undress. She was wondering why her father had called. Bob usually phoned only when he had something to say, like an instruction or some advice to give. But tonight, she remembered, he hadn't said anything. It was as though he had called just to hear her voice. That had been strange. Then she had talked to Karen and Bev. In bed, sleep engulfing her in waves, the two things tangled in her mind. There had been the inconclusive, pointless chat with Bob – but touching, like a piece of bare need. And then there had been Karen. And then. For a moment she was almost fast asleep, but was jolted back by clearer more objective thoughts. Why did Jeremy do what he did? Sleep flooded back, her mind slipped back to Karen and the almost weak voice down the phone line. Then another jerk of wakefulness, sounds of drinking downstairs, and the tide came in again. With each cycle, sleep was stronger.

Something happened. Laura was awake and aware straight away, staring up into the flat darkness, listening. There was a tap at the door.

'Laura? Are you asleep?'

It was Jeremy. She held herself still, not even breathing. Silence. Another tap, and Jeremy said it again. She had her arms by her side. She could feel them squeezed tight against her body. Still she said nothing. She was willing him not to come in, but also curious as to whether he would.

He waited on the landing for five minutes, listening to the silence of the door. Then he mumbled something and stumbled on up the stairs. Laura listened to him leave, waited, then turned on to her side and slept.

CHAPTER SIXTEEN

'What yer having, Tommy?'

It was the first time Aidan had heard the Captain's real name.

'Half of Best'll do me nicely, Michael.'

'What about your friend? What's your poison?'

'Bitter,' said Aidan.

'And a pint of bitter.'

Friday night in The White Horse. A small man with dark hair stood in the corner crooning ballads in a high, quavering voice. He was accompanied by an electric organ. Nobody listened. Later, when the place was packed, there would be a disco.

The bar pumps gushed end-of-the-week largesse. The stout man in the shiny pink shirt who was buying the drinks talked in asides, wagging his finger and playing to the gallery. He was the first to laugh at himself. There weren't many women in yet. Those that were there – cleaned, powdered and perched up on barstools – seemed disappointed that they weren't getting more of the attention. The men were in the first fine bloom of their drinking camaraderie. Women could wait.

Aidan usually avoided The White Horse on Fridays. It was the Captain who had persuaded him to come. Friday night, it turned out, was the only time the Captain went to the pub, and then only for an hour or so, to keep in touch. Aidan had never seen anyone from the warehouse in The White Horse, which was why he went there.

'Here we are young man,' said Michael, and passed Aidan the last of the drinks off the bar. 'That's my daughter there,' he continued to the group gathered round him, and jerked a thumb at the girl who had served him. She had moved off down the bar. 'Just in case you blokes was getting any ideas,' he added, and laughed exaggeratedly, bending his knees, opening his mouth wide and nudging his neighbour. The others laughed too. 'Don't believe me, do you?' he continued. 'Monica!' he shouted down the bar. The girl looked up from the pint she was pulling. 'Am I your father?'

'Eh, Mick, what you gonna do if she says no?' shouted one of the other men, and they all laughed.

'Yeah, what's the name of your milkman?' said another.

Aidan watched the girl frown vaguely at the distraction and turn back to the beer, curling a loose strand of her brown hair behind her ear. She was the barmaid who had started a couple of weeks before. The men around her father had fallen silent, supping on their pints. One of them chuckled quietly and shook his head at the floor, as though he were savouring in his mind some new subtlety in the joke. The Captain was looking round at them with satisfaction, like a chairman noting good attendance at a meeting.

'Tell you something,' said Michael. 'This perishing weather we're having, you're lucky if it doesn't shrivel up completely! Wicked, ennit?'

One of the men – elderly, with a long, angular face – laughed uproariously at this. The one who'd been shaking his head at the floor did it more vigorously, chuckling louder, as though the remark reinforced everything he had been thinking.

Aidan swigged his beer hungrily and watched. He'd had a hard day, unloading heavy crates of VCRs and hi-fis. He was thirsty. He watched the men. Michael was telling a joke now. The other men had formed themselves into a semi-circle around him, listening to him, their pint glasses raised to chest height as though they were paying obeisance to a god.

'And she said, "I thought you meant chop it off!" '

Laughter. Michael was a big chap with heavy eyebrows and a neck that sloped gradually into his flabby shoulders. A gold chain rested on his chest. After crumpling at his own joke, he hitched himself up and puffed officiously at his cigarette. He glanced around the bar, over the heads of the others.

The Captain rocked up on to his toes and said, 'Yeah, there hasn't been a winter like this since – when was that? – must have been 1962.'

'Fucking freezing,' said Michael, not really paying attention and still glancing around the bar. Whatever it was he was looking for, he didn't find it. His gaze returned to the group around him and fell on the Captain.

'How you been doing, Tommy?' he said.

'Oh, you know how it is,' said the Captain modestly. 'Funny old business.'

A mood of boredom had settled on the group of men. One or two glanced away to see what was happening elsewhere in the pub.

'What's a funny old business?' said Michael. A spark of interest. 'People're always saying that, aren't they? "Funny old business," they say, and they could be talking about anything for all you fucking know!'

They chuckled and nodded in agreement.

'The warehouse,' said the Captain impertubably. 'Got another letter from the office yesterday about my retirement.'

'Oh yeah,' said Michael. 'That.'

The boredom returned. Michael looked at Aidan.

'You work there as well?'

'Yeah.'

'Young Aidan and I've got plans, haven't we? He's thinking of setting the business up with me in Dagenham, aren't you, Aidan?'

Aidan frowned. The Captain hadn't mentioned Dagenham for a few days. Aidan had hoped he'd forgotten about it.

'Oh Christ,' said Michael jovially, 'not your cousin's place in Dagenham again.' He stepped forward and put his arm round Aidan's shoulder. 'Tommy there,' he said, pointing at the Captain through the haze of cigarette smoke, 'has been banging on about this Dagenham caper for the past, what, five years?'

The Captain, complacently sipping his beer, didn't answer.

'Five years he's been going on about it, and what's ever come of it? Nothing. I don't reckon the ruddy place exists.'

The Captain, still smiling, just shrugged his shoulders. A familiar taunt.

'Well then . . . what's your name?'

'Aidan.'

'Oh yeah. Well then, Aidan,' Michael gave his shoulders a friendly squeeze, 'so you're gonna set up shop with old Tommy are you?'

Aidan wanted to shake off the big man's grip. They were all looking at him, waiting for a reply – all except the Captain himself, who smiled into the middle-distance, nodding his head happily to the tinkle of the electric organ. Aidan thought, I must say something quickly – anything, make a joke. That way they would forget about it and talk about something else. But it was too late now. It was as though he were being mesmerised by their momentary interest in him, like a rabbit in headlights. And the longer the silence, the stronger the flicker of interest running through the men. Even the Captain glanced at him out of the corner of his eye.

'Well?' said Michael amiably. 'Make your mind up.'

'*No,*' said Aidan. He'd said it louder than he'd meant. It came out sounding strange, like a cry of fright.

An awkward pause. Michael took his arm away.

'Looks like you'll have to find yourself another partner, Tommy,' said one of the other men, and laughed nervously.

Aidan looked at the Captain. He thought he saw him look back reproachfully.

'C'mon then,' said Michael, 'what's all this gloom about? 'Tis a fucking Friday night after all. Tommy, you'll have another, won't you?'

The Captain gave Michael his glass without speaking. The others talked among themselves. Aidan felt as though he'd broken some rule and been ostracised. He moved away to buy himself another beer.

As he waited at the bar, he found himself looking up at the photographs above the spirit bottles. John Fitzgerald Kennedy stared piercingly over the heads of the drinkers. He had a square, handsome face, and his hair was cropped to nothing at the sides of his head. For a moment, Aidan had a clear picture of Morton, who'd had similar clipped hair, only grey. He could hear him drawling out his tales. ('Jack Kennedy had this thing about his brother. Used to talk about him all the time. You must know what I'm talking about, Aidan – you probably have the same kind of thing going with your brother. Anyway, I always said that it was Bobby would have made the great President . . .')

'Do you want a drink?'

It was the big man Michael's daughter, smiling at him from behind the pumps.

'Yeah, pint of bitter please.'

'I saw my dad getting matey with you over there,' she said as she pulled the pump handle.

He looked at her. She had her father's dark eyebrows, but from the rest of her face and neck her father's excess flesh had been lifted away. With a serious expression, she measured the last drops of beer into the glass. Her bare arm bore two moles. She wore a T-shirt and jeans.

'That's one pound five pence. What's your name?'

'Aidan.'

'Nice name.' She rang up the money and turned to the next customer. Her nose was thin and pointed, in contrast to the heavy eyebrows she had inherited from her father. Her black hair curved to the base of her neck, curling behind her ears. Every now and then, as she bent over the pumps to pull a pint, a strand would swing down in front of her face and she would flick it back behind her ear. She had a small mouth.

Aidan forgot about the Captain, Michael and the other men. He stood at the bar and pretended to read a newspaper someone had left among the sodden beer mats. He didn't dare look at her. He felt confused. He gulped down the beer in order to buy another and speak to her, but she had moved to the other end of the bar. He was served by the landlord.

As he grew tipsy, he plucked up the courage to look up from the paper. The Captain, he noticed, had gone. Monica was serving her dad with more drinks. She gave him a quick, business-like smile as he handed her the money. Aidan plunged his head again.

Almost by a kind of sixth sense, he could tell that she was working her way down the bar towards him. At just the right moment, he drained off the last of his pint and looked up. She was there in front of him.

'Pint of bitter, please,' he said.

She took the glass from him and smiled.

'Not talking to your friends any more?' she said as she pulled the pint. She jerked her head at the group that included her father.

'No. I don't really know them.' He noticed that she had a faint Irish accent.

'Well, they'll be a bit old for you, I suppose,' she said, and gave him a matey wink.

Aidan fumbled with the change. He was running out of money. He didn't want to leave things there. He gave her the money and said, 'Are you Irish?' He tried to say it in a light, not-very-interested way.

'I suppose I am. What's it to you?'

'I'm Irish too, well my mum is.'

He expected her to laugh, but she didn't.

'Are you now?' she said. 'You've got a funny way of talking, but it isn't Irish.'

'I'm from near Birmingham.'

'That'll be it, then. When did your mum come from Ireland.'

''Bout thirty years ago, I think. She married my dad.'

Monica laughed. 'You don't say.'

'When did you come from Ireland?' Aidan didn't know why they were talking about this. He just wanted it to go on as long as possible. Monica was wiping beer off her hands with a teatowel while she talked to him.

'I was a baby. But I go back to visit my relations when I gets the chance. I went this last summer. I love it over there.'

'What's it like?' asked Aidan.

'Sorry, I've got to get back to work.' A man further down the bar was banging his glass down to get attention. 'See you later.'

He gulped his beer, elated. She had moved back down the bar. He felt like a different person. He looked up at John Fitzgerald Kennedy, and for the first time noticed the friendly smile on his face.

For quite a while he just stood there at the bar, looking around the pub in a dazed way. Every couple of minutes he allowed himself a glance over the bar at Monica. The pub was full now. The singer had been replaced by a disco. A bank of red and green strobes flashed like mad, multiple traffic lights. A disc jockey with a large, babyish face bounced up and down on a low stage behind his console.

'Yeah Friday night at The White Horse having a GOOD time with the hottest sounds around,' he gushed into the microphone. 'We're gonna GET ON DOWN THERE 'cos we've got the new thing here a single by a new band called WOW! and this is caaaalled . . . WOW!'

Aidan nodded his head stupidly to the beat. A man's voice bleated above the guitar chords, backed by a woman.

> *It's WOW!*
> *What a girl you are*
> *I said WOW!*
> *I'll drive you in my car*
> *I mean WOW!*
> *We could take it so far*
> *Tonight*

Some couples were jigging up and down between the tables. Even Aidan, very drunk now, jerked his knees. He looked round, grinning, to see where Monica was. She was gone. At the same moment, an arm landed heavily across his shoulders. Hot, boozy breath steamed his cheek. He turned his head as far as he could and saw the big man Michael's face up against his.

'Hello, young man . . . Aidan,' the face said, 'thought you'd . . . buy you a drink . . .'

Michael lurched forward and flopped against the bar like a rag doll. Somehow – Aidan was too confused to see how – he bought two pints.

'Good to know you, Aidan,' he said. 'Micky Donahue.' He jabbed a finger hard into his own hairy chest, just below where the gold chain lay, as though he were trying to thrust his own name into himself. 'Micky Donahue,' he said again. 'Everybody knows Micky Donahue.' He gave Aidan an intent, lopsided stare. Then he laughed wildly and did an absurd, comical jig on the spot. For a big man he was surprisingly nimble. But he had no head for drink.

'You're a good man, Aidan. A good man. You've met my daughter, haven't you? Monica!'

Aidan suddenly saw her. She was working her way through the crowd towards them, carrying a tower of empty glasses.

'Monica! Over 'ere! I want you to meet young Aidan. You're a good man,' he added reassuringly to Aidan. 'Monica! Come over 'ere will yer!'

Monica came through the jostling bodies and set the glasses down on the bar. 'I've met Aidan, Dad,' she said.

'The two of you've met!' he cried, delighted. 'You're a good man, young Aidan. A good man.' He gripped Aidan's shoulder with his hand and shook it warmly. Then, with another blind gear-change of the drunk, he started dancing – this time a gross parody of sexy disco dancing.

'C'mon,' he said, ''ave a dance, Monica and young Aidan.' He grabbed them both and thrust them together. Aidan found his face buried in Monica's black hair. Donahue was strong. There was a frightening confusion of clothes, limbs and glasses. Something smashed. Laughter.

'Don't be shy. You're a good man, Aidan.'

> *Gotta be WOW!*
> *To get you where you are*

Aidan could feel Monica pushing him away. He felt he was falling into an underworld of shoes, broken glass, beer and cigarette ends. He grabbed out at anything his hands could reach, as though he were drowning. Somehow, he got his feet beneath his torso, and pushed himself upright. At the same time, he staggered forward, almost instinctively, through the crowd towards the door. He heard Donahue shouting behind him, asking him to come back, telling him he was a good man. He felt vomit well up in his throat and tears of shame and humiliation burst at his eyeballs.

When he burst from the pub door, the freezing cold air seemed to grip him, drag him forward, and throw him down into a snow drift that lay by the side of the road. It was quiet. There was no traffic. He lay still for a moment, his cheek pressed into the snow, gulping the clean, cold air and feeling it fight against the vomit that still welled up his throat. He pushed himself upright, his hands raw red in the snow, just in time for the orange sick to gush up out of him on to the pristine snow. He stood there, stooping, traumatised by the extent of it. His

guts heaved again, and it felt like the thick, vile liquid was being
dragged out of him with a hook. It took ten minutes, standing there in
the biting cold, before his body was rid of it. When he had done, he
walked slowly back to his bedsit. He was sober now. He had almost
forgotten those frightening moments, the shame and sickness. What
he remembered of the evening was the girl behind the bar and the way
he'd felt different after she'd spoken to him. When he got back to his
room he read.

*The woman waited, until she almost felt part of the rock on which she was
crouched. Then, when she saw the lizard move, she hurled her stone down. It
missed. The lizard slithered away to another hiding place and the stone hit the
ground with a tired thud, sending up a puff of dust. Damn. She had been
stalking that lizard for half an hour. It was a big one, heavy with meat.*

*The group had chosen her to hunt lizard in the high country. She had
proved herself to be the quickest and most agile. She could have used a laser
gun, of course, as they all had hitherto. Killing lizards was easy that way,
even if it did make a mess. But the laser guns would become inoperative
eventually, and there would be no replacements. They would have to learn
other ways of killing. On the flat floor of the valley, where there was little
cover, the woman could kill them by chasing them and hitting them with a club.
Over a thirty yard spring she could catch a lizard. But the lizards in the valley
were only small; the big ones were in the rocky crags of the hills, where running
was impossible. Stealth, she decided, was the best strategy. She'd find a lizard
lying, as they liked to do, in the shade of an overhanging rock. Then she'd
climb quietly to the top of the rock and wait. Eventually the lizard would
move, or it could be disturbed by tapping on the rock. When it broke cover, you
threw your stone.*

*At this, her fourth failure, she felt a draining sense of hopelessness. She lay
back on the rock and closed her eyes. At moments like this it was hard not to
think back to the ship. She was picturing in her mind a particular evening some
five years ago when she had had a dinner party to celebrate her selection to the
Planetary Research Unit. Her guests had been some of her new colleagues.
There had been fine food and drink, and to accompany it one of the mild
euphoriates that were popular at that time. (This was before the clamp-down
and polarization.) The talk had been cosy, her career was launched. How
wonderful that seemed now, like a paradise. It was strange; she could hardly
believe it had happened to her, but at the same time she almost thought she
could walk off this hillside and return to it. It was as if this world of rocks and
escaping lizards was transient, like a dream.*

*She sat up again and looked round. She had almost dozed off. What she
needed was a throwing spear – something that would fly faster through the air*

than a stone. She climbed across the rocks for a few hundred yards till she found a large thorn bush, then unsheathed the knife that hung from her waist and, scratching her arms badly, cut out one of the straight, heavy stems from the middle of the bush. She sat high up on a rock overlooking the valley and began working on the stick with her knife, cutting knots away to make a smooth shaft and whittling the point. From where she was now she had a clear view. Even the spaceship looked small from here, a distant glint in the blinding sunlight. Overhead a hawk wheeled in the air currents. A breeze brushed her shoulder. It was one of those moments, there had been many over the past days, when the sheer physical sensation of the planet threatened to overwhelm her. Her eyes felt hammered by light and colour. The smell of the planet was tangible in her mouth, like grit. Even the rocks had their scent. It was hard to believe that she was part of it, even the centre of it. She looked down at her body as though it were the first time it had existed. Her chest was bare and browned. A cloth was wrapped tightly round her waist, and on her feet she wore running shoes. (These would wear out in time – she would have to learn to make sandals from the skin of lizard.) Her legs were streaked with dirt and with blood where she had scraped herself on the rocks. The brute being of all this – the sandy coloured rock she sat on, her body, those reddish rocks over there, that thorn bush below her – flooded in through her eyes. She was still breathing heavily from the climb. For a moment she felt an extraordinary ecstasy – not like the befuddling, excited state engineered by euphoriates, but a sense as clear and deep as a pool of crystal-clean water. Frowning, she bent her head to her work once more and whittled down the point with new energy.

After a few minutes, when the spear was almost finished, she looked up and studied the view once more. The only sign of human life, apart from the spaceship, was far off on the other side of the valley, where a tiny thread of smoke was making its way up into the vast blue sky. That fire must be at least forty miles away, she thought. Probably more like twice that. It was on the edge of the valley just beneath the opposite range of hills. That was what they called South. The colony was beginning to disperse. Perhaps some groups had already started out into those hills. She didn't know. Communications had broken down quickly. The more officious in the woman's group had tried to keep contact with neighbouring groups, but there seemed little point really. As returns to the empty ship became less frequent, contacts became fewer and further between. Things were falling apart. There was nothing organised about the dispersion, just as there had been nothing organised about the groups' constitution. On those first, bewildering nights, people had gathered around campfires. They were neither friends nor strangers (there had been neither on board Xykon), but had clung together out of mutual need. Thus the groups had started.

The woman gazed out across the valley, holding the heavy spear between her fingers. It was strange to know that this was what remained of humanity. After millennia of struggle, of technological development, then after the longest journey and more centuries, they had reached a place beyond knowledge, beyond the furthest projections, and found it to be the most familiar to the collective consciousness of the species: vast, burning skies, and men and women, naked, scrambling over a wilderness of rock and dust, armed with club and spear.

The woman's gaze travelled over the craggy cliff face that tumbled down below her into the valley. She wondered how old those rocks were, how long they had been sitting, waiting, beneath the burning sun. She thought about beginnings. Then, among the rocks, she saw something. It was just a shadow flicking quickly past the corner of her vision, but her whole body tensed. She got up to a crouching position. Then it emerged from behind a boulder, close to her but further down the hillside.

It was a big cat, a lion perhaps, dirty brown in colour, with graceless, flabby skin and powerful limbs. The mouth – open, panting, dripping saliva – dominated the head. It looked like nothing more than an eating machine. The woman instinctively drew back, but she was completely exposed up on the rock. The lion hadn't seen her. It was walking between the rocks with its head hung rather low to the ground. As it came out into the sunlight from the shadow of a large boulder, it stopped and raised its head slightly. The white teeth were prominent in the light against the red of its gums. The woman thought at first that it was listening, but then saw its nose twitching. In the same moment, from the coolness of the breeze blowing off the hill on to her back, she realised that she was upwind of it. The lion looked up and saw her. For a moment they stared at each other. The lion closed its mouth, settling its jaws together. The woman scrambled across the rock, grabbed a stone, and hurled it down at the lion. The stone landed harmlessly to one side of the animal, but surprised it. As it had whizzed past, the lion had flinched instinctively. It took a step forward and stopped again, looking up at her. She grabbed another stone and threw it. This time she hit the lion on the chest. It stepped back a couple of paces, unhurt, then moved forward again – driven now, it seemed, by curiosity. The woman took a whole bunch of stones and threw them all, in quick succession. A couple hit. The lion retreated a few paces, stared up at her for a few more seconds, then turned and continued its journey along the hillside as though it had never stopped.

The woman waited a few minutes, then started back down the hill towards the camp. It took her a while to stop shaking and replaying in her mind the sight of the lion settling its teeth together, dribbles of saliva swinging from its fleshy jowls. By the time she made it down on to flatter ground, the shadows were beginning to lengthen. She was angry with herself at not having caught anything, but at the same time curiously elated. She would be able to catch some small lizards when she was back in the valley.

Not far from the camp, she walked into a clearing between massive boulders and saw a large lizard. It was lying some twenty feet away in the shade, staring at her. She stopped and raised her spear, balancing it in her hand. The lizard stared back. Facing her, it presented a small target. But if she could hit it, its face might be softer than the hard skin on its back. Slowly, she drew her arm back, then whipped it forward again with all her strength. Everything happened quickly. The spear struck and glanced away. The lizard scuttled across the clearing, seeking shelter, and blundered disoriented into a rock. Instead of going off again in another direction, it huddled against the rock, scratching desperately at the earth. The woman dashed across the clearing, scooped up the spear and jabbed it into the animal. The lizard hissed loudly and curled up around the shaft of the spear.

When she got back, she found some of the men of the group building a hut from stones and branches. Others were sitting listlessly in the shade. Many of them were finding it impossible to cope with life off the ship. They just sat gazing at their new surroundings. The woman walked through the camp, the lizard swinging heavy and inert from her spear, to where the well was being dug. They had reached water during the course of the day. She drank some and received the congratulations of those around her on her kill. They would all eat.

She threw the lizard down into the dust and drew her knife out to skin it. She felt pleased and proud. With the well, and the fleshy, dead lizard, it seemed that everything here was provided for, had been waiting for, the humans.

CHAPTER SEVENTEEN

Soho looked like a frontier town. Great banks of snow had piled up along the side of the street. One car was almost buried by it. There was little traffic about, and what noise there was was muffled by the ice and snow. It was eerily quiet.

Jeremy's feet crunched in the snow as he walked along beneath a steel-grey sky. He looked down the straight street, and could almost picture the scene as an Alaskan oil town, surrounded by wintry tundra. Bullshit. What was he doing thinking that, when he was depressed? He stared back down at the icy pavement passing beneath him, and lit a cigarette.

He'd been noticing lately how thoughts just jump into your head without an invitation, without a fucking by-your-leave. Stupid thoughts. Trivial thoughts. Thoughts that had nothing to do with what you were thinking. Haha. It made him angry. He could imagine some bastard shoving them in there from time to time just to fuck up his thinking. What was he doing? All this had nothing to do with it either. This in itself was another one of those fucking thoughts. Completely irrelevant. But to what? Why couldn't he just think those thoughts? Why did he have to think they were a useless distraction from something else? Why couldn't that be all?

Why couldn't that be all? That almost made him laugh. He knew why he was here. He knew what made him unhappy. At the next crossroads, he turned left and entered a doorway. He had been here before. He went to the man in the ticket booth and got some change.

'She's not ready yet,' said the man, hardly looking at him. 'You can wait over there if you like.' He pointed to a couple of orange plastic chairs, like the ones Jeremy had sat on in school assemblies.

Jeremy sat down, puffing on his cigarette. Of course – it was early yet. Barely eleven o'clock. The bloke in the booth was reading his morning paper. All over London people were at work, getting on with their normal lives. He half stood up again. This was ridiculous – what was he doing here? He felt like an idiot. But he slumped down into the chair again. Something seemed to hold him there, to drag him on down this path. He hated it. He hated every fucking moment.

He waited. After a few minutes, there was a sound of someone clattering down stairs. A door opened, and a woman in high heels came out, clutching a tatty fur coat round her. She clattered across to the ticket booth, shivering in the cold, and dragged out an electric fire. The plug bumped across the floorboards. The woman and the man reading the paper didn't speak to each other. The woman dragged the electric fire into the partitioned section, which was lined with wooden cubicles. There was a few seconds pause, then the woman stuck her head round the door and said to Jeremy, with a kindly smile, 'Ready for you now, love.'

Jeremy stood up slowly and walked to one of the cubicles as though walking to the scaffold. He closed the door behind him, fumbled to put his fifty pence in the slot, and watched the peephole cover being mechanically raised.

The woman was crouched down, plugging the electric fire in. She had no clothes on, having put the fur coat on the back of a chair that shared the cramped space with her and the electric fire. When she had got the fire working, she stood up and turned to the thin slit where Jeremy's eyes were. She lifted one leg and swivelled her hips so that he could see better. He felt sick. He wanted to leave right then. He looked at her face. She'd lost her smile completely. She was staring expressionlessly at a point somewhere above the peephole. It was an ageing, slightly worried face. He felt misery well up inside him again. Again, he wanted to leave right away. But the situation held him. His disgust with himself, a feeling of horrible pity and fascination, held him, stooped, with his face pressed to the perspex. The woman turned round and bent over, so that he could study her bottom. God I wish this was over, he thought. I wish this would go on for ever. It was over after one minute exactly. The peephole cover, like a divine overseer, closed automatically. He hurried out of the peep show into the silent street. Mixed with his sense of relief that it was over was a hunger for more. He lit a cigarette and glanced up and down the street.

His mind was bowling down its own path now, the same things coming up again and again, in the same sequence. He went into a booth that showed porno films, flicked through magazines, went to another peep show. The same images again and again. The same distractions. His mouth was dry with excitement and disgust. And all the time: Why am I doing this? Why can't I just stop? Sometimes the question would drive him on, as though just this next one, just this next time, and he would reach a state of satisfaction, plenitude and bliss. But at the same time (so his thoughts went round and round) he knew that there was no end, that this wasn't a path that was going anywhere, but a treadmill turning on the spot. Once or twice, this thought literally paralysed him, and as he blundered out of another lurid doorway, geared to a yet higher pitch, he would stop dead still in the snow. Disgust, remorse, desire for more. Disgust, remorse, desire for more. It was like a spiral, a cork-screw drilling down and down and fixing him, panicking, to the pavement. He looked up and down the street, searching for another neon sign that could give him escape. He lit a cigarette, savouring the scorch of smoke in his dry mouth. Then he could move. He was on his way again.

Eventually, like a fairground ride that has terrified a child, the process wound down and came to a stop. Jeremy, as though woken from a dream, stopped and looked around him. It was lunchtime. The streets were busy. At some point – Jeremy hadn't noticed – the sun had come out. It was still very cold, but the bright sunlight, reflected off the snow, lit the faces in the crowd that spilled on to the street. People laughed, clouds of steam floating up from their mouths. Jeremy felt a momentary sense of relief, as though a heavy burden had been lifted off his shoulders.

He had stopped near Tony's office. He crossed the street to the building and started up the stairs. Everything in his mind had turned over. Instead of that dark descent, digging down for more punishment, he felt he was reaching up for forgiveness. He wanted to be accepted. Desperate to talk to Tony, to anyone, he dashed up the last flight of steep stairs and burst precipitously into the room.

He stood for a moment in the doorway. Tony looked up at him, startled and annoyed. The man sitting with him, smartly dressed, raised the glass he was holding and smiled broadly at Jeremy.

'Hello, Jeremy,' said Tony coolly. 'Take a seat. Have a drink.' He poured some whiskey into a tumbler and handled it to Jeremy.

'We were just toasting a deal,' said the other man in a booming, posh voice. 'Putting a seal of approval on it, so to speak.' He raised his glass and gave Jeremy another warm, friendly smile.

Jeremy, still dazzled from the light and snow outside, breathless from running up the stairs, sat down and smiled back.

'This is Sebastian,' snapped Tony. He didn't like his companion discussing their business.

'Sebastian Parsons,' said the other man, heaving himself out of his chair and giving his hand to Jeremy. 'Good to meet you.' He slumped back into the chair and gave another broad smile. The cold winter sunlight, flooding in through the window beside him, lit up his attractive blue and white stripped shirt, his shiny blond hair. Everything about him was relaxed, healthy and happy. Under normal circumstances, Jeremy would probably have detested him at first sight, hated him for his strapping good looks, expensive clothes and dull good nature. But now, emerging from the dark tunnel he been in the last couple of hours, this clean, friendly presence seemed like that of a saviour. It was as though when he had burst into the office, he had been like a chick which struggles from its shell and latches on to the first object it sees as its source of succour.

'What do you do, Jeremy?' said Sebastian. 'I'm in advertising. My card.' He flicked a card out of his pocket and handed it to Jeremy. Everything he did he did with confident ease. 'Parsons Winthorpe & Crewe', the card read, 'Advertising and Public Relations'. 'Tony and I were just wrapping up—'

'Jeremy here manages Wow!' interrupted Tony. 'Remember – that video I showed you.'

'Oh yah,' said Sebastian, 'I loved it, Jeremy. Absolutely loved it. I thought it was really good. So you were behind that, were you? Interesting.' He sipped his whiskey and looked at Jeremy with satisfaction.

Jeremy, almost blushing with pride, took a drink himself, and felt the whiskey give him a nice warm feeling inside. 'Yeah,' he said, 'well I thought up the kind of concept—'

'Marvellous,' Sebastian interrupted, 'very . . . sixties.'

'Yeah,' said Jeremy enthusiastically. 'That's what I was trying to get at. You know, plug into the nostalgia thing. I'm really pleased you noticed. I wanted the whole thing to be kind of '67, but not too heavy.' He laughed. 'You know, cut out all the druggy crap and the heavy stuff and keep the colour and the image. Make it light.'

Sebastian nodded. 'Loved the bandannas.'

There was a pause. Tony, bored by the conversation, was looking out the window. There was a market in the street at the back of the building. He often liked to watch it, perhaps out of some obscure nostalgia for the old days. Even in this cold and snow, the stall holders had got their barrows out. He could see them, stomping their feet and bellowing out their wares to keep themselves warm. The crowd shuffled past through the slush. The whole scene, even from high up at the window, was radiant.

Tony, looking down at the people go past, suddenly leant forward and studied something more closely. 'Talk of the devil,' he said, 'there's Laura down there. Perhaps she's coming here.' He grinned at Sebastian. ''Fraid she ain't got her bandanna on today.'

Sebastian laughed. 'What a shame,' he said, 'I'm sure she'd look sweet in one. Who is she, this Laura?'

'She plays the sax in the video,' said Jeremy. 'You remember, she's the one who puts the flower in the barrel of the gun.'

'Jeremy's bit,' Tony added, with a wink.

Sebastian accepted all this information with satisfaction, smiling placidly and sipping his whiskey. 'I'm sure she's lovely, old boy,' he said, propping his glass high up against his chest again. Jeremy had seen his father hold his glass that way.

'Well, it looks like she's coming this way,' said Tony, watching her progress from the window.

Jeremy's black mood returned. 'Christ,' he muttered, 'what does she want?'

'You'll soon find out.'

'It must be great working in advertising,' he said to Sebastian, desperate to use the remaining time.

'Jeremy,' said Sebastian in a serious tone, 'you really should think about going into it yourself. Do you know how old I am? I'm twenty-six. I earn thirty thou', I've got a GTI and I'm a company director. Not bad, eh? I don't know another field where a bloke can get ahead like that. I'm right, aren't I, Tony?'

'Maybe,' said Tony. He was still looking out of the window.

'Plus,' Sebastian continued, 'it's, you know, a rewarding and creative job. You're not just fiddling around with share prices, you're doing something, you know, creative.'

'That's right,' said Jeremy. 'That's right. Advertising is *the* radical art form now. We live in the age of the image, don't we? Ephemera, right? The moment.' He laughed. He could almost see his thoughts reflected in the blank, bright sunlight. A parade of images flickered before his eyes. But this time their trajectory was not that dark, descending spiral of earlier. Now they danced upward like the play of sunlight on the snow outside.

'Oh, absolutely. I think you've got something there,' said Sebastian, thinking that Jeremy was a decidedly odd sort of chap.

Footsteps on the stairs outside. Tony and Toby listened. Jeremy still had his dreamy, excited expression. 'It's all about *irony*,' he began to say, but at that moment the door opened and Laura came in.

'Hello, Laura,' said Tony. 'Have a seat. Have a drink. Join the party.' He'd resigned himself to this invasion of his business premises.

'Can't stay, I'm afraid,' said Laura. 'Hi, Tony. Hi, Jeremy.' She leaned over to look at Jeremy, who hadn't seemed to have noticed she'd come in. He glanced at her and nodded.

'Sebastian Parsons,' said Sebastian, heaving himself out of his chair and shaking her hand. 'Good to meet you. Thought the video was great. Thought you were gorgeous, really gorgeous.'

'Thanks,' she said, looking at him a little uncertainly. 'Tony, I just dropped in to get a couple of things from you. I want to borrow a copy of the video for a couple of hours. Is that OK by you? I also want Karen's telephone number. I promised to call her.'

'OK.' Tony gave her a copy of the video and wrote down Karen's number on a piece of paper.

'Thanks.' Laura stood in the open doorway. 'Sorry to have burst in on you guys like this. Enjoy your party.' As she closed the door, she saw Sebastian Parsons give her an indulgent smile. 'Thing is, Sebastian,' Jeremy was saying, 'it's all a question of *irony* . . .'

She hurried down the steep staircase, relieved to get away. There had been something strange about the atmosphere in the room, something she hadn't liked. She had seen that sparkling, glazed look in Jeremy's eyes again. She almost ran from the door into the street, splashing through the slush on the pavement. The sun was at its brightest, the day at its most glorious. It was bitterly cold, and the sun blazed down, so that even the grey mush beneath the feet of the passing crowd sparkled dazzlingly.

Clutching the video and the piece of paper with Karen's number in her gloved hands, she stood in the middle of the road, where the snow was still powdery and white. There was no traffic. Above her, a wide expanse of electric blue sky arched over down the length of the straight street. Until today, she hadn't thought of London as a northern city. It had been very cold for almost two weeks now, but only today did it seem truly Arctic. It was as though with the appearance of the sun, the ice and snow and freezing cold were being confirmed and celebrated as a permanent condition. She could imagine it never changing. For a moment, standing in the snow, the London crowds around her disappeared. She was remembering vividly a plane journey she'd made as a child with her father, from Chicago to Edmonton in Canada. It had been a small plane, flying low, and seemed to take hours to get there. It had been spring, but everywhere there had still been snow. They had flown over hundreds of miles of snow and forest, broken only by the occasional isolated town, as night drew in across the emptiness. And when they landed at Edmonton, there had been gigantic piles of snow along the side of the runway, shining under the floodlights.

A car hooted. She picked her way through the snow to the side of the road to let it pass, then started down the street towards her father's office.

He had called her a couple of days ago to ask her to lunch at the office. She had been pleased he wanted to see her, but hadn't known what he wanted to see her about. Of course it had to be *about* something. It was always *about* something with Bob. Only the last couple of times she had talked to him, the conversation had been kind of directionless. That was what had made them so disturbing and strange, that they had been pointless.

So as she walked up from Piccadilly, she had suddenly thought of the video, and remembered that Tony's office was nearby. The thought of taking the video along to show Bob made her feel more secure. It would give them something to talk about. It seemed to fit things into a pattern she knew from childhood, a pattern of distance, of mutual criticism and approval. Now, holding it in her hand she felt more confident about meeting him.

When she got to the NWBC offices, that confidence began to fade. The thick glass doors shut out, silently and completely, the bright, cold air and the bustle of the street. The rituals of admittance, the oily receptionist and pinging lifts, seemed to suck her into a world far removed from the winter day outside. She wandered down a wide, thickly carpeted corridor. There was soft, hidden lighting. It was warm. At intervals there were big, squashy seats, in case you felt like sitting down and taking a rest. Like all corporate buildings, it was designed to emphasise the smallness, the dependence, of the individual, and the tasteful, all-providing power of the institution. She reached her father's office, and knocked.

'Yeah, come in.'

She discovered him sitting at his desk, gazing out at the snow. For a moment he appeared rather dwarfed by the large, plush furniture around him. Behind him was an enormous, practically empty bookcase, and beside the desk stood a television set as big as a small movie screen. He took his pipe out of his mouth and leant across the desk to kiss his daughter. Between them was a large dish of sandwiches. He pushed them towards her.

'I ordered these up,' he said. 'I hope they're OK.'

'Great.' She took one and ate. With the first mouthful, she discovered that the cold had made her very hungry. She quickly took another.

'Isn't this weather something?' Morton was looking out of the window again. Beyond the glass was a vista of snow-capped roof-tops, and the blinding white sun.

'Sure is. I was just thinking about that time I went with you to Edmonton.'

Morton took his pipe from his mouth again. '1970. Alberta state elections. Nice trip, no story.' He grinned at her, and she smiled back. There was another silence.

'How's the burnt house coming along?' said Laura.

'The house? It's OK. Pipes have frozen. I shower at work. I'm thinking of melting snow for cooking. Plenty of good, clean snow in the garden.' He clamped the pipe back between his teeth.

'What about the repairs?'

'Not much happening on that front right now. Trevor's got the 'flu. Anyway, I kind of like it how it is. Or I might sell it. I don't know.'

'Sell it? But you can't sell it. You've only just bought it.'

'OK, I might stay there. I don't know.'

'You're crazy, Bob. I don't know why you bought that place in the first place. You're only here a year. You'll be going back to the States in the summer. We'll both be going back. What are you going to do with it then?'

Morton didn't answer. He took a sandwich and began eating it, turning it over in his hand and examining it as he ate it, the way children do.

Laura watched him, suddenly very angry and confused. 'You mean you might stay here? I thought NWBC only wanted you here for a year.'

'Who's talking about NWBC?'

'But that's your job.'

Morton shrugged his shoulders, relit his pipe, and looked out of the window again. His face was wreathed in smoke. 'And how are you, honey?' he said. 'How are you enjoying London town?'

'I'm not.'

'You don't like London?'

'I don't know.' She shook her head. Everything was going wrong. 'I almost forgot,' she continued, trying to be chirpy, 'I brought you our video. I thought you might like to see it.' She wanted to show him that London hadn't defeated her.

'Sure. Stick it in that.' He pointed to the television set.

They rearranged the chairs in front of the screen and turned the video on. The screen crackled to life, the familiar guitar chords thundering out. Laura had heard the song so many times she was sick of it. It sounded out of place in this office, with her father listening to it. She was having misgivings about showing the video to him.

> *WOW!*
> *I'm where it's gotta be*
> *I said WOW!*
> *Won't you give it to me*
> *I've just gotta be free*
> *WOW!*

Laura, hardly recognisable at first in a flowery mini skirt, was running across a field. There were trees in the background. Her hair had been frizzed out somehow, and was held in tight to her head at the top by a bandanna. The wobbly, hand-held camera moved in to intercept her. Morton was suddenly, queasily reminded of the dream he'd had about Sammy. Laura did a couple of twirls in front of the camera and made a V-for-peace sign. Cut to the rest of the band, in another part of the field, dressed first as hippies, then in aggressive punk gear, miming to the chorus. Here was inserted some footage of sixties flower children cavorting, laughing, then cut to a close-up of the men in the band, all spots and safety pins, thrashing their guitars. On the sound track, the turn of Laura's solo had come. The film showed her miming it in a derelict street. A young skinhead approached and put a flower into the bell of her saxophone while she played. Cut to Laura putting a flower into the barrel of a gun. Cut to footage of students putting flowers into the gun-barrels of young National Guardsmen. (Morton recognised the film immediately – '68, the Democrat Convention in Chicago.) More footage, of a National Front demonstration, then back to the band. The last chorus was completely different – the whole band, including Laura, was on stage, dressed in snappy suits. This was normal, the 'real' them. Cut to enthusiastic audience. End.

'Well?' said Laura. 'What do you think? Pretty crazy, eh? That first bit was filmed in Richmond forest. I was so cold in that skirt!'

'Hmmm.' He switched off the video player. 'I couldn't quite see what the music had to do with all the stuff on screen.'

'Quit stalling. Did you like it?'

'Let's have some coffee.'

'Did you *like* it?'

Her father didn't answer. He poured out two cups of coffee very carefully, intent on what he was doing. Laura felt ashamed. She didn't know why she was getting so anxious and petulant. She had got up from her seat and followed him across the room to the coffee percolator. Now she sat down again and said, 'God, this place is so confusing. Nothing's ever easy here.'

'Why should it be?' said Morton cheerfully. 'The world wasn't made for our convenience.'

'Are you seriously going to give up work?' said Laura, who hated it when he got pompous. 'What's the matter? Are you retiring? I can't believe they're not paying you enough money.'

'It's not that. I'm sick of having cameras pointed at me.'

She laughed. 'I think you've been living in that house by yourself too long.'

'You said it, honey.'

'Oh no. I'm not going back there. I'm surprised you haven't got some terrible wasting disease in this weather.'

'It's character building.'

'I like my character just the way it is, thanks all the same.'

They smiled at each other.

'I thought the video stank,' he said.

'Thanks. I could tell. Why?'

'It was nothing. It was just a bunch of images thrown together. And it was pretentious.'

'What does that matter? It was only a goddamn pop video.'

'You asked.'

There was another, more disconsolate silence.

'And it makes me mad to see footage used like that,' Morton continued. 'Those were *real* people going through *real* things. It's exploitative to take their images like that and just use them to sell a record.' He got up from his desk and started pacing the room. 'By using their image like that, you're denying their essence. You are stealing something. And I thought they were exploiting you, Laura. What did all that have to do with being a musician, with being a saxophonist?'

'It's all part of it.'

'It's not part of it. It's an excrescence. It's a kind of crud that floats on the top. Everything that's pure and real – ' his hands grasped nothingness and shook it, as though trying to mould the air to his words, 'everything that's pure and real is spoiled by it.'

Laura looked at him in amazement. 'What are you talking about?' she said. 'Television? *You* are actually accusing people of being used by television? I don't believe I'm hearing this.' She stood up, facing him. 'And what's this "they" which has been exploiting me? We made that film ourselves. There wasn't some corporation like NWBC behind it. It was just us and Tony and a couple of other guys. If you want to find someone who's been exploited by some amorphous "they", then maybe you should take a look at yourself.' She felt furious. She started talking quickly, without thinking or believing in what she was saying. 'And you say it was "just a bunch of images thrown together", and you can't even see that that was the *whole point*, 'cause . . . 'cause that kind of fragmentation of images is telling an essential truth about the society we live in. Like Jeremy says, there's more truth in the images than in the things they represent.'

'Then he's a goddamn idiot and so are you for believing him.'

Laura burst into tears. 'Fuck you. Fuck you,' she cried. She turned and ran from the room. As she escaped down the carpeted corridor, she could hear Morton coming after her, calling to her. She ran faster, past the lifts, down the stairs and out through the foyer, beneath the censorious gaze of the receptionist.

Outside, the street was as she had left it. The sun still shone. But something inside her had broken, and all the confusion and unhappiness that she had been keeping out flooded in. She wandered down the street, down another, and found herself in a street market. The London voices, the market people calling out what they were selling, sounded foreign – but not in the cute way they had before. They sounded ugly and threatening, with vowels that grated in the cold air.

CHAPTER EIGHTEEN

Morton called after his daughter a couple of times, then turned and walked back along the corridor to his office. He was annoyed with her, annoyed with himself, annoyed with whatever it was that had caused this argument between them. He slammed the office door behind him, but the loud noise that he wanted to make was deadened by the carpets and upholstery. He frowned, and marched over to his desk. But there was nothing to confront. He tapped some dead ash out of his pipe, banging the ashtray unnecessarily hard so that it made a petulant, ringing noise. Then he sat down in his chair and allowed a smile to suffuse his face.

He was finding it hard to take his own irritation seriously. During the course of his conversation with Laura, the sun had rounded the neighbouring office block, and now its light, magnified to a brilliant whiteness by the snow, was streaming across his desk. He shuffled through his papers, but found himself looking more at the play of light across the whiteness of the pages than at the words. He even threw a few smaller memos up in the air, and watched them float slowly down again on to the desk. It seemed like the kind of day when anything was possible. He looked around the warm, stuffy office, with its fug of pipe-smoke and departmental reports. He saw a lack of possibilities.

'Jean,' he said into his telephone, 'I'm taking some work home this afternoon. You can call me there if anything urgent comes up.'

He pushed the papers together into a rough pile. For a moment, he thought of putting them into his briefcase, then decided the hell with it, left papers and briefcase, and hurried out of the building.

When it had first started getting cold, Morton had scoffed at the way the British kicked up such a fuss. In New England nobody batted an eyelid if they got a few days in the minus tens. Then, as he started to read the papers and look around for himself, Morton saw that all the British fears were justified. Nobody was prepared for it. In New England, an army of snow ploughs would have been out even as the first big fall settled. In Britain, the response was slow and inadequate. Many parts of the country, and not just isolated regions, were cut off. Much of the housing was utterly unsuited to freezing conditions, with no insulation and poor heating. Up and down the country, old people were dying of hypothermia, while ministers and bureaucrats in their hot-house Whitehall offices quibbled about whether temperatures had fallen enough to trigger 'cold weather' welfare payments.

On the positive side, it brought out, in a self-conscious kind of a way, the famed 'Dunkirk spirit'. As Morton waited at the bus stop, still exhilarated by his flight from the office, he fell into conversation with two pink-faced, muffled-up old ladies. The subject, of course, was the weather. In America, the tone of such a conversation would have been practical, and perhaps angry at the incompetence of the authorities. This London conversation, which was exhaustive and detailed, because the bus took a long time to arrive and even longer to worm its way up to the Euston Road and beyond, amazed Morton by its mood of jaunty fatalism. He had never heard so much gloom so cheerfully expressed. The conversation washed backwards and forwards between the three of them as they gazed out of the window at the pedestrians falling like skittles on the pavement. Morton was enjoying himself. By the time the bus reached his stop, and they had to go their separate ways into an uncertain world, they were like old friends.

As the bus pulled away, Morton stumped off up the hill towards the burnt house. The air was clear, and the snow beneath his feet as hard as rock. It was not yet three o'clock, but already the sun was low and shadows long across the icy road. He was still thinking about the two old women on the bus, smiling to himself as he turned over in his mind things they had said. Since coming to England, Morton had rediscovered what it is to listen to 'ordinary' people. In the States, he could look in the window of a bar and see them talking with each other, each with their own concerns. But as soon as he walked in the door and was spotted, all everyday behaviour would cease. He would become the centre of attention. Even in sophisticated places, where no one would be so gauche as to rush up to him for his autograph, they would forget for the moment their own lives and watch him out of the corners of their eyes, following his every move as though some of the magic they saw in him might rub off back on them.

When he did walk through that bar door, he would shield himself from the bonhomie and intrusive intimacy by pre-emptive buddiness of his own. He would slap their backs before they could slap his. But that was tiring. Often Morton had wished he could shed his skin, like a snake, and be born again, incognito.

That shedding of a skin was what had happened to him when he came to London. It wasn't something he had thought of while preparing for the trip, and for the first month or so, when he had been so busy buying the burnt house, he hadn't noticed it. He had just been aware of a great change in his life, a feeling of freedom and lightness. Then he realised what it was, and he revelled in it. It was as though in London he were seeing the world for the first time as it actually was, not how it was after his presence had affected it like a dye.

All the 'Morton on Britain' programmes except one were finished. Two had already been transmitted back home to good ratings. The last one had been scripted, and they were just putting the finishing touches to the filming schedule. Morton had rather lost interest in the whole thing. The house excited him more. He liked its emptiness and the silence it gave off on these intense winter afternoons. He liked the feel of the cold plaster against his hands and the bare boards beneath his feet. The blistered paintwork, the mottled grey stains up the wall left by the smoke of the fire, gave the place the strange magic of something that had been through trauma. Sometimes in the mornings, Morton would wander from room to empty room, just looking and feeling the presence of the house.

The cold air snapped with the ring of the phone. Morton, his mood unbroken, walked slowly up the stairs to answer it. It was dark on the first floor landing. The phone was sitting on top of a large tin of paint. Morton sat at the top of the stairs and picked up the receiver.

'Yeah?'

'Hello. Could I speak to Aidan Fowler please?'

'Aidan? Aidan doesn't live here any more.'

'He doesn't live there?'

'No.'

There was a long, strange silence. Neither of them said anything. Morton was shivering slightly on the draughty staircase.

'Are you Mr Morton?' the woman said.

'Yeah.'

'I'm Aidan's mother.'

'Mrs Fowler, it's good to speak to you. I'm afraid I don't know where Aidan is. I . . . I kind of assumed he'd gone back to live with you.'

'And Aidan's not living with you any more?' the woman asked again. She hardly seemed to have taken in what Morton had been saying.

'No, I'm afraid not.'

'Do you know where I could get hold of him?'

'I'm afraid not. I don't know where he moved to.'

'He was with you at Christmas. He rang us on Christmas Day, in the afternoon.'

'He was here then. He moved out soon after the New Year.'

There was another pause.

'Did he say where he was going, Mr Morton?' she said.

'I'm afraid not. He didn't say anything.'

'But his job . . . I thought he was working for you?'

'He was. He left that. I'm afraid I don't know where he is.'

'I'm sorry if he caused you any inconvenience, Mr Morton. He should have given you proper notice.'

'That's not important. I just wish I could be more help.'

There was another silence on the line between them. It seemed to draw them together down the miles of cable.

'I hope he's all right,' she said. 'We hadn't heard, you see, so I thought I'd ring. And this dreadful weather, you do worry a bit. You like to keep in touch.'

'Sure,' said Morton softly.

'Well I'm sorry to have bothered you, Mr Morton.'

'Wait, don't hang up.' Morton couldn't think what to say. 'Listen, let me see if I can track him down. The guy he worked with might know something about where he is. Give me your number, and I'll call you back when I know something. And don't worry.'

Morton took down the number, and they hung up.

The meeting had been called for the late afternoon, when the shadow of the big rock reached the other side of the main clearing. Most of the group were there long before, sitting in the shade and discussing the question that was to be debated in the meeting – whether the group should move or stay where it was. A few members of the group strolled into the clearing at the last minute. The woman had been making spears. She had found a good, strong thorn bush not far from the camp, and had made five spears and, from lizard skin, a quiver for carrying them. By the time she returned to the camp, the man who was in charge of the meeting had begun speaking. She picked her way through the seated people to the front, and sat down to listen.

'. . . *calling to order extraordinary meeting of North Group Two,*' he was saying, '*to discuss issue of future location.*' Somebody shouted from the back for him to speak up. The crowd was restless. The lucky ones had managed to get into the shade, but the others were left out in the sun, which burned hot even this late in the day. There was a good deal of fidgeting and whispering. Dust rose from feet that scuffed the ground. '*To discuss issue of future location,*' the man continued, louder and rather crossly. He was a round-faced person of about fifty, who pursed his lips very exactly when he wasn't speaking. On the ship he had been a Grade 2 Administrator, but had seen which way the wind was blowing, and had kept his position, when many around him were losing theirs, by supporting the idea of making a final landing on the planet. Now he had put himself in charge of '*North Group Two*'.

'*I've heard much talk recently,*' he continued, '*to the effect that the group should move out of the valley up beyond those hills. I've called this meeting because it is essential that we should make a collective decision and act together as a group. Already a few –* ' he reached for the right word – '*maverick individuals have deserted the group and gone off by themselves. Well, I'm sure they won't survive long out there by themselves.*' There were murmurs and nods of approval from some of his supporters. '*It is essential that decisions are properly arrived at and implemented, and that such decisions as we make are coordinated with neighbouring groups with which we are in contact. North Group One is presently situated, we believe, some five miles in that direction –* ' he pointed away from the setting sun – '*though I think it's been a few days since we sent anyone that way to have a look. However, no matter what the difficulties are, it is my strong belief that every effort should be made to coordinate our activities with those of other Xykon colonists. Remember, this is a colonising mission. What was envisaged by landing on this planet was not some chaotic and degrading free-for-all, but an orderly colonization. And that cannot be achieved if we go taking off into the hills at a moment's notice.*'

There were louder murmurs of approval.

'*Now it may well be that this valley won't prove the most advantageous site in the long run. In time, we shall send out properly organised exploration and survey parties to find better sites. But this valley has one over-riding advantage: it is where the ship is. It is true, as many people have pointed out, that we have not made extensive use of the ship's resources since landing. And we have moved rather further away from it. But we must call a halt here, while it remains within reach. For when we have evaluated our needs, we will want the technologies that the ship has to offer. Otherwise we will be devoid*

*of even the most basic of amenities, of electricity and power generation
and good tools. Over the past few weeks, we've had a taste of that kind
of life, and I think I know what most of us here think of it.'* More
murmurs, and some clapping. *'Colleagues, fellow colonists, we must consoli-
date. If we go into those hills, we will be surrendering ourselves to a life of
barbarism.'*

When he had finished speaking, many of the people clapped. The ones
who clapped clapped hard, but their applause sounded hollow as it was lost
upwards into the great emptiness of the desert. The applause was followed by a
strange silence. Nobody spoke, or moved. From up in the hills came a distant
howl. It was one of the wild dogs that roamed the high country. Always at
night, when they were awake and alone in the darkness in their tents, the
colonists would hear that howling. It would set them to thinking for sleepless
hours about their aloneness in the desert on the vast, unknown planet. But in
the morning they would never talk to each other about what they had thought.
Now, as the strange hush fell over the assembly, the dogs were howling early.
It was not yet quite dark.

A man cried out from the middle of the crowd, *'What about the Explosion?
What's all this about consolidating? What's the point of doing anything, when
the Explosion's coming?'* No one answered him. Only, in the distance, the dog
howled. Then a second joined in, answering it. It was colder now, as the sun
fell to the distant lip of the horizon. A wind blew. Its soft, bottomless roar
seemed almost like the sound of the planet's silence.

The woman stood up to speak. She didn't want to. As she looked
round, at the people, she felt the words coming together in her mouth only
with difficulty. Since being on the planet, she had spoken little. It wasn't
just that it wasted energy. The muteness of the desert and the rock seemed
to be entering into her.

'This man is wrong,' she said slowly, stumbling with her words. As she
said it, her hand made a quick, indicative gesture towards him. *'Things will
not go on as they were. Everything changes now. This is end and beginning.
Tomorrow I leave at dawn. Come with me.'* She gathered up her spears and
walked out of the clearing, hearing not a single voice from the crowd behind
her. She would sleep that night in a secret place away from the camp.
Something told her that was for the best.

At the first glimmer of light across the broad sky, she returned to the
camp. There were about thirty waiting for her. Soundlessly, they made their
way into the hills. When the heat of the day flooded the land, they were up
on the high plateau. The walking was rough, over stone and rock, through
scrub. For three days they walked, living off the flood they had brought with
them. They killed lizard.

'Can't you stop reading that sodding thing?' said Donahue.

Aidan looked up 'What's the matter?'

'It's distracting is what the sodding matter is. I'm trying to watch the telly, and you're sitting there reading a fucking book.' In front of them, on the screen, a group of horses galloped through a blizzard. The commentator's voice was a drone interrupted by spat consonants. 'What do you want to read that sodding book for?'

'It's good.'

Donahue gave a deep, despairing sigh, and reached for his cigarettes. He lit one, still gazing fixedly at the screen. Aidan watched him till it looked like it would be OK to read again, then lowered his eyes.

On the high plateau, the air was cooler and thinner. The woman felt strength in her limbs for running and climbing.

'Christ, I've had enough of this,' said Donahue. He heaved himself up out of his armchair. 'C'mon, young Aidan. We'll go down The White Horse for a pint. Oy,' he shouted through to the tiny kitchen, where Monica and her mother were preparing the Sunday lunch, 'Aidan and me's going down the pub for a bit.'

'You make sure you're back by two,' Monica's mum shouted back. Your lunch'll spoil.'

'Shuts at two anyway, dunnit?' said Donahue, and lumbered out of the flat, trailing Aidan in his wake. The TV played on to an empty living room.

Aidan had been going out with Monica for nearly three weeks now. Since the night of the disco in The White Horse he'd been able to think of little else. She lived on an estate not far from the warehouse. Aidan had been amazed the first time he went there. You couldn't see it from the road because it was tucked away out of sight, but it was enormous. There were half a dozen long blocks, ten stories high, laid out in two quadrants with one end open for a children's playground. Hundreds of people lived there, piled up on top of each other, next to each other. Something about it fascinated Aidan. He liked going there.

They hurried through the snow, past the half-hidden form of the kiddies roundabout. The swings stood out gaunt like a scaffold against the snow and slate-grey sky. Donahue hunched against the soft flakes as he walked, cursing under his breath. Aidan, walking along beside him, hadn't wanted to come out. But Donahue wasn't the kind of bloke you said no to, especially if you were going out with his daughter.

In The White Horse it was warm and cosy. Donahue took his jacket off, and Aidan noticed for the first time that on his arm he had a tatoo of a snake twined round a sword.

'Still working in that warehouse?' he said, handing Aidan a pint.

'Yeah.'

'Like it, do you?'

''Salright.'

'How d'yer get on with Tommy? He treat you all right, does he?'

'The Captain? He's OK.' Aidan hesitated. ''Cept he keeps trying to get me to set up business with 'im.'

'What, that stupid warehouse idea of his? I thought you told him you weren't interested.'

'He won't take no for an answer. Getting to be a real pain in the arse.'

'You don't wanna take any notice of him. He's like a fucking old woman. Like I said, he's been talking about that for years, and he's never done anything about it.'

'He goes on about it every day at work, thinks I might change my mind. The other blokes've started taking the piss.'

'Bah, you wanna get out of that place. What kind of a place is that for a man to work, anyway? Sitting around in a bloody warehouse all day, shuffling invoices? You wouldn't catch me doing that. 'Ere, lets 'ave a look at you.' He pulled Aidan out into the middle of the room and looked him up and down. 'Bit scrawny,' he said. 'Reckon you could climb a ladder with a hod of bricks on yer shoulder?'

'Dunno. I could 'ave a go.'

'You'll have to do more than 'ave a go, or you'll do yourself an injury. Well I'll see what I can do.'

'Do what?'

'Get you a job. Soon as this fucking weather gets better, they'll be taking on more men at the site where I work, won't they? Brickies'll be taking on new blokes.'

'What for?'

'Christ, to carry the bloody bricks up. Hod-carriers.' He shrugged his big shoulders. 'Better money than that fucking warehouse,' he said. 'You leave it to me. I'll see what I can do.'

Aidan shrugged his shoulders. It sounded all right. 'It's two o'clock,' he said, 'Think we ought to get back?'

'Nare,' said Donahue. 'You're not gonna close yet, are you, John?'
The landlord chuckled and gave a wink. 'There you go. Don't you
worry, young Aidan.'

Aidan was bored of all this. 'Think I'd better get back there,' he
said, and headed for the door.

'Bah, don't be such an old woman,' said Donahue. 'Oy, tell 'em
I'll be back soon.'

'Got you tied to the apron-strings,' laughed the landlord.

Aidan shut the pub door and started back through the snow.
He got sick of all the boozing sometimes, just standing around in
a circle with a bunch of blokes rabbiting on about nothing. Besides,
he wanted to get back to see Monica. When he wasn't with her, he
thought, she was like a flame that kept burning right in the middle of
him, underneath all the shit that the world flung at him on top. It kept
right on burning in there. Then, when he was with her, all that shit
would just disappear, and it would be like he was seeing everything
for the first time. Even all the colours round him seemed brighter,
like they did to the woman in *The Voyage Beyond Infinity* when she
landed on the planet. And Monica herself, well he couldn't imagine
anything more real than she was. He was in love.

He took a deep breath of air as he hurried in to the estate. The air
smelt rich and sodden. A thaw was setting in, and the dry, freezing
weather was over.

Monica and her mother were waiting at the dining-room table.

'Where's that husband of mine?' said Mrs Donahue. 'I'll bet he's
still down at the pub. Is he?'

'Sorry, Mrs Donahue. He said he'd be back soon.' Aidan slipped
into the chair beside Monica. Under the table, she reached her hand
out and gave his leg a squeeze.

'Soon, soon.' Mrs Donahue shook her head and began carving
the chicken. 'I don't know what you're sorry about, Aidan. It's not
your fault. I don't know what you must be thinking. The man of the
house should do the carving.'

'Don't be sexist, Mum,' said Monica, looking and smiling all the
time at Aidan. Aidan was looking back at her. They were staring at
each other, dazzled and delighted.

Monica's mother went on carving, her head bent intently to the
quivering carcass. 'Sexist, eh? It's sexist, is it, to expect your father
to stay away from the pub for more than half a day at a stretch?
He's like a big fat baby, that man. If he can't have his beer, he's
like a big baby sulking for its bottle.' She plonked a wing down on
a plate and handed it to Aidan. 'There you are Aidan, help yourself

to vegetables. Take as much as you like. I don't see why we should save any. Look at you two, what a couple of love-birds. I can almost hear you cooing at each other.' She went back to her carving. 'Sexist, eh, Monica? Well I'm all for this women's lib. I just wish they'd had it in my day. I was brought up to believe a woman's place is in the home.' She paused, and looked out of the window. 'Home,' she said, and laughed grimly. 'Sometimes when I was in this flat by myself, when you and your brothers were small, I felt like I was completely cut off from the rest of the world. It was worse in summer. Summer afternoons I'd be in here, and if there wasn't a kid screaming you could listen and hardly hear anything. Only the traffic in the distance. Everyone was somewhere else. You felt so isolated, it was like this flat had floated off into the sky or something. Meanwhile, your dad was down the boozer.' She attacked the chicken again.

When it was dished out they sat and ate in silence, while the clock ticked on in the hall.

'Quarter to three, and the bloody man's still not back,' said Mrs Donahue. 'Pardon my French, Aidan. I get that from him, effing and blinding all the time. I hope you two aren't thinking of getting married.'

They both laughed nervously, happily.

'No, don't get me wrong, Monica. I'm quite the women's libber nowadays. 'Cept it's too late for me now, of course.'

Mrs Donahue's hair was rinsed a dark red. She had a small face and a kind smile. She did everything with nervous concentration. Now she was picking and scraping at a chicken leg.

'Mind you,' she said, 'he wasn't always like he is now.' She waved her knife in the direction of the door without looking up from her plate. 'When we was growing up in Castlebar – that's in Mayo, in Ireland,' she added to Aidan, 'he was the finest boy in the town. Captain of the school football team, and all the girls wanted to marry him. Well, I married him, and he got an apprenticeship and everybody said what a great future we had. 'Cept no one had a great future in a place like Castlebar in the fifties, however hard they worked. So we did what all the young people did, and left. Came to London. And we've been here ever since, Aidan, God help us.' She munched her food, thinking.

'It was London that changed him. This is an evil city, if you ask me. The things it does to people. You're not a Londoner, are you, Aidan? No, I could tell. Before we came to London, Michael had hardly stepped across the threshold of a pub. For goodness sake, we even used to go to mass every Sunday. Tell that to people now, who didn't know him in those days, and they'll laugh in your face. We haven't seen the inside of a church for twenty years, 'cept weddings and funerals.'

'Aidan's mother's from Ireland,' said Monica. 'I told him how I went to Mayo last year.'

Her mother stopped picking at the chicken bone and looked at her daughter with her kind smile. 'Yes, I expect you did,' she said. 'Perhaps you'll go there together one day.'

Monica and Aidan beamed at each other.

CHAPTER NINETEEN

Later that evening, Monica and Aidan made love for the first time. Donahue had come back towards five, drunk and combative. When the argument started in earnest, they had slipped out and gone walking along Regent's Canal. It had stopped snowing, and was colder again in the gathering darkness. A mist hung over the water. They went back to Aidan's room, creeping past the landlord's sitting-room, and sat on the floor before the electric fire. They kissed, and later they took off their clothes and lay together on Aidan's narrow bed.

Even when Monica was naked, Aidan noticed, she drew her hair back behind her ear as she always did. They watched each other, unspeaking. 'I'll have to go now. I love you,' she said softly. She made to lift herself off him, but then fell back, laughing. They held themselves together for a few moments, limp and happy.

He helped her dress. They did everything together, slowly and carefully, as if it were a ritual. Once or twice they laughed quietly together, almost nervous, when a piece of clothing got caught and they had to fumble together with their hands to untangle it. When they had done, they stood close to each other in silence, almost awkwardly. Aidan was still naked. Monica could not resist touching him one last time before she slipped out of the door and walked back through the snow towards the council estate.

For a long time, Aidan lay in the orange-lit glow of the electric fire, following his thoughts. His mind, his whole body, felt like it had been released. It felt like it had a life of its own, like an animal moving swiftly through a jungle. For a long time he imagined Monica hurrying back through the snow, creeping into the flat that hummed through the night to Donahue's snoring. Then other thoughts crowded in, then others, until his head was teeming with life. He picked up his book.

On the third day, the bluish haze that they had seen ahead of them on the plateau realised itself as a vast plain. They reached the edge of the plateau in the middle of the day, when the heat scorched everything and the insects and lizards screeched madly in the shadows, when the distance was a wash of dust and heat vapour, and light was bent and swam in the dazzling sun. But they could see enough. Below them the ground fell away in a series of giant steps, as the ancient rocks tumbled into canyons that veered slowly downwards towards the plain. On the plain was shrub and dust and shrub, and then in the further distance there was green grass, thin at first, then thickening, with huge overspreading trees dotted here and there, before the whole landscape was swallowed up in the furnace of the heat haze.

There was a breeze here on the lip of the plateau where the warm air currents spiralled up from the hot rock. Nobody spoke. They were glad to rest for a moment, slapping a thigh where an insect had landed or adjusting the rags of clothing tied round their bodies. The woman stood at the front of them, looking out at the plain and thinking a wheel of unvoiced thoughts. Heat and stillness, she thought. Time is like this. It goes nowhere, is still and utterly without end. It sits on the earth as solid as the heat. The heat was so intense that it seemed to support the woman's body as she strode down the first scree slope towards the plain. The others followed. Hunger clawed their guts.

That night they camped at the edge of the plain, lighting fires and banging sticks to keep away the lions and dogs that loomed in and out of the wild darkness. Next day, tired and bewildered, they walked on and saw small mammals, rodents and rabbits, then a herd of black cattle, and gazelle that ran away from them. The grass was thicker, till they were wading in it sometimes up to their chests. They had stopped speaking – now they just signalled and made noises to each other. They thought constantly about food, about eating and being eaten.

Laura toyed unhappily with her pasta. She and Jeremy had been in the brasserie for half an hour and had said only two sentences to each other. He was looking around the crowded room, gulping occasionally at his wine.

'Pretty noisy in here,' she said dispiritedly.

'Mmmm?'

'I said . . . it doesn't matter.'

'What doesn't?'

'I said *it doesn't matter*.'

Jeremy shrugged his shoulders and started looking round again at the crowd. He was humming to himself. 'Lot of film people in here tonight', he commented, half to himself and half to Laura.

'Oh Christ, this can't go on,' said Laura. 'Listen to me Jeremy. I can't go on with this.'

He looked at her, suddenly very seriously. 'What, you mean with the band?'

'No . . . well, yes, I guess I mean that as well. But I meant I can't go out with you. I can't *see* you any more.'

'Why not?'

'Because . . .' She was stuck. It hadn't occurred to her that she would be asked to justify herself. How did you *justify* feelings? All she knew was that to begin with Jeremy had interested and excited her, and that now the whole thing was turning weird in a way that she couldn't quite define.

'I don't know, Jeremy,' she said. 'I just know I can't go on like this. I mean, our relationship isn't going anywhere.'

He laughed. 'That's priceless. It sounds so fucking American. "Our relationship isn't going anywhere," ' he mimicked. 'It's a relationship, not a fucking aeroplane.'

Laura could feel tears prick her eyes. 'Well, what do *you* think of . . . of us?' she said. 'What do *you* think is happening?'

'Happening?' he said. 'I don't know what's happening. Why do you have to analyse everything? You Americans are always analysing everything, talking about relationships and all that crap. Why can't you just *do* things, act naturally?' He looked round, drank some more wine. His eyes were sparkling again.

'Is that what you think you do – behave naturally?'

He froze for a moment and looked at her. 'Yeah,' he said.

Neither of them spoke. The clash of plates and conversation crashed into their silence.

'You're a sonofabitch,' said Laura. 'You really are. Why do you have to tease me all the time about how American I am? I *am* American. I can't help talking like an American. That's what I am. Can't you just accept that? I don't get at you for sounding British.'

'Wouldn't bother me if you did. I'm not patriotic.'

'I'm not talking about patriotism. Oh Christ, I don't know why we're having this conversation. *I cannot go on seeing you.*'

'Why not?'

'Christ, I don't have to say why not. I just don't. It's not what I want to do.'

'Want want want. Doesn't it cross your mind what *I* want? Supermarket love – that's what you're after: I want *this* and *this* and *this*.' He mimicked her American accent again.

'OK, OK,' said Laura, her eyes closed. 'What do you want, Jeremy?'

'I don't want anything,' he said acidly. 'We're going out together. I don't see the problem. I don't think you should look at these things like a financial investment. "Gonna pay you a regular dividend." Life's not like that, it's not all apple-pie. You can't live in cloud-cuckoo land, always expect to be spoon-fed and get just what you want.'

'You're twisting my words—'

'Well, what is it then?'

'I don't have to—'

'You owe me an explanation.'

'I don't like you,' she shouted. '*I just don't like you.*'

There was dead silence in their part of the brasserie. Everybody looked at them with interest. Laura squeezed herself out from the table with her saxophone (they'd just come from a Wow! rehearsal), and stomped out.

Jeremy felt a kind of shock at her words, but mixed with it was a creeping satisfaction, as though something he had been working towards had been achieved. There had been a twist. His life was becoming more complicated. He looked around him, and saw some of the other customers smirking, then looking away when he caught their eye. There was a buzz of low conversation. Now he felt angry and excited. He quickly paid the bill and left.

He went to a phone box and called Sebastian Parsons at his office in Mayfair. They arranged to meet late that evening at a wine bar. He wanted to ask Sebastian for a job in his advertising agency. He had seen Sebastian a couple of times since they had met in Tony's office. Asking about a job had been at the back of Jeremy's mind on these occasions, but he had said nothing. Now, the argument with Laura seemed to change everything, to clear the way somehow. Things had moved on to a new stage.

He was nervous and excited when he arrived, early, at the wine bar. He walked the surrounding streets, chain-smoking. It was just starting to sleet when Sebastian strode out of the darkness and ushered him inside.

'So you want a job?' was the first thing Sebastian said when they had sat down.

'How did you know?' said Jeremy.

'Intuition. And also wishful thinking. We've been thinking for some time of taking on another person. Would you like the job?'

'Yeah, I'd love it,' said Jeremy, amazed.

'Done. Afraid we can only offer you ten thousand to start with. See how you go after a few months. I'm sure you'll prove a great asset to the firm. By the way, your father's Charles Tetchley, isn't he?'

'Yeah,' said Jeremy, 'that's right.' He was hardly hearing what Sebastian was saying. He couldn't believe he had been offered a job just like that.

'You'll have to come and meet the other directors, of course, but I can't envisage any problem. You just talk to them – show them that video if you want.'

'What will I do?'

'Do? Copywriting, initially. That's how we all started. Then you can take it from there. It's a big field, a whole world. Cheers.' He drank some of the sparkling white wine. 'How's that delightful American girl of yours – Laura?'

'She's OK, only we had a bit of a row earlier this evening.'

'Oh dear. Nothing too serious, I hope?'

'No. Just one of those things.'

Sebastian nodded understandingly, and tucked his wine glass up against his chest in the way that he liked to. 'Well, Jeremy,' he said, 'since we are going into business together, I think we should celebrate this evening. Some champagne!'

They drank a bottle of champagne and smoked some cigars, then staggered through the melting snow to Sebastian's car and drove to a little pub he knew in Chelsea. They drove with the roof of the car down, laughing and yelling at the pedestrians. It had stopped raining, and a warmer westerly wind had ripped open the cloud cover. As they screamed down Park Lane, Jeremy reflected with half his mind that until recently he hated the kind of people, Sloanes and Hoorah Henries, who careered around like this. He still did, really. And if his friends from college could see him now – like Bev, who had been at the house in Clapham only a month ago – they would disown him. But that was stupid. What was the harm, really? He laughed, and Sebastian, sitting next to him at the wheel, laughed too and shouted something that Jeremy couldn't hear. Jeremy was trying to relight his cigar, but his matches kept going out in the buffeting wind. Silly, really. The champagne buzzed in his head. They were tearing round Hyde Park Corner now. It would be really awful, of course, if it wasn't for the fact that he could see through it all. He laughed again as he saw himself, son of a Conservative MP, drunk in a sports car racing through Chelsea. So fucking predictable. He laughed again, because of course that wasn't really him. The real him was standing back and watching it all and *laughing*.

The pub was crowded, bursting with braying upper-class voices. Ties were loosened and awry, the jackets of pinstriped suits flung casually back over shoulders. The air was full with the mingled stink of a dozen expensive perfumes. They drank beer, on top of the champagne. Sebastian shouted through the crowd at a couple of girls he knew. They came over, and Sebastian bought drinks for them. They talked about sex, laughing a lot, which made Jeremy hot and excited. At closing time, Sebastian suggested the four of them should go back to his flat. It was just around the corner. Jeremy started thinking about what they might do when they got back to Sebastian's flat.

When they were out in the cool street, Jeremy was suddenly less keen. He was remembering his argument with Laura, and their unfinished business. He wasn't going to let her get away with what she had said. All the excitement he had built up in the pub about the two girls switched suddenly to the idea of seeing Laura and stopping her getaway.

'I've got to go,' he announced as the four of them wandered away from the pub.

'Honestly, Jeremy,' said Sebastian, 'can't you even wait till we get back to my place?'

The girls laughed.

'I've got to get home. Sorry.'

'Come on, Jeremy, don't be such a tosspot!'

'Yeah, toy boy, don't go,' said one of the girls, and they both laughed.

'Sorry, I've got to. I'll ring you tomorrow, Sebastian. Bye.' He walked away quickly, ignoring them as they called after him. In the King's Road he got a taxi, and he had been driven as far as Wandsworth before he discovered that he hadn't enough money for the fare. He asked the driver to let him out, and gave him the little change he had. The driver shouted at him and Jeremy ran off towards Clapham Common.

A dank mist had descended. Here and there on the common were lonely figures, walking dogs or staggering drunk. Jeremy marched along quickly. He could feel his head clear, his resolve harden.

When he got back to the house, the first person he met was Tony. He had come out into the hall when he heard the front door.

'What the hell's going on?' said Tony, blocking his way.

Jeremy was irritated at his sudden appearance. 'Nothing's "going on," ' he said. 'What do you mean?'

'Laura comes storming back here this evening, all tears, and says she's clearing out.'

'Where's she going?'

'I dunno, says she's clearing out and she doesn't want anything to do with the band any more. What's going on?'

'Yeah, well I'm jacking the band in too,' said Jeremy irritably. He made to move down the corridor past Tony. He felt trapped, standing there in the narrow hallway. Someone's bicycle was leaning against the wall beside him, and the naked light bulb was dazzling him after the darkness of the common. He was beginning to feel drunk again.

'Hang on just a moment,' said Tony, blocking his path again. 'If you're serious about this, then you're fucking me about good and proper. You can't just jack it in. I've got money in this thing.'

'Yeah, well . . .' Jeremy's voice trailed off weakly, and he made a gesture of impatience.

'I trusted you. I made an investment.'

Silence.

'Well?'

Jeremy said nothing, looking down at the brown carpet beside the bicycle wheel while Tony glared at him. He was being humiliated, he knew it. It was the price Tony was exacting. Well fuck him, he could have it. Jeremy just stood there, looking down at the patch of carpet and the rim of the bicycle wheel. For two full minutes they stood facing each other in silence. To Jeremy, with his head bowed, it seemed like hours. He had boiling, shamed fantasies about what he might do, how he might leap forward and knock Tony down, or smack him in the jaw. And all the time Tony was eking it out, testing him.

'Might've known I couldn't trust someone like you,' he said eventually, and turned away with disgust towards the sitting-room. 'She's packing her bags upstairs,' he added over his shoulder. 'You can pack yours too.'

Jeremy stuck two fingers up at Tony's back and grinned to himself. Somehow, beneath all the confusion and humiliation, he was almost enjoying himself. His head was reeling with alcohol. So much had happened this evening, he felt like the hero of one of those farcical comic novels who rollicks from one mad situation to another. Nothing could stop him. Perhaps he should have gone back to Sebastian's flat with those tarts. That would have been a good scene.

But even while he thought all this, smiling nervously in the brightly lit passage way, his hands were shaking. He breathed slowly, deeply, and began climbing the stairs. When he got to the door of Laura's room, he didn't bother to knock, but quietly opened the door and entered. She was crouched beside the bed with her back to him, stuffing socks into a bag. Her suitcase lay near her, spilling its contents on to the floor, and beside it was a loose pile of music. Jeremy moved softly into the room. He could hear her sniffing. He didn't know why he didn't cough, or say something. He still felt like he was acting out some absurd role.

He was halfway across the room when Laura, without looking round, said loudly, 'Don't sneak up on me, Jeremy. What the hell do you think you're doing?'

Jeremy froze, jolted out of his fantasies. 'I wanted to see if you were all right,' he said gently, carefully.

'Of course I'm not all right,' she said, and swept her head round to glare at him. 'Are you all right? Yeah, you're always all right.'

'I'm not all right,' he retorted.

She shook her head, and began shoving socks into her bag again, viciously.

'What are you doing, Laura?' Jeremy took a couple more steps forward.

'What do you think I'm doing? I'm packing.'

Jeremy said nothing. He was suddenly feeling very tired, very drunk. He also judged that to say nothing at this particular point might be the best tactic. Laura was packing inefficiently, pulling items out and shoving them angrily back in again. A couple of times she breathed heavily, a cross between a snort and a sigh.

'Well?' she said eventually. 'Did you want something?' She didn't look round, but paused in what she was doing, a pair of tights in her hand, to wait for his reply.

'I just wanted to see if you were all right.'

She gave another one of her snorts, and resumed her packing.

'Your needle's stuck,' she said.

Jeremy winced. He didn't like it when she sounded smart, like her father. Suddenly thinking of Morton made him angry and determined. He took a few more steps towards her, till he was standing over her.

'I'm sorry I teased you about being American,' he said softly. He moved slowly around her and sat on the bed.

She looked up. She looked very tired, and her face was blotchy from crying. She was looking towards him, but not really at him. Her eyes looked self-absorbed. She shook her head slowly, as at a private thought. Something about her had changed a lot in the few hours since they had been together at the brasserie.

'I don't know,' she said. 'I just can't figure things out.' She quickly dropped her head and hid her face in her hands.

Jeremy thought about leaning forward to put his hand on her

shoulder, but then decided it was best to let her carry on.

'I was really psyched up when I came here,' she was saying rapidly. 'Coming to live in London for a year was like a dream. I figured I'd play some music and, you know, experience the city. It started out great, but now it just frightens me.' She glanced up at him, and even smiled absently through her tears. 'It must seem crazy, someone my age getting homesick like a kid.'

Jeremy smiled back and laid his hand reassuringly on her shoulder.

'And I can't talk to Bob about it,' she continued, ''cause we had a big row last week and we haven't spoken to each other since then. He's got so weird since he came to London. I don't get what's with him. Not that we talked much before. Have you got a tissue? It's OK, I've got one. All I ever wanted to do when I was in the States was play the saxophone. It was all so simple. And now I'm not even sure about that any more. I feel like I've hardly played for months. I mean there's Wow, and that's been fun, but . . . oh God, I don't know. Everything seems such a mess, and I don't know how it got like this.' She gestured at the clothes and music strewn across the floor. 'I mean, just look at this mess. I don't want to live like this.'

While she was saying all this, she stopped sobbing and seemed to gain in confidence. But then as soon as she stopped, as though it was just the act of verbalising that was propping her up, she collapsed and started crying again into her hands.

Jeremy moved closer, to the edge of the bed. He was concentrating. 'Don't cry,' he said. 'Look, I'm sorry about what I said. Come and sit beside me.' He helped her up from the floor onto the bed beside him. She felt tight, bunched up, between his hands.

'And that argument we had this evening was such a mess,' she continued. She seemed to be talking to herself, distractedly.

'It was awful. Christ, I just don't understand any of it. Look, I'm really sorry I said that about not liking you. You know I do really. God, it was me that chased after you in the first place, wasn't it?' She glanced at him, but again she hardly seemed to see him. 'I just feel so mixed up and unhappy. I think it's England that's making me so unhappy. Doesn't everybody feel unhappy here? How can you be happy in a place like this?' She picked a pair of knickers up off the floor and flung them in the direction of her suitcase. 'I used to be so happy and together when I was at college. I was even in love with a guy for a while, but it didn't last long. Now everything's just fallen apart.'

She carried on. Jeremy was only half paying attention to her now. It made him feel important, comforting her like this. What a night he'd had – chasing across London, drinking, getting propositioned by girls he didn't know, then these emotional scenes. It seemed like he had only really come alive tonight. Tomorrow he would ring Sebastian and talk to him about the advertising agency. Maybe he could start there really soon. He would never have to have anything to do with that bastard Tony any more.

Laura had stopped talking.

'Where were you going to go to?' said Jeremy softly, putting his mouth into the crook of her neck and shoulder, into her hair.

'Mmmm?' Laura was startled, as though out of sleep. She'd almost stopped being aware of his presence, despite his arm pressed around her shoulder.

'Where were you going to move to?'

'I – ' She hesitated. Something, despite all her confusion, told her to lie. 'I was going back to the burnt house – you know, where my dad lives.'

'I thought you weren't speaking to your dad.'

'Oh, like I said, that's nothing new.'

'What about the house? You couldn't stand living there, remember?'

'Well it won't be for long. I'll be going back to the States in the summer with Bob.'

'Maybe you'll stay longer.'

'Look, this is crazy. It's late. I'm tired.'

He held on to her. 'It's not worth going tonight. I'm getting kicked out of here as well.' He grinned. 'Tony's giving me my marching orders. We could both go to your old man's house tomorrow. He won't mind. I've got a job now, in advertising.'

'In advertising? I thought you never wanted to do anything like that?'

He grinned with excitement, clutching her harder. 'Yeah, it's great, isn't it? It's going to be great, really exciting.' His eyes scoured her face, daring her to contradict him.

Later that night, they made love for the last time. Only it was just Jeremy that made it, and it wasn't love. Laura lay with her head on one side, looking away from him and biting her bottom lip with discomfort. When Jeremy had burst inside her, he was grinning as he fell back and his head hit the pillow. He fell asleep immediately. He slept deeply, so deeply that when the grey light of morning filled the room and Laura woke up beside him, she was able to slip out of bed, finish her packing and leave the room without waking him. She crept downstairs and phoned Karen.

'Karen,' she whispered, 'it's me, Laura. I'm sorry I didn't make it last night after all . . . Yeah, he turned up. I hoped you'd guess what had happened. I've got all my stuff right here. I'll come now. Dreadful, really awful . . . Oh god, Karen, you're one in a million. Yeah, see you soon.'

CHAPTER TWENTY

When Morton got off the bus, he stopped for a moment to look back down the hill. There was a view southward from this corner to a wide swathe of the city. A cold gust of wind flapped at his coat, but he stood transfixed by the spread of streets beneath the grey, leaden sky. Aidan's down there somewhere, he thought, among those hundreds of thousands of people. How did you find someone in a city like London? He had been looking at the index to the *A to Z* the previous night, and worked out there were over a quarter of a million streets in London. It was like a vast wilderness, a desert or an ocean, where someone could be lost for years, for a lifetime, and never be found. How many people had simply disappeared, had gone in and never come out again?

When he got back to the burnt house he tried Trevor's number again. This time it was answered.

'Hi, it's Bob Morton here.'

'Hello, Mr Morton. What can I do for you?'

'It's about Aidan. I'm trying to get in touch with him. Do you know where he is?'

'No. Sorry.'

'He didn't leave a forwarding address?'

'No.'

'You don't know anything? Where's he working now?'

'I don't know. Some warehouse.'

'You don't know the name?'

'No. It's in Camden somewhere.'

'And you don't know where he might be staying? His mother called. She's trying to get in touch with him.'

'Well, the only thing he mentioned was that he got a room through some bloke he'd met at the pub near his work, a place called

The White Horse. That's the only thing he said. It wasn't my place to interfere, was it, if he didn't want to tell me where he was going . . .?'

'Yeah, I know. Thanks anyway. That might be a help.'

Morton said goodbye and hung up. When he looked in the phone directory, he found that there were three pubs in Camden called The White Horse.

The caves were in a bluff at the side of the hills that rose up in the middle of the plain. From their mouths there was a good view across the surrounding savannah. You could watch from there for the approach of game, like a herd of the big, black cattle. By watching the behaviour of the animals down on the plain, you could also predict the approach of a group of hunting lions. You could almost see the ripple of fear spread across the landscape. Except that at night, when the lions did most of their hunting, there was just the pale glow of the moon and a vast blackness filled with the cries of animals and insects. Night was a frightening time.

Below the caves, where the hills spread out into the plain, was a water-hole. It attracted animals in their hundreds. It attracted the humans, who had chosen these caves because of their proximity to the water, and it attracted the lions, who preyed on the animals who came there. The lions were the only animals that the humans really feared, because they were the only ones who would attack them without provocation, to eat them. The lions were intelligent, and had discovered the caves and learnt that if they lay in wait for them there, they could ambush the humans when they returned from hunting and steal their kill from them. For the lions, it was easier than hunting for themselves. The humans had to learn ways of frightening the lions away, and of fighting them if necessary. Already, one of the humans had been eaten. It had been horrible to watch him being dragged, struggling, into the long grass. He had never made a sound.

The caves faced west, into the setting sun. In that direction the plain seemed to have no end. The sun would expand and fill everything with its blood-red glow as it dipped below the horizon. You could see birds, flying home to roost, travel slowly across its electric face. The shapes of the trees turned to black.

The woman liked to sit here at the mouth of the caves and look out at the plain during the long hours when day gradually turned to night. She would always be at some job, whittling a spear or honing down an axe, but every now and then she would look up and her eye would catch something and she would think vaguely about it before her head bent again and her hands continued at their task. Hours went on that way.

To her left, far across the plain, was the line of hills that became the high plateau which they had come from so many months ago. Before twilight, as the sun began to lose its dazzling strength, the distant line of hills would become shrouded in mist. As she looked at their vague, far-away shapes, she thought about that journey across the plateau. It was strange to be reminded of it, because she remembered it less and less as time went on. She turned her eyes and looked straight out across the plain that teemed with life and danger. Even now a group was out there hunting. There were other things that she remembered less and less as time went on. What were they? All about the ship . . . the Explosion, that was the main thing. What had happened to that? Was it not coming? Instinctively, her eyes looked up to the sky, where the moon was just visible and the first stars were coming out. It was hard to believe that that was where she had come from. She knew it, but she couldn't believe it. No, she thought, that was the wrong way round. She believed it, but she didn't know it, the way she knew the layout of the caves or the best way to skin a gazelle. There was nothing in her existence that told her of it, that showed it to her. All she had were her feelings of strangeness in this alien landscape. That was the only thing that told her she had come from somewhere else, that she didn't belong here in the way that the lion and the gazelle did.

Any

'Stop reading!'

'What?' Aidan looked up from *The Voyage Beyond Infinity* into the Captain's rheumy eyes.

'That bloody book. Stop reading that bloody book.'

'Why?'

''Cos this is a warehouse, not a sodding library. That's why.'

'There's nothing else to do. Why can't I read my book?' It was true. That morning's delivery of watches had got held up somewhere on its way from Heathrow, so the men were just sitting around. There was no work for them to do.

'That's right,' said Phil Tait. 'Why can't he read his book? Not doing anyone any harm, is he?'

'Look here,' said the Captain, looking rather flustered. 'I'm not standing for any nonsense from you lot. Stop reading that sodding book.'

'Why should he?' said Phil.

''Cos I said so. If someone from the office comes through that door, it's me that'll have to do the explaining as to why you are lot sitting around reading bloody books.'

'Fuck the office.' Phil jumped off his perch on a pile of boxes and swaggered over to the Captain. 'Why can't you tell them there's nothing to do. That's the truth, innit?'

'They're not to know that, are they? They'll just come in here and see people reading bloody books. And it'll be me that'll have to do the explaining.'

'It's not our fucking fault there's nothing to do. They're meant to be in charge of this fucking place, aren't they?' He turned away in disgust. 'Who gives a fuck, anyway?'

The mood of the warehouse had been ugly for a number of days. The Captain had been needling people, especially Aidan, for no apparent reason.

'Well?' Phil Tait had turned back to the captain, and was approaching him threateningly. The Captain looked scared, 'What's the matter then?' Phil demanded, 'If we haven't got any work to do, he can read his book, can't he? Well? Can't he?'

Luckily for all concerned, there was a roar of an engine outside at that moment, then a hammering on the metal screen entrance. The metal screen was rolled up, and a gust of wind and rain blew into the warehouse. The lorry had arrived.

That lunchtime, Aidan went to The White Horse to see Monica.

'He's pissed off 'cos I won't have anything to do with that Dagenham business,' he said. 'He's mad. I'm getting out of there. Your dad said he could get me a job on his site. Has he said anything to you about it?'

'No. I wouldn't count on him. He's all mouth, my dad. Anyway, I don't think I want you hanging around with him and all his mates.'

'Why not?'

'I dunno, I just don't.

Aidan shrugged, and gave her a grin. When the landlord wasn't looking, she leant across the bar and kissed him.

Jeremy woke with a sore head. He got up and went over to the window, pulled the curtains open, and looked out at the rain gusting across the rooftops. He could remember clearly everything that had happened the previous night. Replaying it in his mind made him feel better. There had been the drive in Sebastian's car, and the girls in the Chelsea pub, then Clapham Common and Tony berating him, the argument with Laura and sex with her . . . He looked round and noticed for the first time that her bags were gone. He went out on to the landing and listened. The house was silent, empty.

He dressed and went upstairs to his room to start his own packing. Of course, he thought, he would have to go back to his parents' now, at least for the moment. The inevitability of that irritated him. Everything seemed closed, like a circle. He thought about Laura. His relationship with her, it occurred to him now, had almost been like a way of breaking out of that. His parents had disapproved of her. She had been a new element. Now she was gone.

He sat on the bed. Laura had been right in what she had said the day before. It had never been clear what their relationship was leading to, or what it was based on. It just happened. But thinking about it, wasn't that what was good about it? It might go anywhere. It was open-ended. Everything else in his life, it suddenly seemed to him in a gout of self-pity, was a system of closed circles. There was his tie to his parents, to whom he could – perhaps always would – go back, who would provide for him. There was his secret life in Soho, that sickening, going-nowhere treadmill. Even as he thought about that, his mouth dried, and he felt a sting of excitement in his guts. Yet his relationship with Laura had been something different from that, something ambiguous.

Jeremy was used to being given things, not having things taken away from him. He couldn't stomach that. He had to get Laura back. He got up from the bed and resumed his packing. As he took his clothes off their hangers and laid them carefully in his suitcase, his mind closed firmly around this resolve. He felt calmer now.

He got a taxi back to Dulwich, where his mother paid the fare. He told her about his job in Sebastian Parson's advertising firm, and she seemed delighted.

'What about that American girl?' she asked. 'Is she still . . . around?

'Yeah,' said Jeremy. 'I'm still going out with her. We just had an argument last night. In fact I'd better go. I've got to talk to her.' He got up abruptly and made for the door. 'I'll be back later some time.'

He went to Soho and spent a couple of hours drinking. It made him feel reinvigorated and restless. He flicked through some magazines in a shop, looking at the photos. He left and went into another place over the road. It was all starting again. His mouth was dry with excitement.

Later, the drink still racing through his head, he took a bus north to the burnt house. Walking up the hill from the bus stop, he found it unnervingly quiet in the street where the burnt house stood. There were just some birds singing, traffic only in the distance. It was late afternoon now, and the light was thin and fading fast. He lit a cigarette, clouds of smoke and steam pouring from his mouth.

The house looked the same as when he had last seen it, at the party before Christmas. There was a black smudge of smoke damage up the facade. The windows were dark, but Jeremy went up the steps

and banged on the door anyway, in case she was sleeping. No reply.
He went back down the steps and stoods for a while on the pavement,
smoking his cigarette and looking up at the house. He hated the way
it looked – completely still, towering over him like an accusation. He
chucked his cigarette down into a puddle and started pacing up and
down the pavement, watching the house. The cigarette rested for a
moment, glowing, on the film of ice that was forming on the surface
of the puddle, then hissed as it sank.

Jeremy paced up and down in front of the house, smoking
more cigarettes, while it began to get dark. He had been there
twenty minutes before he noticed, three houses further on, a small
passageway leading down between the buildings. Checking that
nobody could see him, he went down it. He walked carefully, feeling
his way along the cold wall and trying not to let his feet crunch too
much on the gravel. The passageway ended in a blank wall, but to
his left was a gate into a back garden. It was locked.

It was a high gate, and the wall into which it was set was even
higher. Jeremy stood for a while, looking up at the dark shape of it,
thinking. If he could get over it, and across the next two gardens, he
would be at the back of Morton's house. Then . . . He would think
what when he got there. The main thing was to be *doing* something to
get Laura and to get her back. He had to keep moving. He smiled to
himself in the darkness. He really did feel like someone in a book.

He jumped up at the gate and managed to hook his hands over
the top. His toes just touched the ground, and his body, stretched out
between, felt heavy and useless pressed against the gate. Feeling the
height of the gate like this, he almost gave up. Then he noticed that
at about the level of his chest, alongside him, there was a large iron
knob. It served no apparent function – perhaps it had been used to
open and shut the gate before the latch was fitted – but if Jeremy could
get his knee up to it, he might be able to heave himself up to the top.
He let go with his hands and dropped back down to the ground. He
gave himself a few seconds, looking at the gate, to gauge the height,
then stepped back and took a running leap at it.

He landed against the wood with a thump, his arm bent with the
height he had given himself by the jump. His legs were scrabbling
desperately at the gate as he pulled with his arms. His knee found the
knob, and he pushed and pulled until he had done it, slumped over
the top of the gate with his arms aching. He looked around, worried
that someone might have heard him. Luckily, the house beside him
had all its lights off.

He slipped off the gate into the garden. It was very dark here, hidden from the street lights, and all around him was the rising smell of wet, rotting leaves. The only light to guide him came from the next house along, where a bulb blazed from a ground floor window. There was no moon. He stepped forward, and tripped immediately on some object on the ground. He bent down to examine it. It was a small, blue children's wheelbarrow with a red wheel. He grinned to himself and threw it aside into the leaves. His head was still spinning with the lunchtime's drinking.

The garden was small, but wild and overgrown. Wet grass brushed his legs up to his thighs, and once or twice a bramble tore at his trousers. It was divided from the next garden by a low wicker fence. Beyond it, the light from the window flooded a neatly cropped lawn with a space-age glow.

Jeremy struggled through the last few feet of wilderness, then stepped gingerly over the fence. His left knee felt bruised from climbing the gate, and his wet trousers clung unpleasantly to his legs. He shuffled away from the house, along a flowerbed, to get out of the light. From near the back of the garden, he could see into the room where the light was on. The curtains were open, and standing in the middle of the room were a man and a woman, arguing. The woman was flapping her hands about a lot, and the man, as he replied, tossed his head from side to side as though he were trying to escape from a strait-jacket. Jeremy watched them, fascinated. It was like watching TV, only with an extra *frisson*. He crouched down on the edge of the flowerbed to make himself more comfortable. There was a strong, rich smell of wet earth. He could feel the clay soil sticking to his shoes. The woman had moved closer to the man, and was waving her hands up and down in a strange way. The man, whose long, thin face was rather flushed, had expanded his repertoire of gestures to include a slow swaying of the body and flailing spasms in the arm from the elbow down. Then, suddenly, something crucial was said. They both stood stock still, staring at each other. Then the woman stormed out of the room, slamming the door behind her. Jeremy could hear the door slam, as well as see it. He grinned to himself. It was hilarious. The man slumped down into a chair in the classic manner, his head in his hands. Jeremy waited, watching with interest, but the man just sat there, heaving slightly. Boring.

It was time to move on. Jeremy stepped gingerly out on to the lawn. As his foot touched the grass, there was a terrifying scream from close by to his right. He froze. The scream plunged in pitch and became the familiar miaow of a cat. Jeremy breathed a sigh of relief, then turned, and saw the man coming to the window to find out what the noise was. Jeremy froze again. The man peered out into the garden, straining to make things out through the reflections on the glass. He was looking straight at Jeremy. Jeremy stared straight back at him. The man turned away, back to his private troubles.

The wall at the other side of the garden was only chest high. Jeremy was quickly over it and standing looking up at the back of Morton's house. There were still no lights on. What should he do now? His limbs felt shaky with excitement. He lit a cigarette and studied the elevation of the house. The windows on the ground floor and down in the basement were firmly shut. On the first floor, the window on the right was inaccessible. The one on the left was just within reach of a garden shed that had been built propped against the back of the house. It looked shut, but it was hard to tell in the gloom. It might be worth a try.

Climbing up on to the roof of the shed wasn't difficult, but the roof itself was rather steep and slippery. He had crawled about half-way up it, clinging to the edge of it, when he was seized by a sudden fear of slipping back off. He pressed himself flat against the wet wood and tried to think what to do. He could picture himself losing his grip and tumbling off. But that was stupid. Even if he did, he had barely five feet to fall, on to soft grass. He started up again, and crawled easily to the top. The window was further from the roof of the shed than had appeared from the ground. He could just cling to the edge of the windowsill, his feet keeping a precarious grip on the roof. By gradually shifting his centre of balance, he was able to stretch up further. His fear of falling returned. Laura would be impressed that he'd done all this for her. His fingers crept over the windowsill and found the window itself. It was open a crack at the bottom. He managed to push it up further. Now he just had to pull himself up. For a moment, it all seemed too much. But he had come too far to turn back. Some over-powering will was pulling him on. There was a vent pipe sticking out of the wall to one side that he could use as a foothold, but it was still a hellish operation. He couldn't take a jump at it this time.

His legs scraped against the brickwork, his whole body aching. Eventually he did it. He rested when he was slumped halfway through the window, his legs still dangling down the wall outside. The room was pitch black, but he began to remember it as the room they had used as a kitchen. This was where Morton had turned round and recognised Jeremy.

That memory spurred Jeremy on. His heart was going fast again. He took a deep breath, and began to heave himself forward again into the room. As soon as he moved, there was an explosion of light in front of his eyes, and a voice shouted, 'Hold it right there.' Jeremy froze.

It was Morton, shining a torch into Jeremy's face.

'Don't move a muscle until I tell you what to do,' said Morton slowly.

Jeremy brought his hands up from the sill to shield his eyes, which were seeing throbbing red spots in the dazzling torchlight. 'But it's me,' he began.

'I said don't move,' Morton shouted. 'Get your hands back there, or I'll knock your head into the bleachers.' He brought his arm forward and waved a large baseball bat. 'Shut up and listen. I want you to keep your hands down by your side, and I want you to come in from that window and down on to the floor here. I want you face down with your hands behind your back. Just like they do in the movies. One false move and I'll hit your teeth for a home run. Now do it.'

Jeremy pushed himself forward off the windowsill. His head felt horribly exposed, with Morton waving that bat over it. He could almost hear the crack it would make as it struck his skull. He pushed himself forward, keeping his hands by his side, and fell heavily on to the floor, banging his shoulder against a chair.

'On to your front, with your hands behind your back,' snapped Morton. He kept the beam of the torch pointing into Jeremy's eyes. 'Now who the hell are you, and what are you doing?' Morton peered down at Jeremy's face, all the time keeping the baseball bat raised, ready to strike.

'I tried to tell you,' said Jeremy, his voice breaking slightly. 'It's me, Jeremy Tetchley.'

Morton pushed his face closer to Jeremy's. 'Tetchley?' he said. 'Charles Tetchley's son? Laura's friend?'

'Yeah.'

Morton roared with laughter. 'God,' he said, chuckling, 'I'm sorry. I thought you were a burglar. Hang on a moment.'

The beam of the torch veered away across the room and landed on the light switch. Morton flicked it on, bathing the room in brightness.

'Are you OK?' Morton continued. 'I hope I didn't scare you too bad. Let me give you a hand. You look in a terrible state.'

Jeremy, half lifted by Morton, staggered up on to a chair. He sat there in dazed silence. Morton regarded him for a moment.

'You could do with a drink, young man,' he said. 'In fact I could handle one myself.' He put the torch and the baseball bat down on the table, and poured out two measures of Scotch into tumblers. 'Get this down you.' He gave Jeremy the drink. 'Don't worry, I wouldn't really have socked you on the head with the bat. Christ, you could kill someone with this thing.' He picked up the baseball bat again and weighed it in his hands. 'Given to me in 1975, it was, by the Redsox. This is the actual bat Chuck Smith used in the World Series. Signed by the whole team. One of my most prized possessions.' He winked at Jeremy. 'Wouldn't want any blood stains on it.' Morton chuckled to himself and took a long sip of his Scotch. 'You're really OK, are you, Jeremy? I feel really bad about all this. I must admit I was kind of enjoying myself, although I am glad you're not a burglar. Never got a chance to do that kind of thing before. Thought I did pretty good. See I'd only just come in – I've been walking round every bar in Camden Town this afternoon – and I was just going to switch on the light when I saw someone strike a match down there in the garden. So I waited, and I heard you climbing up on to the shed there. You made a hell of a lot of noise, you know that? I don't think you'd be cut out for a career in crime. Anyway, I got the bat and the torch and took up my position. Even opened the window for you a bit to make sure I'd get you.' Morton chuckled, and took another sip of Scotch. He was silent for a few seconds, looking at Jeremy and smiling, shaking his head in amusement. Then he added, 'What the hell were doing, anyway?'

'I was looking for Laura,' said Jeremy grimly.

Morton laughed again. 'Don't you English know about doors and phones?'

Jeremy suddenly stood up, shifting his weight off his bruised knee. 'Don't fucking laugh at me, Morton,' he said.

Morton fell silent, took his pipe out of his pocket, and lit it.

'You've done all this on purpose, haven't you?' Jeremy went on. He hated Morton more than ever.

'Why don't you sit down?' said Morton calmly. 'I think maybe we need to talk.'

Jeremy stayed standing for a few moments, then sat down, glaring at Morton all the time.

'Look, Jeremy,' said Morton, 'I'm sorry if you thought I was laughing at you. I was really laughing at the situation. You've gotta admit, it's pretty farcical. I mean, it isn't the kind of thing that happens every day, is it?'

'Don't give me that, you old bastard. You planned it all, just to fucking humiliate me. Making me lie down there on the floor. You *knew* it was me. You could fucking *see* it was me.'

'You just hold on there, Jeremy, and calm down for a moment. Of course I didn't know it was you. What reason would I have for thinking you'd go breaking into my house?'

'You saw my face when you turned on the torch.'

'I didn't recognise you. I'll let you into a secret, Jeremy, as long as you promise not to tell anyone. My eyesight's not what it used to be. I'm a vain old man, and I've got used to seeing me without glasses. So has everyone else. I'm too old to get used to contacts. So I try and get by—'

'I don't want to hear your fucking secrets.' Jeremy stood up again. 'I'm not an idiot. I can see things. You were trying to humiliate me, play around with me just like you've been doing ever since—'

'For Chrissake,' Morton interrupted. He put his glass down on the table. 'I don't know what the hell you're doing here – Laura isn't here – but I don't see why I should put up with this crap from you. Hell, you've just broken into my house. Are you living in some kind of fantasy world? You want to wake up, kid. I've a good mind tell your father about all this.'

'You can do what you fucking want,' said Jeremy. 'I just want you to know that I'm not taken in a bit. And you can't hide Laura from me, because I'm going to find her.' He ran his hands through his hair. His hands were shaking. 'I know you want to stop me finding her. I know what you think of me. But I'm not a fucking idiot. Do you know that? I know you saw me coming out of that place in Soho. We saw each other. You pretend not to remember, you pretended you hadn't seen me and it had never happened. But you were just playing games. You knew that I knew you'd seen me. You just wanted to squeeze me as much as you could. You just wanted to humiliate me. Well I'm not playing your games. I don't care. Do you hear me? I just don't care.'

'I'm not responsible for your paranoia, Jeremy.'

Jeremy banged his fist on the table with fury. 'You *saw* me coming out of that strip club.'

They stared at each other silently for some twenty seconds. Then Jeremy ran out of the room, kicking a chair aside as he went. Morton got up and followed him to the landing, and as Jeremy clattered down the stairs to the front door, Morton shouted after him, 'I told you. My eyesight isn't too good.' Then he turned back to the kitchen, shaking his head in bewilderment.

Jeremy ran down the street, trying to light a cigarette as he ran, but the matches kept going out. He stopped for a moment to cup his hands over the flame. His heart was beating fast, and his hands quivering uncontrollably. He had stopped on the corner from where there was a wide view of the city. He looked down at the strings of orange street lights, and the tower-blocks and houses and offices. He was inclined to believe Morton that Laura wasn't back in the house. That meant she could be anywhere down there in that maze of lights. Jeremy could feel the anger rising in him again. He ran on.

CHAPTER TWENTY-ONE

Morton felt confused and depressed after Jeremy left. He didn't like not understanding things. Why did the kid hate him? He had heard the real hate in his voice. What was all the stuff about Soho? And about Laura?

He poured himself another drink and went through to the front bedroom, where he looked out of the window to check that Jeremy wasn't hanging about on the street outside. He had unnerved Morton. There was something especially unnerving about being the object of a hatred you couldn't understand. Like being the victim of racial hatred, thought Morton. The hatred became something purely abstract and negative. Like death.

Morton suddenly needed his pipe badly. He hurried through to the kitchen to get it. As he stood in the kitchen, putting flame to tobacco, he noticed that the window was still open. He was remembering how only a few moments ago Jeremy had wriggled in there, caught in the torch beam. It didn't seem so funny now. Morton glanced down at the wet slope of the shed disappearing into the black night. The wooden roof, streaked green with lichen, was lit by the electric light behind Morton's head. Morton could see the scuff marks Jeremy's knees had made on the roof receding into the darkness from which he had come. Again, looking down into the darkness that Jeremy had come from, remembering Jeremy's anger, Morton thought of death. He closed the window and bolted it.

He went back into the bedroom and sat on the bed. He was suddenly thinking about Sammy's death, about Sammy being dead. That was a funny way of putting it. How could you *be* dead? If you were dead, you couldn't *be* anything. You just weren't. All that was left of Sammy was a Sammy-shaped hole in the universe, and nothing would close that hole up, ever. He could remember how much he'd

223

talked to Sammy about their father, who had died when Sammy was still a baby. Right from when he was a kid, Sammy had quizzed Morton about him. After their mother got remarried, Sammy hadn't felt as if it was right to ask her. So he'd asked his elder brother. And Morton had tried to fill that gap. He had ransacked his memory for the smallest details. They had mourned him together. Perhaps that was why Morton didn't think about his father now, the way he thought about Sammy. Their father they had mourned so much. But Sammy – Morton had hardly mourned him at all. When he got the news, he had thrown himself into work to take his mind off it. And he had got angry about Vietnam. Anything not to have to think about Sammy being dead. Of course, he had even kept his anger bottled up. He was nothing if not professional. Ever since then, for twenty years, everything had been a distraction from Sammy.

Then he had come to London. The work, the distractions, had seemed to fade from his mind. Now he often found himself thinking about how Sammy was dead. It felt good. It even felt good to think about how things might have been different, because that gave a kind of depth and brought things into focus. It was a dark kind of depth, and not at all attractive to begin with. It was like the mottled shadings of grey and black up the walls of the burnt house, a million miles away from the flatly immortal film that was made of him every day. That immortality was a kind of lie. The camera always lied.

His thoughts came back to Sammy's absence. Yes, death was what you couldn't look at directly. You couldn't photograph that. It was behind everything, delineating it and giving it its meaning, just as objects in space were brought into presence by the invisible depths and distances between them.

The phone rang. He got up off the bed and went out on to the dark landing to answer it.

'Bob?'

'Yeah?'

'It's Laura.'

'Hi, honey. How're you doing?'

'Not too bad now, but I was in a real mess last night. I felt awful.'

'Jeremy Tetchley called round here earlier.'

'Oh God.'

'He was looking for you.'

'You didn't tell him?'

'Tell him what?'

'You won't tell him, will you, if he calls back again?'

'No. Tell him what? You haven't told me. Where are you, Laura?'

'Bethnal Green. I'm staying with some friends.' She gave him the address and phone number. 'And don't tell Jeremy if he calls again, please.'

'Sure, if that's what you want. What about that group you were playing with – Wham or whatever it was called?'

'I'm through with that.'

'What are you going to do now?'

'I don't know. I hate London. It's like nothing's gone right for me here.' There was a pause. 'What have you been doing?'

'Today I went on a pub crawl in Camden Town.'

'What's a pub crawl?'

'A pub crawl is what the English jocks do when they go drinking. Neat phrase, isn't it? Pub crawl.'

'Don't tell me. You were with Don Hexter, right?'

'Wrong. I was on my own. And I hardly drank a thing. Well, a couple of beers maybe. I was looking for Aidan.'

'How come?'

'His mother called me. She hasn't heard anything from him for a long time. He's just disappeared. She'd assumed he was here. Now she's worried. *I'm* worried. I'd just assumed he'd gone back home to his family. Anyway, Trevor gave me the name of a pub in Camden Town that Aidan had mentioned. Trouble was, there were three in Camden Town with that name. Hence the pub crawl.'

'Did you find out anything?'

'No. Nobody knew him.'

'Too bad. At least you tried.'

'His mother's coming to London next week. She phoned yester-day and asked if she could see me. I don't know what to say to her. I feel like I've let her down.'

'I don't think you should feel bad about it. You've done what you can.'

'Maybe.' Morton paused. 'But I've got some good news. British TV's going to put out one of the "Morton on Britain" programmes.'

'No kidding! That's great.'

'Yeah, well this particular programme might not see the light of day in the U.S., so I think getting it put on here was a kind of sop to me. My guess is NWBC flexed some corporate muscle to get the British to schedule it. I had a big row about the whole thing with the guys in New York.'

'Didn't they like the programme?'

'Like it? They hated it. Let me give you some idea. Guess what the opening two words of commentary are. "Karl Marx."'

'Do they think you're turning into a communist?'

'They think I'm turning into an intellectual. That's even worse.'

'What about the other programmes?'

'Oh, they're safe. It's crazy, this programme that's stuck in the corporate gullet is the only one I feel anything about. Even so, I couldn't really care whether or not it hits the screens in the States. I'm pleased they're going to do it here. Might cause a stir.'

'What does Don Hexter think about it all?'

'Don? He thinks it's hilarious. He reckons I've lost my marbles. He's thought that ever since I came to London and bought this house.'

'No comment.'

'So are you OK, Laura? It seems like I've just talked about myself.'

'Oh, I'm OK. I guess.'

'Well you give a call if you have any problems. OK?'

'Yeah, I will.'

They said goodbye and hung up.

In Bethnal Green, Laura turned to Karen and smiled. 'Well that's my father all over,' she said.

'He seems very chatty,' said Karen. 'Hardly let you get a word in edgeways.'

'I guess that's just the way he is.'

'What was he talking about?'

'Himself. What he's been doing.'

'But that's rotten. You rang him because you were really upset and wanted to talk about things. And then he just goes on about himself.'

Laura shrugged her shoulders. 'I guess I'm used to it. In fact it's kind of reassuring – you know, that some things always stay the same. I don't know whether I'd be able to cope if he started taking a heart-felt interest in my state of mind.'

'Well I still think it's rotten.'

Laura laughed. You couldn't help laughing when you were with Karen. It wasn't that she made jokes. Her presence just seemed to draw it out of you.

'No, but it is rotten, isn't it?' Karen added indignantly. 'Still, he's probably been spoilt by fame.' They both laughed, though neither of them could have said why this was funny.

The door of the flat banged and Bev came into the room. She sat down without speaking.

'Laura just rang her dad,' said Karen. 'Would you believe it, he isn't even interested in what she's been through. Isn't that terrible?'

'Yeah.' Pause. 'Anyone fancy a quicky at the local?'

'I'd better not,' said Laura. 'It's kind of late, and I hardly slept last night.'

'Yeah,' said Karen, 'you must be really tired. The sleeping bag's in that cupboard. I'll come for a drink, Bev.'

Karen slowly shifted forward in her seat to stand up. 'I still can't believe Jeremy's been so nasty,' she said. 'I always thought he was really nice. It's weird, isn't it, Bev?'

'He's not even worth talking about,' said Bev. 'He's sold out, going into advertising. That's what you said he's going to do, didn't you?'

Laura nodded.

'I meant about how he's treated Laura.'

'Yeah, he's a complete wanker.'

When they had left, Laura laid the sleeping bag out on the sofa, switched the light out, and got into it. For a long time she gazed at the pattern of shadows that the ill-fitting curtains cast on the ceiling, turning things over in her mind. Later, she heard Karen and Bev return from the pub, use the bathroom, and retire to their bedrooms. The worst thing when she thought about Jeremy was the feeling of waste. She had wasted all that desire. It felt like it had been drained out of her. Nothing would bring back that emotion. It had been chucked away for nothing, into a vacuum. It might as well never have happened. It changed nothing.

Things like this – unspoken, felt things – turned over and over in Laura's mind. The flat settled into silence, and Karen and Bev in the other rooms flew off into sleep. Laura turned the same things over and over: how everything had been great when she first came to London, but then had gradually begun to go wrong without her noticing; how she had wasted all that emotion on nothing; how much she missed America and wanted to go back there, where everything was loose-limbed and ranged with space, not cramped and English. Everything had gone wrong. Everything had been wasted for nothing. There was a horrible indeterminacy about it all, in the way that nothing had been settled with Bob, or with Jeremy. Everything was left open-ended.

She slept badly. In the morning, after Karen had gone to work and Bev had gone out for a walk, Laura phoned a bass player she had done a gig with months back, before she had got involved with Jeremy. His name was Arthur Lloyd. He was a black American studying at one of the London music colleges. Laura, feeling curiously high on two nights with little sleep, asked him if he wanted to do some playing. He agreed, and told her to meet him at his college at lunchtime.

She had almost forgotten what he was like. All she could remember clearly was his playing, which was brilliant. Physically, he was compact, with heavy-lidded eyes and thick glasses that made his eyes look unnaturally small. As he led her down the echoing, institutional corridors, looking for a spare practice room, they swapped smalltalk. Each felt happy to be hearing another American voice. Lloyd was a bit uptight and preppy, Karen decided, but nice all the same. He was into old-fashioned politeness, holding doors open for Karen even though he was stooped under the weight of a double-bass.

At last they found a small room with a battered old piano. They unpacked their instruments and played a few numbers, sometimes drifting off into long improvisations. Lloyd knew jazz to the bones. He could make his bass sound like a whole rhythm section, snapping and crackling like drums, sliding and snarling, rippling through runs as though on a keyboard. Laura floated over him, let herself be pulled down, drove beneath him, released herself. For a while he put his bass down and played the piano. He showed her some of his compositions, and they played them through together. After three hours they went and sat in the cafeteria for a long time, drinking coke and chatting. They reminisced about home. They talked a lot about ice-cream. It felt good.

The old woman had died. Gone were the last of the old generation. The young man dragged the body away into the bush, where it wouldn't bring lion to the caves. He had just turned and was beginning to walk away, when something made him pause. He returned to the body and looked down at it spreadeagled unceremoniously on the reddish ground. Laboriously, using the bone-handled flint axe he carried everywhere tied to his waist, he dug out a long shallow pit in the sandy soil, rolled the old woman's body into it, and covered her up. Then he forgot about her.

When he got back from disposing of the old woman, he had a fight with another man about which of them had rights to a particular area at the back of the cave they shared. The argument had been brewing for many days, bursting out not in words but in physical posture whenever they passed each other at the cave's mouth. There had been some shoving, and now there was a full fight. It settled nothing, because nothing could make the cave any bigger. The caves as a whole were now proving too small for the expanding population of the group. And it was proving more and more difficult to make enough kills in the immediate area to feed all the people and the children they were producing.

As these pressures began to make themselves felt, people began to drift away. It was just individuals at first, the ones whose brains had been fried to foolishness by the burning sun. Then small bands began to go together.

The group was breaking up. The young man found himself with some others heading towards the mountains. Over the following day and weeks they drifted across the vast valley, and up into the foothills. If any of the old generation had been alive and been with them, they might have recognised, as they emerged up out of the foothills, the high plateau they had crossed those distant decades before.

The young man knew none of this. He trailed along with the others, drifting backwards and forwards without plan across the great high plateau. Each day was the same. Wake to the cold, then the thump, thump of bare feet hitting the rock and earth. The great sun warming, feeling everything with its all-seeing fingers of light. Sometimes, an animal would start up out of the rocks – a lizard, or, better, one of the stocky goats – and they would be off after it. But even if they made a kill, there was never enough for all of them. They would move on, nagged by hunger, in an interminable quest for food. They found plants from time to time, mountain roses and stringy shrubs whose leaves they sucked greedily for any juice they could extract.

The clouds drifted slowly over them, through the vast blue sky, and the planet span and hurtled through space on its orbit of the sun, and the sun and its planets shot around the galaxy of a hundred thousand million suns. And the cluster of galaxies of which it was just one . . . Of all this the people on the plateau knew nothing.

After three months living on the plateau, they one day found themselves at the edge of an escarpment. Below them, cut deep into the plateau, was a dry canyon. Once, over millions of years, a great river had worn its way down through the rock, carrying boulders, pounding rock with rock. Now the source was gone, only wind flowed down the channel, and the boulders that the water had carried lay unmoving on the canyon bed. The people had climbed down into the canyon in the hope of discovering water, but this was all they found. They walked for two days, following the winding path of the canyon bed. There were a few meagre plants, whose leaves they stripped and ate, but little other food. Every noise they made echoed eerily between the high walls of the canyon. Large black birds nested high up in the rocks, and as the humans passed by far below in the canyon's bottom the black birds wheeled out stark against the blue sky and filled the canyon with their empty, chilling croaks.

On the third day, as the sun was reaching its zenith, they came across something strange. The young man, walking at the head of the file, saw it first. He stopped, gave a grunt, and pointed up ahead to alert the others.

Some six hundred yards in front of them, a huge, strange object was sticking out over the edge of the escarpment. If it was a rock, it was unlike any they had ever seen before. It was elongated, the sun glinting on it. They changed direction, climbing up the side of the canyon towards it. The canyon

*was shallower here, and by twilight they were at the top, on the true floor of
the wide valley into which the canyon was cut.*

*The Xykon had collapsed on to its belly. It was this that had caused
the landing leg to splay out across the canyon. The humans, still breathing
heavily from their climb, gazed at it for a long time, the curved metal hull
towering over them. Much of it had been cannibalised, pieces of it ripped off,
so that it was more like a skeleton than a carcass. It was well-preserved in the
dry desert air, but even here the little moisture there was in the atmosphere was
beginning to do its work. Specks of rust had appeared, which over thousands
of years would grow until by an inexorable process the whole mammoth
object would be reduced to wind-blown dust.*

*After their first dim surprise on seeing it, the humans accepted the ship as
part of the landscape, and thought no more about it. They lacked curiosity.
Only food concerned them, and there was none of that here. They wandered
around beneath the vast hulk, but found nothing. Debris was strewn over a
wide area – objects pulled from the ship's interior that they neither understood
nor cared for. They slowly drifted away across the wide, shallow valley in
which the ship had landed.*

*Next day, at the edge of the valley, beneath the hills, they found the
remains of a camp. That was what it was, but they didn't recognise it as that,
and didn't care. All it was to them was some scorch marks on the ground and
a few old bones. There was nothing there to eat.*

A lorry ground its gears as it turned the corner and disappeared
down the hill towards Camden Town. It was a busy corner this,
on the crossroads of routes from Islington to Camden and Holloway
to Kings Cross. The lorry shuddered away into the thin mist that
glowed yellow round the street lights. It was a mild night, towards
the middle of April now, and Aidan was waiting for Monica. He
liked this corner despite the noise, because at the wide junction,
where the buildings parted and unfolded, there was a wide view
of the starlit sky.

Aidan looked up from his book to the clear, liquid-white disc of
the moon. When they took photographs from space, you could see the
moon as it really was, a massive piece of rock – miraculously, a perfect
sphere – spinning round and round through the void. Bare rock
reflecting the light of the sun. It was strange that it didn't look like that
from here. The moon hung perfectly still over London, like a lantern.
Things weren't what they looked like. And the distance – the moon
was 240,000 miles from the earth, ten times the circumference of the
earth itself. Who could comprehend that from looking at that disc
hanging in the sky?

Aidan had seen the photographs and learnt those figures when he was at school. Sometimes in lunchbreaks he would go down the road to the public library and look at the astronomy books there. He would stare at the photographs of the huge globes as though searching them for some hidden meaning. He would read off the amazing figures to himself – distances, sizes, speeds, eons of time – and wonder. His lips would move, as though the strings of noughts were a rosary being fumbled through his hands. He would have liked to learn astronomy properly, but they didn't teach it at school. Besides, he had been put in the bottom stream for science, and he had hated school.

Now he mostly just read science fiction. He didn't like the stuff that tried to be funny. He liked the books – the long ones, the ones that took a long time to read – that gave him that sense of mystery and wonder. Yet often the fascination with those vast distances and unimaginable stretches of time seemed horrible. It seemed to destroy and ridicule day-to-day things. Aidan hardly explained it to himself in this way, but he felt the depression and hopelessness. It induced a kind of paralysis. He felt it now, as he thought about the rediscovery of Xykon in the wind-swept desert on that planet, this planet, beyond the infinite edge of the universe. He felt it as he looked up at the airless, shining moon and tried to measure out in his mind each of the empty quarter of a million miles that would always separate him from it. Stupidly, he felt tears well up in his eyes.

The door behind him opened, releasing a burst of music and beer-sodden air. He looked round, forcing his tears back down into him. It was Monica. Aidan smiled with relief.

'Sorry I'm late, love,' she said, and leant over him and kissed him. Her hair fell forward from behind her ear and brushed his face. Aidan liked the way she called him 'love'. Her mother called people that as well. 'I was looking for you all over inside.'

She was silent for a moment, smiling and looking into his eyes. Miraculously, the traffic had ceased for a moment. It was perfectly still. 'It's nice out here,' she said.

'Yeah. What do you want to drink?'

'I'll get it. You wait here.' She turned to go back into the pub, and another lorry thundered up the hill from Camden Town.

While she was gone, Aidan struggled to push the universe from his mind. But it wouldn't budge. A deep melancholy had taken root in him, and nothing could pull his mind back from those vast empty wastes to concentrate on the here and now. He looked at his beer. It looked a weird colour under the street lamps.

'You all right?' said Monica as she stepped over the bench to sit at the table beside him. 'You looked really pissed off when I got here.'

'I was thinking about the distance it is to the moon.'

Monica laughed. 'Yeah, it's a real drag, isn't it?'

'No,' said Aidan. 'I mean it. And the moon's nothing. That's like as close as I am to you.' Monica moved up closer to him, put her arm through his, and held his hand. 'Some of the galaxies they can see through their telescopes are five hundred million light years away. That means they're so far away, it takes the light from them five hundred million years to reach us. Some of them probably don't exist any more, they haven't existed for millions of years. But you can still see them. Don't you think that's depressing?'

'What?'

'That they're so amazingly far away.'

She thought. 'I suppose it depends on whether you want to go there. I'm happy here.'

Aidan thought about this. 'No,' he said. 'I don't mean to go there. It just makes you feel . . . funny.'

Monica laughed again, and squeezed his arm. Suddenly, Aidan was confused, and annoyed that Monica wasn't taking him seriously. He made a small but definite motion to pull his arm from hers.

'You just don't understand,' he said.

'What?' she said, still smiling. 'About the stars?'

'About how it makes me feel,' said Aidan crossly. 'You just don't understand.' He gave his arm another little yank away from her.

Monica let go of his hand and withdrew her arm, hurt. 'What, you think I'm thick, do you, because I don't talk about the stars and stuff like you do?'

'It's not that,' said Aidan, grumpily. 'It's how you *feel* about it.'

'Oh sorry. I know you're *ever so* sensitive. Not like me. I can't get worked up like you about the moon and the stars. You should write poetry, you should, because you're *ever so* sensitive.' She glared at him, but he wouldn't be provoked into a response. This made her angrier. 'I think you're really self-centred,' she added.

He said nothing.

'Why've you got to make all this stuff about the stars something to do with you? So what if they're a long way away? What difference does it make?'

'It does make a difference. You just don't understand.'

'I don't think you're even interested in the stars. You're just interested in yourself. All this stuff about the stars is just an excuse for being self-centred. Why should I have to put up with it? I was being really nice to you, and then you just turn on me for no reason. You don't think about me at all, do you?'

'Yes, I do,' Aidan replied gruffly. He flicked his hair away where it had fallen in front of his face, and stared steadfastly out at the road. The warm, moist wind had blown cloud across the sky, hiding the moon. They sat in silence for a couple of minutes.

'I think it's just an excuse,' Monica continued. 'You can spend all your time thinking about the stars and how amazing they are and how old and far away they are, but it's just an excuse because you're too lazy to think about what's around you. It's just a way of escaping from the present.'

'Don't see what's wrong with that. What have I got? Stupid, boring job. I'll probably be on the dole before too long, back at home like my brother. What's wrong with escaping from that?'

'Thanks a lot. And what about me? I suppose you want to escape from me too?'

'I didn't say that.'

'Besides, do you think I'm happy pulling pints in that pub? You're not the only one doesn't like their job. I hate listening to those blokes moaning on about their wives, fending them off when they've had one too many. Don't think I'm satisfied with that. But don't think I want to drift off into a daydream so's I forget what's going on around me. If I did that I might end up in that pub for the rest of my life. That's your trouble, Aidan Fowler. You're always drifting away from things so's you don't have to face up to them. You're always trying to escape. It's so childish. Like you ran away from that American bloke you were telling me about. And your family – you never keep in touch with them.'

'They don't want to know.'

'That's just an excuse. You're all excuses. I'm sick of you. Why don't you just look at your stars by yourself?' She got up, leaving her drink untouched, and marched off down the street, towards home.

Aidan didn't call after her. He crossly picked up *The Voyage Beyond Infinity* and yanked it open. But he didn't really feel like reading any more.

CHAPTER TWENTY-TWO

Terence Healy locked his arms rigid against the steering wheel, pushing himself smugly up against the back of the driving seat. 'Tell you something,' he said, narrowing his eyes at the road ahead, 'that Yank'll get a surprise when he sees me.'

Silence in the car. Barbara Fowler was gazing dreamily at the tower blocks flick past. She hadn't heard him.

'Barbs?'

Mrs Fowler looked round at her brother and smiled.

Healy, for her benefit, leaned up against the back of his seat again and said, 'That Yank'll get a surprise when he sees me.'

'You really didn't have to drive me over, Terry. I could have found my own way.'

'No,' said Healy firmly. He pressed his foot down on the brake. 'I'd rather be with you when you see him.' They had stopped at traffic lights. 'Never let it be said that I don't look after my little sister.' The lights changed, and Healy revved the engine and jerked off the clutch, attacking the road with renewed vigour.

Barbara Healy couldn't remember the last time she'd been to London. She and Frank used to come down a lot, years ago, before the boys were born. They'd come two or three times a year, to a show – the Palladium or maybe a musical. That was in the day when she used to sing and dance herself. *Salad Days*, that had been the pinnacle of her career. And Frank had helped with the lighting. She smiled to herself. Why had they ever stopped? Now there was just the telly.

'Penny for 'em.' Healy glanced at her. They had stopped at lights again, in the heaving, grinding traffic of Kingsland Road.

'I was just thinking about how we used to come to London, Frank and me. Remember us dropping in on you a couple of times, with the boys, when they were small?'

'Course I do. We went up to Epping Forest one time and had a picnic. It was summer.'

The traffic was moving again. They sat in silence, remembering.

'Terry,' said Barbara, 'I just wanted to say that I'm grateful for what you did for Aidan – putting him up and giving him a job like that. I wish it had turned out better. I wish I knew where he was now. But I wanted you to know I'm grateful.'

Healy straightened his back again. 'Don't be daft, Barbs,' he said. 'I like the kid. 'Sides, you've got to look after kith and kin. Never let it be said I don't do that.'

Mrs Fowler smiled and shook her head. 'Well I do hope he's all right.'

'Don't worry, Aidan can look after himself. He's all right, basically. He just falls into bad company. Happens a lot with kids these days.'

'But why doesn't he get in touch for months?' said Mrs Fowler, suddenly distressed. 'Not even to let us know where he is? I know we've never been a close family. I don't know why not. You do all you can for them, and then they just disappear like that, as though all those years when they were growing up had never happened.' She began to cry, then pulled out a handkerchief and wiped her eyes. 'Sorry about that, Terry,' she said. 'I think it's coming down to London that's unsettled me. Too much excitement. Furthest I've been in the last three years is Birmingham, since Frank got layed off.'

'Don't worry,' said Healy, 'I'll help you get the boy back. What I want to know is, what part Morton had in all of this. I never trusted him right from the start. I warned Aidan against him. Now it looks as if I was right. I hate to think what kind of nonsense he might have put into that boy's head. You know what these Americans are like, with their big ideas. Arrogant bastards, if you want my opinion.'

'He's been very helpful, Terry. He said he'd look for Aidan. He said he might be able to find him. Let's just see what he says.'

Healy looked at the speedometer sceptically.

When he pulled up outside the burnt house, Healy glanced up at it and said with satisfaction, 'Well this place looks as mucky as ever.' He switched off the engine. 'Look, Barbs,' he said earnestly. 'Let me do the talking. I know this Morton. He's a slippery customer. I wouldn't trust him too far.'

'Well, he was nice and friendly on the phone,' said Barbara Fowler, and she got out of the car and breathed gratefully the damp, fresh air.

Healy scrambled after her, grinding his cigarette out beneath his shoe. 'That's exactly what I mean,' he hissed across the roof of the car. 'You have to watch that type.' He slammed his door.

Morton had been expecting Healy to turn up with his sister. When Barbara Fowler had called him briefly the previous evening to fix up when she'd come, she'd mentioned that she was staying with him. It didn't take much to figure out that Healy would want to come too. It was a perfect opportunity for him to win some psychological points back, under the guise of playing protector to his sister and nephew. Sure enough, when Morton opened the door, there was Healy standing next to his sister. He had a pious look on his face.

Awkward moments. Shaking of hands, much mumbled greeting and apology. Studying of floorboards. Morton ushered them into the still bare and bleak main room. Healy looked around him sniffily.

'Good to see you, Terry,' said Morton. 'How's the business doing?'

Healy examined the proffered, double-edged olive branch, and remained on his dignity. He sniffed again, pointedly prodding a squeaky floorboard with this toe.

'Very nicely thank you. Do you mind if we get down to the business in hand, Mr Morton? Barbara and I have come about the boy, Aidan. We're both very worried about him. I entrusted him to your care, and I was expecting you to take responsibility for his welfare.'

'Hold on just a moment,' interrupted Morton. 'Let's get a little perspective on this. I'm worried about Aidan too, but he's nineteen. He's not a child. And I don't really see how I'm to blame if—'

'You're not, Mr Morton,' said Mrs Fowler. 'Don't be stupid, Terry. Mr Morton, did you find out anything from the gentleman you mentioned who was working here with Aidan?'

'Trevor said that Aidan had got a job somewhere in Camden Town. He didn't know where, but he said that Aidan had mentioned a pub, The White Horse. There are three White Horses in Camden. I went round them, showed some people a photo I've got of Aidan, but I'm afraid I drew a blank. Sorry.'

Mrs Fowler looked crestfallen. Healy, for other reasons, didn't look too happy either.

'Nothing else?' she asked.

'I wouldn't trust that Trevor, neither,' said Healy.

'Say,' Morton said, 'why don't we check out those pubs again? Perhaps we'll find someone who knows Aidan. It's the only lead we have. I'll drive you over, Mrs Fowler.'

'That's all right,' said Healy, 'we can go in my car.'

'Don't worry, Terry,' said his sister. 'Mr Morton and I can manage. You've taken enough time off from work as it is.'

'Yeah,' said Morton with a faint smile, 'your business needs you.'

'But I am worried,' said Healy, ignoring Morton. 'This is more important, Barbs.'

'Oh, very well,' said Mrs Fowler impatiently. 'You drive.'

Healy gave Morton a triumphant glance. 'Right then, let's go.'

'There were a couple of things of Aidan's I wanted to give you, Mrs Fowler,' said Morton. 'He left them here.'

'Well don't be too long,' said Healy, feeling he had now successfully taken charge. 'I'll be turning the car round.' He went out, leaving them together.

'I'll get them,' said Morton, and he went upstairs for Aidan's two records, the Mahler and the Bob Dylan. 'He used to play these a lot,' he said when he returned. 'He never got tired of them. I can't think why he left them behind.'

Barbara Fowler took the records and looked lovingly at the photograph of Bob Dylan. Morton looked at her, at her brown, greying hair and her dreamy, worried face.

'I remember when he used to play these at home,' she said. 'He'd race home from school and put them straight on the record player. It drove Frank and me up the wall.'

Outside, Healy was hooting his horn.

'We'd better go,' said Morton. He was suddenly, uncomfortably, aware that they were talking about Aidan as though he were dead.

Aidan had never felt more full of life. It was early summer, and he was in the heart of the city now, working on Donahue's building site. Below him, beyond the site, men in pinstriped suits, women in tailored jackets and skirts, filled the streets to overflowing. Around him, office blocks tore up out of the tangled streets. Around him, too, were the shouts of men perched on girders, scaffolding, ladders, against a background grind of a generator. A lathe screamed at the early-morning sky. Aidan paused for a moment to take it all in, feeling the balance of the hod on his shoulder. The air was damp and fresh. The clay mud clawed at his boots. He stepped on to the first rung of the ladder, adjusted his balance again, then started upwards.

His legs were still tired from the previous day's work. The muscles in his calves felt taut and springy. He swung himself round the top of the ladder on to the wooden platform, squeezed past one bricky, and delivered his bricks to the next one along the line. With

one deft movement, he jerked the hod, with its heavy load, off his
shoulder and caught it, balancing it in his hand. Then with a second
movement, gripping the stem of the hod high up, he lowered it safely
on to the floor of the platform, and began unloading the bricks. The
bricky, whistling the same snatch of meaningless melody over and
over again, ignored him. Aidan watched as the bricky scooped some
mortar up and, with four wipes of his trowel, manipulated it across the
bottom and ends of the brick. He tapped the brick twice with the edge
of the trowel, always in the same way, almost like a ritual, and laid it in
its place. All down the row trowels hit bricks like the fall of metallic
rain.

The bricky, conscious of Aidan lingering at his side, looked
round. Aidan turned away, grinning to himself, and started down
again. At the bottom of the ladder, he took his hard-hat off and
scratched his scalp, letting his hair fall down and his head breathe. He
hated wearing his hard-hat, but that was the rule. When he had started
at the site, the foreman had made him tie his hair back into a ponytail,
too. Some of the blokes laughed at him, called him a hippy, so when
he was at work he usually kept his hair crammed up underneath
his hat.

He looked at the yellow plastic hat with disgust, then scooped
his hair up into it and wedged it on his head. He started back across
the mud towards the stacks of bricks. Monica's dad gave him the
thumbs-up from the cab of his digger. Aidan waved back. There
was a kind of hierarchy on the site, and Donahue, as an operator of
one of the big, expensive diggers, was a member of the aristocracy.
Aidan trudged on through the mud and loaded his hod with bricks
again. He was near the open main gate of the site, and he could see
passers-by out on the pavement stop and gaze in at him. Except for
those few lingering figures, pausing for a moment to take him in,
the city churned on around the men on the site, oblivious to their
presence behind the high wooden barriers. Viewing slits had been cut
into the barriers, but not many people made use of them.

The days were getting longer. Aidan watched the walls grow
higher, and the higher the walls grew the further he had to climb with
the hods of bricks. He took the mortar up too, in buckets. The mortar
was delivered by lorry at the main gate, ready-mixed and poured
into large tubs. Each tub was covered with a sheet of heavy plastic
to stop the mortar drying out. Laid out side by side, packed with the
grey mortar, they looked like obscene cake tins. Aidan peeled back
the plastic and shovelled the stuff into his buckets. He had to work
quickly. The brickies got paid bonuses for the amount of wall they

laid, and if they ran out of brick or mortar, they gave Aidan and the other hod carriers a hard time. They were kept scurrying up and down the ladders. Not that they ever got a bonus themselves.

Sometimes Donahue would give him a lift back to Camden in his car, but more often, because they were knocking off at different times, or because Donahue couldn't be bothered to come and find him, Aidan would get the tube. By the end of the day, he was so dirty and sweaty that the men and women in suits would try to stop their clothes touching him in the crowded carriage. Sometimes, when they were squashed like sardines, Aidan was the only one who had room to breathe. Work started at seven, so on week nights all he did was have a bath and sleep. He saw Monica at weekends.

Donahue he hardly talked to at work. One time he invited Aidan along with some mates for a lunchtime drink at a local pub. It turned out they went there every week, for the strippers. The place was packed with men. There was loud music, and the curtains were drawn to keep out the sunlight. The stripper, who looked about Aidan's age, stood waiting behind the bar in frilly underwear, half laughing and half scared. When she went up on to the stage, the whole pub whistled and clapped. Donahue shouted something, and all his mates laughed. Aidan wasn't interested. The air was hot and smoky, and the whole thing seemed stupid. He finished his drink quickly and slipped out without anybody noticing.

It took them forty minutes to find the first White Horse, which was a smart place on a main street, with plotted plants and green upholstery. Unfortunately, the man behind the bar was the same one that Morton had spoken to the week before. When Morton showed him the photograph again, he started getting suspicious, looking from Morton to Healy and Aidan's mother. Who were they? he wanted to know. Police? No? Who then? Healy stepped in at this point, aggressively. Argument raged for a couple of minutes, then spluttered out for want of fuel. There wasn't really any argument to have, since the man didn't know what Healy was talking about. They trailed dispiritedly back to Healy's car, which he had parked on the pavement round the corner. He had got a ticket.

At the next White Horse, they decided on different tactics. They all had a drink. They all needed one, after the arguments and aggravation of the last hour. It was an Irish pub, this one. Morton noticed with amusement the photographs of JFK and the Pope over the bar. Healy saw someone he knew sitting at one of the tables, and left his sister and Morton at the bar. Morton bought drinks. He was served by a girl who hadn't been there when he had come in the week before. He was going to show her the photo, but before he got a chance she disappeared. She didn't come back.

'Thanks again, Mr Morton, for all you've done to help find Aidan,' said Barbara Fowler. 'And sorry about my brother. He means well.'

'That's OK. Call me Bob, please.' Morton smiled at her. She seemed to spend all her time thanking and apologising.

'Aidan talked about you a lot,' she continued, softly and slowly. 'He came home to visit last autumn, just for the weekend. He talked about you then.' She paused. 'Well, he mentioned you. I don't mean to be rude or anything. I just mean he never really talks much. But I could tell he liked living in your house. I suppose it was a kind of adventure for him. Anyway, he liked it very much. We asked him about it, you see, because we were a bit worried, what with him moving out of Terry's place. So he told us a bit about you, about how you're from America and you work on the telly. He's never been a great talker. Takes after his father that way. We've always, you know, kept ourselves to ourselves as a family. Never made a great show of things. That's why I feel so bad about all this happening, dragging you into this when you must be so busy.'

'Don't worry about that, Mrs Fowler. Things are pretty quiet right now.'

Morton called the barman over and showed him the photograph of Aidan.

'Sorry, mate, can't help you,' said the barman, giving the photo a quick glance. Like the barman in the first pub, he seemed suspicious, as though Morton were trying to involve him in some criminal enterprise.

Morton shrugged, and was just taking the photo back again when the old man standing next to him at the bar tapped him on the arm.

'Let's 'ave a look at that,' he said. He had a long, angular face that made him look almost mournful. He was one of the men who had been with Donahue that Friday night back in the winter when Aidan had come to the disco.

He looked at the photo for a couple of seconds, then pronounced, 'I've seen this chap in 'ere. I remember he came in once with old Tommy Trotter. I reckon he works with him at that warehouse.'

'Which warehouse?'

'You know, the one just down the road there . . . what's it called . . . Yukido Electronics, something like that. Japanese. Well they all are, these places now, aren't they?'

'It's near here?'

"Course. Turn out of the pub and it's just down on the left. You can't miss it. Big white building.'

'Thanks, pal. Well, Barbara, looks like we might've tracked him down at last.' Morton swigged off the last of his drink triumphantly. They made for the door. They had completely forgotten about Healy in the excitement. He intercepted them.

'Oy! Where are you two going? You're not going without me?'

'Mr Morton's found out where Aidan is,' said Mrs Fowler. 'It's just down the road.'

They bundled out of the pub and down the road, excited and slightly tipsy from drinking in the middle of the day on empty stomachs. The sun had come out. It suddenly felt hot. Mrs Fowler took off her coat and carried it bundled under her arm. Healy carried his slung back over his shoulder.

'You'll never guess who I met in there, Barbs,' he said. 'An old mate of mine from way back, Micky Donahue. He's a laugh. We used to work together.' He chuckled at some private recollection. 'So where's this place Aidan's hiding?'

They were there. 'Yukido Electronics', read the big red letters above the entrance. Sitting against a wall in the sun, eating sandwiches, were three young men. Morton, Healy and Aidan's mum stopped in front of them. The street was quiet.

'Excuse me, gentlemen,' said Morton. 'Do any of you know a guy called Thomas Trotter?'

'Howdee,' said Phil Tait in a fake American accent. The others chuckled, munching away.

'Do you know Thomas Trotter?'

'Blimey, I think it's the sheriff.' The others laughed. '*I shot the sheriff,*' Phil sang, encouraged by their response, '*but I did not shoot the deputy.*'

'Who's this idiot?' Healy muttered in disgust.

'What was that?' snapped Phil. He looked hard at Healy, and began slowly to stand up, uncoiling himself from the hot pavement.

At that moment, the Captain came out of the dark entrance of the warehouse. 'What's going on out here?' he began, then saw the three strangers and stopped. 'What can I do for you?' he asked stiffly.

Phil Tait spoke up. 'They was looking for someone called – what was it? – Thomas Pig-Trotter, and we told them there's no one here called that. That's about the size of it, Captain. All present and correct.'

'What can I do for you?' said the Captain.

'Are you Trotter?' asked Morton.

'Yes.'

There was an explosion of incredulous laughter from behind the Captain.

'The Captain's called Pig-Trotter,' Phil Tait cried with delight.

'Thomas the tank engine,' shouted another. Another gale of laughter swept through them.

'What can I do for you, Sir?' the Captain repeated, pretending to ignore the jibes from behind him.

Morton looked at him sympathetically. He had grey hair, watery blue eyes, and a clipped, military moustache above his pursed lips. He looked like an Edwardian gentleman fallen on reduced circumstances.

'We were looking for someone called Aidan Fowler,' said Morton. 'This is his mother, and his uncle. We were told he maybe worked here.'

'Used to,' the Captain corrected tersely. 'Mr Fowler,' he continued with dignity, 'is no longer in the company's employment.'

'Since how long?' said Morton.

'He left six weeks ago.'

'Where did he go to?'

'Went and joined a commune, didn't he?' put in Phil Tait. 'Heavy, man. He's a fucking hippy. Stonehenge, man. Heavy.'

'I'm afraid I don't know of his present whereabouts,' said the Captain. 'He left without warning.'

'What about you guys?' Morton turned to Tait and the others. 'You know anything? You know where he's living?'

'Look here, sheriff,' said Phil, in his American accent. 'This town ain't big enough for both of us.'

Morton, ignoring him, stared at the others. His seriousness, and that of Healy and Barbara Fowler, must have impressed them, because this time they didn't laugh at Phil, but merely shook their heads.

Morton, Healy and Barbara Fowler walked back to the White Horse. They were disappointed, but somehow it still felt like they had taken a step forward. They were not disheartened. The old man with the long face was still sitting at the bar. He commiserated with them.

'Still,' he said, 'I expect he'll turn up.'

For a moment, it seemed like he might.

'Where's Micky gone?' said Healy, looking round the pub.

'Micky Donahue?' said the old man. He left just after you did. Had to get back to work. He's on a site down in Aldgate. Big job.'

Healy shrugged his shoulders, sorry to have missed his old friend. To cheer everybody up, Morton bought another round of drinks.

'Karen! It's for you.' A braceleted arm held up a telephone receiver.

'Put it through, can you, Sue? I don't think I can move. It's all that pasta.' Karen patted her stomach. The girls in the office had just returned from their fortnightly jaunt to the local *trattoria*. They were all feeling comfortable and woozy with wine.

Sue tapped out a number on her telephone. 'Here he comes,' she shouted across the office. 'He sounds *terribly* tall, dark and handsome.'

Karen was still laughing when she picked up the receiver.

'Hello? Is that Karen?'

'Yeah.'

'Hello. It's Jeremy Tetchley here.'

There was a pause. Karen was taken aback, slow to register. 'Hello, Jeremy. This is a surprise.'

'Why?' He sounded suspicious.

Karen laughed nervously. 'I don't know really. I'm a bit tipsy, actually. Don't take any notice. We've just been out for lunch.' Out of the corner of her eye she could see a couple of the girls smirking as they listened to her.

'Have you seen Laura recently?' said Jeremy.

'Yeah, I . . . saw her the other day.' Karen was hesitant, suddenly feeling sober.

'Did she tell you where she's living?'

'She . . . No, she didn't.'

There was a silence. He obviously didn't believe her. 'Can I meet you for a drink, tomorrow?'

'What for? I mean, it'd be really nice to see you, of course.'

'I want to give you a note for Laura – in case you see her.' Was there a note of sarcasm in the last bit? It was hard to tell on the phone.

'Well, OK. Pick me up here at six o'clock. You know where it is, don't you?'

'Someone's gonna be washing their hair tonight,' said one of the girls when Karen put the phone down. But Karen only managed a weak smile. Somehow the day had gone sour.

All afternoon, and going home on the tube, she worried about Laura and Jeremy. Was she right to see him and take his note? Why hadn't she just told him where Laura was? Something told her she had been right not to do that. But it was all stupid. He probably just wanted to say he was sorry to her. Karen still found it hard to believe he had been as nasty as Laura said he had. He had always seemed really sweet, not like so many blokes you came across. He was probably upset and wanted to make it up to her.

This was the conclusion she came to, rocked backwards and forwards on the tube. But even so, something stopped her telling Laura about the phone call when she got back to the flat. She would wait until tomorrow and see what Jeremy had to say for himself. Besides, Laura was being difficult these days, sulking around the flat and hardly speaking to anyone. The only time she seemed to come alive was when she was playing her saxophone or talking about how nothing here was as good as it was in America. Bev was getting well sick of it, and had started muttering about asking Laura to leave. Karen had vetoed that, because Laura was obviously still upset about Jeremy. But even Karen was beginning to get fed up, despite the fact that she liked Laura.

Next day, Jeremy picked Karen up from the office and took her for a drink. He behaved very sweetly, and as they sat in the wine bar all Karen's doubts and worries dissolved. They hardly talked about Laura, except that when Jeremy gave her the note he said he was really sorry and wanted to make it up to her. That made Karen feel much better about seeing him and passing on his note.

CHAPTER TWENTY-THREE

Years passed. Hundreds of years passed. The rust on the hulk of the Xykon spread. It started as specks, then gradually grew as stains across its dark, bright surface. With almost infinite slowness, the corrosion ate into the metal. The thick plates that had withstood being flung across the universe with unimaginable violence, warped across the grain of space-time, now succumbed to a simple chemical process and crumbled to dust.

Thousands of years passed. As the main metal casings crumbled away, the skeletal frame of the spaceship, the massive girders that held it together, were revealed. The interior of the ship was laid bare to the sun, and to the slow, eroding forces of the desert air and wind. Metal structures collapsed, wind swept dunes of sand and dust through the hollow hulk, gnawing at plastics, paring everything slowly down. The sun burned fiercely.

Ten of thousands of years passed. Finally, the great metal girders creaked apart, and the spaceship fell open like an egg. The wind continued its work, wearing down, covering up, until the whole of the ancient spaceship was destroyed and obliterated.

Across that vast duration since the ship had landed on the planet, time had been measured out by the slow destruction of the ship. Now that was done, the measure had gone, and all that was left was the wind sweeping down the valley, and the slow beat of day and night. Hundreds of thousands of years passed.

There were other rhythms too. During that time, people had passed through the valley. Generations had come and gone, families and larger, looser associations that had crept along the hot floor of the valley and come upon a mysterious, unnatural object, half hidden by sand. They would stop and stare at it for a while, without interest but with a spark of gratitude that something, anything, had broken the tedium of the desert. Then, seeing nothing there to eat, they would move on.

The generations had their own rhythm, but it was not like the spin of the planet or its orbit of the sun. This rhythm was chaotic, spreading in fits and starts, broken sometimes by disease or disaster. The population, spread out across the wide desert, began to reach at its furthest fringes the grasslands and forests to north and south.

For this was Earth. This was Earth as it never had been, as it always is, as it always had been, as it always would be, for ever and ever, over and over again. As the last traces of the Xykon were blown away by the wind, on this other Earth, this Earth, man once again walked out from the blazing deserts of Africa.

Aidan looked out at the late spring drizzle. No chance of blazing deserts here. But perhaps one summer it would start getting warm, then just continue getting hotter and hotter. Perhaps this year . . .

'You're not thinking about that book again, are you?' said Monica.

It was early evening, in Monica's bedroom. They had made up after their quarrel about the stars. She was sitting beside him on the bed. Next door, Monica's mum and dad were watching telly. The drone came through the wall. An American accent, English accents.

'What's it about, anyway, this book?'

Aidan continued looking out of the window, thinking. 'It's about how everything's circular, it all comes back to where it started from.'

'That sounds pretty daft,' said Monica. 'You'd never get anything new.'

'No,' said Aidan, 'it's more like everything's repeated.'

'Like the telly, you mean?'

Aidan grinned. 'I suppose so,' he said.

'Well, I don't understand.'

'Here,' he said, 'it's got it in this thing in the beginning.' He opened the book at the epigraph and read carefully. '"All that is straight lies. All truth is crooked; time itself is a circle. Nietzsche."'

'What's nichee?'

'The person who wrote that.'

She looked at him for a long time, giggling quietly to herself. 'You're mad,' she said.

'Yeah,' said Aidan. He flicked some hair proudly from in front of his face. '"Course I am.'

She leant over and kissed him. Through the wall, the drone of voices continued.

'Jeremy darling! You're going to miss your father on television. It's that documentary Mr Morton made.' Margaret Tetchley's voice rang up the wide staircase of their Dulwich home.

'Yeah, OK,' Jeremy yelled back. He flung down the magazine he was reading and lay back on the bed. He was loath to join his parents in the lounge and gloat with them over his father's appearance on TV. But he did want to see Morton, who held a horrible fascination for him. He had been made a fool by him, humiliated by him. Jeremy tended his hatred like something precious. Watching him on telly would feed it. He got up from the bed and went downstairs.

Charles Tetchley looked happy and relaxed, his wife by his side. They were waiting for the programme to start. He was a vain man, and watching himself, knowing that his image was being multiplied millions of times, excited him. Since becoming a junior minister, he had had many opportunities to indulge in this pleasure. When his son joined him to watch, it added greatly to his contentment.

'Hope you're taking notes, Jeremy,' he said amiably, and nodded at the adverts flicking past on the screen. His son smiled morosely. 'They're terrible clever, some of these ads. Can't pretend I understand what all of them are about, but you can see they're quality products. Must be a highly competitive field.'

If Jeremy had an answer to this, it was forestalled by the end of the commercial break.

'And now,' said a disembodied female voice, 'another in the occasional series, 'From The Outside In', in which we look at Britain through foreign eyes. Tonight, one of a series of documentaries on Britain and the British by American broadcaster Bob Morton.'

The channel's logo was replaced immediately by a shot of the Thames, with the House of Commons on the opposite bank. A figure was walking towards the camera from the middle distance. It was Morton. When he reached the camera, he said, 'Karl Marx once wrote, "History occurs twice. The first time as tragedy, the second as farce." In the nineteenth century, Britain was the greatest power on earth, with a great Empire abroad, and great riches at home. Now, in the 1980s, some Conservatives are calling for a return to "Victorian values" and a revival of Britain's Imperial role abroad. Is this a genuine British renaissance, or an illustration of Karl Marx's cynical dictum? Tonight I'll be looking at some possible answers to that question.'

The opening credits began, to a loud fanfare.

'I do hope this isn't going to be one of those unbearable socio-logical things,' said Charles Tetchley, settling himself comfortably anong the cushions on his chair.

In Function Room 2 of NWBC's corporate London headquarters, a party was in progress. As the names unrolled on the opening credits, there were cheers and jeers. People shouted for quiet. People shouted back. The last words to appear on the giant screen were 'Producer Don Hexter'. There were more cheers, and Morton, standing at the front of the crowd, clapped his old friend on the back and cracked a joke. On the other side of Morton, smiling weakly and looking down at the floor, was Laura. She felt unhappy and uncomfortable. She wished she hadn't accepted Bob's invitation. She looked up at the screen again just as the image flicked from the credits back to Morton. His smile filled the screen, towering over her. She almost visibly cringed. The chatter in the crowd gradually died down as the Morton on the screen started talking. Only at the back was there laughter and tinkling of glasses. Laura gazed miserably up at the screen, vacantly watching the programme go by. The picture had flashed to old, grainy footage of men in white shorts with funny white hats pointing sticks at crowds of natives. Sometimes the white men were on top of elephants, beneath elaborate awnings. The movements on the film were jerky and comically quick. Morton's voice bounced on over the old film, then his face popped up, talking some more. More news footage, modern this time, of an aircraft carrier pulling out of a harbour, and hundreds of people on the quay cheering and waving the British flag at it. Then there was shaky film of a bleak landscape, some water, and a black dot shooting across the sky. The camera followed the dot, shuddered, the dot dipped down below the horizon, and the camera cut to a plume of black smoke rising from the distant stretch of water. All the time Morton's voice. Laura tried to shut it out. She felt in her pocket for the piece of paper, as she'd already done this evening several times, but this time she pulled it out. Surreptitiously, she bent her head and reread the letter.

> Dear Laura,
>
> I'm sorry things seemed to go wrong between us. I'm sure they can be put right if only we could get back together again. I think of you day and night, all the time. I tried everything to get in touch with you. Your father's probably told you how I came to his house looking for you. That's how much I love you and need you. I'm distraught without you, and I think sometimes I'm going mad or will do something drastic. I won't stop till I get you back,

Laura. That's how much I miss you. Please ring me.
I'm back with my parents. I must see you.

love,

Jeremy

Guiltily, Laura shoved the letter back into her pocket and looked
back up at the screen.

'For the answers to some of these questions,' Morton was saying,
'I turned to Peter Bradmore, Professor of Sociology at Oxford
University. Professor Bradmore is author of an historical study of
British patriotism.'

'What did I tell you?' exclaimed Tetchley, slapping the arm of his
chair with a mixture of triumph and outrage. 'A bloody sociologist.
I knew he'd get some bloody trendy sociologist. What a lot of
poppycock. Didn't I say—'

'Shut up, Dad,' said Jeremy.

It was over a week earlier that Karen had brought the letter back
to Laura. They had had a row. Laura had felt betrayed, and refused to
believe Karen when she said she hadn't told Jeremy where she was.
Karen had started crying. Laura had thought she was safe in the flat,
but now it looked like she wasn't safe even there. The letter showed
that. 'I won't stop till I get you back, Laura.' Why did he want her?
The way he expressed his feelings for her, they were so hard and
abstract they could just as well have been hate.

She had come to dislike the sound of British voices. What had
first struck her as strange and wonderful now sounded strange and
grating. Like this man, she thought, looking up at the enlarged image
of Professor Bradmore, with his sinking, sneering voice. British
intonation seemed to carry with it a whole baggage of self-pity and
negativity. The picture changed to a cut-away of Morton. She had
never got used to seeing him on TV. She didn't like sharing him with
the viewers. It felt as if they were stealing him from her. Up there on
the screen, he looked further away than ever. It had been stupid, her
coming to England to get close to him. Now everything was a mess.
She used to be so *together*, so proud of her life, carrying it around like
something precious, sometimes holding it out carefully for people to
admire. It used to be such a beautiful thing, her life. It felt like it was
England itself that had spoiled it. Every time she heard that downbeat
English accent, she imagined she heard in it some maliciousness that

had reduced her to this state. She even thought she heard it nowadays in the voices of Bev and Karen. It was as if a malicious English force was hunting her down, even there.

'You OK, honey?'

Morton's question broke her miserable train of thought. 'Sure, I'm fine.'

'Say, Don, you wouldn't believe a daughter could be so depressed by the sight of her father on television, would you?'

Don laughed. 'It's not that, is it, Laura? You just don't like to see your father make a fool of himself.'

Laura smiled weakly as Morton feinted a blow at his buddy. Their attention was drawn back to the giant images moving on the screen above them. Laura couldn't bear it, everyone was so cheerful. She wanted to cry. Morton had been joking and fooling around all evening, but in an agitated kind of way, especially since the film had started. It was as though it made him nervous to watch it.

It was the end of the first part. The adverts came on.

'Thank God,' said Morton loudly. His colleagues laughed.

'Thank God for that,' said Charles Tetchley, and his wife laughed. He got up and went to the drinks cabinet to top up their G & Ts. 'What about you, Jeremy? Will you join us?'

His son nodded, smiling painfully.

All across the country the people turned inwards to watch the TV. Only the TV itself, with its millions of screens positioned across the country, seemed to be turned outwards. Only the flat screens looked out. The people – Monica's mum and dad in their Camden flat, those at the NWBC party, Mr and Mrs Tetchley, sipping G & Ts with their son – gazed at the adverts as though their brains were being sucked in through the screens, rushed up into an etheric vortex, transformed to twitching conductors of pulse and signal, their eyes as open and all-receptive as satellite dishes.

Mrs Donahue closed and rubbed her eyes, then got up out of her chair and went through to the kitchen. The sitting-room was lit only by the flickering, sepulchral glow from the television. In the kitchen, she filled the kettle. The jet from the tap thundered against the metal bottom of the kettle. There was something infinitely reassuring about that sound. As she stood at the sink, she suddenly felt that things weren't so bad after all. She went along the corridor to Monica's room, to see if she and her young man wanted tea. She was about to open the door, then hesitated and knocked instead. Inside there was a scuffling noise, and a couple of frantic whispers. Then her daughter called out, 'Yes? Who is it?'

'It's me. Do you two want some tea?'

'No, Mum. Thanks anyway.'

Mrs Donahue smiled to herself and turned away, retracing her steps along the corridor to the small kitchen, where the kettle was just beginning to boil. Next door, the adverts had finished, and the programme was just about to start again.

Morton was standing in a studio now. Alongside him and behind him, picked out dramatically from the darkness, was a receeding row of scenery flaps, on which were various blown-up photographic images. Some of them were modern, street scenes and public events, and some were from the last century. As he started talking, Morton walked forwards. The camera withdrew before him, revealing to the viewer more and more giant photographs.

'Welcome back,' said Morton. His pitch was perfect, sincere but listener-friendly. 'In the second part of tonight's programme, we're going to turn our attention from foreign policy, and Britain's role in the world, to domestic issues. In recent years, some Conservatives here have been calling for a return to "Victorian values", to the kind of attitudes that, they claim, formed the basis of Britain's might in the last century. They'd like to see a revival of the entrepreneurial spirit that was behind the Industrial Revolution, and they'd also like to see the family take a prominent position again as the fundamental building block of society. For many of these Conservatives, the sexual permissiveness of the sixties went much too far, and has threatened to undermine the very basis of British society. I talked about some of these issues with Charles Tetchley, a Conservative Member of Parliament, and one of the leading younger members of the government who has been speaking out on this issue of Victorian values.'

His father's face flashing up on the screen gave Jeremy a shock of recognition.

'I asked Mr Tetchley first,' Morton was saying, 'if what we were seeing was a genuine backlash against the sixties.'

Charles Tetchley's image thought for a moment, then responded to the question. 'Personally I don't like the word backlash,' he said, 'but I do think that people have come to reconsider in a mature, responsible way the extent to which permissiveness can be allowed to go. You see, if you throw all constraints out of the window, what you're doing in effect is destroying the basis of civilization. I believe very strongly in freedom. But freedom, remember, does not mean licence. Our society is built on the sanctity of marriage and the family, and I think things like pornography and the open encouragement and flaunting of certain sexual practices put a great strain on society. They also put a great strain on the human body, and I do think that with this AIDS crisis we are reaping the whirlwind. Of course, I'm not pointing the finger at anyone or moralising about AIDS in the way that some people have done. AIDS is a very serious medical problem that requires all our expertise and compassion. All I'm saying, to put it bluntly, is that there's no such thing as a free lunch, and AIDS is just one of the prices our society is paying for excessive permissiveness.'

That camera cut to Morton. As he spoke, there was a quick cut-away to Charles Tetchley, nodding sagely with his fingers formed into a steeple.

'OK, Mr Tetchley, I understand what you're saying. But I want to try to put you on the spot now. You're helping a bill through Parliament right now which would severely restrict the kind of material broadcasters can put out. Yet only three months ago you yourself voted against a measure that would have stopped national newspapers from putting topless models on their pages. Isn't there some kind of contradiction there?'

The picture cut back to Tetchley, who laughed in a way that was intended to say, 'Oh no, not this old chestnut again!' He straightened his face and began: 'All these questions are ones of where you draw the line. They're matters of judgement, of getting the balance right. I do think that there's a real difference between sexy pin-ups and the kind of thing that the present bill is aimed at stamping out. What the bill I support is trying to do is prevent children and young people from being exposed to perversion through the medium of television. I think we've got the balance about right.'

'If I might press you on this point, Mr Tetchley.' The camera cut back to Morton. 'One of the newspapers which features topless girls the most is *The Sun*, which is owned by Mr Rupert Murdoch. Mr Murdoch, and *The Sun* newspaper, is one of the most valuable sup-porters the government has. Has that fact got nothing to do with your more lenient attitude towards this particular kind of pornography?'

Cut back to Tetchley, who was doing his dismissive, weary laugh again. 'I can assure you, Mr Morton, that I hold no brief for Mr Murdoch or *The Sun* newspaper. I personally don't find the kind of material you're talking about to my taste. But we come back to this question of where you draw the line. I would dispute your use of the word pornography for this kind of pin-up. For the most part, I think it's pretty harmless, and I think it's rather misleading to make some simple equation between it and the real pornography that one finds oneself and one's family subjected to by television and the cinema.' He smiled.

Laura, looking up at his face looming over her, saw in him a resemblance to Jeremy. He was a handsome man, with the same swept-back eyes and bold facial bones as his son. He was flatteringly lit. She suddenly felt very angry at the way the two men were sitting discussing pornography so comfortably.

'Say, didn't you have any women on this programme?' she hissed at her father.

'Sure,' he whispered back, flapping his hand for her to be quiet, 'later.'

Later could wait. Laura had had about as much of this as she could handle. She slipped quietly to the back of the crowd, past the bar, and out the door.

Up on the screen there had appeared a spread of lurid tabloid papers with their bold, childlike headlines. Morton's voice was talking over: 'Charles Tetchley is keen to draw a distinction between the pin-ups in the pages of *The Sun* and the kind of pornography that he sees as undermining family life. But let's take a closer look at *The Sun*, which is Britain's biggest-selling daily newspaper. Because the irony about *The Sun*, from the point of view of Conservatives, is that it's very much a child of the sixties. Right from the outset it exploited the permissive atmosphere of the times to capture a mass audience through a mixture of titillation and irreverent attitudes to traditional British institutions like the monarchy.'

There followed a quick-moving collage on the screen, made from old film, street scenes, clips from advertisements, fashion shows, rock concerts. Above it, Morton's voice-over: 'So there is a paradox about *The Sun* newspaper. It is one of the bastions of support for the Conservative party, and yet at the same time it is a product of the permissive society the Conservatives love to hate. This paradox can be seen in other institutions too, like the advertising industry or the pop music industry. Advertising saw an enormous expansion in the affluent sixties, and since it has come to exploit to the utmost the youth culture that grew up at that time. It also epitomises everything modern Conservatives value most highly: aggressive capitalism, the power of the consumer, public relations, and the dream of limitless consumer choice. Perhaps it's in the advertising industry that we see most clearly the strange interconnections between the cultural freedoms that are the legacy of the sixties, and modern Conservatism.'

'Well, he's lost me,' said Tetchley, and he stood up to go over to the drinks' cabinet again. He glanced down at his son, who was staring at the TV screen with a peculiarly intense expression on his face. 'Do you know what he's going on about, Jeremy?'

'Yeah,' said Jeremy. On his face was the strange, grim smile he had worn all evening.

His father shrugged his shoulders and went over to the drinks' cabinet. 'Top up, anyone?' he asked, but the other two were absorbed by the programme. ('For answers to some of these questions,' Morton was saying, 'I turned to journalist and writer Madelaine Tweed.') 'Still, I think my interview went all right, don't you think?' His wife nodded distantly. Tetchley turned back and poured himself some tonic. He was wondering whether the PM had been watching.

Laura had gone a few yards down the corridor when she stopped. Why was she running away? She was always running away these days. She had run away from Bob once in this building already. She wouldn't do it again.

She had stopped by the entrance to a kitchen. The bright strip lights were on, and there were cartons of fruit juice and wine bottles on the sideboard. It had been used to prepare for the party. For some reason, rather than stand in the corridor she went into the kitchen and poured herself a glass of apple juice. She stood up against the sink, sipping the juice. She was missing her mother this evening. She wanted her very much.

Suddenly, something momentous happened to Laura. She realised that she would go back to the States as soon as possible. She would do it as soon as she could get a ticket. There was nothing to stop her. It was absurd – what had been preventing her doing it before now? It was as though some catch inside her had been released, allowing her whole view of everything to flip over, so that now she wasn't looking backward, inward and self-pityingly, but outward and ahead. She could feel a buzz of excitement in her stomach. A strange blues lick suddenly came to her, and, still with a serious, intent expression on her face, she whistled it out at the bright, empty kitchen.

'So the entrepreneur of 1980s Britain is more likely to be an advertising executive, or maybe even a producer of blue videos, than an iron master. And that's what makes all the talk of Victorian values so strange and anachronistic. As Madelaine Tweed has said, the steam is already going out of the government's moral crusade, not only because of a couple of recent sex scandals within the government's ranks, but also because it was obviously a non-starter with the general public. The British dislike being told how to behave by their politicians just as much as Americans do.'

Morton gazed up at his image on the screen. Sure, he'd made the right decision. Already he was looking at the screen with a kind of nostalgia, a separation. Soon he would be free.

His alter ego's face suddenly loomed larger, the camera cutting to close-up for the classic 'personal opinion' shot.

'At the same time, the Victorian values issue, in one form or another, is unlikely to disappear completely, because it's symptomatic of a profound – though unspoken – doubt in Conservative circles about the world they're in the process of creating. The permissiveness of the sixties, after all, was in part the product of the consumer society. To have consumers, you've got to have appetites, appetites for as much and as many things as possible. It will take more than a few politicians talking about Victorian values to stem that tide of appetite. British Conservatives have started getting queasy about the monster they're helping to create. Many of them would like to return to a mythical simpler age, when people lived in pretty cottages and did what they were told. The trouble is, they also want unfettered consumerism, in which any appetite, however ugly it may be, is nurtured and encouraged, so long as it has cash backing it up. It's the kind of contradiction that old Karl Marx would have appreciated. Good night.'

There was pandemonium in Function Room 2 of the NWBC offices as the film came to an end – cheers, laughter, applause, some heckling, someone shouting 'Yay, Ho Chi Morton' from the back. Morton walked out below the screen, turned to the audience, and waited for quiet.

'Well, ladies and gentlemen,' he said, 'I thought I'd better say a few words, first to thank everybody who helped on the series, either on the production side or in the back-up' – applause – 'You're a great bunch of guys to work with' – more applause, cheering – 'and second, to make a personal announcement. But before I get to that, I just want to say something about this programme which we've just been watching, whose screening by British TV is kind of the excuse for this get-together. Mission control in New York are still stalling on whether they're going to run it in the U.S. of A.' Hisses, boos, cries of 'shame'. 'They're afraid it might offend in some obscure way the delicate sensibilities of the Great American Public. Or rather, of the advertisers. All I can say is this: if you come across any of the big boys from Sixth Avenue, just get in there and kick some ass for me.'

Laughter and cheers. 'OK, OK. Before we get down to the serious business of drinking, the personal announcement. This series is the last Bob Morton Special, in fact it's the last Bob Morton anything, because I'm retiring.' Always the showman, Morton left a dramatic pause here. You could have heard a wine glass drop. 'Yeah, even as I speak my letter is winging its way across the water to that building in Manhattan we all know and hate. But the bad news for you guys is that you haven't seen the last of me. As many of you know, I bought myself a place here last year – a few of you thought I'd gone completely off my rocker when they saw the state of it. Well, I love it. And what's more, I actually *like* London, and I'm gonna stay here. Maybe I'll write my memoirs. Whatever. Anyway, I just want to say I hope I'll see you all again outside this building, and thanks for being such great people.'

The applause at the end of Morton's speech was muted by surprise. There was a hum of conversation. Laura, who had come back into the room right at the end of the film, and had listened to Morton from the back, by the door, now worked her way throughout the audience. She tapped her father on the arm and said quietly, 'Can we talk?' He detached himself from the group of people who had surrounded him, and followed her to one side of the room.

'Why didn't you tell me first?' Laura demanded, turning on him. 'I'm your daughter. Why not talk to me before you decide something like this? Why did you have to tell all these people before you told me?'

'Honey, I thought you knew. I thought you realised from that time we talked up in my office and you walked out on me.'

'Well I didn't.'

'I'm sorry. I thought you did. Don't be angry.' He took a step towards her.

'Angry? 'Course I'm fucking angry. You're a selfish bastard.' She raised a fist and hit him lightly on the arm. There were tears in her eyes. She tapped him a couple of times more with her bunched fist – it was a strange, obsessive gesture – then unclenched her fingers and reached forward and hugged him.

Charles Tetchley marched up to the television with a slight stagger in his step. 'What a lot of nonsense,' he said, and punched the Off button with his finger. The closing credits disappeared. 'Utter rubbish.' He was feeling tired, hot and rather drunk. He hadn't quite followed everything that Morton had said on the programme, but he'd been able to follow the general downbeat, dispiriting drift of it. 'It's that kind of programme,' he said, jabbing the air in front of the television, 'which shows why we need proper regulation of broadcasting.'

There was a brief silence, then Jeremy burst out laughing. It was hard, derisive laughter. Tetchley gazed blinking at his son for a few seconds, then turned away in disgust. God knows what he'd done to deserve a son like that.

CHAPTER TWENTY-FOUR

Laura left England two weeks later. As soon as the plane was off the ground and heading out west across Britain, Laura felt a black weight fall away. The sunlight danced on the roof of the clouds all the way back across the Atlantic. She had a seat by the window, and one of the entertainment channels was playing Count Basie hits. She felt so happy, it was as if her time in London had been a ghastly dream. None of it seemed real any more. Her mother met her at Kennedy and took her into Manhattan to have lunch or breakfast or supper or whatever it was at her favourite Chinese restaurant. They stayed there until the waiters began glaring at them and Laura was so tired and hoarse she couldn't talk any more.

Morton, left behind in London, retreated into the burnt house. He had started on the first draft of his memoirs. When he had let slip to Don Hexter what he was doing, Don had ribbed him about it, said it was a sign he was all washed up. But Morton had never felt more full of life. He had almost told Don he saw it as a final victory of the word over the image. But he had thought better of that. Don would only have laughed at him.

Spring was slow to undo the damage that February had done. For weeks, even with the warmer weather, there had been no sign of green on the trees. Then tiny leaves appeared. Morton worked in the yard, digging the flowerbeds and laying new turf. Don accused him of becoming British. The days were getting longer, and after reliving his life at his typewriter, Morton would spend the lingering evening turning over the wet, rich-smelling soil, turning over the words he had been writing, reworking them in his mind. His arms would ache, his breath would pour clouds of steam into the darkening air, and his head would feel tired from searching through all the words he could use to describe things. He felt as though he had never known the joy of real work before. When it was too dark to see outside, he went inside and read. He would go to the public library once a week and get books. For the first couple of weeks after he had resigned, there had been a lot of calls from the States – old colleagues asking what was up and reporters looking for a story. He answered most of their questions. There was no story. The calls had tailed off now. For a brief moment he had been a point of focus, then the big, blinkered eye of the media had moved on to other targets. That suited him fine. In Britain there had been a short-lived fuss about his programme. Tories had held it up as an example of anti-government bias in the media. Labour people had gleefully called attention to the participation of Tetchley. But the affair was generally deemed not to have set back the career of a promising young minister.

Morton had decided to get rid of the old lean-to shed at the back, the one Jeremy Tetchley had climbed on to that strange night weeks back. It would have been a job for young Aidan, if he had still been around. Barbara Fowler had gone back to the Midlands, but had promised to call if she heard anything from the boy. Morton still thought about him. Before his mother left London, they had had one more outing to Camden Town, but had learnt nothing more. Terry Healy hadn't bothered to come along that second time. Morton guessed he thought he had made his point.

One day, instead of going to the café as he usually did, Aidan walked down through the City. The sky was clear, with a damp, warm wind blowing from the west. Funnelled down between the imposing buildings, it flapped the expensive raincoats of the people who hurried past Aidan. He had no particular destination. The streets were very clean and echoey here, lined with large windows and massive letters spelling out the names of companies. Aidan had walked for half an hour through the maze of crowded streets. He came round a corner, and suddenly, unexpectedly, the world opened up around him. He had come out at the river.

Aidan knew about the Thames, of course, but he had never seen it. The world he had moved in in the year since he had come to London had been limited to a small area in the north and east of the metropolis. Only glimpses, like the view from the attic room of the burnt house, had shown him a world beyond. He had quite forgotten that there was a large river running through the middle of the city, the way many Londoners forget it until they come round a corner and find themselves in what looks like a picture-postcard, foreign city.

Aidan stood on the bridge and tried to take it in. But it was too much. The worlds of water and building resisted one another, refusing to be encompassed by a single look. The river moved down in a great curve between the buildings, an enormous elemental force chopped into wavelets by the breeze that swept down its surface. Overhead, gulls wheeled across the opened-up sky, squawking, dived down to the water and rode up again on the wind. Aidan could hardly believe that there was all this, just yards from the closed-in streets and reflecting windows. In a flash, the city's meaning had been transformed for him. It had become the adjunct of the river, the outgrowth of the river's low banks and of the hills to north and south that emerged from the banks. At its heart was the river, which others might call arterial, or vital, but which for Aidan defied all analogy, all words. It was simply there, more than anything else he had ever seen.

After that occasion, Aidan came down to the river as often as he could. He came in lunchbreaks, hurrying back so as not to get into trouble, and he came after work, at sunset, when the homebound traffic roared by behind him on the bridge. He ignored it, and simply watched the massive water move by beneath him.

Jeremy toyed with his pen. He had just written the first draft of an advertisement for a photocopier, and he was pleased with it. Writing was easy. Since he had started working at Parsons Winthorpe & Crewe, he had been amused at how one got complimented and rewarded for doing something that was so simple. All you needed was a subject, to start the ball rolling, and then the words took off with a life of their own. He liked words that had a spin, a buzz, which could send them flying off on a trajectory of their own. His facility at copywriting was encouraging him to try other kinds. Maybe he would do some journalism, perhaps poetry. The technique was basically the same, only instead of selling photocopiers, wrapping them up with words to make them look attractive, you were selling stories, or an image or idea. His ambitions ran on a thread, like the silken words that spun themselves out across the page.

He had been gazing out of the window while thinking all this. Now he looked back at the draft, and felt a twinge of dissatisfaction. But it would do. He'd send it down for typing and see what they thought of it at the meeting tomorrow morning. He pulled a pile of magazines across the desk and started flicking through them. This was part of his job too, to run through the press looking at what the new ideas were, the buzz words, the buzz images. He flicked the pages quickly, his eyes flitting over the gloss. Now and then he smiled knowingly.

He hadn't given up looking for Laura. She had never replied to his note, so last week he had rung Karen again. Karen wouldn't say anything about her, but in the end she had agreed to meet him for another drink. That was tomorrow night. He was going to get out of her where Laura was. And if she really wouldn't say, or really didn't know, then maybe . . . Karen was bloody attractive, after all. Jeremy smiled to himself again, licked his fingertips, and flicked over some more pages. Sometimes it felt like the whole world was at his fingertips.

Just as a crowded city looks peaceful and utterly still from far up in the sky, so from our perspective there is a kind of calm and stillness about the vast stretches of prehistory. The great changes – use of fire, the development of tools, agriculture – appear necessary, delineated and singular. Yet, of course, the things described in the books, the notions which we use to arrest an unfathomable reality, never even happened.

A young girl, sent down to the river by her mother, scoops water with the thick shell of an ostrich egg, just as everybody else in her world does. As he has done at dawn for as long as he can remember, a man beneath the baobab tree pounds two hand-axes together until a spark flies from them on to the pile of grasses. His leg still aches from the fall he took the day before. And hundreds of miles away, thousands of years away, the woman whose baby died just two months earlier pounds the grain and carefully puts some aside to plant for next year.

These moments are lost to us. We merely try to swallow them in our understandings. But of course they're not lost, they're only lost to us. In their own time, in their own place, they still happen. They are unenclosed, open-ended. The man still stands up, rubbing his leg vigorously, and watches with pleasure as the smoke rises to mingle with the morning mist. The significance of that moment, more than all the words we might toss in its direction, is that it still happens.

'Everything goes, everything comes back; eternally rolls the wheel of being. Everything dies, everything blossoms again; eternally runs the year of being. Everything breaks, everything is joined anew; eternally the same house of being is built. Everything parts, everything greets every other thing again; eternally the ring of being remains faithful to itself. In every Now, being begins; round every Here rolls the sphere There. The centre is everywhere. Bent is the path of eternity.'

And what of the moment when the Xykon descended like a miracle out of the hot, blue sky and landed on the desert floor, with one of its legs crashed into a canyon? What of that moment? It was also written: 'There is a great year of becoming, a monster of a great year, which must, like an hourglass, turn over

again and again so that it may run down and run out again.' That moment was
the turning, the point of switch-back, when end came to meet and obliterate
beginning, and complete the circle. For out of that spaceship would walk, on to
the blue planet, the creature that would tell this story.

'Why do you frown when you read? You've got your face all screwed
up. Like this.' Monica tugged the corners of her mouth down.

Aidan grinned. 'I dunno. It's getting hard to follow this book.' He
tossed it into the grass.

'Don't know how you can stare at a book on a day like this. Let's
go up on the hill again. No, let's stay here.' She stretched back
luxuriously. 'How hot do you reckon it is?' She leaned over and poked
him in the side with a finger. He rolled away a couple of yards, then
crawled back to her.

'I give up,' he said, and she laughed and then suddenly closed her
eyes and pretended to sleep.

Aidan looked up through the trees at the green back of Parliament
Hill. His head felt dizzy. He felt like laughing all the time. He looked
back the other way, at the sunlight dancing on the surface of the pond.
There was a splash somewhere, and some kids laughed.

Morton had spent the morning working. But the sunshine had been
calling him all the time, the way it does when you're a kid, and at noon
he had packed up his typewriter and headed out. It was the first day of
high summer, the first day when the sunshine and heat felt, for a
moment, like it was immovable, installed forever. Morton had
wandered along the baking pavements, choosing always the routes
that were unfamiliar, until he was lost. A bus with 'Hampstead' on its
front had moved slowly out of the swimming heat. He had got on it,
enjoyed its musty coolness, then got off and asked the way to the
Heath.

Now he was standing on the top of Parliament Hill. There were
kids flying kites above him. London was spread out like a map,
completely still in the heat, while round him, running in the breeze
that caught the top of the hill, kids shouted with joy and excitement.
He could have been one of them. Morton could remember when he
was a kid in Chicago and he would look up at a fathomless blue sky
and something in him would kind of strain, and he would want to yell,
just because that seemed like the only way the surplus life could burst
out of him and fill the world.

As Morton watched the kids run round and round him, he made
plans for the evening. He would pick up some salad on the way home

and eat it in the garden. Then there were a few notes he wanted to make about Sammy and what he had been like before he went to Nam. He felt like he could face Sammy squarely now, but he liked to do it in the evening, when darkness drew everything in. The burnt house seemed to accept the darkness. Morton liked that.

He took a last long look at the view. Far away, the other side of London, there seemed to be hills rising out of the plain on which the city rested. Perhaps it was simply a cumulative effect of the haze that hung in the air. You couldn't tell. He turned away and started across the hill. Down to one side, he had noticed a glitter of water through the trees. Perhaps he would check it out.

Despite the sunlight streaming in through the windows, Jeremy had his desk lamp on. It was a Saturday afternoon, but he had to get everything right for a presentation on Monday. Before him was a large sheet of paper. He was pencilling in his copy, getting the arrangement of it with the artwork just right so that he could make a successful presentation. Playing around with the different patterns that he could make with the words absorbed him. When he had finished, he gazed vacantly out at the streaming sunlight. His room faced north, and even through the slight heat haze he could see right across the rooftops to the Post Office tower and beyond. The city lay at his feet, like a little empire. It was late in the afternoon. Perhaps he'd go down into Soho and look around. He felt good.

'Did you ever phone your mum.'

　　'Yeah. I did it this morning.'

　　'Are you joking? This morning?'

　　'Yeah.'

　　'Why didn't you tell me?'

　　'Dunno.'

She pulled him down beside her. They were still on the bank above the pond.

　　'You don't know anything, Aidan.' They both laughed. 'What did she say?'

　　'She asked if I was all right.'

　　'Are you going to see her?'

　　'I said I'd go home. Visit them, like. Do you want to come?'

　　'Visit your parents?'

　　'Yeah.'

　　'Won't they mind?'

Aidan shrugged his shoulders.

'Maybe,' she said.

As Morton walked slowly down the hill, pressing back on his heels to stop himself accelerating down the slope, a kid rolled past him, screaming with delight. Below him was a wood, and through the trees a pond with a few people walking round it and some kids bathing.

He was thinking about the letter he had got from Laura that morning. She was applying to do a graduate course at a music college in Boston. She sounded much happier. He quickly found himself thinking about other things, half-formed thoughts about the kids who were shouting out in London accents around him. He let his pace quicken down the hill towards the pond, where there was a young couple standing, looking out across the water.

'Don't forget your book.' She picked it up and tossed it to Aidan.

'Oh yeah. Thanks.'

'You've been reading that ever since I met you.'

'It's a long book. Too bloody long.'

'I'm sick of the sight of it.'

'Seems like I've been reading it for ever.'

'Have you nearly finished?'

'Never seems to end.' Aidan looked at the book for a moment. 'Here Monica, come over here.' He took her hand and led her down to the edge of the pond. They walked along the bank out of the wood, into the open.

'Watch this.'

He drew back his arm and threw the paperback out as far as he could. The pages opened and flapped as it sailed through the air, white against the blue sky, so that it looked for a moment like some weird bird trying to take flight. It soared in a great arc, and hit the water without a splash. The kids, who had stopped swimming to watch, cheered and laughed, then returned to their games.

'There,' said Aidan.

Monica hardly seemed to hear him. She was gazing out across the water, smiling. He looked as well. The book was resting on the surface. Its wood pulp was soaking up the water. It sat heavily on the surface for a few moments, then sank out of sight. It sank slowly through the water. As it fell, the pages detached themselves and floated their own way down through the weeds to the mud from which they had come.